THRIVE

ALSO BY KENNETH OPPEL

Bloom

Hatch

Inkling

Every Hidden Thing

The Nest

This Dark Endeavor

Such Wicked Intent

Half Brother

The Boundless

Airborn

Skybreaker

Starclimber

Silverwing

Sunwing

Firewing

Darkwing

Dead Water Zone

The Live-Forever Machine

THRIVE

KENNETH OPPEL

ALFRED A. KNOPF
NEW YORK

FOR JULIA

S eth spread his arms and ran.

Speed.

He pushed off and skimmed low over the ground.

Lift.

He angled his arms, felt his feathers parting the air. With a shout of jubilation, he climbed into the sky.

Faster.

He felt the swift ascent in the pit of his stomach. Leveling out, he squinted against the headwind, blinking tears from his eyes.

Nothing dragging him down. Nothing holding him back.

Esta soared alongside him, laughing with delight, and he followed her. Both of them, dipping and banking and learning how to fly. To be with Esta, wing tip to wing tip, doubled his joy.

Hadn't he been having this dream his whole life?

Flying, with others like him: *belonging.*

This time, it wasn't a dream.

ONE WEEK EARLIER

CHAPTER ONE

HIGH OVERHEAD, THE WINGED cryptogen circled tightly, its golden wings glinting in the sunlight that shafted through the clouds.

Anaya squinted up at it, stunned. This was the last thing she'd expected to emerge from the ship that had just crash-landed. Not a runner, or a swimmer, but a flyer.

The enemy.

Where was Terra? Or maybe there had *never* been a Terra, or any rebels, and she'd been mistaken all along. Why had she trusted them?

She'd stupidly thought this was going to be a peaceful encounter between humans and three cryptogen rebels, to form an alliance. To work together and make a weapon that would defeat their mutual enemy.

That was a fantasy, a lie, and it was her fault.

Terrified, she watched the flyer face off with the helicopter that had fired the missile. The spiky crest on the creature's helmet shimmered with a sickly violet light and emanated an ominous whine. Even all the way down here, Anaya heard it. Everyone around her winced at the sound: Seth, Petra, Dr. Weber, Colonel Pearson, the lone soldier. She knew that whine could swell at any moment, to crush people and decimate buildings.

"Why is there a flyer?" Pearson shouted at her.

"I don't know!"

"Is that helmet a weapon?"

"Yes!"

"They said they'd come unarmed!"

—You attacked!

This voice had never been inside Anaya's head. Definitely it was not Terra's. It came from the flyer. The words carried an angry whiff of gasoline and had a jagged metallic taste like she'd just bitten her own tongue.

—It was a mistake! she called back desperately, and hoped the flyer believed her anguished words.

"Don't fire!" she shouted at Pearson, suddenly hopeful. "I'm talking to it."

"Tell the flyer to stand down!" Pearson barked.

Anaya didn't think they were in any position to give orders.

"We fired first! We promised we wouldn't! Get the helicopter out of here!"

Pearson said nothing. It was a standoff, and all it would take was for the helicopter to open fire again, and the flyer would destroy it—and then the rest of them on the ground.

Suddenly the noise from the flyer's helmet evaporated, and the flyer turned away from the helicopter.

"Look!" Petra shouted.

She wasn't pointing into the air, but at the smoldering cryptogen ship on the field. From the hatch a second creature was emerging. At first it looked so much like a human astronaut that it took Anaya a moment to realize the creature was wearing a synthetic white skin that covered almost its entire body.

From the hood protruded a furred face that tapered into a long muzzle. Fitted across its large nostrils was a breathing mask, with tubing that fed into a slim pack on its back. Earth air wasn't right for these cryptogens, not yet. The creature stood tall on its two powerful legs, then took a step across the field toward Anaya.

In her mind, she saw a flare of familiar amber light, smelled damp soil—and instantly felt a flood of recognition, and relief. This was the person whose voice had filled her head so many times over the past days. And now here she was. Suddenly Anaya's cheeks were damp with tears of relief.

"It's Terra!" she told everyone.

"You're sure?" Petra asked.

Instinctively, Anaya was walking closer, to greet her.

—*You promised you would not attack!*

Terra's silent words vibrated with bewilderment and hurt, but also anger.

—*I'm sorry!* Anaya replied. *It was one soldier, acting alone. We didn't order it!*

She felt a stab of guilt that she'd been so quick to lose faith in

Terra. Still, the sight of the flyer had been so shocking, so terrifying, what else could she think?

"Keep your distance, Anaya," she heard the colonel say.

"It's fine," Anaya said.

Nonetheless, she stopped a little distance away from Terra. The two of them regarded each other. Even in her white suit, Terra bore an uncanny resemblance to a kangaroo. A kangaroo without a tail. Her thighs were massive, and the lower half of her legs very skinny, almost bonelike. Long toes stuck through the synthetic white skin, and Anaya took in the wickedly sharp black claws—they made her own look puny.

—*Are we safe?* Terra asked her.

"Anaya, are you talking to them?" Pearson bellowed.

"They want to know if they're safe! You should get the helicopter to land!"

"Not with that flyer still airborne!"

—*Why is there a flyer?* Anaya asked Terra. *You didn't tell me there was a flyer!*

—*He is a rebel, like us.*

Was it a lie? But as always, everything that passed into her head from Terra felt like the truth. She took a big breath and turned to Pearson.

"The flyer's a rebel, too. It's safe!"

Anaya couldn't make out Pearson's expression, but she guessed it was annoyance. Nonetheless, he spoke into his radio and said, "Stand down."

Immediately, the helicopter tilted and headed back to Deadman's Island.

—*You're safe,* Anaya told Terra, and saw her shiver. *Are you cold?*

The sky had darkened with clouds, and Anaya smelled rain. But with her own thick hair, she was still perfectly warm, sometimes too warm, now that it was summer.

—*Your atmosphere is cold, for us. These skins help keep us warm.*

As always, Anaya understood more than just Terra's individual words. *Skins* meant the white fabric she wore. It was some kind of microfiber that regulated her body temperature. After so many early, clumsy conversations with Terra, the two of them had somehow forged a common mental language, like a forest path that got easier the more it was walked.

Terra made a sound that Anaya realized was a sneeze.

—*Are you sick?* Anaya asked worriedly.

—*Allergic.*

Of course! Terra had the same kind of allergies Anaya had suffered from all her life. It was strange, imagining the cryptogens having weaknesses, but this was not their world. Not their air, or sun, or pollen.

—*Where is the third rebel?* Anaya asked.

—*There.*

And as Anaya watched, another cryptogen emerged from the ship.

PETRA HATED IT INSTANTLY.

It walked on all fours. The head that jutted from its weird white bodysuit was long and sloping, like an alligator's. Maybe a dolphin's—if she was being super kind. Its eyes were set way back. She couldn't see ears. Its feet had long webbed toes. From its rear end curled a long tail. When its mouth opened, Petra saw sharp teeth.

Like the runner cryptogen, the swimmer had a mask fixed over its nostrils, which were slit-like holes in front of its eyes. When its gaze locked with hers, Petra looked away. She didn't want to talk to it. She was scared its words would appear inside her head.

When the missile had hit the cryptogens' ship, she'd been shocked, but hopeful, too. She wanted them destroyed. And then when she saw the flyer—she feared that she and all her friends had been lured here to die.

She still felt far from safe. Her eyes darted between the three cryptogen species. She remembered those pictures in Seth's sketchbook, the ones he'd shown them long ago. His dream creatures from another world. She'd hated them then. But seeing the real creatures now, right in front of her—that was a different thing altogether.

She caught herself stepping backward.

She shared *half* her DNA with these things.

She didn't want to look at them. She didn't want to *be* like them.

Was this what awaited her?

The webbed feet. Walking on all fours.

Would her body one day flip down to the ground? And she'd scuttle around, trying to hide her sharp teeth?

Every muscle in her body was telling her to run. She felt a light pattering of raindrops on her bare arms and hurriedly brushed them off, knowing they'd start her itching. To her surprise, she caught the swimmer doing exactly the same thing, rubbing its face, swishing its tail against the earth to dry it.

"It has the same water allergy as me!" she told Dr. Weber.

"We need to get them all inside the biodome," Dr. Weber replied. "Anaya, can you explain to Terra?"

AWE: SETH WASN'T SURE he'd ever properly experienced it before now.

In the light rain he watched the flyer swoop down and land nimbly beside the other two cryptogens, its massive feathers folding back along its arms. It was the tallest of the three by far. Its broad shoulders and deep chest tapered to a slim waist and skeletal legs, also feathered, that ended in clawed feet. Seth saw the talons flex, gouging the ground.

The talons startled him. They made the flyer seem even wilder than he'd imagined in his drawings. Power emanated from the flyer, and incredible danger, too. Heart pounding, Seth couldn't stop staring. He got the sense that he was being examined, too. His own wings felt shabby compared to the spectacular golden spans of the flyer. He hadn't seen its head yet, and waited, breathless, for the flyer to remove its helmet.

With both clawed hands, the flyer gripped its helmet on either side and pulled it smoothly off.

In his sketches, Seth had sometimes given his flying creatures the heads of humans, sometimes the heads of birds. But the reality was something altogether different.

The eyes were large and dark, though there was definitely a hawklike intensity in them, and in the upswept angles of its brows. It was hard to tell if it had hair or downy feathers, but there were certainly silver and gold feathers in the amazing crest that rose like a crown from the back of its head.

It had no mouth.

It had, instead, a beak. Its tip had a downward hook and was wickedly sharp.

Like the other cryptogens, it wore a mask fitted over its round nostrils above the beak.

Seth longed to talk to it, and at the same moment, was terrified by the idea. Words abruptly seared the inside of his skull.

—*You've damaged our ship.*

—*That wasn't supposed to happen,* he replied.

Silence. Seth wasn't sure he was believed. He could feel the energy of this creature, like an unstable charge of electricity, ready to strike like lightning. He knew what the flyer could do with its mind, the destruction it could inflict.

—*Were any of you injured?* Seth asked.

—*No.*

"Anaya," Dr. Weber said. "Tell them what's going to happen next."

Seth heard Anaya silently tell all three cryptogens about the place that had been prepared for them. The dome on the other side of the trees. It had the right air and water. The right plants, too.

Seth followed the flyer's gaze across the field to the biodome and sensed that the cryptogens were talking among themselves, blocking him out. Then the three of them went together to examine the damaged hull of their ship.

"Tell them," Pearson said to Seth, "that we'll help repair it."

When Seth relayed this to the flyer, the reply was mocking.

—*You cannot repair it. Only we can. And if we fail, our battle may already have been lost.*

CHAPTER TWO

PETRA WAS GRATEFUL FOR the windowless walls around her. She needed walls. Something to put between herself and everything that had just happened outside. Walls were good. Walls were normal.

On the field, she'd watched as the cryptogens were escorted inside an armored personnel carrier and driven to the biodome. She and Seth and Anaya had followed in a jeep. Inside the building, Petra was relieved they hadn't been taken to the observation level. Instead Dr. Weber led them downstairs to a conference room in the warren of unfinished offices. She told them to wait there and unwind, then disappeared to join Colonel Pearson.

Unwind?

Petra went straight to the bathroom and locked herself in a stall. More walls. Dr. Weber had given her a pack of hypoallergenic wipes, and she started scrubbing her face.

Outside, just before the cryptogen ship landed, they'd been attacked by a huge rhino thing with tentacles and a cratered mouth. And a tongue. A very long, yellow, sticky tongue that

14

had dragged her *by the head* across the field. Her face still had tongue goo on it, and she was desperate to get off every last bit.

She'd held it together when they fought and killed the rhino thing, when the spaceship landed, and when the three cryptogens emerged. That was a long time to hold it together, and now her whole body began to tremble.

She'd had weeks to get used to cryptogenic plants and bugs, and after all that, you'd think *nothing* would shock her. But the real cryptogens made her feel like the entire world was flying apart. They were like *people,* despite their wings and claws and beaks. They were intelligent—more intelligent than humans, or how could they cross the galaxy to get here?

Now that she'd finally laid eyes on them, there was no way she could trick herself into thinking they didn't exist. They were real and the entire world was different now—and maybe coming to an end.

She could practically hear her panic echoing around the bathroom stall, so she opened the door and walked out. She stood in front of the sink, thinking she might throw up, and took ten deep breaths.

When she returned to the conference room, Anaya was perched on the table, Seth was pacing, and they were talking telepathically. Petra was instantly barraged by their conversation. They were going fast, talking over each other, like they had to get out all their words before they ran out of breath.

—*When it flew out of the ship*—

—didn't know what it was. That helmet—

—and the crest!

—looked like a freaking angel, its wings—

—and the flyer's voice, it was so—

—smoke and gasoline. Felt like I had a bleeding lip—

—didn't expect the legs to be so thin—

—confused by the white skin when I first saw Terra—

—who expects aliens to wear clothing, but I guess—

—it was like meeting, I don't know, a different version of myself, Anaya said.

—Yeah, agreed Seth.

"Are you serious?" Petra said aloud. She had never been as good at telepathy as the others, and she definitely didn't feel like using it now. "They're aliens! Real aliens!"

She sat down, trembling. Even her teeth were chattering.

"Are you freaking out?" Seth asked.

"Yes, I am freaking out!"

"How can I help?" Anaya asked.

"You can freak out, too! Why are you so calm?"

"I'm not calm, believe me."

"Everything's happened so quickly," Petra said. "Oh my God, we really just met them!"

Seth sat down next to her and held her hand. All her attention went to her hand, his warm fingers wrapped around her icy ones. Some of her panic drained away. She didn't understand how Seth could make her feel calmer so easily. But he did. He smelled bad, but she didn't care.

She was embarrassed by how much she'd thought about what it might be like when he returned. Maybe he would hug her. Maybe he'd tell her how much he'd missed her. Maybe he'd kiss her.

Now here he was beside her at the table; it was enough that he held her hand for a few seconds before giving a squeeze and releasing it. Everything slowed down a bit, and they could talk at normal speed. There was a lot to talk about.

She listened as Anaya told Seth about the code that the rebel cryptogens had hidden in the DNA of every hybrid kid, and how they needed it back, to make a weapon to defeat the flyers. She told him about the cure she'd been given for the mosquito bird plague. And about the pesticide Dr. Weber had invented, which worked on the bugs.

"But that rhino thing you killed on the field?" Petra said. "That did not hatch. It was a live birth. The spray didn't work on it."

It almost set her teeth chattering again, wondering what other new monsters might start appearing on the planet.

A soldier came in with a cardboard box filled with sandwiches and bottled water. Petra didn't feel remotely hungry, but Seth grabbed one of the sandwiches and started eating ravenously. Anaya checked inside a couple of the sandwiches and picked one she wasn't allergic to. Petra opened a bottle of water and took a long drink.

Seth had already told them a tiny bit about what had happened after they got separated escaping the bunker. Now he told them about his journey in more detail. The freight train he'd hopped was bad enough—with one of those stilt bugs hatching inside, and Vincent getting kicked off—but things only got worse once they reached Washington State.

"We went into a Spray Zone," Seth said, "and found a superstore to buy some stuff, and I saved a kid from this weird armadillo bug, but then everyone saw my wings, and we had to run for it."

The police had trapped them on a bridge. Siena, who had a broken collarbone, got caught; Charles had escaped but no one knew where he was.

"Me and Esta jumped off the bridge," Seth said.

"Are you serious?" Petra exclaimed.

"We glided. It was so amazing." He paused, and Petra could see he was reliving the moment with a sense of wonder. "And then we met up with Darren and made it to a marina. And stole a boat."

But out on the water they'd had a fight over where to go, and Esta had accused Darren of ratting them out to the police. And then Darren had stung Seth with his tail.

Petra looked at the rip in the center of Seth's windbreaker.

"You were paralyzed? That must've been so scary!"

"Thought I was dying for sure," he said.

"But it just wore off?"

"In a couple of hours!"

That made her feel a bit better. Back in the bunker, during their escape, she'd stung a guard and worried she'd killed him. So he hadn't died—unless he'd been eaten by something while paralyzed. Like a pit plant. Or a giant worm. But she couldn't exactly be responsible for that.

"What happened to Darren?" Anaya asked.

"Esta made him jump."

Petra said, "You mean she blasted him with sound until he threw himself overboard."

Seth gave a nod.

"How close were you guys to shore?" Anaya asked, her eyes wide.

"He would've made it," Petra said. "He's a swimmer. You really think he snitched on you guys?"

"I don't know," said Seth, "but Esta was sure. Maybe she was right. The marine police seemed to find us pretty easily."

"So they got Esta?" Anaya asked.

"They jumped aboard and kidnapped her."

Petra saw his face flinch at the memory. Her tail thwacked jealously and startled Seth.

"Sorry," she said, trying to tuck it out of sight.

"I have no idea where they took her," he continued. "I was pretty close to the border, so I don't even know what country she's in."

"Pearson might be able to find out," Anaya said.

Seth snorted. "He won't help."

Petra hoped he was right. "I was so worried about you," she said, then quickly added, "We all were."

She was hoping he'd say something like "I was worried about you, too" or even "It's good to be here."

He said nothing, just sighed wearily. He reminded Petra of the withdrawn kid who'd first arrived at Salt Spring Secondary School a few months ago. His face was guarded. She blamed Esta. She'd poisoned his mind and probably convinced him that he could never trust her, or Anaya, or any of the grown-ups around him again.

Dr. Weber came into the room with fresh clothes for Seth.

"These should fit," she said.

"Thanks."

Petra felt calmer with Stephanie Weber in the room. The doctor had a steady, even comforting, presence—or maybe it was just that Petra was missing her own mom. Dr. Weber was a microbiologist with the Canadian Security Intelligence Service, and when Petra had first met her, back on Salt Spring Island, the doctor had definitely *not* been calming. She'd been the one, after all, to helicopter them to the army base on Deadman's Island. And tell the three of them that they were cryptogen hybrids.

Half alien. Which was not a comforting thing to hear. And yet, Dr. Weber had been through an awful lot with them, and Petra trusted her.

She knew Seth didn't feel the same, though, and it made Petra heartsick. It was so obvious to her that Dr. Weber thought of Seth as the son she'd lost—she'd even asked if she could become his foster mother. But that was before the second rain, Ritter's terrible bunker, and Seth getting left behind by rescue helicopters.

Dr. Weber looked like she wanted to say something to Seth—an explanation, another apology—but couldn't find the right words.

"There's a towel here, too," she said. "And a shower in the bathroom if you want."

Petra felt like a shower herself, but she doubted the water here had been treated so it was safe for her. She needed acid water that would burn normal people. That was the kind of girl she was now.

After Seth went off to the bathroom, Dr. Weber said, "We've already talked to your parents. They know you're okay."

"Thanks," said Petra. Her dad had probably been freaking out with worry. Everyone at the base must've heard that missile exploding against the spaceship and imagined the worst.

"How're you guys holding up?" Dr. Weber asked.

Petra looked at Anaya and couldn't help spluttering out a laugh. "Good, yeah. Pretty great."

"How're they doing?" Anaya asked Dr. Weber.

They meant the cryptogens, especially Terra, with whom Anaya had been communicating for days. Petra was starting to wonder if her friend was getting a little too close to Terra. Frankly, how the cryptogens were doing was the furthest thing from her mind.

"They're inside. We got their ship in, too. We just sealed the loading bay doors, and we're getting the temperature and atmosphere levels stabilized. When I left the observation room, they were still examining their ship."

"They seemed pretty angry," Petra said.

"Can you blame them?" asked Anaya.

"I was sure that flyer was going to blast us!"

"It was Terra who stopped him, I'm pretty sure."

"The colonel wants to get started right away," Dr. Weber said to Anaya. "With the interviews."

It was the only reason she and Anaya had been permitted at the landing. They were needed. As hybrids, they were the only ones who could communicate with the cryptogens.

Dr. Weber looked at Anaya with motherly concern. "Have you had something to eat? You need a little more time?"

"I'm good."

Petra gave her friend a sympathetic smile. She knew that Colonel Pearson and Dr. Weber had spent the last couple of days making lists of questions for the cryptogen rebels. And Anaya was expected to be the translator.

"I've told the colonel we'll need to take frequent breaks," said Dr. Weber.

"I can help," Seth said, returning from the bathroom in fresh jeans and a hoodie. They were virtually the same clothes Petra had first seen him in, except now he wasn't a gangly kid anymore. His barrel chest and bulky feathered arms made him look like a football player in a padded uniform.

"It'll save Anaya having to do all of it," he said. "And it'll be way faster."

"Thanks," Anaya said gratefully. "Will the colonel go for it?"

"I can ask," said Dr. Weber.

"Why don't all three of us do it?" Seth asked. "The telepathy's strongest between the same types, right?" He looked at Petra, like he expected her to back him up.

Startled, she looked at Dr. Weber. "I don't want to talk to them!"

She wasn't even sure she was happy about the cryptogens surviving the crash. She absolutely did not want to spend any more time with them.

"Petra, if you're uncomfortable, I won't volunteer you," said Dr. Weber. "We can return you to the base."

The idea of being left out made her feel wimpy. *Sent back to base.* Like a kid who couldn't handle a field trip. If Seth and Anaya were doing it, she didn't want to be the weak link.

She forced herself to take a few deep breaths.

"No, I'm fine," she said. "I'll translate, too."

She had some questions of her own she wanted to ask.

CHAPTER THREE

THROUGH THE WIDE OBSERVATION window, Anaya peered inside the biodome.

When the Vancouver Aquarium had designed this building, it was supposed to house four different environments: a boreal forest, a subpolar region, a Pacific marine habitat, and a tropical rain forest. Now it was a cryptogenic landscape of high black grass, berry-laden vines snaking from buried pit plants, and seed-spitting water lilies floating serenely on a pond so acidic no human would dare swim in it. And amid it all, like some giant mollusk, was the cryptogen ship itself. It had been transported to the biodome on a flatbed truck and moved inside with a crane.

And then there were the cryptogens themselves.

Anaya watched the swimmer, now free of its white protective clothing and mask, circling through the pool, snapping up water lilies.

At the top of the dome, the flyer circled restlessly. Gone were the scary helmet and the silver armor, but the beaked face still radiated violence, like the lingering gasoline scent of his silent voice. *His.* Without thinking, Anaya had chosen a pronoun for the flyer cryptogen. She couldn't explain why, any more than how she'd sensed that Terra was a she. At the same time, she also knew that the cryptogens might not even use words like this for themselves or each other.

As she watched, the flyer plunged down on the dead body of the rhino thing that had been moved in for food. With his talons, the flyer ripped off a hunk of flesh, transferred it to his hands, and ate it furiously.

Near the grove of black grass, Terra jumped high to pluck sprigs of berries from some vines. Next she slashed down a stalk of grass. With the tip of a claw, she slit it lengthwise, and peeled back the hard outer coating to reveal softer matter inside.

Anaya had a sudden memory of the wild grass she used to suck as a kid, how sweet it was. She realized her mouth was watering, just watching Terra eat the black grass. It was strange to think of the black grass as food. When it had first appeared on Salt Spring, it was spiky and relentless. When burned, it sent up toxic smoke that choked people. And yet, to the runners, it was nourishment—and judging by Terra's enthusiasm, it tasted really good.

It was like Terra hadn't eaten in years. Maybe none of them had, Anaya thought with a start. All that time aboard their spaceship, traveling to Earth, orbiting for years, they must have gotten *some* kind of nourishment—but it probably wasn't freshly grown food like these plants from their home planet.

Still chewing, Terra curiously examined one of the chairs that had been moved into the biodome ahead of the cryptogens' arrival. The furniture looked out of place: a bizarre living room in the middle of a jungle. No one had really known how to make the cryptogens feel at home, so they'd brought in an arrangement of chairs, beds, and side tables from the army base.

Terra now tried to sit in a chair, but the seat was too narrow, and her mighty haunches cracked the whole thing apart. Pieces clattered to the ground.

—*Apologies,* she said silently.

—*No worries,* Anaya replied, grinning.

Like some extraterrestrial Goldilocks, Terra warily examined a couple of other chairs, then patted a mattress and made a few tentative bounces.

Anaya found it hard to tear her gaze away from her cryptogen parallel. She was extraordinarily beautiful. She no longer wore her white astronaut clothing and hood, and Anaya could now see how tall her ears were. The way they stuck up attentively made her look even more kangaroo-like.

Colonel Pearson's voice pulled her attention back inside the observation room.

"You three are crucial to this operation," he said, handing out wireless headsets to her and Seth and Petra. "We'll feed you the questions, you relay them to the cryptogens, then translate their answers for us over the mic. I can't stress enough how important it is that you leave nothing out. Be as accurate as you can."

"I haven't even talked to one of them yet," said Petra nervously.

"It's okay," Anaya reassured her. "It's not so different from the way we silent talk. It'll be a bit clumsier at the start."

Along the back wall of the observation room, officers in headsets waited at their laptops, ready to make transcripts.

"You'll only speak to your parallels," Pearson said. "For ease of reference, the runner is C1, the swimmer C2, and the flyer C3."

Anaya looked at Pearson in dismay. "Do we have to do that?"

"That's pretty much how Ritter labeled us in the bunker," murmured Seth.

"I don't care," said Pearson. "It's efficient. Let's get started."

"Let me go inside, at least," Anaya said. "It feels weird talking to them from out here, like they're prisoners. Especially with these guys around." She nodded at the three armed soldiers stationed in the observation room.

"The cryptogens are not in prison," Pearson said irritably. "They're in a specially sealed habitat by their own request."

Still, Anaya didn't like the idea of a window between her and Terra. It felt like a zoo.

"You really want to go inside?" said Petra, looking horrified.

"I wouldn't advise it," Colonel Pearson said. "We don't know what the cryptogens are capable of."

"If they wanted to hurt us," said Seth, "that flyer could've killed us on the field."

"Is it safe for them?" Pearson asked Dr. Weber.

"The toxicology screening on the ship's hull was clear," said Dr. Weber. "And the air samples we're getting from the biodome aren't triggering any pathogen readings. Nothing that would hurt the kids."

"What about the atmosphere itself?" Pearson asked.

Anaya already knew the atmosphere in there would not be good for regular humans, but she figured that as a hybrid, she could handle it.

"It's just a little hotter, with a little less oxygen, right?" she said.

"What about the plants?" Petra reminded her.

Seth shrugged and rustled his feathers. "Nothing we can't cut through."

"You want to go in, too?" Petra demanded.

"We have protective eyewear," Dr. Weber said, "in case the water lilies start spitting. If you begin feeling light-headed, you come right out. You're sure about this, you two?"

"Yes," Anaya said at the same time as Seth, and she smiled at him.

"But maybe they don't want *you* inside," Petra said.

Anaya thought this was a fair comment. "Can I ask Terra?"

Pearson was starting to look like a grumpy grandfather. He nodded.

—*Can we come inside? To talk?*

Inside the biodome, Terra turned toward her, as if called.

—*Yes.*

"Terra said it's okay."

"All right," said Pearson. "Take them in."

At the end of the observation room, a soldier opened a door and led her and Seth down a short corridor that dead-ended at a windowless door.

"When that light goes green, you can go inside," the soldier told them, and left them alone.

Her pulse thumped at the base of her throat and she felt her ears pop as the pressure changed. She looked at Seth, suddenly glad she wasn't alone.

"Did you ever think . . . ," he began, his lips dry.

"No," she said. "Not in a million years."

"It's like we're explorers or something."

"Yeah." Anaya could see his knees shaking. "You okay?"

He gave a quick nod. "Feel like I've been waiting my whole life for this."

The light over the door went green. Anaya turned the handle and pushed. Hothouse air poured over her, but she shivered with nervousness. She stepped into the biodome. It felt unreal. She'd been *out there,* and now she was *in here.* She inhaled deeply. The air was good.

And not just good.

It was *better.*

Whatever was in this new atmosphere, it made her lungs feel bigger.

"Do you notice it?" she asked Seth.

"I feel stronger," he said softly. "This is what the whole world will be like one day."

"Unless we stop it."

"Yeah," said Seth, but he'd faltered before saying it. Anaya looked at him worriedly. He didn't want Earth turning into *this,* did he? Did *she?* With air like this, she felt like she could run even faster, and jump higher. It troubled her that she was even thinking this way.

She tried to tidy her thoughts.

Stepping into the biodome was a bit like entering someone else's house, with its own definite scent, strange but not totally unfamiliar. Near the grove of black grass, Terra watched her approach. Anaya was anxiously aware of the flyer watching, too, from atop the carcass of the rhino creature. The swimmer was still in the pond, though its head was clear of the water, and its eyes were on her. Anaya avoided the vines questing across the ground, and steered clear of the pond. A few water lilies perked up and leaned their way.

She only now realized how quiet the cryptogens were. They didn't seem to have any spoken language. She hadn't heard grunts or chirps, or anything. Telepathy must be their only way of communicating.

When she was a comfortable distance from Terra, she stopped, but Seth angled off, going deeper into the biodome toward the flyer, who now stood protectively atop the mollusk-like ship.

—*Good luck,* she said to Seth.

—*You too,* he replied, glancing back to return her nervous smile.

Terra now approached her in long easy strides, half walk, half lope. Anaya felt herself tense. When Terra stopped, they were no more than six feet apart.

They beheld each other. Anaya sensed that her wonder was matched by Terra's. Both of them, creatures from across the universe.

Terra's large eyes were remarkably beautiful. They had no whites but were amber, with gold-flecked irises, and pupils that were not circles, but horizontal slits. Despite the hair covering the runner's entire body, the way she held herself was uncannily human.

She was taller than Anaya, but not by so much. She had narrow sloped shoulders, long arms held attentively in front of her. Her tapered hands were amazingly nimble-looking and graceful, despite the claws. Her powerful legs were constantly bent, as if ready to spring at any moment. She stood with an expectant forward tilt. There was something strangely regal about her.

Anaya felt suddenly ridiculous, like a stuffed toy version of the real thing.

—*Afraid?* Terra asked.

—*Yes.*

—*I am also afraid.*

From a nearby vine, Terra tore a sprig of berries and offered it to Anaya. When she accepted, their hands touched briefly. Terra's fingers were warm and softly furred.

Anaya chewed on the berries. Terra smiled. Her face was such a different shape, but it was unmistakably a smile, the ends of her mouth pulling back, the lips parting slightly. Anaya returned the smile.

The scent of Terra's fur was somehow comforting. Anaya was reminded of the gentle, friendly smell of the horses in a stable back on Salt Spring she'd sometimes visit.

Anaya saw Terra's nostrils flare and realized she was being sniffed, too. With a flash of self-consciousness, she wondered what *she* smelled like. Terra tentatively stretched out an arm and touched Anaya's long hair. The urge to touch her back was over-whelming. Anaya reached up to touch one of her ears, because it looked so soft. It felt exactly as she'd imagined.

Anaya jerked when an officer's voice came over her headset.

"We need to get started."

"Oh, right, okay."

Terra looked at her curiously, surprised by the sudden sound, not knowing what had been said.

"Ask C1 what its rank is," the officer instructed her.

It was such a brutally unfriendly way to open a conversation—and it definitely sounded like an interrogation. It was the wrong start.

—Are you comfortable? she asked Terra instead. *Warm enough?*

—Yes.

—Is there enough to eat here?

—Yes. The ship gave us what we need, but this is true food.

"Anaya," came her officer over her headset, "are you asking the question?"

It was jarring, shifting from telepathy to human words.

"Yeah, in a sec."

—They want me to ask you questions. Is that all right?

—Yes. We have many of our own.

—They want to know your rank.

She concentrated on the answer—with all its tendrils that carried much more meaning than clumsy words—then relayed it.

"She was trained as a scientist and a pilot. She flew this ship."

She was surprised, and weirdly comforted, that Terra did the same jobs as her parents. She glanced over at Seth and saw him looking intently up at the flyer. They seemed to be in conversation, too. Was he getting fed the exact same questions as her?

—Explain the nature of your mission to our planet, she asked Terra now. *I'm sorry: these aren't my questions.*

—A pioneer mission.

Her gut told her this wasn't a good translation, but it was as close as she could get. *Pioneer* sounded too innocent. Just some friendly alien pioneers hankering after fresh air and wide-open skies to plonk down a homestead. Then she realized this was no different from what humans did. It was never innocent. Wherever humans had settled, there were always people already there. People who got overthrown or wiped out altogether.

"The cryptogen leaders are here to make Earth their own," she reported into her headset when Terra was finished. "Once all the flora and fauna are established, and the atmosphere's set up, they'll come down. They're hoping that most of us will already be dead by then. The survivors will be killed or enslaved."

She knew this plan wasn't Terra's, but even uttering such terrible words made her feel sick.

Nearby a chair tipped over with a bang, pulled down by a restless vine. Drawn by the noise, a water lily unleashed a volley of seeds. Anaya was glad of her protective glasses.

Another question blurted over her headset.

—*How many are carried aboard your vessel?* she asked Terra.

She listened, eyes closed. She still found it easier to concentrate without her vision distracting her. Words, thoughts, images flared in her mind.

—*Most are still sleeping.*

She was inside an enormous chamber of the cryptogen ship orbiting the planet. Attached to the walls by throbbing red cords were hundreds—no, thousands—of long, fleshy pods. And Anaya understood that this chamber was just one of many aboard the vast ship. A quick mathematical calculation took place in her head.

"Almost seven hundred thousand," she said quietly into her

headset. "Most of the soldiers are still asleep in these weird pods that look like giant gray corncobs. There's a small team of cryptogens awake who supervise the day-to-day operations of the ship. The flyer was one of the senior officers on duty."

"How many active rebels are there, total?" was the next question.

—*Not many,* came Terra's terse reply, carrying a number with it.

Anaya felt a gulp of despair. Just three hundred? Out of a million? Could you even call that a resistance? Or was it just a group of doomed people?

—*We are not the only rebels who landed on your planet,* Terra added.

When Anaya passed all this on to her officer, she heard a rustling sound over the headset, and then Pearson's voice.

"How many landings were there?" he barked.

—*Ten,* Terra answered. *In locations on the planet where our rebels were able to communicate with sympathetic hybrids.*

It was ridiculous, but she felt a prick of hurt. Why had she assumed she was the only one contacted by a cryptogen? She'd come to think of Terra as a friend, but maybe the cryptogen only saw her as a particularly useful specimen.

—*You were one of the first we could reach,* Terra said. *One of the first who talked back. Many were too scared. It was difficult to find ten.*

Anaya wasn't surprised. Lots of the other hybrid kids in the bunker had hated it when they'd discovered they had telepathy. It freaked them out. Even here, in the safety of the Deadman's Island army base, some of the kids refused to use it. And if you didn't want to talk silently with a hybrid friend, you sure wouldn't want an alien species in your head.

"Anaya!" Pearson said impatiently. "You need to tell me everything you're told."

"She said there were ten landings."

"Did you know about this?"

"No!"

"One landing sounds like a diplomatic mission," Pearson said, "ten sounds like military scouting parties."

"What do you want me to ask her?" Anaya said. She felt thrown by this news, and nervous, too, standing there in front of Terra. A vine slyly slid over her shoe, but Terra, with one of her clawed toes, casually impaled it and flicked it aside.

"Are they in contact with the other rebels?" Pearson wanted to know.

"No," Anaya told him. "They need to stay silent so the main vessel doesn't pick up any of their signals."

"Can they at least tell us where the other rebels landed?"

—*We won't tell you,* Terra replied bluntly after Anaya asked.

—*Why not?*

—*To keep our other landing parties safe. We need to be sure that none of you will use this information to attack them.*

This seemed fair to Anaya, but she knew Pearson wouldn't be happy about it.

"I don't imagine they'll get a warm welcome in most places," Pearson muttered.

"We didn't give them a warm welcome here," Anaya reminded him.

"Are all their missions identical?" the colonel wanted to know.

—*Yes,* Terra replied. *We need to extract the code from the hybrids' blood. From this we will make the weapon.*

—*What form does this weapon take?* Anaya asked. She already knew that the cryptogens had hidden a code in her DNA, and the DNA of every hybrid child they had created.

—*A chemical substance,* Terra explained. *We sent ten teams, because we do not know how successful any one will be.*

It occurred to Anaya all over again what a risk the rebels were taking. They were putting themselves at the mercy of the humans. She wasn't sure this was a good idea. But what other way was there?

—*Do your leaders, I mean the ones in charge of the invasion, do they know where you are, right now?* Anaya asked Terra.

—*No. All our landings were cloaked.*

That was very, very good, Anaya thought, and passed it on to Pearson.

"Thank God," the colonel said. "But presumably they know ten ships have left the orbiter ship."

—Most likely they will think we have left for another world, to avoid the fight. They will not think we've come to Earth.

"And there are other rebels still aboard the orbiter?"

—Yes, waiting for our orders.

"Ask her when the invasion is planned," Pearson told her.

—Thirty-eight planetary rotations.

That was just over a month. Not much time for Earth to prepare. But lots of time to get weaker. They had an herbicide and pesticide now, yes, but the plants and bugs were relentless, and now there were cryptogen animals being *born* on the planet. Her father had also said the atmosphere was changing fast and would eventually make humans weaker still.

—What will they do once they invade? Anaya asked fearfully. *How bad will it be?*

—They will be virtually impossible to defeat. Our hope is to stop them, before the invasion begins.

—HELLO? PETRA BEGAN TENTATIVELY.

She felt like a wimp, hanging back in the observation room when Seth and Anaya were there in the biodome. But she wanted very thick glass between her and the swimmer cryptogen.

It was still swishing around in the pond. It looked less ugly when it swam, cutting effortlessly through the water. It had an unusual way of swimming, undulating its body head to tail like a wave. With a start, Petra remembered she'd swum exactly the same way, last time she was in the harbor. The time her mother died. She tried to push the thought away, but it stayed in her mind like a darkening sky.

Now that the swimmer had removed its weird white bodysuit, its skin tattoos were on full display. They were the same black-and-gold colors as hers, but their pattern was more complicated, like the spiraling interior of a tropical seashell. Really, it was quite beautiful.

Still, Petra thought it was unfair she got the cryptogen that looked least human. Anaya's was graceful, even though it had monster thighs and a very big bottom; Seth's had a terrifying magnificence to it.

—*Hello?* she said again, trying to form her silent words very clearly. *My—name—is—Petra.*

The cryptogen gave no sign of hearing her.

"I don't think it hears me," she said, looking at the officer assigned to her.

Maybe this swimmer thing wasn't even that smart. The other two cryptogens looked alert, but hers? It didn't look like it could cross a parking lot on its own—much less the universe.

"Keep trying," the officer told her.

She didn't even want to be doing this. She wasn't good at silent talking. She wasn't even good at French! She felt overheated, as if all that hot air they'd pumped into the biodome was seeping through the observation window.

She tried once again:

—*Hello?*

The swimmer propelled itself gracefully out of the pond. On all fours, it stumped closer to the observation window. Its feet had five webbed toes. In the water it was elegant, but on land it lumbered. As it got closer to the window, Petra couldn't help taking a step back. Just how thick was the glass?

Head tilted up, the swimmer glared balefully at her. A word suddenly took murky shape inside Petra's head. It had a bluish light around it and tasted of seaweed.

—*Ugly.*

Had she heard right? Had this thing just called *her* ugly?

—*What did you say?* she demanded.

The answer came more clearly this time:

—*Ugly.*

—*At least I walk upright,* she retorted.

She had no idea how her words would be translated, but suddenly the swimmer cryptogen reared up. Amazing how much more human a creature looked when standing upright. Petra gave a squeak of surprise. Its new height was startling, but even more startling was the blaze of color from its belly and chest. Its black-and-gold pattern flashed an aggressive red. It tilted its head skyward, as though to make itself taller still, and its barbed tail lifted threateningly. Petra felt her own tail spike high defensively.

—*Good,* the swimmer said with satisfaction. *You are not defective.*

The swimmer's words lingered in her head, along with their unique light and smell. She remembered Anaya explaining that these sensations must be like the cryptogens' names. Her friend had also sensed that Terra was a she. Maybe Petra wasn't very smart telepathically, but she didn't get a strong sense of *he* or *she* from the swimmer. It felt weird and wrong deciding pronouns for someone, but maybe she could use *ze* and *zir.*

The swimmer's belly faded from red to black and gold, and when ze leveled zir gaze at Petra, she was startled to see that zir eyes had two pupils each. As ze peered into the darkened observation room, zir pupils dilated and merged together into a crescent. Intelligence blazed from these eyes.

"You two talking yet?" Petra's officer asked over her headset.

"Oh, we're talking," she replied.

"Let's get going, then," the officer said, and fed her the first question.

—*They want to know your rank,* Petra told the swimmer.

A word took shape in her head.

"Scientist, I think," she reported back.

Anaya was right: when you used telepathy, the meaning didn't come with just the words; there were images and associations, too. In this case, *scientist* also meant *builder* and *designer.* And what exactly did ze design? The answer trembled through her.

—*You made* us, *didn't you?* she said. *That was you?*

—*Yes. I was part of the project.*

Project? Like a science fair project? More like a Frankenstein project. Anger flickered inside Petra. Another question was being fed to her over her headset, but she ignored it. She had her own questions, ones she'd wanted to ask for a long time.

—*Were you there when it happened? To my mother?*

Her anger must've been clear because she saw the swimmer's head tilt back, and the chest fill and deflate. Was that defiance, or guilt?

—*Yes.*

Petra's eyes were wet. Her poor mother.

—*No harm,* the swimmer said, zir words stinking like seaweed on a hot beach. *A simple injection.*

No harm? Yeah, being jabbed with a needle full of cryptogen DNA, that was no big deal at all. Her mom had been unconscious. She hadn't said yes. None of them had, not Anaya's mother, not Seth's.

—*How many?* she wanted to know.

—*Thousands. Across the planet.*

—*You came down in ships like that one?* Petra pointed at the one inside the biodome.

—*The same ones, yes. They are swift and undetectable.*

—*It was monstrous,* she said.

—*It was vital.*

Over her headphones, she heard the officer yapping, telling her to stay on task.

"Shush!" she snapped back, wiping away tears. She wasn't done with her own questions, not by a long shot.

—*Vital to you, maybe*, Petra raged. *What about us? We didn't ask for this! You've made us freaks!*

She was aware that the more emotion she put into her silent talking, the better the swimmer seemed to understand. It was a kind of talking with your whole self. And she felt like she was understanding zir a bit faster now, too.

—*We needed you*, ze said. *As a safe place to keep the substance.*

The substance. That was the word that Terra had used to describe Anaya's blood—and whatever special thing was in it that the rebels needed to make their weapon.

—*And we also needed you as translators*, the swimmer added.

It was so one-sided, Petra fumed. All they cared about was what *they* were getting out of it. They were as bad as Ritter with his insane bunker experiments.

—*What will happen to us?* she demanded. And then she asked a more precise question. *Will we turn into you?*

The silence went on a worrying length of time.

—*No. You will not become like us.*

—*Then what? Will I keep changing?*

—*I do not know*, ze said.

—*What will I look like when I'm done?*

—I do not know.

She snorted in frustration.

"Petra." Her officer stood beside her. "Follow the script and report your answers!"

"Just a second! This is important."

She took a breath and asked the question that had been throbbing at the back of her mind.

—Can you fix us?

With all their advanced technology, it had to be possible. Here on Earth they could chop off her tail, but it might grow back. And they could never change the stuff inside her brain, or the DNA in every single one of her cells. But maybe these guys could.

—Fix? said the swimmer, obviously confused.

She was about to say, "Turn us back to the way we were," but she and Anaya and Seth had never been normal, not for one second of their existence. They were conceived and born as hybrid creatures. She needed to be more precise.

—Remove all substance of you, she said. *Make us like the other people on this planet.*

—Then we could not talk to you.

—Okay, but could you do it?

—That is not possible.

—Why not? she asked, her hopes wilting.

—You are already built. You cannot be unbuilt.

—*YOUR RANK, PLEASE,* **SETH** asked.

He'd added the *please.* The flyer was definitely someone you said *please* to.

The cryptogen glared down at him from the hull of the damaged ship. Seth wasn't sure he was going to get a reply. But then, inside his head, the answer came like a spark blazing into flame.

—*Warrior.*

With that single word came the flare of a gasoline-scented image inside Seth's mind: the flyer in crested helmet and silver armor, leading more flyers into battle. Their helmets shimmered with a violent sonic energy. On the ground, buildings and living creatures were obliterated.

Inside the biodome, Seth was aware of his heart pumping hard. So the flyer was some kind of leader, a general. And Seth's instincts told him that the flyer was also a he. The flyer jumped and landed on the ground, only a few feet from Seth.

The cryptogen's arms were almost skeletal, little more than anchors for his amazing feathers. Despite how thin he was, his shoulders and head—his entire being—radiated power like a raging fire. Seth's gaze was drawn immediately to the silver-and-gold crest flaring from the back of his head.

He couldn't help touching the back of his own head but felt no sign of waiting feathers.

It was uncanny, looking at the flyer. His face was both unearthly and weirdly familiar. Maybe from his dreams and drawings. He felt like he was looking at a relative he never knew he had.

Now that he was closer, Seth noticed for the first time the scar on the cryptogen's face, a thick cord curving around his left eye.

"He's a military leader," Seth reported through his headset. "Super powerful. A general."

Over his headset: "Ask him why he became a rebel."

Nervously, Seth relayed the question to the general, hoping he was shaping his message clearly. With Esta, the silent talking had become second nature, but this was new and more difficult. Still, there was an unmistakable flicker of light, bridging the gap between his mind and the flyer's. They were, after all, genetic relatives.

The thought made him shiver. He wondered if the general was, in some strange way, his father.

A metallic word hammered itself together in Seth's head:

—*Disgust.*

He didn't understand, but instinctively shut his eyes to focus on the images rapidly flooding his mind. A battle. In the water and on the ground, the runners and swimmers were being decimated, their buildings imploding and sinking, as the flyers unleashed a hurricane of sound.

Seth saw the general get hit in the face by some kind of harpoon. He spiraled, senseless, to the ground.

Another image: the general, his head bandaged, being offered food by two runners who worked in some kind of field hospital. Seth understood that the general had temporarily lost his ability to use sound as a weapon. Inside the hospital were wounded swimmers and runners. Outside the hospital was the wreckage of a city.

Yet another image: the hospital being overrun by flyers, and the general being rescued. All his runner caregivers were killed.

—*Disgust,* came the word again. And now Seth fully understood.

For perhaps the first time in his life, the general had been helpless, and had felt the same terror and misery as the swimmers and runners. The runners had saved his life. He'd seen their decency. And after the flyers had killed his runner caregivers and rescued him, he was disgusted by everything he'd done in the past. He'd become a spy for the rebels, and eventually one of their leaders—but the other flyers still thought he was loyal.

After Seth relayed all this over the headset, Pearson came on.

"It's a good story," the colonel remarked, and Seth got the sense he wasn't convinced. "Was he responsible for sending down the rains on us?"

Seth asked and waited for the general's answer. When it came, it took him a long time to fathom it all.

"Yes. He was a senior officer in the acting crew. He gave the order to start the rains." Seth could practically hear Pearson's anger in the quiet hiss over the headset. "But he had to do it!

If he hadn't, he would've given himself away. And the rain was necessary. It was always necessary!"

"How?" demanded Pearson.

"The rebels needed us, the hybrids, to start changing. The way we did after the rain. So they could communicate with us—and with you."

"Why does he want to communicate with us?" Pearson asked.

—*We've come here to fight a war,* the general said after Seth relayed the question. *Against the flyers. Against tyranny. We want to form an alliance with you.*

The general's words echoed forcefully in Seth's head, and the taste of them, too. He told the colonel what he'd been told, and Seth heard Pearson conferring with some of the other officers in the observation room.

The general flared his wings briefly, light glinting off their metallic edges. Seth took a step back.

—*Answer my questions now.*

It was not a request. Seth felt the hot crackle of his impatience.

—*Are you willing to help us?*

"He wants to know if you're willing to help them," Seth said to Pearson.

"Tell him we need to know we can trust them."

"But they've already—"

"Do what I say," Pearson snapped.

Reluctantly Seth echoed Pearson's words.

—*We already sent you a cure,* the general answered, gouging at the ground with his taloned feet. *We came down at huge risk to ourselves. You attacked us. We have not attacked you.*

Yet. Seth felt that word hanging in the air. He looked fearfully at the general's feathered head, knowing what his brain could do. He could probably kill every human in the building before a single shot was fired.

Seth relayed the flyer's words to Pearson.

"We need to know what kind of weapons they have. We need—"

The general was already talking in Seth's head, drowning Pearson out.

—The only weapon of importance is the one that we must build together. We hid the code inside you. Now we need it back.

Seth frowned. *If you had this code all along, why didn't you make the weapon yourselves?*

—We tried. It needs to be grown in a living creature. And it would not grow inside us. It died inside us. But it will grow inside you.

Seth didn't like the sound of this.

—So what happens now?

—We will extract it, then let it produce a virus.

—And what will the virus do, exactly?

—If successful, it will permanently destroy our ability to use sound as a weapon.

The news was so momentous that Seth had no words. He felt his breath entering and leaving his body. This would change everything. Without sound, the flyers would be no more

powerful than the other cryptogens. Maybe weaker. Yes, the flyers had flight and razor-sharp wings, but the runners had claws
that could punch through metal, and the swimmers had stingers
with paralyzing venom.

—*What about your helmets, though?* he asked the general.

—*No. They merely amplify our sound many times over. But if we
cannot make sound, the helmets are useless.*

"Seth!" Pearson barked over his headset. "Talk to me!"

He looked back through the glass and saw Pearson glaring.

—*And me?* Seth asked. He was half cryptogen, after all.

—*Yes.*

In some ways, it was a relief; the sonic weapon had always
terrified him. But right now, it might be the only thing keeping
him safe.

He took a few minutes to tell Pearson everything he'd just
learned. The colonel fed him yet another question, but Seth
ignored it. He had one of his own he wanted to ask first. It had
been worrying away at the back of his mind.

—*Will I be able to fly?* he asked the general.

—*You will never fly.*

Seth felt as though someone had struck at his heart with a
chisel.

—*How do you know?*

—*You are not us. You will never fully become like us.*

—*But I can already glide, and—*

—*Gliding is possible, but not actual flight. I have studied you.*

You are too heavy. Your legs, your torso, your head and bones. It is too much to take aloft.

Seth looked at the general's tall limbs, as fine as a bird's, and his massive muscled chest. Seth's own body was all wrong for flight. He'd worried it was, and now he knew. But he still felt like someone had broken a wordless promise to him. A promise made years ago and repeated over and over again, in his dreams.

—*I DON'T UNDERSTAND,* **ANAYA** asked Terra. *How can we* stop *the invasion?*

She was completely thrown. Maybe she hadn't understood properly. Had Terra truly said there was a chance of defeating the flyers *before* they arrived on Earth?

—*If we can make the weapon in time,* Terra said, *we will take it back to the main vessel. Our laboratories will grow more of it. Then we can deliver it throughout the ship while the winged ones are still asleep.*

Anaya imagined the flyers in their pods, a chemical weapon passing through those long umbilical cords that fed them.

—*After they are infected, they will be unable to strike with sound,* Terra continued. *Then we will overpower them and seize control of the ship.*

—*So we wouldn't get invaded at all!*

—*Correct.*

Anaya had always assumed there was no stopping an invasion. This news seemed too much to hope for. If they could make the weapon, all they needed to do was get it back to the cryptogens' main vessel in outer space—

She looked across the biodome at the scorched hull of the small landing ship.

—*Can it still fly?* she asked.

—*No.*

Without it, even if they managed to make this weapon, there was no way of delivering it.

—*Can it be fixed?* she asked desperately.

—*No,* said Terra, *not with any materials on your planet.*

CHAPTER FOUR

"PASS THE RICE, PLEASE?" Anaya asked Seth.

The apartment was filled with the delicious smell of the ratatouille they'd all made. Mom had put everyone to work. She and Dad had sliced peppers and some very squidgy eggplants—none of the vegetables were the freshest, but these days they were lucky to get any at all. Petra and Seth had peeled and chopped the onions and garlic; Mr. Sumner and Dr. Weber had started the rice steaming, drained the chickpeas, and set the table.

Anaya found the familiar clinking of cutlery and glasses incredibly comforting. When Seth passed her the rice, her claws clicked against the ceramic bowl and it wobbled a bit. She was still getting used to them. Simple things were hard, like holding a fork, or a hairbrush, or tying her shoelaces.

"We could file them down, if you like," Dr. Weber suggested.

It would've been much easier, yes, but the claws made her feel stronger. She didn't have Seth's razor-sharp wings, or a sound weapon that could drop people; she didn't have a poison-tipped tail like Petra. But she could jump high, and kick people across the room—and these claws of hers, they could pierce and slash. She needed to know she had fight in her. The hair on her face, she shaved. But her claws, she kept. She just had to be very careful when she scratched her nose.

"She doesn't want to get rid of them," Petra said, spooning ratatouille beside her rice. "Same reason I'm not getting rid of my tail."

Anaya nodded and smiled back. When Petra had first felt her tail growing, she'd freaked out and wanted it hacked off. But after the water striders attacked the army base and killed her mother, she'd stopped asking for her tail to be removed. She didn't even try to hide it anymore. She knew it was a weapon, and there were a lot of things on the planet trying to kill them right now.

Inwardly Anaya sighed. Preparing the meal had been so relaxing, and she was hoping this feeling of normalcy—this *illusion* of normalcy—could go on just a little longer. She could tell, though, that her parents, and Petra's father, were desperate to hear about what had happened today—on the landing field, and inside the biodome. They had too many questions. And how could she blame them? As exhausted as she was, her own mind was still buzzing with everything that had happened.

To finally see the cryptogens. To touch Terra's hand, her fur.

And to learn the full reason why they'd come.

Across the table, Dad uncorked a bottle of red wine he'd found in a cupboard. He poured hefty glasses for all the grown-ups, then splashed a little into the teens' tumblers, too.

"Quite a day," Dr. Weber said.

"So," Dad began, looking at her, and then the others, "how much can you actually tell us?"

No parents had been at the landing site, or inside the bio-dome during the interviews. Colonel Pearson had told Anaya and Petra and Seth that everything that happened with the cryptogens needed to stay secret—which meant no talking about it to anyone on the base: not the other hybrids, not even their own parents. So far she'd kept to that rule, and up till this moment, none of the parents had asked.

Anaya looked over at Dr. Weber, waiting for her to reinforce Colonel Pearson's stern warning.

"Technically, the information is highly classified," Dr. Weber said before taking a deep sip of her wine. "But I don't care about any of that. As far as I'm concerned, your kids can tell you whatever they want. You have the right to know."

"Honestly?" Anaya asked in relief. It had been torture not telling Mom and Dad anything.

For the rest of the meal she and Petra and Seth told their stories. The wine made her feel pleasantly warm. She'd only talked with Terra, and she learned new details from her friends. She told them about the rebels' plan to take the weapon back to the main ship and use it to destroy the flyers' ability to attack with sound.

"But if their ship's grounded," asked Mr. Sumner, "how're they going to get this weapon back up there?"

"Can they repair it?" Mom asked.

"Some of it," Anaya said. "Terra told me they can heal the damage to the hull."

"Heal?" said Petra. "Makes it sound like the ship's alive."

"The way Terra described it was like a skin graft," said Anaya. "Maybe more like 3D printing, using material from another part of the ship."

"So far so good," said Mom. "Is there another problem?"

Anaya took a breath. "The levitation system."

"That sounds pretty major," said Seth.

Anaya nodded. "It got destroyed and there's no way they can make a new one down here."

"But there're other rebel ships, right?" Mom said. "Couldn't they use one of those?"

"They won't give away any rebel locations," Anaya reminded her. "But Terra did say there might be another ship they could salvage. Sixteen years ago, when they first came here, one of their ships crashed."

"You mean when they were abducting women and making little hybrid babies," Petra said scathingly.

Anaya had been trying very hard not to think about this fact. She worried it would make it harder to like the rebels, no matter how much they were doing to defeat the flyers and stop Earth from being invaded. She pressed on:

"Terra said if they can find that crashed ship, they can salvage the part they need from it."

"Do they have any idea where it is?" Dad asked.

"Not yet. But there's equipment on their ship they can use to try to locate it."

"Well," said Mom. "It seems there's good reason to be hopeful. A possible weapon to overthrow the flyers. And a plan to stop the invasion." She raised her glass. "We have a lot to celebrate tonight."

PETRA WASN'T SO SURE about that.

"Except there's no way of us ever going back to normal," she said. "The swimmer said it was impossible."

She could still smell the swimmer's seaweedy words, like they were trapped in her nose. But it didn't stop her from taking another helping of ratatouille. She hadn't eaten since breakfast, and she was famished.

"The flyer said it was impossible for me to fly," Seth said quietly.

Petra put down her fork. "He really said that?"

Somehow this seemed even worse than her predicament. She wanted normal. Seth had wanted *less* normal. He wanted to go *all the way*—so that his feathered arms really could take him into the sky. Even if she couldn't understand that, she understood how important it was to him. After everything, it seemed too cruel to deny him flight.

"I worried it'd be that way," he said. "I'm built wrong for it. Too heavy."

"Oh, Seth, I'm sorry," she said.

"There are other ways to fly," Mrs. Riggs said kindly.

Seth didn't look up from his plate. "Become a pilot like you. That's something, I guess."

Petra had kept a close eye on him through the meal. Of the three of them, he'd talked least. He pushed some uneaten food around on his plate.

"We need to help Esta," he said, finally looking up.

"I have news about her," Dr. Weber said.

Petra saw Seth sit up straighter.

"Colonel Pearson said she's being held in a detention center. In the US."

"Can he get her out?" Seth asked.

Petra's tail tapped irritably against her chair back, and she made it stop.

"I don't think it's going to be that easy," Dr. Weber said.

"Why not?"

"They still think the hybrids are security risks."

"Pearson can change their minds about that," Anaya said. "Right?"

"Even if he could, they're holding Esta on criminal charges. They've accused her of murdering Dr. Ritter."

Petra watched Seth's eyes dart desperately around the room, like he was trying to find something solid to grip onto.

"No," he said quietly. "She didn't do it. It was me."

Petra felt like the room had suddenly tilted. "Seth, that's not true! I was there. I saw her do it!"

Inside that terrible bunker, during their escape, Ritter had been about to operate on Seth to remove the part of his brain that controlled telepathy—and the sound weapon. She and Anaya and Esta and some of the other hybrids had burst into the surgical suite just in time. While they were rescuing Seth, Petra had seen Ritter writhing on the floor in agony as Esta hammered him relentlessly with sound.

"She's innocent!" Seth insisted. "Get Pearson to tell them. They need to release her!"

"She's not worth it, Seth!"

The words were barely out, and already Petra wished she could snatch them back. It made her sound cold and cruel—she could tell by the surprise in Dad's and Dr. Weber's faces. But they had no idea what Esta was like.

"She saved my life!" Seth said, his voice hoarse with feeling.

"*We* saved your life, too!" Petra reminded him. "Me and Anaya! And I'm not letting you take the blame for Esta! You did *not* kill Ritter!"

Seth frowned, confused. "I was hitting Ritter with sound, too.

It's hard to control. When you do it, it just comes out. . . ." He trailed off, looking from one face to another, then said, "Anyway, Ritter was about to saw my head open!"

"You're named as an accessory," Dr. Weber said reluctantly.

"That's crazy!" Petra didn't care what Seth said; she didn't believe he was capable of killing someone, not even Ritter.

"We can keep you safe here," Dr. Weber told Seth. "But Pearson's not willing to do anything about Esta, not right now."

Petra saw Seth pull back inside himself. Those long weeks in the bunker, she'd worried he was slowly drawing away. Only Esta and the other flyers had made him feel safer. And after the escape, all the flyer hybrids got left behind—abandoned—and forced to fend for themselves.

Still, Seth had made his way back to them—that had to mean something. He must have some feeling for them, for *her*, didn't he? Or maybe he already regretted his choice. Maybe he wished he'd been captured with Esta.

Calmly, Seth asked, "Where's this detention center?"

Dr. Weber looked at him carefully. "Pearson didn't tell me that."

"We need to get her out," Seth insisted, the feathers on his shoulders making a metallic rustle. Petra saw her dad looking at him warily. "Can't be very far. I'll go by myself."

"Seth, don't," Petra said. "It's too dangerous!"

"Believe me, I know what it's like out there."

"We need you here, Seth," Dr. Weber said.

"Sure," Seth said bitterly. "Everyone needs us. Ritter needed us as lab rats. You guys need us as translators. And turns out the cryptogens need us, too, because we're walking memory sticks with a magic code."

Petra had rarely seen him this angry, and she couldn't blame him. It actually stoked her own anger—which was never hard to ignite these days. All of them had been abused, Seth more than anyone.

Dr. Weber said, "You're right. No one should have to go through the things you have. There's no way of undoing what's happened. But everyone at this table wants you here. I couldn't forgive myself if I lost you again."

Petra saw Seth's expression soften, but he said, "Esta and I took care of each other out there. She trusted me and I trusted her. I *promised* her."

Petra felt like something very cold and blunt was being shoved into her chest.

"I'll bring it up with the colonel again," Dr. Weber said. "Can you promise me you won't do anything until then?"

Seth waited a good long time before he said, "Yes."

The oven timer beeped, and Mrs. Riggs went to take out the chocolate lava cakes she'd made (gluten-free for Anaya, of course). Petra had been smelling them baking all through dinner. She helped Mrs. Riggs dust some confectioners' sugar on top and bring them to the table. She wouldn't have thought the sight of a little round chocolate dessert, still steaming, could make her feel so much better, but it did.

She was about to take her first bite when there were three quick knocks on the apartment door. They were the kind of knocks that didn't promise good news. She was closest, so she got up, and opened the door to Colonel Pearson.

SETH COULDN'T THINK OF a time when Pearson showing up was a good thing. Usually it was the opposite.

"I apologize for disturbing your dinner," Pearson said. "I was told Dr. Weber was here."

"Come in," said Mrs. Riggs. "Join us for dessert?"

The colonel looked genuinely surprised, like no one had invited him to dessert for a long time.

"That's very kind, thank you," he said, entering.

"Is everything okay with Terra?" Anaya asked worriedly.

"Yes, all three cryptogens are fine. We've got personnel in the observation room at all times."

Mr. Riggs pulled over a chair and everyone made room around the table. Seth felt weird having someone in military uniform squish in next to him. It was sort of like meeting your teachers outside of school and feeling like they were totally in the wrong place. And Pearson was hardly his favorite person—Seth doubted whether he was anyone's favorite person right now.

Mrs. Riggs placed a lava cake in front of the colonel. He took a bite.

"This is excellent," he said appreciatively. His gaze lighted on Seth and then moved across to his friends. "I gather you've told your parents everything that happened today."

Petra choked a little on her wine.

"Of course," said Anaya. "Everything."

Seth couldn't help smiling. When had Anaya become so daring? He looked back at Pearson, ready for an angry ticking off.

"That's fine," said Pearson, brushing some confectioners' sugar from the corner of his downturned mouth. "I expected as much. If we can just keep it to this room, please."

"Of course, yes," said Mr. Riggs, looking surprised himself.

"We've been picking up some intelligence chatter from other countries."

"Chatter?" asked Seth.

"News," said Dr. Weber. "Secret news."

Pearson put down his fork. "Two other small cryptogen ships were shot down. One over North Korea, the other over the Suez Canal."

"But how?" said Anaya. "The cryptogens would've been talking to hybrids first and—"

"—and those hybrids must've told people who were not willing to trust the cryptogens."

"Were the crews killed?" Anaya asked.

"We don't know. We've also had a report of a cryptogen landing in Mexico. The crew were quarantined, and interrogated. One of them has died, apparently."

"What about other countries?" Mr. Riggs asked. "The Americans? There must've been a landing there."

"We're not hearing anything so far. It may be there was a landing and they're keeping it quiet. Just like we are."

"But why? If the cryptogens are getting hurt or killed," Anaya said, "we need to tell people they're here to help us!"

"I can use CSIS back channels," said Dr. Weber, "to try to find out which countries had a landing. They might be willing to talk . . ."

"No," said Pearson.

"Why not?"

"The world can't even accept that the hybrids are friendly yet. Every country—including our own, officially—still considers them a huge security threat. They're put into internment camps and treated as enemy spies. Ritter wasn't the only one performing experiments on the hybrids."

"We've got to stop it!" Anaya said again. "We can't just sit by and let this happen! To the hybrids—*or* the cryptogens!"

"If you tell the Americans the hybrids are safe," said Seth, "they can let Esta out."

He watched Pearson for his reaction, barely needed to hear his answer.

"If I called my American counterparts right now and told them I was harboring hybrids and now cryptogens, I can guarantee a combat force would be sent to take over my base. And if they didn't do it quick enough, another country might take care of it for them."

"Keeping quiet is the only smart thing to do," said Petra's father.

Seth felt his feathers rustle angrily.

Anaya shook her head. "I don't get it. It's obvious the rebels aren't dangerous. What if you told them they gave us a cure for the mosquito bird plague—"

"I can't take that chance right now," said Pearson. "The cryptogens say they can make a weapon. I don't want to jeopardize that by losing control of my base. We'll work with them in secret. Once we have a functional weapon, then we can think about telling other countries."

"So you won't help get Esta out," Seth said.

"No."

Seth got up and left the apartment. He stalked down the corridor, left the building, and headed back to the barracks, where he shared a room with Adam and Paolo and a couple of other hybrid kids who'd escaped from Ritter's bunker.

When he'd first come to the army base with Anaya and Petra, they'd all shared the same apartment, but now all the bedrooms were taken up with parents. Still, being separated from his friends felt like another abandonment.

"Seth."

He turned to see Dr. Weber hurrying after him. He sighed and let her catch up.

"What I'm going to say stays between us," she said as they crossed the base. "I have counterparts in the US, people who work for the intelligence service, who want to free the hybrids, too. It's just a question of convincing enough people that they're innocent. It's slow going and we have to be careful, but we will get everyone released."

"Because we're such useful assets, right?"

"Yes," she said frankly. "And also because it's the right thing to do. I'm going to make inquiries about Esta and see if I can speed things up."

He listened but said nothing.

"I don't expect you to trust me right now," she said. "But I hope you will, eventually."

What could he say? "I hope so, too" or "Not likely"? She was doing her best, he knew that.

"Thanks," he said.

He felt her gentle hand on his back. "Okay. Try to get some sleep."

CHAPTER FIVE

IT WAS SEVEN A.M. when Anaya entered the biodome's observation room with Seth and Petra, and the place was already buzzing with the smell of coffee and loud officers at their laptops, volleying questions and answers and suggestions to each other.

"Propulsion systems . . ."

"We need to know the detonation velocity of . . ."

"Is there a frequency that . . ."

Beyond the window, Terra and the other two cryptogens were working on their ship's damaged hull. It looked worse than she remembered: a scorched and melted mess at the rear—although she wasn't absolutely sure it was the rear. The organic contours of the ship were confusing. Terra was crouched over a machine that was connected to the hull with a series of tubes. They looked a bit like electrodes and IVs for a human patient.

—*How are the repairs?* she asked Terra.

It was the general who replied, his terse, metallic words making her molars tingle unpleasantly.

—*The damage is worse than we thought. It will be slow.*

Terra's voice entered her head next.

—*We need to start making the weapon now.*

Anaya glanced at the cooler that Dr. Weber had filled with her blood samples earlier this morning.

—*Yes. We have blood for you. I'll bring it in.*

—*No, you must come inside the ship for the extraction.*

Startled, Anaya turned to Dr. Weber. "Terra says they need me inside the ship."

Dr. Weber frowned. "Why?"

"Extraction."

Back in the bunker, Dr. Ritter had planned "extraction" procedures for the hybrids, and this sounded ominously similar.

—*I thought you just needed my blood,* she said to Terra.

—*Not just your blood. Something we seeded inside it. But we don't know where it is.*

—*How can you not know? You put it there, didn't you?*

—*Yes. But we don't know where it has hidden.*

Anaya hoped this was just a bad translation. Terra made it sound like there was something scurrying around inside her.

—*What exactly is it?*

—*You must be inside the ship for us to find it.*

Anaya was seeing a new side of Terra: evasive, and unbending. If she'd thought they were friends, maybe she was mistaken. It was one thing to go inside the biodome, another to go inside the ship. The idea of having some kind of procedure in there made her stomach give a cold swirl.

"Maybe you should ask your parents," Petra said after Anaya had explained what Terra had told her.

Anaya considered and shook her head. Telling her parents would only make it harder. She could already imagine their responses: Mom would be outraged and worried, and Dad would tell her she didn't have to do this, that she'd done enough. And she would have to convince them there was no other way—and that would be exhausting.

"I'm sixteen, I don't need their permission anyway."

Petra said, "Maybe someone else should volunteer. I mean, I'm not volunteering myself, but maybe one of the other kids—"

"It should be me. I'm the one who's been talking to Terra. I brought them here. I'll do it."

"I don't like it," said Colonel Pearson, coming over.

"Me neither," said Dr. Weber.

"She goes inside the ship, they could take her hostage."

"Whoa," said Petra. "Hostage taking?"

"I want to know what they're doing," said Dr. Weber. "I'm coming with you."

Anaya felt a huge swell of relief and gratitude.

—*We're coming,* she told Terra.

She waited while Dr. Weber got fitted with a canister of oxygen and a mask, and then they went inside. Seth came with them, to continue his interview with the flyer. Pearson's staff had come up with an even bigger list of questions than yesterday's.

Terra escorted them across the biodome toward the ship while the flyer slashed away any aggressive vines in their path. The swimmer slipped into the pool to distract the water lilies from spitting acid-coated seeds. Anaya was surprised by how normal this new landscape already seemed, but she sensed Dr. Weber was on full alert, head and eyes moving all the time, watching every step she took.

When they reached the ship, Anaya marveled at the material. From a distance it had looked gray and featureless, but up close it looked almost like shell, with an intricate texture. She couldn't help touching it.

The moment her hand grazed the hull, a tone appeared in her head—not just a sound, but almost a song. She felt like there were words, too complicated to understand. Startled, she withdrew her hand.

—*It talked to me!*

—*Yes,* Terra replied.

—*I don't know what it said.*

—*Much of our technology is sound-based. We use our minds more than our hands.*

Terra touched the tips of her claws against the ship's hull and a hatch opened. The runner ducked inside. Anaya hesitated. This was a big step.

"I'm with you," Dr. Weber whispered beside her.

She entered. She'd expected dark metal tunnels, like in basically every sci-fi movie she'd ever seen. Instead she was greeted with open space. An even light emanated from curved window-less walls.

Instantly she was aware of the ship's smell. It wasn't unpleasant exactly, just incredibly different. She must be smelling things that didn't exist on Earth: substances, chemicals—maybe even new elements?

"Could you tell Terra," Dr. Weber said, "that I want to know exactly what is happening, every step of the way."

"I'll try," said Anaya, "but I'm not sure she'll cooperate."

It was strange to hear their human voices in this very alien space. Where were the controls, the examination tables, the cockpit?

Terra touched the wall, and from the high ceiling, a pit plant dropped and hung suspended, trailing vines.

Anaya gave a cry and jumped back. Dr. Weber protectively shielded her, even though she was far more likely to be hurt than Anaya.

—*What is wrong?* Terra asked, looking alarmed.

—*It's a pit plant!*

—*No.*

Anaya looked more closely, then relaxed. What she'd thought was plant flesh was actually fabric; the vines were really tubes and cables that fed into the ship's ceiling.

"It's not a plant," she told Dr. Weber. "It's like the pods they travel in, asleep. Inside the big ship."

—You will need to go inside, Terra said.

Anaya was startled by how abrupt Terra had become.

—You can't just . . . take my blood right here?

—You must go inside.

A small rebellion flared inside her. She'd had enough. She'd given enough blood to feed all the guests in Dracula's castle ten times over; she'd been evaluated and measured and slimed and *bitten.* But she did not want to get inside that weird womb-shaped pod.

—What exactly happens inside this thing?

—We inserted a code in your DNA. That code will have created an organism that will produce the chemicals we need for the weapon. But we do not know where the organism will have chosen to grow.

Anaya remembered the shock of seeing the organ in her brain, like a tiny sea polyp, that made her telepathic. Now she had another weird little visitor in her body.

—This machine will find the organelle, then extract it. You will be very comfortable.

She actually laughed. She doubted that. She brought Dr. Weber up to date.

Terra unzipped the side of the pod.

"I want to look inside first," Dr. Weber said.

Obligingly, Terra parted the opening, and Dr. Weber leaned in.

—Is this where my mom was taken? Anaya asked Terra.

She could feel Terra's hesitation like white noise in her head.

—*Yes.*

For the first time, she doubted Terra's kindness. Maybe all along she'd mistaken the cryptogen's urgency for personal concern. These creatures had abducted her mother and countless other women and put them inside sacs like this so they would later give birth to hybrid children. And these were the *nice* cryptogens.

Now they'd come back for the final part of their project.

And just like her mom, she was getting into this thing. Only, she was awake, and something was going to be taken *out* of her.

Dr. Weber pulled back. "There's nothing sharp in there, not that I can see anyway. Obviously there must be all kinds of tech woven into it, for imaging and administering things percutaneously."

"Through the skin?" Anaya asked.

"Yes. It's up to you, Anaya."

Not really, she thought. When you could do something that might save the human race, you really didn't have a choice anymore.

She gritted her teeth and climbed inside the sac. She'd expected it to sag under her weight, but it held its shape, making it easier for her to sit, knees bent, facing the opening. Her last view was of Terra, zipping her in. The darkness was total.

—Lie down, Terra told her.

Her heart was beating too quickly. She felt breathless. As she stretched out her legs and leaned back, the sac contracted to mold itself against her. She gave a muffled cry as the fabric pressed over her mouth and nose—and yet right away she could breathe. Dr. Weber was right. The material was porous and must be feeding oxygen right into her nostrils. And it was warm, too, like a cozy flannel blanket. The pod wanted her to relax, and she did, despite herself. She breathed.

—We are scanning now, Terra said.

She didn't see or hear or feel anything. Was this what it was like, being a baby in a womb? It occurred to her that she'd actually started her life inside this thing—*maybe this very one*—inside her mother, a tiny collection of cells.

She dozed off and dreamed of caves and climbing a steep slope. When she reached the top, she had no idea how to get back down.

—We've found it, came Terra's voice in her head. *We're removing it now.*

She prepared herself for pain, but all she felt was a tiny prick in her lower back. Then the pod was moving her back into a sitting position. Suddenly the darkness was slit as Terra opened the sac. Unsteadily, Anaya hopped out. Dr. Weber put a hand on her arm.

"How long was I in there?" she asked.

"Ten minutes, maybe. I watched the scan on a monitor." Dr. Weber nodded at a section of the ship's wall that had a subtly different texture. "Their technology is, well, as expected. Centuries ahead of us."

In Terra's hands was a small translucent disk, about the size of a hockey puck.

—*It's in there?* she asked Terra. *The stuff to make the weapon?*

The surface of the disk changed its tint, and Anaya realized it was magnifying what was inside. She saw first a small collection of dots, which grew into molecules, which grew into cells, which became something larger. They were going closer and closer at a dizzying speed until Terra touched the tips of her claws to the surface and spun the image, zooming in until Anaya could see a fibrous tangle.

—*It's like a little nest,* she said.

—*Yes. It has been dormant. Now we need to wake it up and encourage it to start growing.*

—*What will grow there?*

—*A virus to attack the brain cells of the winged ones.*

Winged ones. Those were the words Anaya's brain had chosen as a clumsy translation. What she really experienced was like a flare of light, a fleeting scent and taste that were as unique as any fingerprint, or face. But it was unmistakably the name that the cryptogens gave the flyers.

—*The virus will steal their ability to strike with sound,* Terra said.

The runner pushed the disk against the wall, and the material of the wall adjusted itself so the disk nestled within it, glowing faintly.

"Ask her how long the incubation period will take," Dr. Weber said.

"A day or so," Anaya replied when she got the answer.

—*And now we will try to find the crashed ship,* Terra said. *Unless we can return to our primary vessel, our plan is useless.*

WHEN HE'D WOKEN THIS morning, Seth had thought about refusing to help. Staying in bed. Going on strike.

Why should he be helping them, the humans, if they couldn't do anything for him? "They're just using you," Esta would say, if he could reach her. He imagined conversations in his head all the time. What she'd think of things. How she'd react. How she'd reply. And she'd think all this was crap.

In his bed, he'd tried to reach her telepathically. It was the last thing he did before sleep; the first thing on waking. And every time, silence was the answer. She was too far to hear him, or *unable* to hear him, which was much worse.

He wanted to talk to her so badly. The general's words from yesterday still echoed inside him like a curse.

You will never fly.

Part of him desperately hoped it wasn't true. But he needed

to tell Esta. Only she would understand his torment. More than ever, he wanted to be with her.

But he was here; she was out there.

He was safe. And she wasn't.

He'd promised himself he'd find her. But all he'd done was *ask.*

And all they'd done was say no.

In the end, he'd gotten up, had breakfast, and come to the biodome with Anaya and Petra.

Because he thought the general might be able to help him.

Everyone was calling the cryptogen flyer "the general" now. Seth had introduced the name just to piss off Pearson, who was only a colonel. But the name fit. If anyone should be called general, it was this flyer. He seemed haughty and severe and like he would never take no for an answer.

Seth had entered the biodome with Anaya and Dr. Weber. The two of them had gone inside the ship, but he'd stayed outside with the general. Close enough to reach out and touch him—not that he'd ever dare.

He was taller than Seth, but thinner, and Seth figured he weighed more than the cryptogen—not that it mattered. The general could fry his brain without even twitching an eyebrow.

He counted the general's feathers (twenty-six on each arm), and watched how they folded together seamlessly. If the cryptogen angled his arms a certain way, you could almost mistake him, from a distance, for a human with very brawny, tattooed arms. His torso was not feathered, but covered in a fine silvery hair. His legs, too, had a full complement of feathers, which were folded against his limbs right now. The clawed feet were as disturbing as ever.

Over Seth's headset Pearson fed him the first question of the day.

—They want to know about your weapons, Seth told the general.

—I would be surprised if they did not.

Before he'd entered the biodome, they'd given Seth an electronic pad and stylus, in case he needed to draw or write down anything complicated.

—I will show you, said the general.

Seth waited as the cryptogen went inside the ship and returned wearing his helmet.

Every muscle in Seth's body tensed for fight. It was instinctive. That helmet changed everything. Its angles were brutal, and the way it swooped backward into a sharp crest made Seth think of a bird of prey, poised to dive.

"Seth, what's going on?" came Pearson's anxious voice over his headset.

"It's okay," he croaked, but was it? "He's just showing me the helmet. You wanted to know how it works, right?"

—Would you prefer I removed it? the general asked, as if he could sense the tension in the observation room.

—I think so, yes.

The general pulled it off and held it out to Seth. Nervously Seth took it in his hands. It was quite heavy. The inside lining was still warm from the general's head. Touching it was strangely personal. He felt a glimmer in his own head, like there was a connection between him and this helmet. The urge to put it on was strong, but also a bit terrifying.

—*When you strike, the helmet strikes with you. Only the winged ones can use these helmets. They are useless to the others. This weapon is so powerful, it has enabled us to dominate our planet.*

His words were tinged with regret.

"How many helmets did they bring?" Pearson wanted to know.

"Only the flyers can use them," Seth replied.

"What about you?" Pearson asked him.

—*Would I be able to use it?* he asked the general.

—*Strike me,* the flyer instructed him. *So I can see.*

Seth shook his head.

—*I need to see how powerful you are.*

He wasn't angry right now, but it was never hard for him to find anger. He thought of Ritter and his big meaty hands, the way he chewed through words, the dead gaze he fixed on him. He thought of Esta being dragged off the boat. He thought of Pearson refusing to help him find her. In his head, he saw that dangerous, vibrating string of light. He pulled it like a bowstring and let fly at the general.

He saw the flyer wince and step back.

—*Stop,* the general said. *You are more powerful than I thought. Yes, you would be able to use the helmet.*

Seth realized he was glad, even though the idea sickened him.

"Ask him if there is any way to block it," Pearson prompted. "Maybe with some other frequency."

—*No,* the general replied.

"Would the blackout hoods work?" Seth asked, and then tried to describe to the general the hood Ritter had put over his head, which stole his telepathy and his power to strike with sound.

—*I doubt it. If such a thing were possible,* the general said, *it would need to be put over the flyer's head and helmet. You would never get close enough to a flyer to do such a thing.*

"What about other weapons?" Pearson asked. "What do the runners and swimmers use?"

—*It will be easier to show you,* the general told Seth.

Words and images and diagrams flowed into Seth's mind, and he scribbled them down onto the pad. It was a torrent of information. He lost track of time.

The swimmers used a chest-mounted harpoon rig that could shoot explosive spears underwater, or into the air to strike flyers. The runners had long rifles with two gauntlet-like grips, designed for their long hands. The tips of their claws slid into special trigger slots. They shot pulses of energy deadlier than bullets. Just as the harpoons were designed specially for the swimmers, the rifles could only be used by the runners.

After this, the general had questions of his own.

Seth volleyed the questions and answers between the two military men.

"Can we make these weapons on Earth?"

—*No, they require materials only found off-world.*

"What are the exact numbers of flyers and swimmers and runners?"

—*If the invasion force was launched, there would be ten landing ships, each carrying sixty thousand warriors. Of those, five thousand would be flyers, the rest swimmers and runners.*

"That's good, Seth, thank you," Pearson said to him afterward. "Come back to the observation room for a break."

But he had something of his own he wanted to ask the general first.

—*Can you find someone for me?*

—*Why?*

And he found himself telling the general about Esta. Which meant telling him a bit about Ritter and the bunker, and the way the hybrids had been treated. The general listened carefully and then seemed to consider his request. Finally he said:

—*No.*

—*Why not?*

—*If I were to send out a powerful signal, it might be traced back to us. Or detected by monitoring equipment on our primary vessel beyond Earth. And give away our location here.*

It was all said matter-of-factly, without any tinge of regret. The general was more similar to the colonel than he'd thought. Neither of them had one speck of sympathy for Esta. Or him.

—*WE FOUND THE CRASH* site.

The swimmer's briny words silently filled Petra's head. Once again, she'd stayed behind in the observation room. She still wanted a barrier between her and the cryptogens.

Last night Anaya had kept talking about how good the biodome air was—and Petra worried that she'd like it, too. Maybe she'd be tempted to hop right into the pond and paddle around, munching water lilies like the swimmer.

Ze certainly liked to eat, that was for sure. When she'd arrived this morning, ze and the general were tearing into a stilt-legged bug that some soldiers had killed and dumped inside the biodome. Fun fact: flyers and swimmers were omnivores; Terra was happy with just plants.

"They found the ship that crashed," Petra told Pearson now.

Everyone's attention was focused on her, in silence for a second, before a volley of questions was fired at her.

—*Where is it?* she asked the swimmer.

—*Look.*

She had to concentrate now, because a borderless map of Earth appeared in her head, rotating and enlarging, like she was plunging through the sky. She recognized where she was.

"I need a map of northern BC!" she called out.

It was quickly summoned on a wall monitor.

"There," said Petra, pointing. "Zoom in there."

Petra blinked, trying to match her mental map with the one on-screen.

"Stop." She went over and touched the monitor. "Yeah, right here."

"Northeastern British Columbia," said Colonel Pearson. "Middle of nowhere. What do we know about this area?"

"The terrain is mostly muskeg. Swamp, basically," said one of his officers, consulting her laptop. "Which means if a ship crashed in there, it might be underwater."

Pearson grunted. "That's going to make a salvage a lot harder."

Satellite images came up on the monitor.

"Looks like there's a lot of black grass," Petra said, eyes roving across the screen. But it wasn't just grass. There were all sorts of other shapes she didn't recognize, and they didn't look like normal trees or scrub.

"Can we get closer?" Pearson asked.

"That's as close as it gets," the officer said. "We don't normally have a satellite tasked for this area. It's lucky we have any images at all."

—*Is the ship in water?* Petra asked the swimmer, then concentrated, because the answer involved measurements, and those were always tricky to translate.

"It's underwater," she told the room. "The hatch is, maybe, twenty feet under. I think. And the water's very acidic."

"We can get a crew to the site," said Pearson, studying the map, "with a helicopter and extra fuel, but the swimmer has to come to lead the salvage. He knows the exact location—"

"Sorry," said Petra. "Sorry to interrupt, but the swimmer's not a he. Or a she, for that matter."

Pearson looked at her with both incomprehension and annoyance. Before he could chew her out, she added:

"So I've been using *ze* and *zir* pronouns. If that helps."

Pearson looked like he was about to say something cutting, but then just took a breath and said, "The swimmer needs to go, because only . . . ze knows exactly what ze is looking for. Also, ze can handle that water."

—*I will go,* said the swimmer when Petra relayed this to zir. *But you will need to come with me.*

Petra felt a kick of fear in her chest.

—*Why me?*

—*I need a translator. And someone to work underwater with me. You will come.*

So far today, her conversation with the swimmer had been civil—at least ze hadn't called her ugly or insulted her—but Petra didn't like being ordered around. Why should she do anything ze said? She couldn't get past the fact that ze had abducted her mom sixteen years ago—midair when she was a passenger on Mrs. Riggs's floatplane.

"The swimmer will go," Petra told the room. "But ze wants me to come, too."

"Not a chance," said Dr. Weber forcefully.

"Exactly what I said," Petra said, then felt a sudden spasm of sadness. Dr. Weber had sounded like her own mother just then. Mom would've chewed Pearson out for even considering such a plan. And Pearson definitely was considering it. Petra could tell by his impassive expression.

"There hasn't been a single spray up there," Dr. Weber warned the colonel. "Not herbicide and certainly not pesticide."

Petra knew what that meant. The black grass would have grown and grown. The vines and pit plants would've spread. The water would be seething with venomous lilies. And the bugs. Without any pesticide it would be a totally alien landscape, swarming with things that wanted to crush, slice, and drink her. And those were the things she'd already seen. She didn't want to think about what brand-new cryptogenic monsters might have been born up there now.

"We need a translator," said Pearson. "To communicate between the swimmer and my soldiers."

"We have promised these kids and their parents that they're safe here," Dr. Weber reminded Pearson. "Petra is doing vital work here. Sending her out there is too dangerous."

"What isn't dangerous?" Colonel Pearson said wearily. "We need that ship, and we need a translator."

"Well, it's not going to be me," said Petra. "I've been with your guys in a helicopter before, and it did not go well. I got you the location, okay? I'm not leaving this base. Get one of the other kids, or just send the swimmer alone. Ze knows what ze's doing."

She looked away from Pearson then, not wanting to weaken under his disapproving stare. She wasn't being unreasonable or selfish. If Pearson thought he could strap some kid into a helicopter and send them into a war zone, he was way out of line.

"All right," the colonel said. "We'll work around this. Let's start prepping a salvage team right away."

CHAPTER SIX

"I CAN'T BELIEVE YOU went into that pod thing," Petra said. "They just zipped you up inside?"

Anaya shuddered inwardly. "I wasn't crazy about it, believe me."

It was after dinner and the two of them were walking across the base toward the barracks to meet Seth. He hadn't come to the apartment to have dinner with them, which was unusual, and Anaya was worried about him. Leaving the biodome today, he'd barely said a word, aloud or silently.

"So they did surgery on you," Petra asked, "and it didn't even hurt?"

Anaya shook her head. "And Terra got what she needed. Which is the important thing."

"Yeah," Petra muttered, "they're great at getting what they need."

"It's what we *all* need," Anaya reminded her.

The army base's field must have been mowed earlier that day, because the scent of fresh-cut grass still lingered in the air. As far as Anaya was concerned, it was one of the best smells in the world, even if it did make her sneeze. Since returning to Deadman's Island, she was back on allergy meds, because the base was a Spray Zone. Which meant it was clear of cryptogenic plants. Which meant real green Earth grass had a chance to grow again.

She took another deep breath and closed her eyes. A seagull's cry carried on the fresh breeze. It was such a familiar sound to her—and a hopeful one now, because so many birds had been eaten by the cryptogenic plants and animals. All she needed now was the sound of a lawn sprinkler, and she might trick herself into thinking this was a normal summer back home on Salt Spring Island.

"I want ice cream," she said, opening her eyes.

"From Scoops," Petra said with a grin, as if she'd been thinking the exact same thing. "Burnt marshmallow, two scoops on a sugar cone."

"Ginger rhubarb," Anaya said.

"I can't believe you like that one."

"So good. You've got to try it."

Her friend sniffed ruefully. "When will that be?"

Anaya lifted her gaze to the protective netting that covered the entire base, to keep out mosquito birds. She took in the guard towers. The decimated Vancouver skyline across the harbor, where buildings had been toppled by giant borer worms. And they were lucky here. This was one of the safest places on the planet. Before she'd left the apartment, their parents had turned on the news. So many numbers. The wounded. The sick. The dead. It seemed almost wrong that it was such a beautiful evening.

"We've got Terra and the others on our side now," she said.

"You don't feel like they're just using us?" her friend said. "Like everyone else. We're such great *assets.*"

"Petra, they're helping us!"

"They're helping themselves!"

"Same thing," said Anaya, "if it stops an invasion!"

"Well, maybe they could've done their whole civil war thing somewhere else," Petra said. "Like another galaxy or something? I mean, our planet isn't even that great for them. They have to change the entire ecosystem and atmosphere!"

She had a good point. "Maybe you never get a perfect planet," Anaya said after thinking a moment. "Maybe Earth is as close as it gets. Anyway, it's not like the rebels had any say in the matter."

"Give us your blood! Get in this sac! Come find a crashed ship for us!"

"Well, we did wreck theirs," Anaya pointed out.

"I don't want to go on their stupid salvage mission. It's not my problem!"

"Oh, come on. It's everyone's problem!"

Anaya could tell Petra was feeling guilty—the guiltier her friend felt, the louder she argued. Well, maybe she *should* feel guilty. Was it such a big deal, to go along and translate for the swimmer? If it meant stopping an invasion of the entire planet? Everyone needed to help.

"They're not doing anything for me," Petra persisted.

"Saving the world!"

"I meant *fixing* us. The swimmer said they can't, but come on! They must be able to do *something*."

"Even if they could, it'd probably mean going inside a pod, and I'm pretty sure you wouldn't be into it."

That made Petra pipe down, but only for a second.

"They just order us around," Petra muttered.

Anaya had to admit this was true. "It was weird," she said. "I felt it, too, with Terra. Maybe it's just the way things get translated sometimes. Or they're just scared like us and know we don't have much time."

They reached the barracks. Inside, a surly guard directed them to the third floor, where all the hybrids were bunked. Upstairs it was like a bizarre house party. Music spilled from open doorways, and teenagers filled the corridor, talking, playing cards, tossing Ping-Pong balls into cups of ginger ale. Hairy teenagers with clawed feet; teenagers with colored, patterned skin, and tails. Like Anaya, they were all escapees from Dr. Ritter's bunker, rescued by Pearson's helicopters.

She talked to some of the kids she knew best, was lured into a game of pong (she won), but really, just wanted to find Seth. When she literally bumped into one of his roommates, he said Seth must've gone out for a walk.

Anaya felt a twinge of uneasiness. A walk? Or an escape?

Everyone knew how unhappy he was. She told Petra, and the two of them hurried out of the barracks. In her mind she searched for Seth's telepathic beacon.

—*Where are you, Seth?*

To her huge relief, his reply came almost at once.

"He's on the roof," she told Petra.

"On the roof?"

Anaya shielded her eyes and looked up at the building they'd just left. "There!"

The building was three stories tall and Seth was standing right at the edge.

"What're you doing?" Petra shouted at him.

"Hey, kid!" a guard from a nearby sentry tower hollered. "Get off of there!"

"Okay!" Seth said, and threw himself off.

Anaya gasped, and Petra clutched her arm. Seth spread his arms, and his colorful feathers fanned out magnificently. He wore shorts, and on the lower half of both legs, more feathers deployed. He glided and did a few circles over the field, and then Anaya saw him pumping his arms up and down furiously.

"He's trying to fly," Petra whispered.

But he didn't seem to be gaining any altitude. And then something happened. He tumbled, a chaos of arms and feathers.

"Oh my God!" Anaya cried, and bounded toward the place where he'd crash.

Before she got there, Seth recovered. His arms steadied, his feathers caught the air, and he leveled off. He was low now, and came in to land.

"He was never very good at landing," Petra said, watching tensely.

Skimming low, Seth dropped his legs and touched down perfectly, running a few meters to slow down as he folded in his wings.

"You're freaking crazy!" the guard shouted at him through his megaphone. "Do not do that again!"

With Petra, Anaya sprinted the rest of the way to Seth. He saw them coming but didn't even wave. Hands on hips, he was still puffing to catch his breath.

"I couldn't fly," he said. "The general's right."

Anaya didn't know what to say. It felt wrong to encourage him if the thing he wanted was impossible.

"Maybe he's just trying to discourage you," Petra said. "Doesn't want any competition. It's not like they really care about us."

"That's not fair," Anaya objected.

Seth said, "I asked the general if he could find Esta for me."

"You did?" Petra asked.

"He wouldn't do it. Said his signal might give away his location."

"Well, sure, he's right," said Petra, singing a different tune now. "That's a good point. But still," she said to Anaya, "they can't be bothered to do anything for us."

"You need to trust them a little more," Anaya said.

"Maybe you'd feel differently if it was your mom they'd killed," Petra snapped.

Anaya felt her lungs wither. That wasn't fair. It wasn't the rebels' fault, what had happened to Petra's mom. But Anaya knew her friend still blamed them for the water striders' attack on the base. It didn't have to make sense.

Now it was Anaya's turn to feel guilty. Of course her friend was going to have harder feelings toward the rebels.

"I'm sorry," Anaya said. "I'm stupid. I have no idea how it must feel."

Which wasn't entirely true. Her own mom had been bitten by a mosquito bird and almost died. So she did know that terrible, despairing feeling that moaned through you.

"It doesn't even feel real," Petra said, looking slightly panicky. "I know that Mom died. I mean, I was there, and I saw her buried later. But it's like I'm ignoring it. There's too much other stuff to think about. Like aliens landing, and the world about to end. Or maybe I'm just afraid to think about it."

Anaya gave her a hug. Seth squeezed her hand.

After a moment Petra asked, "What happens afterward? If the rebels win."

"Wow," Anaya said, genuinely surprised. "I hadn't thought of that. That seems so . . . far off. It would be a good thing, though."

"But I was just wondering, were they planning on blasting back into outer space, or *staying* here?"

OUTSIDE COLONEL PEARSON'S OFFICE, Seth slipped the narrow tip of his feather into the lock. When he felt the fine barbs settle into the grooves, he rotated his wrist. The lock opened, the doorknob turned, and he was inside.

The last of the daylight filtered through the blinds. He didn't need to turn on the light. He went to the colonel's desk. There was no computer, not even a laptop. Pearson didn't strike him as a tech-savvy kind of guy, and that was good, because it meant there might be an old-fashioned paper record of where Esta was.

He'd promised he wouldn't abandon her. And that was exactly what he'd done. Now she was jailed somewhere, and who knew what was going to happen to her. What they'd *do* to her.

Pearson would never help him rescue her; not even Dr. Weber could help. He was tired of asking and being told no. He was tired of *waiting* to be given what he wanted.

Now he was going to *take*.

On the desk were tidy stacks of file folders. He started going through them. He'd never done anything like this before, wasn't even sure what he should be looking for. Maps. Something with Esta's name on it.

Nothing.

Nothing.

More nothing.

Then a boring piece of paper with so little on it he almost slid over it. It was a printout of an email:

Confirm A3 detained . . .

A3.

That was Esta's ID number in the bunker!

From the hallway came voices, and one of them was Pearson's unmistakable baritone rumble. Seth's heart pounded at the base of his throat. He cast his eyes desperately around the room. There was a closet crammed with file boxes, and he pushed himself inside and tried to shut the door after him. It wouldn't close all the way, despite his twisting and turning. He shuffled as far away as possible from the sliver of light coming in—

Which grew suddenly brighter as the office door opened and the overhead light snapped on. Seth picked out two sets of footsteps.

". . . when will they have enough for a test?" Pearson was asking.

"It's hard to know," came the reply. Dr. Weber. "All the information I get is through Anaya. She's very thorough, but I'm left guessing at the cryptogens' procedures, and their technology. Right now they're still waiting to produce their first culture of the virus."

"And then?"

"We need to talk about that," Dr. Weber answered.

Seth heard the colonel exhale—he knew that sound of exasperation.

"It's clear who we test it on," Pearson said. "It needs to be a flyer—or a flyer hybrid."

"You mean Seth."

Seth felt an icy surge through his veins. Stupid that he hadn't thought about it until now. Obviously they'd need to test the virus to make sure it worked.

"We can't test it on the general," Pearson said.

"I don't agree."

"He's too valuable to us."

"It should be tested on a real cryptogen. From every point of view."

Pearson's voice was unflinching: "If it works like we hope it does, the general loses his ability to strike with sound—and we need that power as long as possible. He's like a missile launcher. I'm not losing that."

"We don't know what this virus will do to anyone, much less a hybrid, and a teenager."

"We have no options, Dr. Weber."

"It has to be the general."

"Unless you can find a different hybrid, or kidnap a winged cryptogen elsewhere, Seth is our test subject. All the virus does is take away the sound weapon, yes?"

"If it works as they hope. But this is a first trial. If it doesn't work, it could be extremely dangerous. It might kill him."

"Yes."

There was a very long pause. Seth wished he could cover his ears; he didn't want to hear any more. He was terrified of what Dr. Weber would say, or not say. Would she keep arguing, or just give up? Even if she fought, she'd lose. There was no way she could win this fight against Pearson. She couldn't protect him.

"He's been through too much," she said. "They've all been through too much."

"I agree. But I also can't see any other logical alternative."

"I won't allow it."

"You know I'm right."

He heard the door open and close, and Dr. Weber's footsteps faded down the hallway. That left Pearson alone in the office. Seth heard a weary sigh, the creak of Pearson's office chair as he sat down behind his desk. Papers rustled. Then silence. Seth couldn't remember if he'd closed the file folder before hiding. Had he left it open? He heard the colonel stand and approach the closet.

Seth's forehead throbbed with feverish heat. It wasn't hard for him to find that angry vibration in his head: he was ready to strike.

The footsteps passed the closet, and Seth heard Pearson open his office door. The lights went out, and the door closed after the colonel.

Seth counted to thirty before stepping out. He rushed back to the desk, hoping Pearson hadn't taken away the file folder he needed. There were fewer now, all of them neatly restacked. He started opening them frantically and exhaled with relief.

Confirm A3 detained County Sheriff Point Roberts.

Point Roberts—where was that? He'd heard that name. Excitedly, he turned to the big map on the wall. His eyes ricocheted around. Yes! Below Vancouver, below the ferry terminal at Tsawwassen, a rectangular peninsula jutted south into the Strait of Georgia. The bottom half of it actually belonged to the United States, this weird little hunk of America totally cut off from the rest of the country.

Esta was there! Not even fifty kilometers away.

She'd been so close all along.

Now all he had to do was get her back, whatever it took.

IN DARKNESS, WET FROM her swim, Petra squeezed through the gap in the fence.

She'd found the spot a couple of nights ago when she couldn't sleep and had gone for a walk. It was a sheltered bit of the harbor, between Stanley Park and the yacht club marina. There was no guard tower nearby.

The urge to swim was too strong. She hadn't told anyone about it. Everyone would freak out. She barely wanted to admit it to herself.

She'd stayed inside the Spray Zone—mostly. She might have gone just a touch beyond, just far enough to eat a few water lilies. Tonight, she'd even come across a stray water strider egg underwater. She ate it. She was doing everyone a favor. Yes, it was delicious, but devouring it also gave her a deep satisfaction: this particular water strider would never grow into the kind of terrifying monster that had killed her mother.

She could still taste the egg's saltiness as she dried her hair with the towel she'd left near the fence. Crossing the base, she stuck to the shadows of buildings as she made her way back to the apartment. She rounded a corner and nearly screamed when she came face to face with Seth.

"What're you doing out here?" he asked, squinting at her wet clothes. "Were you swimming?"

There was no point in lying. So she told him. He listened carefully.

"More like them than you think, huh?" he said.

"Just please don't tell anyone."

Then she noticed that he was wearing long pants and a hoodie and a backpack over his shoulder.

"No," she said.

"You keep my secret, I'll keep yours."

"You don't even know where Esta is!"

"I found out."

"Don't," she said.

"I'm going."

"You are *not* leaving," she said. "I'll wake up the whole base."

"Don't make me stun you," he said.

"Go ahead."

He looked at her pleadingly. She knew he hated using sound as a weapon. It wasn't in his nature to hurt people. He would never hurt her. Or so she believed.

"If you tell them," he said, "they'll put one of those hoods over my head. They'll lock me in the basement again. You know I'm right."

He was, and she knew it.

"Is that what you want for me, Petra?"

Her insides knotted. "You will *die* if you go out there."

"I've been out there before."

Slyly she lifted her tail, ready to strike and paralyze him.

She winced with the sudden pain that throbbed through her head.

"Don't make me," Seth said.

She let her tail drop. "How can you do this to us?" she said, and heard her voice catch. "There's a lot of people who care about you, you idiot."

"Not really," he said bitterly.

"How can you say that?"

"I overheard Dr. Weber talking with Pearson. They're going to test the cryptogens' weapon on me."

She just stared. This couldn't be right.

"Yeah, to make sure it works."

"Dr. Weber wouldn't let them!" she protested.

"She's not in charge. There's nothing she can do, even if she wanted to."

"That's not true. If you disappear, it'll break her heart."

She saw him frown. "My heart, too," she blurted.

The bewilderment on his face told her what a total surprise this was to him. He was completely clueless about her feelings. She almost laughed. All his thoughts were about Esta; there really wasn't any space in his head left for her,

"I didn't—" he mumbled.

She cut him off. "Are you coming back?"

His reply took too long. "Yes."

He must love Esta so much, if he was willing to do this. Leave the base, go out there where monsters and humans both hunted him. She'd basically told him she loved him, and he didn't care one bit: he was still desperate to go to Esta. How could she stand in his way?

"Go, then," she said.

She wrapped her arms around him and squeezed tight. He squeezed back.

"I could still sting you with my tail," she whispered in his ear.

"Go ahead and try."

She hugged him harder.

"Go find her," she said. "But come back. I just want you to come back."

CHAPTER SEVEN

ANAYA LOOKED AT HER friend in bewilderment.

"Last night? And you didn't stop him?"

Petra's face was blotchy with tears. A bubble of snot burst from her nose and she started sobbing anew.

"I tried!" she hiccupped.

"Tried?"

Anaya felt Dr. Weber's hand on her shoulder, like she was being restrained. Which was a good idea, or she might have grabbed Petra and started shaking her. How could she have let this happen? And why had she waited so long before saying anything?

They'd eaten breakfast in the apartment—not a peep from Petra. They'd waited together for the jeep to take them to the biodome—not a peep from Petra. When Seth wasn't on it, Anaya started worrying. Still nothing from Petra.

It wasn't until they were inside the biodome, in the observation room, and Pearson told them Seth was missing and a motorboat had been stolen that Petra fell apart and confessed.

"I couldn't stop him!" she said. "He said he'd stun me!"

"Oh, come on," Anaya said impatiently. "Seth wouldn't do that!"

"He zapped me with sound! To warn me! You didn't see how he was!"

"You could've told someone when you got back inside," said Dr. Weber. "Pulled the fire alarm!"

"I know," said Petra miserably.

"And he'd be here right now!" Anaya said.

"I know!" Petra wailed. "Okay, I know, I screwed up!"

"What time was all this?" Pearson asked.

"Maybe around one o'clock," Petra said.

Anaya wondered why she'd been out in the middle of the night but knew it wasn't important right now.

"Seven hours ago," said Pearson. "He could be a lot of places."

"He went to rescue Esta," Petra hiccupped.

Anaya frowned. "He doesn't even know where she is."

"He said he found out."

Anaya caught Pearson's eyes slice across to Dr. Weber, then dart about, like he was piecing something together.

"You should've told us, Petra," said Pearson. "This is a serious security breach."

"Security breach?" said Petra. "Seth's out there by himself! *That's* what we should be worrying about."

Dr. Weber muttered, "I still can't believe you let him go."

"He doesn't want to be here with us, okay?" Petra said. "He only wants her. He's in love with Esta!"

And then Anaya understood fully, and her anger with Petra

grew. Petra had let Seth leave because she felt rejected. She'd been too proud to beg him to stay. So she'd let him run away.

"How could you do it?" she shouted at her friend. "Just because he wasn't crazy about you? Like everyone else in the world? He's going to get killed out there!"

"Why're you so mad at me!" Petra shouted back, then pointed at Dr. Weber and Colonel Pearson. "These guys practically forced him out!"

"What're you talking about?" Anaya asked, glimpsing the uneasy look on Dr. Weber's face.

"Seth said they were going to test the new weapon on him," Petra said.

"Is this for real?" Anaya gasped, feeling sick.

"He must've heard us talking," Dr. Weber said. She felt behind her for a chair and sat down. Anaya had never seen anyone's face go pale so quickly.

"He must've broken into my office last night," Pearson said. "I wondered if someone had been through my desk."

Anaya didn't care about any of that. "You were actually going to use him as a guinea pig?" she asked Dr. Weber.

"No," said Dr. Weber.

"Yes," said Pearson.

"After all those promises to keep us safe?" Anaya cried.

For the first time, she realized how silent everyone else in the observation room was, all the staff officers studiously looking at their monitors and files.

"None of this matters right now!" Petra said. "Can't we go get Seth?"

"You've made that very difficult," Pearson retorted. "He's been gone seven hours."

"Yeah, well, he got out, right past your super-duper guards. Who clearly are not so super-duper!"

Anaya could see that the fight had returned to her friend.

"All you needed to do was report it!" Pearson said.

"This wouldn't have happened if you'd rescued Esta right away, like he wanted. You guys have screwed him over so much, no wonder he doesn't trust you!"

"This isn't helpful," said Dr. Weber. "Have either of you tried to reach him, telepathically?"

"Of course I have," Petra said. "All night. But if he can hear me, he's not answering. My range sucks, though."

"But you know where he's going, right?" Anaya asked Pearson.

Pearson said nothing.

"This is our fault," said Dr. Weber. "We failed him. We should've rescued Esta. We should've picked them *all* up, that night at the bunker. No one should've been left behind."

"So we'll just go get him, right?" Petra looked hopefully from Pearson to Dr. Weber. "And bring him back!"

"No. A3 is being held on American soil. And Seth might already be there."

"Can't you call them?" Anaya asked.

"If I call the facility," said Pearson, "they'll wonder how I know about Seth at all. They might think I've been harboring him, and if they trace him back here, *all* of you are at risk."

"Maybe now is the time to stop keeping secrets," said Dr. Weber. "We need to start talking about the hybrids and the rebel cryptogens and convince everyone they're trustworthy."

"Not yet," Pearson said. "And Seth might make that more difficult if he hurts anyone else. It'll be nearly impossible to convince people the hybrids are harmless—much less the cryptogen rebels."

In a small voice Petra said, "He was really angry. He'll do whatever it takes."

Anaya thought of his razor-sharp wings, which could slash through chain-link fences and bulletproof vests. She thought about his sonic weapon, which could drop guards screaming to their knees. She saw Seth, furious, doing terrible things, and it made her groan in despair.

"What he's done is extremely reckless," Pearson said. "He's putting himself in danger, and our entire war effort. If he's captured, and he tells them we're harboring hybrids and rebel cryptogens here—"

"He wouldn't do that," said Anaya. "That's the last thing he'd tell them!"

"Maybe he's not even there yet," Petra said. "Why can't we go ourselves, try to head him off?"

"You were the one who let him get away!" Anaya wanted to say, but didn't.

"I can't spare the personnel," Pearson said. "Right now, we

need to focus on making this viral weapon, and we need to find and salvage a ship. That's what we need to be doing. Be unhappy, be angry about it, but accept it. This is a war, and our enemy is not using a rule book. We can't afford to either."

It was a pretty good speech for Pearson, and Anaya and everyone else were silent for a few seconds.

"This is my fault," said Petra, her shoulders drooped in self-loathing. "I screwed it all up. I'm sorry."

Dr. Weber passed her some hypoallergenic wipes for her tear-blotched face and gave her shoulders a squeeze. Anaya couldn't bring herself to comfort her friend, not yet. But what Petra said next melted her heart.

"I'll go on that salvage mission with the swimmer," Petra said. "I'll be the translator."

SETH HAD EXPECTED A small police station, but this building looked like a warehouse, big and windowless and surrounded by a chain-link fence tipped with razor wire. In the grubby yard were stacked freight containers and impounded cars and trucks. Early-morning sunlight glinted off their windshields.

Parked right outside the unfriendly main entrance were several police motorbikes, the kinds he'd seen before, with sonar arms that detected pit plants in the road ahead.

Hidden behind some pines in the neighboring vacant lot, Seth took all this in. He also saw two armed guards in masks, helmets, and protective clothing, patrolling the yard.

—*Esta!* he called silently. *Esta!*

But of course he heard nothing back. They'd have her in one of those blocking hoods, or someplace underground.

Getting through the fence wouldn't be hard. His wings could cut through the chain link, no problem. Then what? He supposed he'd have to stun the guards with sound, handcuff them, use one of them to get through the main doors. He had no idea how many more guards would be waiting inside.

From one of the trees came a queasy, sticky sound. Cautiously he walked around the trunk and found a big hollow at shoulder level. Inside was an egg the size of a softball, trembling slightly, as if ready to hatch. He was about to hammer it with sound when he had a better idea.

He reached inside and pulled it out. Immediately another egg plonked down into its place. It was like a gumball machine, and you wouldn't know what your prize was until you opened it.

Luckily he wouldn't be nearby when this happened. The egg vibrated unpleasantly in his hand. Leaning out from behind the tree, he lobbed it high over the fence, then grabbed the second egg from the tree and sent it flying, too.

They made a few big bounces, and then a few smaller bounces, and then came to a squishy halt. Seth counted four beats of his fast heart before both eggs burst open like jack-in-the-boxes. They were the same kind of creature he'd fought on the freight train: a long narrow body held high by stilt-like legs, and a triangular head with bulging eyes and a pair of very eager mandibles.

The bugs charged the guards. There was cursing and shooting. Either the guards were terrible aims, or the bugs' bodies simply gobbled up bullets without harm. Seth lost sight of them all as they disappeared around a corner of the building.

He pulled up his sleeves to free his feathers and slashed through the chain link. Peeling it back, he heard another sticky noise from the gumball tree. When he looked, there was a third egg.

"You, my friend, are coming with me," he muttered, and snatched it up.

He pelted across the yard to the main door, the egg cradled against his chest. It was starting to tremble worryingly. Opening the door a crack, he peeked in and saw a dingy lobby. Behind a desk sat a guard.

Seth recognized him instantly: the guy who'd snatched Esta from the boat. The guard saw him and stood abruptly with a shout.

Seth rolled the egg in like a bowling ball and slammed the door. He heard a few gunshots and then counted twenty seconds of silence. He waited another twenty and opened the door. He saw the desk, and a human shape crumpled behind it, and no sign of the bug.

Seth hurried inside and locked the door behind him. Locked inside with an alien bug, a great life choice. He peeled off his hoodie so all his feathers were free. He rustled them to their full length. Fists clenched, he approached the desk and peeped at the guard's body. He was dead. Pieces of him were missing.

Trying not to look, Seth bent down and snatched the guard's security pass from his belt. He didn't take the gun because he'd never used one and didn't trust himself to do it right. Anyway, he had a better weapon—inside his head.

He heard chewing and looked around to see the bug on top of a vending machine, eating something with its mandibles. It sprang down to the floor and advanced on Seth.

"Not me," said Seth, and jabbed the bug with sound.

It faltered, came at him again.

Again, Seth pulsed it sharply. The bug hesitated.

"Not too great, is it?" Seth said.

A slow learner, the bug came at him a third time, and he delivered the harshest blow yet. The bug's joints creaked, and it swayed unsteadily.

Seth looked at the bug. The bug looked back, stationary.

"I think you get it now, right?"

Keeping his eye on the bug, he walked to the security door that led inside the station proper. He beeped it unlocked with the pass, pulled it wide open so it stuck, then stepped back.

"Now go and make some new friends," he told the bug.

Seth heard voices from inside. The bug must have heard them, too, because it hurtled through the doorway and down the corridor.

Before it rounded a corner, Seth saw it run effortlessly up the wall and continue its charge, upside down, along the ceiling.

Seconds later, Seth heard curses and wails of panic.

"Holy sh—"

"How the hell'd it get inside?"

The voices were soon drowned out by wild gunfire.

Seth crossed the lobby to a second security door. He buzzed himself through and followed the hall past some maintenance closets and bathrooms and then to a promising set of double doors. He pushed them open a crack and took a peek.

It was a vast warehouse. He stepped inside. There were cars and trucks arranged in orderly rows, and high rows of stacked crates. He wandered through them.

Near the middle of the warehouse was a clearing, and in it were six freight containers, like the ones you saw stacked on trains. They were arranged in a row with big gaps in between. Attached to the side of each container was an air-conditioning unit, buzzing faintly.

There had to be people inside.

For the first time, he realized there might be other hybrid kids here.

—*Esta!*

Nothing.

He opened up his mind, searched for a flicker of her light. Anyone's light.

He thought of shouting aloud, but that might bring a guard running.

Near the freight containers was a desk with an empty chair. Maybe the guard had been called away to help deal with the bugs, inside and out. Seth hung back in the shadows of the aisles and then made a dash for the desk.

On it was a monitor, showing black-and-white security footage of six identical rooms. They had to be the interiors of the freight containers: long and narrow, with a hard bed. A stainless steel sink and toilet. No windows.

Two of the rooms were empty, but in the other four were people. He couldn't see any of their faces because their heads were hooded. They all wore nondescript sweatpants and short-sleeved shirts. One of them had a tail; the build suggested someone muscular. Seth studied the pattern of tattoos on his arms.

Darren.

He was surprised at his relief. Darren had tried to kill him on the boat. Still, when Esta made him jump off, Seth had feared the worst for him. They'd been a long way from shore. The water was cold and full of water lilies. But Darren was a swimmer, like Petra, and he'd made it—to land, at least. After that he'd been caught—or maybe he'd given himself up, too exhausted and scared to keep running.

In another container paced a kid with furry arms.

Could it be Charles?

The third kid had one arm in a cast, the other in a sling. Definitely Siena.

The final kid had casts on both arms. Another flyer, absolutely. Seth's pulse picked up.

It had to be Esta.

Which container was she in? The rooms on the monitor weren't labeled, and neither were the containers. It didn't matter. He felt a rush of fellow feeling for all of them. He'd rescue them all, even Darren.

He ran to the nearest container. The door had two halves, each with poles and bars and catches. He'd had no idea opening it would be so complicated. There was probably a special order to it, and he was doing it wrong and running out of time. He should've forced a guard to do this. He felt a panicky fury building in him, and it was all he could do to keep from shouting and swearing.

A hood plunged down over his head in one swift pull. In darkness, off-balance, he spun around, slashing out with his feathered arms. But whoever had done this to him had skipped out of reach.

"Stay still," a voice said, "or I'll shoot you."

CHAPTER EIGHT

AS THE HELICOPTER'S ROTORS began to turn, Petra buckled up. On her right were two soldiers: a woman with a small hard mouth and a guy with sleepy eyes, who Petra hoped was not really that sleepy.

Across from her was the swimmer, stretched across three seats. Sitting was not an option with that long, thick tail. It really put Petra's own tail problems into perspective. The swimmer wore the same synthetic white clothing ze'd worn when Petra had first seen zir, and some kind of tool kit belted across zir chest. Ze kept jostling and flopping zirself around on the seats.

—*This is not comfortable,* ze said to her.

—*What do you guys usually sit in?*

—*A formfitting synthetic membrane.*

She thought of the pod Anaya had gone inside to have her blood extracted. Maybe they slept inside those things, too. Creepy.

—*Oh. Well, I'm very sorry we don't have a bag to put you in.*

And maybe the swimmer could understand sarcasm, because ze sent her a baleful look and sniffed behind zir breathing mask.

Petra thought: *I'm in a helicopter with a grumpy dolphin thing.*

This was the first time she'd been so close to zir—without anything between them. She caught herself holding her breath, like she was afraid of breathing zir in. When she did, ze was actually odorless, which was a relief. She'd worried ze might smell like rotting seaweed or fish guts or something. It made her wonder how she smelled to zir.

She envied Anaya, having a name for her cryptogen parallel. It definitely made it easier to talk about someone when they had a name. But Petra would've felt like a copycat, calling her cryptogen Aqua or something. Anyway, it would be weird making up a name for zir—it was somehow personal, like a nickname for an old friend.

As the rotors spun faster, Petra put the headphones on. She looked out the window at the soldier waving a baton. They lifted off, and she forced herself to take a deep breath.

Here she was. With Seth gone, she didn't feel like anything was that important anymore, including herself. She'd basically told him she loved him (so stupid!) and he'd gone and left anyway. It was like the universe had given her a quick glance and said, "Meh."

So why not go on the salvage mission?

Anyway, she owed it to everyone. She needed to do her part to—it sounded so crazy—*save the world.*

Against her better judgment, she glanced out the window and saw the army base falling away. They'd swooshed up through a temporary hole in the netting, and now she saw it close back up, and then they were skimming high over the harbor.

Vancouver's skyline looked like a row of smashed teeth. Entire buildings had collapsed after being undermined by the worms. Others were covered with dead vines.

And this was one of the lucky cities. It was in a Spray Zone and trying to drag itself back to some kind of normal. Her dad had told her that hospitals were full and had overflowed to school gyms and church halls and indoor rinks and parking garages. So many people with the mosquito bird plague, or pit plant burns, or broken bones and lost limbs from bug attacks.

Down along West Hastings Street, she glimpsed a dead worm, its rotting carcass as big as an eighteen-wheeler. A small victory. But she wondered how many more were tunneling under the city right now.

Outside the city, she saw a tractor moving among neat green rows of crops, and Petra's heart lifted. Mr. Riggs had talked about how farmers were planting things that grew fast: baby carrots and peas and bush beans, kale and spinach and other leafy greens. Things they could harvest before fall.

They climbed higher. Some mosquito birds pattered against the window and were gone. The helicopter flew over foothills, then mountains proper, headed northeast. Outside the Spray Zone, the landscape went black.

Black grass.

Vine-strangled forest.

She thought of all the plants and animals that the cryptogenic plants had choked out. Mr. Riggs had used phrases like *habitat destruction* and *species loss*. Things that they might not ever get back. Extinction. Whatever human beings had already been doing to the planet through pollution and climate change, the cryptogens were doing much, much better.

They passed over a small town where people had tried to rig up protective netting. It hung in tatters over a school and a skating rink. Vines coiled like snakes through the abandoned streets. In a parking lot a bonfire burned.

"It's like this most places," the sleepy-eyed soldier said. "Outside the Spray Zones."

There was only so much herbicide and pesticide to go around. She was glad she wasn't the one who had to make the decisions. They needed to protect main roads and railways. Industrial farms. Cities with their hospitals and hungry people. Power-generating stations, and corridors for electricity transmission towers. Factories desperately trying to make *more* spray.

There were so many things that needed to be kept plant-free. It was a constant struggle. And even after they sprayed, new pollen would blow in and start everything growing all over again. It was like using sandbags to stop a tsunami.

She felt a surge of anger toward the ungainly swimmer sprawled opposite her. *Look what you did,* she thought.

It was unfair, but so what? If the cryptogens hadn't come here, none of this would have been happening. Out of all the places in the universe, what cosmic bad luck they'd picked Earth.

A signal flare arced into the sky and she traced it back to a rooftop. A couple of figures jumped up and down, waving desperately.

"There's people down there!"

"Nothing we can do," said the female officer with the mean mouth, not even looking.

"We could land!" Petra protested.

"Colonel's orders. We don't stop. We have just enough fuel. We can't carry more people anyway."

Petra had to look away, trying not to cry.

"Hey," said Mean Mouth, pointing at Petra's tail, which had strayed toward the soldier's seat. "Keep that thing away from me, you got it?"

"Sorry." Petra curled her tail back, feeling humiliated on top of everything else.

"What a crap assignment," muttered Mean Mouth, folding her arms. "Babysitting Barbie and a crypto."

Petra watched her worriedly. Why had *she* been selected for this mission if she hated the cryptogens so much? Or maybe she hated them *less* than most of the other soldiers. Either way, it made Petra nervous. A rogue soldier had fired a missile at the cryptogen ship as it came in to land—she didn't want Mean Mouth here doing anything crazy.

The cabin got colder as they passed over the mountains. Petra zipped up her hoodie and tipped her forehead against the window. Black grass bristled through the snow. Only the very summits were free of it.

She looked up into the huge sky and didn't see a single jet trail. She felt cold and gloomy and very alone.

—*If you beat the flyers, what will you do?* she asked the swimmer.

The question had come up yesterday with Seth and Anaya, and had circled the edges of her thoughts, like a skater in a darkened rink.

—*We will take the primary vessel back to our own planet.*

Petra felt she could suddenly breathe easier. They had no plans to stay on Earth. But she couldn't imagine the runners and swimmers getting a happy reception if they returned home.

—*But won't you get attacked when you return?*

—*Before we land, we'll send a rain that contains the weapon. We will hope for peace, but if we must fight the winged ones, we will at least fight as equals.*

Petra wondered how the runners and swimmers would ever be able to trust the flyers again. She looked out the window some more.

After the mountains, more sweeping plains of black grass, more ruined towns.

She must have slept a bit, because she woke up to the pilot over her headset:

"Getting close."

With surprising grace, the swimmer stood and bent zir head to the window.

—*Tell them to take us lower,* ze told her.

As they dropped closer, the earth became a mosaic of countless dark ponds, separated by boggy strips of blighted land. Petra whistled softly. She'd expected lots of cryptogenic plants, but no one had warned her it had turned into an alien theme park. Cryptopia! Bring the whole family! Complimentary oxygen and masks!

Mosquito birds flew in churning black clouds that contracted and expanded across the sky. A haze of pollen swirled in the air.

The helicopter went lower still, and Petra saw two massive water striders rowing themselves across a pond. When the bugs reached a thicket of black grass, they leapt up the stalks and walked across the spiky canopy. Smeared across it were big frothy blobs that looked like spit.

—*What the heck are those blobby things?* Petra asked the swimmer, pointing.

She moved out of the way so the swimmer could peer out the window.

—*A parasite. It feeds off the juices of the grass and excretes foam to conceal itself from predators. When immature, it is harmless.*

—*What about when it's not immature?* Petra asked.

—*It becomes troublesome.*

Troublesome? Was the swimmer being ironic? The last thing she needed was a cryptogen trying to have a sense of humor.

—It grows and can fly, the swimmer said unhelpfully. Then quickly added, *This is the crash site, here.*

"Ze says this is the place!" Petra told the pilot over her headset.

The helicopter turned sharply to circle back, then hovered.

The soldiers told them to sit as they slid open the door. Below, it was very marshy. The rotor blades shattered the water into ripples, blowing water lilies into the shallows, their black swan heads bent. The soggy ground was snaked with vines—which meant pit plants everywhere. From various ponds rose large messy structures that looked like a cross between wasp nests and beaver dams.

"What the hell are those?" Mean Mouth shouted above the din of the rotor blades.

—What are those? Petra asked the swimmer.

—Habitats built from the creatures' own saliva and organic matter.

—What creatures?

—They are reclusive. More worrying is what might be in the water.

—Hang on, what lives in the water?

"Man, what a stink!" said Sleepy Eyes, whose eyes no longer looked remotely sleepy. He winced as he leaned back from the door.

It startled Petra that she hadn't noticed the smell sooner—as if her body was used to the sulfurous stink. She'd encountered it first at the eco-reserve on Cordova Island when they rescued Anaya's father. Whatever the lilies exhaled, it was changing the chemistry of the water—and slowly but surely, the atmosphere, too.

The swimmer removed zir respirator mask, and zir nostrils flared as ze took a deep, grateful breath. Petra supposed this must be a lot like the air on zir home planet.

"You'd better put your masks on," she told the soldiers and two pilots.

She remembered what Anaya's father had said about how the cryptogenic air would eventually become faintly toxic to humans. She didn't want the pilots getting groggy and crashing their ride home. They all must've been briefed, because they wasted no time starting a drizzle of oxygen into their masks.

"I think I see the ship," the co-pilot said over Petra's headset. The helicopter drifted to the right, and directly below, she saw what she would have mistaken for a mossy rock beneath the surface of the black water.

—*Most of it is submerged,* the swimmer said.

"Shut the doors, we'll do a couple of passes to spray," the pilot said.

Petra sat back as the helicopter unleashed its pesticide and herbicide over the crash site. She hoped it would be enough.

—*The creatures in those habitats?* she asked the swimmer. *Are they bugs or mammals?*

She wasn't sure if *bugs* and *mammals* meant anything to the swimmer, but she wanted to know if they had hatched or had been born, like the rhino thing. But ze seemed to understand, because in Petra's mind flashed an image of a creature with oily fur, a viciously sloped head, and sharp teeth that didn't all fit inside its mouth. It had no legs, just hairy tentacles. It looked like half mammal, half fish.

—*Your planet must really suck,* she said, not expecting zir to understand, but the way she said it must have made her meaning clear.

—*Our planet is beautiful,* ze replied, with such sincerity and wistfulness that Petra looked at zir afresh. Ze had a home ze loved, one ze hadn't seen in years and years. Ze was homesick.

"I'm not loving this terrain," the pilot said. "There's no good landing site."

When Petra passed this on to the swimmer, ze replied:

—*Tell them to hover low and we can jump out.*

—*Right into the water?* Petra asked, picturing the black murk.

—*Yes. It is deep enough.*

—*What about those things in the water?*

—*With two of us we will be safe. Tell the pilot we will jump.*

Petra sighed. "Can you just go low and let us jump out?"

The pilot turned back to her. "You sure?"

"Just stay close, okay?" she said pleadingly.

Mean Mouth looked as if she'd like nothing better than to dump the two of them here permanently.

"We'll keep you covered," Sleepy Eyes said. "Anything that's not dead from the spray, we'll make dead."

Ruefully, Petra remembered the last time a soldier had told her everything would be a piece of cake. It ended with a crashed helicopter and four dead soldiers.

"I saw water striders back there," she said, dragging off her hoodie and shoes. The wet suit underneath had been specially altered so her tail could stick out. "Oh, and there's hairy wolverine-squid things in those freaky towers."

"No problem," said Sleepy Eyes.

The soldiers pulled open the doors on either side and lifted their rifles as the ground approached. Everything was now coated with a fine white mist of herbicide and pesticide. The water lilies drooped. The vines were already starting to yellow. A water strider turned over dead in the water, its legs clenched. Good. Petra wondered how much time the spray would buy them. There were a lot of things out here that could coil around a landing strut or, worse, jump right aboard.

"How long can you hold your breath?" Sleepy Eyes asked her.

"About twenty-five minutes."

"We'll be waiting."

When they were five feet above the water, the swimmer said to her:

—*Are you ready?*

—*After you.*

Ze launched zirself headfirst, slicing gracefully into the water. Ze didn't reappear. Petra's turn now. What amazed her was she didn't feel more hesitation. Despite the murkiness of the water, she still wanted to swim.

She held the diving mask firmly in place, took a last deep breath, and jumped. The water was a cold slap. She was blind at first, but slowly her eyes adjusted. All around her was a dark soup of decayed plants and floating animal bones.

She caught the bright undulating shape of the swimmer and followed zir to the sunken ship. It was resting askew on the silty bottom, its hull covered in slime.

—*Why did it crash?* she asked.

—*The hull is not breached. Systems malfunction or pilot error. I do not know.*

The swimmer wiped slime from the hull and took a tool from the belt around zir chest.

—*We need to go inside. Move back and wait till the ship has flooded fully.*

Ze pushed the tool against the hull and a hatch slid open. Petra kicked back as water surged past her into the ship. Air burst out, soaring upward in long skinny balloons.

It took only moments for the ship to fill, and then the swimmer entered. Petra held back. It was like the mouth of a cave. She hadn't gone inside the ship in the biodome, and she certainly didn't want to go inside this one. There'd be dead cryptogen bodies—and maybe worse. Would there be humans in there, too? Women who'd been abducted?

From the corner of her eye she thought she saw something move—and that decided her. She kicked her way inside the ship.

The space was cluttered with cables and sacs swaying and bobbing in the water. She didn't want to look at anything too long, in case it was horrifying.

—*Over here,* said the swimmer.

A cone of light emanated from zir chest—some kind of fancy lamp on the tool belt—and Petra followed zir to a section of wall.

—*Am I keeping watch, or are you?* she asked zir.

—*We should both be vigilant.*

Floating horizontally in the water, ze held out a tool to her. She was impressed by how well ze manipulated things with webbed fingers.

—*We need to remove the wall to reach the levitation system.*

Petra watched as ze began to cut, and did the same. The tool didn't look sharp, but it sank into the wall as effortlessly as a scalpel. When they'd cut a narrow rectangle, they plunged their fingers into the incision and pulled. The panel peeled away neatly. What was revealed behind looked more like living tissue than machine. It was fleshy, crisscrossed with wires and tubes that resembled veins and arteries. Petra spied something shaped a bit like a heart, and shivered as it trembled.

The swimmer delicately patted several places and then, without ceremony, plunged zir arm straight into the wall. Oily purple fluid leaked into the water like ink. Like the ship was bleeding.

—*I can't reach it,* ze said to her. *Your arms are longer.*

Ze pulled out zir arm and tilted zir head at the wall. Swallowing back her revulsion, Petra pushed her hand into the opening ze'd made. It felt like the inside of a pumpkin.

—*What am I looking for?* she asked.

—*A cylinder.*

She pushed deeper, up to her elbow, before her fingertips grazed something hard. With her fingernails she dug it out and held it up to the swimmer.

—*This tiny thing?* she asked in amazement. *This is the entire levitation system?*

—*You appear surprised.*

—*It doesn't even look important!*

—*Without it the ship can't fly.*

—*Something this important should be bigger than a lip gloss, is all I'm saying.*

—*What is lip gloss?*

Something tightened around Petra's leg and pulled hard. The cylinder jolted from her hand. She twisted around to see a long tentacle curled twice around her lower leg, dragging her feetfirst toward a vicious head full of teeth.

The swimmer flashed past her, zir belly a furious red, and bit through the tentacle holding her. Petra kicked herself away from a wolverine-squid, which was thrashing in the swimmer's jaws, vainly trying to wrestle itself free with its remaining tentacles.

—*Find the levitation system!* the swimmer shouted silently.

Desperately Petra cast about, searching. It was so murky in here. How was she supposed to spot something the size of a AA battery? From the corner of her eye, she caught a smudge of movement. Another squid thing had just jetted inside. Her eyes ricocheted around the ship's cluttered interior. So many dangling cables and sacs, it was hard to tell what was machine and what was animal.

The levitation system, there! Fast, she kicked down and grabbed the cylinder. A tentacle grabbed her wrist. More tentacles looped under her shoulder and around her waist and wrenched her around so sharply, she lost her grip on the cylinder. She saw it float straight into the jagged mouth of the wolverine-squid bearing down on her.

Petra's tail whipped out to sting but was batted away by a tentacle. She pulled it back and lashed out again from her left. This time she felt the satisfying slap of the tip hitting flesh. A hot flush went through her as her venom pumped into the creature. Almost instantly it went still, tentacles rigid, jaws frozen open. Inside, she saw the cylinder. It hadn't been swallowed. Wincing, she pushed her hand past the rows of motionless teeth and plucked out the levitation system.

—*Got it!* she cried silently, tucking it inside her wet suit.

When she turned, the swimmer was hovering placidly in the water, chewing on a tentacle of the wolverine-squid ze had just killed.

—*You're eating? Now?*

—It's been a long time since I ate food such as this.

—Hang on, were you just eating as I got attacked by that other one?

—You had control of the situation. And now we have the levitation system.

—Yes.

—You might want to taste the tentacle, the swimmer said, offering her a bit. *I think you would find it very pleasing.*

Suddenly she felt breathless. She'd lost track of time down here.

—Need air, she told the swimmer, and kicked for the hatch.

But the hatch was gone. In its place was a writhing nest of tentacles. It took her a second to realize that something was in the process of entering. A tentacle, so much longer than the ones she'd already seen, curled inside. A second shot in, almost hitting Petra, and slammed against the far wall.

The swimmer grabbed her arm and tugged her to the other end of the ship. She looked back to see more tentacles splayed out inside the ship, and then the torso and head entered. The massive wolverine-squid took up most of the ship.

Petra's urge to take a breath was building to panic. She needed out, she needed air!

The swimmer plunged a tool into the ship's fleshy ceiling, and a smaller hatch opened.

—Go! ze told Petra.

She didn't need any convincing. She kicked through. She

looked back just once and didn't see the swimmer coming. Had something happened? She couldn't stop and check.

Air air air!

She broke the surface and gasped. Then she whipped her head around, looking.

The helicopter was gone.

CHAPTER NINE

INSIDE THE BIODOME, INSIDE the ship, Anaya stood with Terra and Dr. Weber, staring at a translucent disk that glowed like a crystal ball.

Magnified within was the same nestlike tangle she'd seen before. This time, however, emerging from the nest was a small army of headless spiders.

—*What're those?* she asked.

"Viruses," said Dr. Weber and Terra at the same moment, one aloud, one silently.

It was hard for Anaya not to think of them as monsters. They were hairy and muscular and mindless—yet they moved with such intent.

"Those things came from *my* body?" she said, feeling like she wanted to wash every inch of herself.

Dr. Weber's face mask hissed quietly as it drizzled supplemental oxygen. "You just carried the blueprints for them," she said reassuringly, but Anaya still felt sick. Just when she thought she'd come to terms with her mutant body, there was always something new to spice things up.

—*The nest was productive,* Terra announced.

This was good news, and she should've felt happier, but her thoughts kept circling back to Seth. What was happening to him out there? And Petra had just taken off on the salvage mission. Anaya regretted how harshly she'd spoken to her friend. Before the helicopter lifted off, she'd said she was sorry and told Petra she didn't need to go, but Petra wouldn't change her mind. Petra was not one to back down.

—*We will do a test now,* Terra said.

Anaya looked at Dr. Weber. "She says they're ready to do a test."

Dr. Weber nodded. They hadn't yet told Terra that Seth was gone, and Anaya did it now. When she heard Terra's reply, her eyes stung with tears.

"What's wrong?" Dr. Weber asked her with concern.

"Terra said they'd never planned to test it on Seth. It was always going to be tested on a full cryptogen."

If only they'd known this earlier! Why hadn't they talked it through? Seth would never have overheard that argument between Dr. Weber and Pearson—and maybe he'd still be here right now.

"I'm so sorry, Anaya," Dr. Weber told her. "This is my fault."

Her eyes were shiny, and she sounded like she had a cold.

Maybe it was just allergies, and exhaustion, but Anaya didn't think so.

"It's not your fault," Anaya told her. They'd each had to make so many rushed decisions without knowing all the facts. All they could do was blunder through this together as best they could.

—Does this mean you're going to test it on the winged one? she asked Terra.

No reply was needed, because the regal flyer cryptogen had just stepped through the ship's hatchway.

—Is it time?

The general's words carried a powerful scent of skid marks and firecracker smoke. Anaya checked on Dr. Weber and saw her stiffen in fear, so close to the flyer. Anaya didn't blame her. But in a strange way, the general's bearing reminded her of the stern, gaunt presence of Colonel Pearson. Both military men, just from opposite sides of the universe.

"They're testing it on him right now?" Dr. Weber asked.

Anaya nodded, then jolted as a synthetic sac fell from the ceiling. She'd never get used to those things popping out.

"The colonel won't be happy about this," Dr. Weber said. "He thinks the general is one of our best weapons."

—Is he willing to lose his power? Anaya asked Terra.

She was surprised when the general answered for himself.

—It is an acceptable loss, to defeat tyrants.

If she had any lingering doubts about Terra and the rebels, they were vanquished now. The general had lost his power once before, injured in a battle, and now he was willing to lose it permanently.

The general climbed inside the sac and Terra zipped it up. Anaya watched as the sac molded around the winged cryptogen while he reclined. The vinelike cables migrated to the area around his crested head.

Terra tapped the wall and an image floated to its surface and became crystal clear: a mosaic of bright red pebbles, jostling tightly.

"Brain cells," Dr. Weber murmured. "The general's brain cells."

—*This is the region that produces the sound,* Terra explained to Anaya. *The virus should alter it. The sound it generates will never leave the skull.*

—*So what happens?*

—*The sound will only harm the individual who makes it.*

—*You mean they'll feel the pain?*

—*Agonizingly.*

—*So they'll stop right away.*

—*Or if they persist, they will die.*

"Wow," said Anaya, and told Dr. Weber what she'd learned. There was certainly poetic justice to it. The weapon turned against its user.

Terra tapped the translucent disk that contained Anaya's blood.

—*I am delivering the virus now.*

On the monitor, Anaya saw a torrent of the headless spiders muscle their way among the general's brain cells. Spellbound in terror, Anaya watched one of the little spiders latch onto a brain cell with its sharp legs and squeeze. The brain cell exploded. She winced and glanced worriedly at the general inside the sac, expecting him to cry out, but he was very still.

When she returned her gaze to the monitor, things shaped like boomerangs were swirling among the brain cells and viruses.

"What're those?" Anaya asked aloud.

"Pretty sure those are antibodies," said Dr. Weber. "An immune response."

With incredible aim, the boomerang things chopped off the legs of the spiders before they could latch onto any more cells. Severed limbs drifted everywhere, then dissolved. The spiders had all been destroyed. Hardly any of the brain cells had been ruptured.

—*What just happened?* Anaya asked in bewilderment.

—*The virus should have destroyed far more brain cells.*

—*So it didn't work at all?*

—*No. This was a failure.*

SO STUPID, SETH RAGED at himself, *just letting them sneak up on you.*

Hooded, blind, he heard the pounding of footsteps as more guards entered the warehouse.

"How'd he get past you guys?" demanded the guard who'd just hooded him.

"Bastard brought a bug in here," another voice answered. "Set it loose in the hallways. It took down Carlson."

"Tom's in bad shape, too," said a third voice. "But we finished it off."

"This freak was on the boat with her," the first guard said. "I recognized him."

"Let's cuff him."

Seth thought of slashing out with his arms, but he knew there were at least three guards, maybe more, and they'd have guns trained on him the whole time. If he tried anything, he'd only end up getting shot. And then he'd be even more useless.

"Stay still!" the first guard barked at him.

He let them manacle his hands behind his back, telling himself there'd be another way out, he'd think of a plan. But right now he couldn't think of anything except what a terrible mess he'd made of this.

Someone gave him a shove and he staggered forward. He heard the door of a freight container creaking open. No doubt one of the empty ones he'd seen on the monitor. Like it had been waiting for him all along.

He stumbled up the steps and inside. His feet clanged on a metal floor.

"How long we supposed to take care of these freaks?" one of the guards asked.

"Until the doctor comes."

Seth felt a hot rash of panic sweep across his neck.

"The guy with the eye patch?" another guard asked.

Seth turned around so quickly he almost fell over. "What doctor? What's his name?"

His answer was the slamming of the door, and the crack of bolts being shot.

PETRA TREADED WATER, LOOKING around wildly for the helicopter.

Beside her, the swimmer crested the surface.

—*Where is it?* ze demanded.

—*Great question!*

They'd left them! She'd never trusted Mean Mouth. The woman obviously hated all the cryptogens and wanted them dead. But to leave them out here like this? In the middle of a squid-infested swamp?

She had to get out of the water.

She dragged herself closer to the shore—if you could even call it that. It was a big mushy mess, and she bellied up onto it, hands and knees sinking into muck.

The swimmer gracefully skimmed ashore beside her. Petra was glad to pull her legs onto land. She could still feel the hideous pressure of those tentacles around her.

Hoarse and breathless, she looked around the muskeg. Had

the helicopter crashed? She couldn't see any wreckage. No smoke. They were a million miles from anywhere.

Anxiously her eyes strayed to one of the weird hive towers poking up crookedly from a nearby pool.

—*How many things live inside those towers?* she asked.

—*They can make themselves very small.*

Which didn't answer her question but still made her shiver. There were many small openings in the tower, and from one of them, just above water level, the tip of a tentacle jutted out and was quickly retracted. From another little window she caught the angry flash of an eye.

Petra slid her gaze across the muskeg, from one tower to another. She counted four. In the distance she caught sight of a water strider, not coming closer, but not moving any farther away either.

—*We are basically surrounded,* she said.

—*There is a human settlement,* said the swimmer.

—*Where?*

—*To the southeast.*

—*How far?*

—*In your distance, two hundred miles.*

—*I don't think we'll make it two miles!*

Out in the murky water the hairy face of a squid thing broke the surface. It didn't move, just stared malevolently at them. Petra scuttled farther back onto solid ground, which was not really very solid at all.

A droning noise pulled her attention to the sky. Rotors! Coming closer. She sighted the helicopter, flying erratically.

"Over here!" she cried, jumping up and down, scissoring her arms above her head.

Then she heard the patter of gunfire. Two huge winged things harried the helicopter.

—*What're those?* she asked the swimmer.

—*The parasites whose eggs you noticed earlier.*

Those weird eggs in the spittle on the plants? They grew up to be the size of flying manta rays? One flew straight at the copter's windshield and splashed against it.

When the copter turned straight toward her, Petra could see that the creature had plastered itself flat against the windshield, and the glass was smoking. Was it melting?

The helicopter slewed closer. Sleepy Eyes was leaning out the doorway, firing at the other winged thing attacking the helicopter. With another patter of gunfire, it dropped aslant through the air and hit the ground.

Worriedly, Petra glanced back at the water. The wolverine-squid that had been watching them from the shallows had moved a bit closer. Suddenly it rose straight up from the water, first its head, then its furred torso, and she realized that this thing was walking upright on its tentacles. Ten feet tall, it tippy-toed onto shore like some deranged eight-legged ballerina.

"Holy *crap!*" Petra screamed.

"Get on!" Sleepy Eyes shouted, hurling scramble netting down the side of the helicopter.

Petra threw herself at the netting and climbed.

With zir shorter legs, the swimmer was slower.

As Petra clambered inside the cabin, Mean Mouth let fly with a torrent of bullets. Petra looked back to see a tentacle curled through the netting. The wolverine-squid had hooked a ride.

The soldiers might as well have been shooting into a ball of clay, for all the good it did.

"Take us up, up, up!" Sleepy Eyes wailed at the pilot. The helicopter lurched higher, but the squid thing held tight, climbing up. One of its tentacles looped around the swimmer.

"Don't fire!" Petra shrieked at the soldiers, afraid the swimmer would be hit.

The squid thing was all over the swimmer now, tentacles everywhere, and the swimmer was chewing off as many as ze could.

"We're cutting the netting loose!" Mean Mouth said, bending down for the release buckles.

"Don't!" Petra cried.

"They're too heavy!"

The helicopter tilted and Petra grabbed a handle to avoid getting dumped out.

"Sit down!" Mean Mouth shouted at her.

—*Sting it!* she yelled at the swimmer.

—It has my tail pinned!

Before the soldiers could grab her, Petra swung herself out of the cabin and onto the netting. Wind blasting against her, she clung on for dear life. She went as close as she dared to the wolverine-squid, then struck it with her tail. The stinger hit the creature's back, and she pumped out venom until her heart thudded with exhaustion.

The swimmer shrugged free of the paralyzed squid and sent it spinning down into the muskeg, but not before biting off one last tentacle. Petra grabbed the swimmer's hand or foot or paw—she wasn't sure what it was called and didn't care—and helped bring the swimmer inside. Ze spat the severed tentacle onto the cabin floor.

"What the hell's this?" said Mean Mouth.

"Food," Petra told her. "You have a problem with that?"

"We can't see!" the co-pilot was shouting from the cockpit. "We need to clear this goo off the windshield!"

"Whatever you do, don't land!" Petra said, looking down fearfully at the dozens of wolverine-squids performing some kind of terrifying ballet around the paralyzed one that had plunged from the helicopter.

—Tell the pilot to stay level, the swimmer said.

Then, without ceremony, ze climbed out of the cabin on all fours and walked along the outside of the helicopter's fuselage to the windshield.

"What's going on?" the pilot bellowed.

With zir jaws, the swimmer scraped off the splattered bird thing that was melting the windshield. Ze licked it clear with zir tongue, which was a very disgusting sight to behold. Still chewing, ze walked back with zir weirdly sticky feet and returned to the cabin. Mutely, Sleepy Eyes slammed shut the door.

—*Good job,* Petra told the swimmer.

—*You saved me,* the swimmer told her, zir silent voice tinged with surprise.

Petra was surprised, too. She'd just instinctively risked her own life to sting that wolverine-squid and save a cryptogen.

—*You saved me underwater,* she admitted truthfully.

—*Here.* The swimmer held out the tentacle. *It is very pleasantly flavored.*

Ze sounded like one of the cooking shows her mom watched to unwind after work.

—*Do you ever stop eating?*

—*It has been a long time since I consumed fresh food!*

With a sigh Petra took the offered tentacle and had a bite. She was famished. It was indeed pleasantly flavored and she eagerly had more.

When she caught the soldiers looking at her, she said:

"What? You guys never get hungry? Don't you have a protein bar or something? I'm not sharing."

"Sorry we had to leave you back there," Sleepy Eyes said. "Those winged things came flying at us, and we tried to lose them, but they literally stuck to us. You get what you needed?"

"Yeah, we got it." She held up the little cylinder.

The swimmer reached for it and deposited it carefully in a pouch in zir tool belt.

Mean Mouth asked, "Does it understand when we talk?"

"*Ze*. Not *it*. And no, I don't think so."

"You really trust these guys?"

"About as much as I trust you guys," she replied. "A little more, actually."

She took another bite of tentacle. There was something satisfying about eating something that had just tried to eat you. She closed her eyes and made herself more comfortable on the seat.

They'd gotten the levitation system. They could fix their little ship. They would make this new weapon. They would win and save the world.

She fell asleep.

CHAPTER TEN

AT DINNER, ANAYA CHEWED her food without tasting it.

"Dr. Weber said she'd never seen an immune response so fast," she told her parents and Mr. Sumner. "The general's antibodies just wiped the virus out."

"Well," Dad said, "the good news is the virus knows its target. You saw it lock on and destroy the brain cells."

"Hardly any, though," Anaya replied.

This was a failure.

Terra's words reverberated in her head.

"It's only a first trial," Dad said. "These things can take time."

Anaya nodded, trying to feel reassured. Her father was a botanist, and he knew about lab trials. And after all, he'd helped Dr. Weber design the herbicide that was killing the cryptogenic plants.

"We don't have much time, though," Mr. Sumner pointed out.

"Terra said she was going to grow a second culture from my cells," Anaya said. "Under different conditions. To see if the viruses are faster and more aggressive."

"We'll get there," Dad said.

The table lapsed into silence. It had been a somber dinner. Anaya had been hoping to bring home much better news from the biodome. And she was also missing Petra. She glanced out the window—a few more hours of daylight—and then back at Mr. Sumner, who hadn't said much during the meal. He must be worrying about his daughter. They hadn't had any kind of update on how the salvage was going, but Pearson had warned them ahead of time: the helicopter would be out of radio contact almost the entire mission. Still, everyone was hoping they'd be home before nightfall.

Anaya lapsed back into her own thoughts, which were split between Petra's salvage mission and the virus tests. Both needed to be successful or the rebels' plan would fail.

As they were cleaning up, Mom asked, "You okay?"

"Hmm?" She looked up from the sink.

"You hardly ate anything."

"Sorry. It was really good."

She didn't want to tell her mother that she'd already eaten in the biodome with Terra: berries from the vines, stalks of black grass sliced open. She was still full.

"You're pretty quiet," Mom said.

"Just tired." After a day in the biodome with Terra, it was strange talking aloud. Back in the bunker, when she'd first started silent talking, it felt totally abnormal and hazy. Now the opposite was true. Normal talking was jarring and imprecise. And slow. She found herself getting impatient, listening to people speak aloud. Telepathically, things came faster, and with greater complexity.

Anaya dried the last plate and put it away in the cupboard.

Mom said, "The bathroom's free if you want to have a shower."

"I'm okay," Anaya said, and then paused, embarrassed. "Are you saying I *need* a shower?"

"No, no," Mom said quickly, "it's just I know the bathrooms are in high demand sometimes."

With the pads of her clawed fingers, Anaya touched her face and felt the pleasing velvet mat of fine hairs. She'd forgotten to use the hair-removal cream for a couple of days. Or shave her legs and arms. Or any other part of her body.

Or maybe she just hadn't bothered.

It didn't seem so bad to her anymore. But perhaps no one else agreed. She'd been wearing pants and long sleeves to hide her arms and legs, but the thick hair under the fabric did make her look bulkier.

"Do I smell bad?" she asked, self-conscious now.

Had she been stinking like a wet dog this whole time? And everyone was too polite to say anything? That was too awful! Terra didn't smell mangy, but maybe Anaya hadn't noticed because *she* smelled the same.

"Of course not," her mother said.

"You doing okay, Anaya-lator?" Dad said.

Anaya smiled at her dad's old nickname for her. He hadn't used it for a while, and it made her feel homesick.

"Yeah, I'm fine," she told him.

"We're kind of worried about you."

She blinked, surprised. "Why?"

"You've been a bit withdrawn," Mom said.

"Sorry."

"Is it too intense, spending so much time in the biodome?"

"Well, yeah, of course it's intense." She was communicating with another species, and translating for Dr. Weber and Colonel Pearson, and trying to help create a weapon that might save the planet. "But they need me in there."

"We thought we'd ask Stephanie Weber if she could use some of the other hybrid kids to translate."

"No!" said Anaya, surprised by the force of her reaction. "I'm used to it now. It'd take them too long to get good. Anyway, some of the kids definitely don't want to use silent talking. It freaks them out."

"Maybe it freaks them out for good reason," said Mr. Sumner, wiping down the counters.

Of all the adults, Petra's father was the least sympathetic to the whole project. It wasn't surprising, Anaya thought. His wife had been killed by the cryptogen bugs. And he worked in the base hospital and saw, every day, the terrible injuries and diseases meted out by the plants and bugs.

"Look, I'm okay, really," Anaya said. Did they think she was getting weird or something?

"Well, we'd still like to bring it up with Stephanie anyway."

"Don't, please," she said. "Terra's used to me now. We're really fast."

She had fallen into an easy rhythm of translating back and forth for Dr. Weber. Also, she didn't want to get shut out of what was happening. Mostly, though, she knew she'd miss Terra's voice inside her head.

Dad said, "We're only trying to—"

"I know, and thank you, but I don't need to be monitored or anything, I'm fine."

"Sure," said Dad. "But maybe we could limit it."

"You're worried I'm turning into a cryptogen—just say it."

"No, no," Dad said hurriedly. "But you do seem different lately. Like you're barely here. You're only sixteen years old, and this is too much for any person."

"I can handle it."

Translating was easy, compared to being imprisoned in a bunker and breaking out. For the first time she felt irritated with her parents. It was nice being cared for, but they didn't need to get in her way. She was trying to help the entire world. So what if she got a little tired?

She rubbed her itchy eyes. "If I'm tired, maybe it's just my allergies coming back."

They didn't bug her inside the biodome. There she felt great.

She wanted to be back inside right now, sharing food with Terra. But she couldn't tell this to her parents. Especially if they were worried she was going to turn into a cryptogen.

"Your eyes," Mom said, cutting a worried glance at Dad.

"What? They're just a bit red from my allergies."

She went to the hall mirror and had a look. Were her eyes bloodshot, or were the whites darkening? She focused on her pupils. They weren't quite round anymore. They were flattened at top and bottom, more oval now.

More like Terra's rectangular pupils.

Instead of panic, she felt a bizarre twinge of pleasure.

"I can't help what's happening to me," she said, turning back to her parents and Mr. Sumner.

Seth had left. Petra was elsewhere. Anaya felt alone, and weirdly ganged up on. Mom came over and enveloped her in a tight hug. Dad put his arms around both of them.

"We know, sweetie," Mom said. "Everything's okay."

She sneezed and eased out of the hug to grab a tissue. She didn't like it that she had allergies again. She didn't want to go back to acne and a snotty nose and asthma attacks. She wished she had an immune system like the general's. She pictured those boomerang antibodies exploding red across the monitor and decimating the spider-like virus.

An idea flickered in her head.

"Dad," she said, "allergies are immune reactions, right?"

"Yep. Your own body attacks the allergen, whatever pesky thing it might be. Pollen. A fungus. Certain foods."

"Okay. Maybe this is crazy," she said. "But if someone's having an allergic reaction, would their immune system be weakened? Or, say, *distracted*?"

"*Overactive* might be the better word." Her father looked at her, puzzled but intrigued. "What are you thinking?"

"If we could trigger an allergic reaction in the flyers, and *then* hit them with the virus, would their immune systems be too overloaded to kill the viruses as fast?" She winced. "Is that totally unscientific?"

"Not necessarily," said Dad, his eyes drifting thoughtfully as he mulled it over. "But what are the flyers allergic to?"

"That's what I was wondering," Anaya said. "Terra has the same allergies as me. The swimmer, I guess, ze'd react to regular water the same as Petra. But the flyer—"

"Are they even allergic to *anything*?" said Mom. "Seth isn't, is he?"

"One thing!" Anaya said excitedly, turning to Dad. "The soil on the eco-reserve. Remember, he got an itchy rash. All three of us did. So if *we're* allergic, chances are the flyers are, too!"

Dad was nodding. "It wasn't a very severe reaction, though."

"Maybe Terra could make it stronger."

"Tell this to Dr. Weber," Dad said.

"You think it might work?"

"Maybe. It's definitely worth exploring."

Anaya grinned. *Maybe* was a lot better than a failure.

PETRA WOKE TO A deepening vibration through the helicopter. It felt like they were about to land.

"We back already?" she asked Sleepy Eyes.

"Had to make a detour," he told her. "We need to refuel. We burned too much back at the muskeg, trying to shake off those bird things."

Petra's heart picked up speed. "So where are we?"

"The exact coordinates," said Mean Mouth, "would be 'the middle of nowhere.'"

When Petra peered out the window, the sun was low in the sky. She saw trees mostly, then fields rampant with black grass, then some overgrown streets of a town that looked forlorn and utterly deserted. And now, directly below them, was an unlit gas station. Vines had grown over the main building, but the pumps themselves were pretty clear.

—*We're landing,* she told the swimmer when she caught zir wondering look. *We're out of gas.*

—*Gas?*

—*Fuel.*

—*Your machines are terribly inefficient.*

She clenched her teeth as the pilot set them down gently on the asphalt. She didn't think she would ever stop worrying about pit plants growing underneath school fields, or parking lots, or highways. If the helicopter fell inside one of those things, it would be game over.

As the blades slowed, the pilot unbuckled and ducked into the main cabin.

"Did you have to turn it off?" Petra asked.

"Got to turn it off to fuel it up," he said. To Sleepy Eyes, he said, "Come with me." To Mean Mouth, he said, "Guard the helicopter."

"You think there's any gas here still?" Petra asked.

"There better be. We've only got five minutes of fuel left. And that doesn't get us anywhere close to the base. You two stay inside with Daniels." He nodded at his co-pilot, who was absorbed in some kind of checklist.

Peeping through the window, Petra felt stressed out. There could be pit plants, there could be mosquito birds, there could be so many kinds of bugs and stuff she hadn't had the pleasure of viewing yet.

Outside, Mean Mouth was doing slow circuits of the helicopter, looking all around, gun at the ready. At the helicopter's nose, the pilot opened a compartment and unspooled a narrow hose. He and Sleepy Eyes walked it across the station, past the fuel pumps, to a manhole cover. They heaved off the cover and knelt down. The pilot shined a light into the hole, then looked back at the helicopter and gave the co-pilot the thumbs-up sign.

—*There's fuel,* Petra told the swimmer with relief.

The co-pilot flipped a couple of switches, and Petra heard the sound of a small motor that must have been pumping the fuel up into their tank.

"How long will it take to fill up?" she asked the co-pilot.

"Six minutes."

This was good. They'd be on their way fast.

"You planning on paying for that gas?"

Petra heard the voice before she saw its owner step out from around the side of the gas station. He was dressed in hunting gear, though he carried no gun that she could see. He was a stocky, older man, his hair and sizable beard streaked with gray.

"Sir," said the pilot, standing, "we are on a military mission for the Canadian Armed Forces. We just need to refuel."

"Sure, sure," the man said. "Army, doing important work and all."

Petra wondered if he was crazy, wandering around out here all alone.

"Must be wonderful, helping all those people," the man said conversationally.

"We'll be on our way shortly," Sleepy Eyes replied.

The old man stuck his hands in his pockets and rocked back and forth on the balls of his feet. "I don't remember getting much help up here, though. None, in fact. We tried calling. But no one came. Had to manage on our own. Our own weapons. Our own food and water. Our own gas, which you are now stealing from us."

Petra swallowed. The man's tone was no longer remotely pleasant. She could see Sleepy Eyes holding his gun more tightly.

The pilot said, "We'll replace the gas as soon as we can."

"Oho! I bet you will. I bet you'll just add that to your little to-do list."

"Just enough to return to base, sir," said Sleepy Eyes.

"Must be nice, having a base," said the old-timer.

"There's more of them!" called out Mean Mouth suddenly, and Petra saw men and women with guns surrounding the helicopter, like they'd just materialized from the shadows.

From the cockpit the co-pilot swore and drew his service revolver.

"Everyone, just let's calm down now," said Sleepy Eyes, gripping his gun very tightly. "We are all in this together."

"I am very glad to hear you say that," said the old-timer. "Because we have a simple request. We have eight very sick people, six of them children. They got bitten by those flying insects. We want you to take them to your base for treatment."

"We can't do that," the pilot said. "We don't have the room, but we can radio our base and get them to—"

"Your helicopter looks plenty big to me," said the old-timer. "Six little kids don't weigh much."

Petra felt her heart tearing. It seemed completely reasonable to her. But she knew the soldiers didn't want anyone seeing *her* and the swimmer. These people almost certainly thought hybrids were evil, and who knew what they'd do if they found a real live cryptogen.

"Not possible," the pilot said. "We're overweight as it is."

"Well, maybe we can take some of that weight out. If you've got other passengers in there, we will take real good care of them here, so we know you'll bring *our* people back to us safe and sound. Let's just have a look at what you've got inside."

"You get back!" Mean Mouth shouted at them. "Or I will open fire!"

"Steady, steady!" said Sleepy Eyes. "There's no need for violence!"

Petra sank back into her seat and tried to hide her tail. Faces pressed up against the windows, and then the door was yanked open, and a man in a couple of wool sweaters poked his rifle inside, then his head.

"Who're you?" he asked, not unkindly.

"Petra."

"Need you off the helicopter. Now. And what's this?"

With the barrel of his rifle he poked the large tarp she'd quickly spread over the swimmer.

"Just some supplies," she said.

"Well, we'll need those off, too. Let's just see—"

He pulled off the tarp and saw the swimmer.

"Holy—"

He fumbled with his rifle but didn't get a shot off before the swimmer struck him in the chest with zir stinger. The man fell backward out of the helicopter and hit the earth, gurgling.

"What'd you do to him?" someone shouted.

—*Did you kill him?* Petra asked.

—*No.*

"Out, out, out!" voices shouted at them. The opposite cabin door was pulled open and more guns jabbed in at them.

"Don't shoot!" Petra cried, trying to shield the swimmer.

"They've got one inside!" a woman cried. "A cryptogen! And a hybrid girl!"

—*Should I strike?* the swimmer asked.

—*No, wait.*

"We're not going to hurt you!" Petra shouted. "We're trying to help you."

"Out!"

Slowly Petra edged out, followed by the swimmer, onto the asphalt parking lot.

"Well, this is something," said the old-timer. "What the hell's going on here?"

Petra looked at Sleepy Eyes and Mean Mouth and the pilots, but they weren't talking, so Petra did.

"It's a lot to explain, but this cryptogen's a rebel. On our side. There's lots of rebels, actually, and they're helping us. They're going to stop the invasion."

Petra could smell a lot of tense people all around her, most of them holding guns, but so far no one was firing.

"This is crap," one of them said. "I don't buy it."

"Me either," said someone else.

"Here's what's going to happen," said the old-timer. "You and you"—he pointed at the pilots—"get back inside. You two"—he pointed at the soldiers—"you're going to put down those guns and stay with us." To some of his own people, he said, "Get our sick people inside the helicopter, and as many others as'll fit, with guns. We're going to a hospital. And these two"—he was looking at Petra and the swimmer now—"they will stay here and we will deal with them as we see fit."

—*What is happening?* asked the swimmer.

"It doesn't have to be like this," said Petra. The soldiers were not putting down their guns, and she sensed there was going to be a terrible eruption of violence, and she realized she was crying. "We'll take the sick people, it's okay."

Things came out of the woods so quickly that Petra didn't even know what they were. She only caught glimpses of mandibles and long tongues grabbing several townspeople and dragging them back into the shadows.

"Bugs!" shouted the old-timer, pulling a pistol from his waistband and opening fire.

The pilots ran for the helicopter.

"Get inside!" Mean Mouth shouted at Petra.

"Don't you move!" cried one of the townspeople, her rifle swinging between Petra and the swimmer.

With astonishing speed, the swimmer's tail stung the woman, and her hands froze before she could pull the trigger.

But there were gunshots everywhere now. Sleepy Eyes grabbed Petra's arm and dragged her into the helicopter. Before the swimmer could leap in after them, two bullets blasted small craters in zir back.

"No!" cried Petra, and lunged to help the swimmer as ze struggled aboard.

Mean Mouth slammed shut the cabin door. Instinctively Petra pressed her hands hard against one of the swimmer's gunshot wounds. The blood was red, just like hers. She was dimly aware of the growing noise of the rotor blades, bullets pattering against the fuselage.

Sleepy Eyes dropped down beside her, tearing open a medical kit. He seemed to know what he was doing as he pushed Petra's hands away and applied field dressings to the swimmer's wounds.

—*Are you okay?* Petra asked silently. Ze didn't look okay. The patterns on zir skin were faded, and ze was taking small, raspy breaths.

—*I will survive,* ze replied. *The ship will heal me.*

If they got back in time.

They were rising now, and she noticed that the co-pilot's seat was empty.

"Where's the—" she began, but Mean Mouth just shook her head.

Petra took a last glimpse out the window at the chaos in the parking lot. Whirling bugs, peopling shooting, running for their lives, bodies motionless on the asphalt.

"But the kids," Petra croaked, and she knew it was hopeless, and she was sobbing because everything was so terrible, and it made people do terrible things to each other, and she hadn't thought things could get any worse, but they just had.

SETH HEARD THE DOOR of his freight container opening and whirled to face it.

Still hooded, both his arms now in casts, he was powerless in every way.

Footsteps. Two people. One with a limp: he could hear a foot dragging a bit along the metal floor. It was accompanied by the thump of a cane. Someone either very old, or recovering from an injury.

"Hello, A4."

The voice was slightly slurred, and he couldn't place it. But the greeting sparked terror in him nonetheless.

A4 was the ID number he'd been given inside the bunker.

"I'm amazed you came back to rescue your friends," the voice said. "It seems you nearly succeeded."

The thick words reminded Seth of one of his long-ago foster parents, who'd had a stroke and was doing therapy to get her speech back to normal.

"But I'm very grateful you did try," the voice continued.

The skin on Seth's arms crawled.

"Because now I get to finish the work I started."

Seth had been unsure at first, but now he was certain.

The voice belonged to Dr. Ritter.

CHAPTER ELEVEN

IT WAS THE MIDDLE of the night when Petra got back to the base. She was hugged and congratulated, but she couldn't relax until the swimmer was in a jeep with Dr. Weber and headed to the biodome, where the other cryptogens could take care of zir.

—*You'll be okay, right?* she asked as the jeep drove off. *They'll put you in one of those special pod things?*

—*Yes. Do not worry.*

And after that, Petra felt so exhausted it was all she could manage to have a shower, get into bed, and pull the covers over her head.

She slept for a long time, and when she woke up, the light was bright beyond the blinds and Anaya was gone. Probably already at the biodome. Beyond her bedroom door, the apartment sounded quiet. She didn't want to get up. Partly, she was still wiped out; mostly, though, she wanted to stay here forever, cocooned in her blankets. The world could go on without her, couldn't it? It was doing such a great job on its own.

And still no word from Seth. It was one of the first things she'd asked last night when she returned. She tried to reach him telepathically now. More nothing. Just another reason not to get out of bed.

But in the end, she did. She wanted to check on the swimmer.

She put on clean clothes and made herself a breakfast of toast and cereal. Outside she found a soldier to drive her over to the biodome.

When she entered the observation room, it was the usual crush of people and bad breath and coffee and everyone talking with each other and into headsets. Inside the dome itself, Anaya, Dr. Weber, and Pearson were gathered around the ship.

"I'm going in," Petra said to whoever was listening.

She grabbed a headset and went through the pressurized doors.

Anaya was right: the air inside was amazing. Careful of roving vines, and attentive to water lilies in the pond, she made her way toward the others.

"Hey," said Anaya, turning in surprise, "you decided to come inside!"

"Well, this place is totally tame," Petra said, "compared to what I saw up north."

"Pretty bad, I hear."

Petra nodded, and she must have looked haunted, because her friend wrapped her up in a hug.

"How's the swimmer?" Petra asked Anaya.

"Ze spent the night in one of the pods. Terra's just checking zir over—oh, there ze is."

From the ship's hatch the swimmer emerged, and Petra was startled by how happy she felt. Ze looked completely healed. She couldn't even see any scars on zir back.

—*You're all better!* she exclaimed.

—*Of course.*

Petra wished she had one of those pod things.

—*And the levitation system?* she asked. *Does it work?*

—*We will soon find out,* ze replied. *The others are preparing to test it. But the hull still needs time.*

Petra followed the swimmer to where a masked Dr. Weber and Colonel Pearson were examining the breach in the ship's hull. It looked like a wound that was starting to form scar tissue.

"How long before it's completely fixed?" Pearson asked.

Petra relayed the question and told the colonel, "Two more days, maybe. Before it's ready to go back into space."

—*Stand back now,* the swimmer told them.

"They're going to see if it can fly!" Petra said. "We should move away."

The ship hummed. Tensely, Petra counted seconds. Then, silently, miraculously, the ship lifted, hovering a few feet off the ground.

"Well, look at that," said the colonel with a rare smile.

"It works!" Petra cried, beaming at Anaya and Dr. Weber.

—*We can rise again,* the swimmer said.

INSIDE THE SHIP WITH Terra and Dr. Weber, Anaya watched the red-pebbled world of the general's brain cells.

Her stomach was in knots. The cryptogen ship could fly again, and now they were about to find out if they'd have a weapon to carry back to the primary vessel.

"Terra says she's disguised the virus," Anaya told Dr. Weber, using a pad to draw the images Terra was creating inside her head.

A lot of what Terra communicated to her was very complicated, and diagrams were often the best way of telling Dr. Weber what was going on.

"Okay, I think I see," said Dr. Weber, her voice muffled within her breathing mask. "It's a bit like a Trojan horse. The virus sneaks in, hidden inside the allergen. Well done, by the way—that was a very good idea of yours."

Anaya felt her cheeks heat with the praise. "Thanks."

"So the flyer's antibodies attack the allergens and bind to their exteriors. Meanwhile, the virus just squirts out in all the confusion and starts wiping out the brain cells."

Within his pod, the general hung suspended from the ceiling.

The sight still made Anaya's skin crawl a bit. It was like a body shrouded for burial.

Terra was touching various surfaces, and Anaya sensed that she was sonically communicating with her laboratory machinery. It made Anaya realize anew how much of the cryptogens' technology was based on sound—and how far beyond theirs it was.

—*I am releasing the virus now,* Terra said.

"It's starting," she told Dr. Weber.

The viruses stormed into view. They didn't look like headless spiders this time. They looked weirdly bloated, like they were wearing armor. Anaya supposed they were—allergen armor, designed to trick the general's immune system.

"Look at them all!" Anaya said.

It was strange to be rooting for little monster viruses that crushed brain cells, but she was.

Boomerang antibodies whirled onto the screen and plastered themselves against the allergen armor.

Inside the pod, the general twitched.

—*Is he all right?* Anaya asked Terra.

—*It should be short-lived,* Terra said.

"It's the allergic reaction," Dr. Weber said. "Remember how you felt when the soil was on your skin? Itchy as anything. It'll be like that, only more intense."

Anaya found it upsetting, seeing the general writhe in distress.

She looked back at the wall monitor. The antibodies had completely coated the viruses, like barnacles on a rock.

—*Nothing's happening!* said Anaya.

—*Wait,* said Terra.

The general's body relaxed inside the pod.

On the monitor, from each of the barnacled viruses, a headless spider jetted out like a torpedo.

"They're out!" Anaya cried.

The viruses plunged among the general's brain cells, unleashing destruction. The image on the monitor quickly dissolved into a terrible red smear. The view pulled back, and Anaya felt like she was looking down at a battlefield from a helicopter. Total devastation.

She looked worriedly over at the general in the pod. She half expected to see blood seeping through the fabric, but he was eerily still and silent.

"It's working," Dr. Weber said.

—*Your idea was effective,* Terra said to Anaya.

She should've felt pleased and elated, but she couldn't quite. She was partly responsible for the damage to the general's brain.

—*Will he be okay?* she asked Terra.

—*The work is done. The virus was designed to attack only the brain cells that transmit sound.*

This didn't answer her question, and she sensed Terra's unease. Anaya watched as the runner unzipped the surgical sac. The general swung his legs out. In the light his feathered face was dewed with sweat. Maybe Terra had silently told him to take things slow, because he sat for a few moments. His chest rose and fell. He looked like he'd undergone a dreadful ordeal.

Then he stood, chin tilted high, as if trying to restore his dignity.

—*I will need to try it to make sure,* Anaya heard him say.

—*Remember,* Terra told him. *The weapon is turned against you now. It will cause you pain.*

Anaya watched as the general's chest swelled and he suddenly clutched his head and staggered. Terra steadied him.

—*We have triumphed,* he said.

But his words carried an aching disappointment. He had sacrificed a part of himself—yes, a very dangerous and violent part of himself, but still something that made him who he was. Anaya felt a pang of sympathy for him.

The general and Terra embraced. Anaya sensed they were talking privately. Maybe Terra was thanking him, saying he had done a great thing.

"The trial was a success," Dr. Weber reported over her headset. "The virus works."

Over her own headphones, Anaya heard the eruption of cheers and applause from the observation room.

"We're going to win," Anaya said.

It felt risky to be hopeful. Too much hope, too much to lose. But she wanted joy right now, even if it was short-lived. For a little bit she wanted to believe things were going to be okay.

Through her feet, through the ship's hull, she felt a vibration.

"Anaya," came Pearson's voice. "Are they doing something with the ship?"

—*What's happening?* she asked as Terra and the other two cryptogens rushed to various glowing surfaces around the ship.

The general's smoky words filled her head.

—*It's beginning.*

CHAPTER TWELVE

"NOW?" PETRA CRIED. "I thought they weren't supposed to invade for almost a whole month!"

Everyone in the observation room was talking at once, calling out coordinates.

". . . second sighting over the South China Sea . . ."

". . . have a visual over the English Channel . . ."

". . . multiple entries reported now . . ."

The entire room trembled. A couple of years ago there'd been an earthquake, and Petra had heard the old wooden banister in their house rattling, and then the pictures on the walls. She'd stood there, frozen, knowing that some massive force was at work and she was absolutely powerless against it.

Dr. Weber and Anaya hurried in from the biodome, and Petra grabbed her friend, just to hold on to something.

"It should be right over our heads in ninety seconds!" someone said.

"Let's get some eyes on this," Pearson said, heading for the exit.

Petra felt like all the bones had suddenly been removed from her body. Oh my God, it was really happening.

"Come on," Anaya said, tugging her along. Petra was glad to move, afraid if she stayed still, she'd literally collapse. Ahead of them, down a corridor, Pearson threw open a metal door and walked out onto the fire escape.

Blinking in the light, Petra found space on the metal platform with Anaya and tilted her face to the sky. The entire sky echoed. She felt the low rumble in her molars. She felt the vibration in her eardrums, making her dizzy.

She saw it.

It was like a lid sliding over the top of the sky.

The ship was gray, curved like a rose petal, curling slightly at the edges. It wasn't smooth like a flower, though, but rough-textured like some kind of volcanic stone. High against the clouds, the ship's dimensions were a mystery. She remembered the gigantic vessel she'd seen in outer space, a flower with an array of petals. This was just *one* of those petals. What was it Ritter had said—the length of three football fields? It had no lights, no engines, no doorways, no jet trail.

But she knew what was inside. Anaya had described all those rows upon rows of pods plugged into the fleshy walls. Thousands of slumbering cryptogen soldiers. Were they still asleep? Or wide awake and ready?

The ship moved with eerie slowness. When it blotted out the

sun, a huge shadow dashed itself against Earth. She imagined a sound accompanying it, like a clash of cymbals. She shivered.

Everyone from the observation room was now crowded on the fire escape and metal staircase, faces turned upward.

"We have ten reports so far, ten ships," an officer with a headset was saying. "Sightings from Baltimore, Mexico City, Rio de Janeiro, Brussels, Cairo, Jakarta, Mumbai, Seoul, Shanghai. And here."

"They're picking human population density," said Pearson. "Putting themselves within striking distance of multiple targets."

"Sir," said another officer, holding a phone to his ear, "we have incoming fighters from CFB Comox."

"No!" cried Anaya. "They'll get annihilated!"

Two warplanes tore strips through the sky, trailing vapor from their wing tips as they closed on the cryptogen ship. Each veered off sharply after releasing a pair of missiles.

Petra wasn't sure they even touched the ship. There were small pulses of purple light, and the missiles exploded, but when the flame and smoke cleared, there didn't seem to be any damage to the vast ship at all. It moved on, as indifferent as an elephant to a mosquito.

"Must have some kind of shielding," Pearson said.

Payloads spent, the fighter jets disappeared. The ship hadn't even bothered to return fire—which Petra thought was worrying. Weren't they even *concerned* that the human warplanes might come back with something more powerful?

As the ship passed directly overhead, Petra staggered, light-headed. She sat down, the world spinning.

"It's a low-gravity field," said Dr. Weber, crouching beside her.

"We've lost comms," Pearson said. "Power's down, too."

"Probably an electromagnetic pulse," said Dr. Weber.

Petra wrapped her arms around herself and held on tight. It seemed to take an eternity for the ship to glide over Stanley Park, then the harbor. It cast huge shadows over the ravaged buildings of Vancouver. People watched from balconies and rooftops as the ship headed south.

She couldn't help feeling relief that it was moving on. She'd feared it would hover over Vancouver and unleash a torrent of destruction.

"Did we get an estimated landing site for this one?" Pearson asked an officer.

"Based on trajectory and velocity, somewhere between Vancouver and Seattle."

Grimly, Pearson said, "Easy striking distance of both."

And Seth, Petra thought.

SETH WOKE UP, CONFUSED.

They must've Tasered him, or drugged him, because he couldn't remember going to sleep. He was on his back, and his wrists and ankles were tied to side rails. This was a different bed, a hospital bed. And he didn't think he was in the freight container anymore. The acoustics were different.

And there was someone here with him.

"They tell me that helicopters came to rescue you from the bunker. Who sent them?"

The slurred voice belonged to Dr. Ritter.

"I don't know. I wasn't on them."

"Ah yes, left behind. Maybe your friends will tell me when I question them."

"I thought you were dead," Seth said.

"Who told you that?" Dr. Ritter asked, and Seth knew he'd made a mistake.

It was crucial he not mention anything about Deadman's Island, the hybrids, or the cryptogens hiding there.

"You weren't moving, on the floor," he said, saving himself.

"Ah yes, they thought I was dead at first. I was in a coma for some time, on a ventilator. But I woke. I'm told all my motor skills will return in time. But for now I am a little shaky."

Things were being shoved around the room. Things on wheels. Clinking metal things.

This had all happened before.

"In case you're concerned," Ritter said, "I won't be performing the surgery myself. I have a very able colleague working under my direction."

Seth didn't feel one bit relieved by this news. He wanted to see Ritter, to look him in the eye, to strike him with sound, again and again.

"Shall we begin?" Ritter asked, and Seth realized with a start that there were now multiple people in the room.

His entire body was trembling, but it wasn't him. The bed was actually shaking, and maybe the floor, too. He heard a growing hum.

"What the hell's that?" said someone.

Everything was vibrating: his teeth, his bones, the very air. An awful dizziness swept through him.

He heard heavy footfalls, and someone burst, gasping, into the room.

"There's a ship!"

"What're you talking about?" someone demanded.

"A cryptogen ship. And it's landing!"

"Where?"

"Here, dammit, can't you hear it!"

"We need to get out of here!"

A stampede of footsteps.

"Hey!" he called. "Don't leave me here!"

"I'm still here, Seth." It was Ritter. "I'll take care of you. I don't want you falling into enemy hands."

Seth's terror burst from him like a panther.

"Stay away from me!" he roared, sensing Ritter drawing closer.

His whole body felt suddenly weightless. His first thought

was that he'd been jabbed with a tranquilizer, but then he heard a grunt of surprise from Ritter. Something—a foot, a hand?—glanced off his shoulder, and he realized that his bed was drifting at the strangest angle across the room. He thrashed against the restraining belts and felt the bed slew and roll. He might have been upside down but wasn't sure. He heard and felt other things deflecting off him, but nothing seemed to be tipping over and crashing to the floor. He was certain that he was truly floating, along with everything else in the room.

Gravity came back like the flick of a light switch. With a sickening crack, his bed hit the floor at an angle and tipped over on its side. His head struck the railing hard, but one of his wrist restraints must have broken—

Because his right hand was free.

He ripped off his hood and saw Ritter disappearing out the door before he could strike. The floor was strewn with medical equipment, and within reach he spotted a scalpel. Snatching it up, he cut through his other restraints.

He leapt off the bed, fury pounding at his temples. He found surgical scissors and cut open his casts to release his feathers. He was glad to see he still wore his clothes.

The corridor outside was abandoned. He guessed at a direction and opened doors until he found the warehouse. The thunderous vibration from outside shook him as he ran to the row of freight containers, all of them resting crooked, as if a giant had flicked them around.

He picked the nearest one and wrestled it open.

Be Esta, he thought.

He made a heck of a lot of noise opening up the doors. His heart sank when he saw a boy with tattooed arms and a tail that had some kind of cap on it.

"What the hell's going on?" Darren demanded. "Earthquake or something?"

"It's me, Seth."

"What? Seriously?"

"We're getting out of here." He walked inside and yanked off Darren's hood.

"Holy crap, it *is* you," Darren said, and he looked so happy and grateful that Seth's heart softened a bit.

"Come on, we've got to get the others!"

"What others?"

"You don't know?"

"How would I know?" Darren said, hurrying after him. "I've been in a box for weeks!"

"Look!" Seth said, pointing at the other freight containers. "Help me open them up!"

"What's that noise?" Darren said as he started opening one of the doors.

"The cryptogens are landing."

"Is that a joke?"

"No. Hurry!"

Seth yanked open a door and saw a kid with hairy arms.

"Charles? It's me, Seth!"

"Seth!"

He pulled off his hood and dragged him out. Darren had freed Siena from the other container. He ran to the last one.

"Hang on, hang on," Darren said. "Who's in there?"

"Esta."

Darren planted himself in his path. "Dude, do not let her out! She tried to kill me. She's crazy!"

Seth glared at him, and Darren swallowed and stepped aside.

Seth swung the doors wide and there she was. He told her it was him, and when he pulled off her hood, he felt like he'd just unhooded a falcon. Her intense eyes blazed. She threw herself into his arms and he wrapped her up tight, breathing her in.

—*Thank you,* she said.

—*I promised.*

Things felt possible again. They were together. He wanted to tell her everything. Mostly about how the general had told him he would never fly—*they* would never fly—and he wanted her to tell him it wasn't true, but there was no time.

"We've got to go. The cryptogens are landing—here, now!"

By this time the room was shaking as if it would crack open and start spewing lava. At the back of the warehouse was a set of fire doors, locked with a chain. He slashed through it with his feathers and pushed his way outside.

The sky was gone.

It had been replaced by something else. Seth nearly fell over, the effect was so disorienting. Not a hundred feet overhead was something vast and gray. Eventually he found its outer edges.

It was one of the petal-shaped ships that came from the big one in space. And it was landing right here, half over land, half over water. The air tasted metallic.

"Let's go!" Darren shouted.

Esta was staring up at the ship in amazement, and Seth tugged at her.

"Esta, come on!"

She turned her challenging gaze on him. "You think they'll treat us any worse?"

"I don't know! But come on!"

He started running, wanting to get out from underneath the massive ship. To his great relief, Esta kept pace with him. Charles was the fastest, already way in the lead. They ran down dusty industrial roads, through vacant lots. He spotted a few other people fleeing and, farther ahead, one of those police bikes with the sonar arms.

Up ahead he saw open sky. A jet streaked past and released a missile. It exploded in a strange purple flash without even hitting the ship.

Charles was bounding back toward them now, looking panicked.

"There's soldiers coming our way. If they see us—"

"There's nowhere else to go!" Darren shouted. "I'll take my chances with humans!"

"What's that?" Siena said, pointing into the sky.

A pillar of indigo light shot from the ship. Seth wasn't sure if he was *seeing* it or just *hearing* it, like a telepathic image.

"I see it," Charles said. "Some kind of energy ray?"

At its very tip, the light thickened and began to pour down through the sky, like liquid down the inside of a glass dome. It fell in a translucent curtain around the edges of the ship and then began to spread outward, slowly but steadily, toward them.

Seth ran with the others until a crack of pain in his leg sent him skidding along the asphalt.

Only Esta noticed, and turned back. "Seth, no!" To him, her voice sounded like it was coming across a lake. Blood welled from a small neat hole in the back of his right thigh.

She dropped down beside him and pressed her hand hard over his wound. Blood leaked past her fingers.

"Who shot me?" Seth asked, dazed, looking around.

About a hundred feet behind them was Dr. Ritter, one hand holding a pistol, the other gripping his cane. A patch covered his left eye, but that hadn't stopped him from nailing Seth.

"I'm going to finish him!" said Esta savagely.

She didn't need to.

Behind Ritter, the strange purple curtain swept toward him. Only now did he seem to notice it; he whirled clumsily and covered his ears, as if shutting out a terrible sound. Seth heard it now, too. More like a pressure in his head, about to make his ears pop, coming from that seeping indigo light.

Ritter tried to run, but he couldn't move quickly enough. The light passed over him like a waterfall, and the moment it did, he collapsed like an empty hand puppet.

"Come on, Seth, we're getting you up," said Esta, trying to lift him.

"Run," he told her. There was no way he'd beat that curtain of light. His blood formed a small puddle on the ground. A cold weakness swept through him. "Just run, Esta!"

He looked at the wall of light, towering over him like a tsunami. He felt his ears pop and clenched his eyes shut—

Pressure built inside his head, and he knew it would soon become pain. But abruptly, the pressure was gone, and the pain never came. When he opened his eyes, he saw that the wall of light had passed right over them.

"It went right through us," he murmured.

"You're losing a lot of blood," Esta said.

Seth watched her wind her hoodie tightly around his leg. He hardly felt he was in his own body. In a daze he stared at the spreading dome of light.

"How far will it go?" he wondered.

Overhead, two helicopters hovered nervously at the dome's outer reaches. Could the pilots not even see it? One came too close and suddenly dropped like a crumpled tin can. The other helicopter veered up and away.

Seth's eyes came back to his leg. He knew he was going to die.

"Something's coming," he heard Esta say.

He looked in the direction of the huge gray cryptogen ship.

Soaring toward him was a flyer. Wings of white and gold and blue spread wide, catching the morning light. He felt himself leaving his own body. He was glad the last thing he would ever see was magnificent.

CHAPTER THIRTEEN

IN HORROR, PETRA WATCHED the monitor in the biodome's observation room. Playing on it was a video feed of the vast cryptogen ship drifting over Point Roberts, just south of Vancouver.

There must have been lots of helicopters and drones taking footage, because the views kept changing: one from directly overhead, some from different sides.

Tree branches lifted skyward as the ship passed overhead. Grit and garbage hung weirdly suspended above the ground. Jets and helicopters unleashed missiles. The air bloomed with fire and black smoke. But the ship slid through the sky completely unharmed. It drifted to a stop, half over water, half over a big park. From the surrounding streets, Petra saw police cars and armored personnel carriers approaching.

And then she saw the people fleeing the buildings and houses and streets shadowed by the massive ship. The angle was too high to make out faces, but one detail caught her attention instantly.

"That's a tail!" she said, rushing up to the screen and pointing. "Look!"

It was definitely a swimmer hybrid. He was with some other kids. Light flashed off something.

"Were those feathers? On that guy, there?"

But the footage cut away to another drone, showing a different angle of the ship.

"Go back to those people! Can we go back?"

"We're not controlling the feeds," said Pearson.

Her first and only thought was: *Seth.*

The image on the monitor shimmered—not all of it, just the parts around the ship. There was a hissing sound, too.

"Why's it doing that?" Anaya asked.

"Just some kind of interference," the colonel said.

"No, there's light coming from the top of the ship," said Anaya. "That color, I saw it earlier when it passed over us. It's kind of purply. Petra, you see it?"

"Yeah."

Like wavy heat off a hot road, it rose in a column from the ship's center. Then it began falling, like water flowing down the inside of a snow globe. It touched the ground, enclosing the ship, and spread outward on all sides.

"What is that?" Pearson demanded. "Ask the cryptogens."

All of whom were inside their own ship, watching the same thing, only with much better technology.

Petra telepathically asked the swimmer about the color around the ship, and volleyed zir answer back to the colonel.

"It's a shield. It's made of sound."

The view changed again, farther back from the ship now. She could see people running away from the light. These people wore uniforms, maybe police, and had rifles.

The shimmering wall was swiftly overtaking them. It was just light, and a pretty color, but there was something terrifying about it. Birds fell from the sky like snipped Christmas tree decorations. Petra caught herself holding her breath. *Run! Run!*

The moment the light touched the running officers, they fell down limp, looking strangely flattened.

"What happened to them?" Anaya cried.

But again the viewpoint changed, and Petra was back to the first group of people she'd seen running from the big warehouse. The purple light was closing on them. Without a doubt she knew that one had feathers on his arms.

"Seth!" she shouted. "That's Seth! Can you zoom in? Zoom in!"

"We can't zoom in!" Pearson snapped.

It had to be Seth. And someone was with him. Was it Esta? Following the two of them was a man, reaching out to them—no, aiming a *gun* at them! But then the light passed over him and he just dropped dead.

Her eyes darted back to Seth. He wasn't running anymore. He was sitting, with Esta, or whoever it was, tugging at him. Why was he sitting?

"Get up!" Petra shouted at the screen.

The purple shimmer slid closer, then passed right over him. He didn't collapse, and neither did the person next to him.

"Is he okay? Can we roll it back to see?"

Pearson ignored her.

The viewpoint changed again, this time to show two helicopters launching missiles uselessly at the ship. They exploded in midair. One helicopter got too close to the shimmery light and plummeted sideways to the ground, like a dented aluminum can.

With a shudder of purple light, the image on the monitor evaporated into static.

"That's all there is," said Pearson. "They lost their surveillance drones after that. I want to know more about that shield."

"It's a kind of sound energy," Anaya said, and by the look of concentration on her face, Petra knew she was talking silently to Terra. "It's generated by the ship. It destroys weapons, makes them malfunction or self-destruct before they hit their target."

"Can we tunnel underneath it?" Dr. Weber asked.

Anaya was silent for a split second, then replied, "No. It extends underground, too. It forms a sphere around the ship. It's fatal to some living things. Including humans."

"But not *us*," said Petra.

"No, not us, because we're half them. Because of the organ in our brains."

Petra released a big breath. "So Seth's okay?"

"The sound wouldn't hurt him."

"Good. That's good."

Petra's eyes stung. She could've stopped him that night. If she'd pulled the fire alarm, he'd be here right now. No one was saying anything, but she knew they still blamed her, Dr. Weber and Anaya especially. Could see it in their tight faces.

She wanted to roll the tape back and see Seth again.

"Something happened to him. He was just sitting there. I think that other guy shot him!" She started to cry. "Can we try to—" And she couldn't finish because she knew how impossible it was, and how they would just say no to her.

—*My friend was down there*, she told the swimmer, and explained who Seth was. *Can you talk to him? Find out if he's okay?*

—*No. They will be vigilant for incoming signals. If we talk to him, the others might track us back here.*

—*Just a tiny message!*

—*We cannot. We will not.*

—*You suck!*

—*What does that mean?*

—*I thought we were friends! After all we've been through!*

"Seth's wounded and the cryptogens are probably going to kill him!" she burst out to the others.

"He might've been surrendering," Pearson said, "or joining them."

Angrily, Petra shot back, "He wouldn't do that! No matter how much you guys screwed him over. He went there to rescue Esta, not join them!"

"We have more important things to worry about right now," Pearson said. "The cryptogens weren't supposed to invade yet. Why are they early?"

Petra put the question to the swimmer, and ze emerged from their ship with Terra and the general. All of them gravely made their way toward the observation window. It was the general who spoke first, his metallic words smoldering in her head.

—*The commander must suspect we are here.*

The commander. Those two words in Petra's head were almost painful, like staring at the sun. She had a mental image of a flyer, a she, with immense power, who ruled over the entire invasion force.

—*But you said they'd think you'd gone to another world,* Petra heard Anaya say. She felt her mind opening to all three cryptogens at once.

—*That was our hope,* Terra replied. *But we have learned that one of our other ships, one that you shot down, sent out an automatic distress call. Before it could be stopped, it must have been detected by the main vessel.*

Petra quickly relayed this to the colonel while still listening to the cryptogen conversation.

—*There is also the possibility,* said the general, *that they have caught one of our rebel compatriots on the primary vessel. They might have tortured them to discover our plans on this planet.*

Petra felt a sick clenching in her stomach.

—*Does that mean they know where you are?* she asked. *Right now?*

The general replied. *I don't think so. If they knew our location, they would have annihilated us instantly. And they have no way of detecting us—unless we send signals beyond this base.*

Petra relayed this to Pearson, who exhaled in relief.

"That's good news. Will they attack immediately?"

—*Unlikely,* the general answered. *Your atmosphere is still hostile. And your gravity is greater. They will wait until conditions are more favorable. They have time to wait. Inside their shield, they are invulnerable.*

Pearson didn't sound convinced by this theory. "If they wanted to wait, why not wait upstairs? I don't buy it. If they're here, it's for a reason."

—*If they have discovered our plan, the commander may have a new strategy,* the general said.

"What new strategy?" Pearson asked.

Petra listened as the general explained, and the fist in her chest clenched tighter. "The rebels can't use the virus weapon like they planned," she told the room. "They were supposed to go up to the main vessel and deliver it to all the flyers while they slept in their pod things. Zap them all in one place. But now everyone's down here, and wide awake."

A GASPING HELPLESSNESS SEIZED Anaya. Everything had changed. And the rebels' entire plan had just been wiped out.

"All right, okay, so we can't deliver the weapon on the main vessel," Dr. Weber was saying hurriedly. "But how about this. If we cultured the virus here on Earth, we could spray it like a pesticide during battle. Would that be effective?"

Anaya volleyed the question straight to Terra.

—It's unlikely you could get close enough to the flyers to deliver the weapon properly before they destroyed you. Its effect would be minimal. Also, I doubt you have the ability to culture the virus quickly enough.

Anaya knew Terra was right. The world was struggling just to make enough herbicides and pesticides and vaccines to keep small pockets of the planet safe. And even if they all switched to making the virus weapon, it wouldn't work. How could a fighter jet or helicopter even get close enough to the armored flyers before getting obliterated by their sound helmets?

She looked hopelessly at Petra. Just hours ago, there'd been so much hope.

They had the weapon.

The small rebel ship was almost repaired.

"Ten of these ships have landed all around the world," Pearson said. "My first priority is figuring out what they're going to do next." He turned to her and Petra. "I need both of you to start asking questions. That shield, how can we take it out? There must be a way."

—Even if I still had my power, the general answered, *it would not be enough to destroy the shield. Its machinery must be destroyed from inside the ship itself.*

190

"So nothing can get through that shield," said Pearson.

"Except the cryptogens," Anaya said, then added, "And us."

—*Thanks for reminding him,* Petra snapped at her.

"Without the shield," Pearson said, "can our weapons damage the landing ship?"

—*Yes,* said the general.

"Okay. That's something," Pearson said. "So if a cryptogen passed through the shield, would they need to get inside the ship, or could an explosive on the outside take out the shield?"

—*A blast in a certain location could destroy the transmission tower. The shield would be disabled until they could construct another tower.*

"We need to take down the tower, then," said the colonel.

Dr. Weber said, "And we finally need to start sharing what we know. With our own military, and any government around the world that'll listen."

The lines in Colonel Pearson's face deepened, but he gave a quick nod. "I agree. We need a huge coordinated strategy: humans, rebels—and hybrids so we can all talk to each other. If we want any chance at all of victory, we need to join forces. Are there rebel forces aboard these ten landing ships?"

Anaya asked Terra, and a number took shape in her head.

"There's maybe thirty or forty rebels on each ship, waiting to turn against the flyers, once they get the signal."

"What's the signal?" Pearson asked.

—*We will raise the lantern,* the general told Anaya.

—What's the lantern?

In her head she saw a beautiful corona of light. Very quickly it changed from cool blue to orange to scorching white, and she could smell the heat coming off it. It kindled, burned, then blazed. It made her heart beat faster.

—It is our signal. It's how we tell who is with us.

—Can I make one? she asked excitedly. It was so beautiful. *And the other hybrids, too?*

—Try.

Before now all she'd done was transmit words. Now she was creating an image in motion. It felt like she was spinning on a carousel, the flash of color and motion dizzying her, speeding up. Blue, orange, white. It was like the sun gloriously shining on her face.

—Yes. That's it, Terra told her, and Anaya thought she sounded proud.

"It's kind of like a lighthouse beacon," she explained to the others. "It gets really bright and sort of sweeps through your head." She inhaled. "It's pretty exhilarating."

—Others will join us, Terra added, *once they see us fighting. When they see us leading the way, they will lead, too.*

"Looks like we were hasty to test the weapon on the general," Pearson said. "We could've used his firepower." He thought a moment. "Can we train flyer hybrids to use those helmets?"

"None of them should be involved in combat," Dr. Weber said, startled.

"Agreed. But they might have to be," said Pearson. "If we can get cryptogen weapons, we need to use them. Not just the helmets, but the swimmers' harpoon guns, and the runners' rifles. And our best chance might be to force them out of their ships earlier, when the cryptogens are still at their weakest."

The general agreed. *Your stronger gravity is in your favor. And until your atmosphere changes fully, we are vulnerable. To your air. To your water.*

"The rain!" Anaya heard Petra exclaim aloud.

"What about it?" she asked her friend.

"Remember it was raining a bit when these three first arrived, and the swimmer got itchy, just like me? Because ze's allergic to Earth water, too. So I think maybe that's how we can deliver the weapon!"

Anaya nodded, swept up in her friend's line of thinking.

"If Terra can get the virus up to the main ship," Petra said, "and make enough of it, couldn't they send it down over the entire planet, just like they did with the seeds and eggs? In the rain! We use their own rain against them!"

THE DARKNESS CLUNG TO Seth like a second skin. Was he dead? Blind and weightless, he kicked and lashed out. But suddenly there was a pleasant scent in his nostrils, and calmness spread warmly through him.

—It's okay, Seth.

It was Esta's voice in his head, familiar and soothing as a drug.

—Where are you? he asked.

—Right here. Beside you.

He felt her hand slip into his and squeeze.

—Why can't I see anything? he asked, still confused.

—You're inside a, well, a big stretchy bag.

—Huh?

—It's healing you. You lost a lot of blood, Esta said.

He remembered now. Getting shot. Sitting down hard, his leg wet. The winged cryptogen, blazing like an angel toward him.

—Esta, are we—

—Yeah. Inside the ship that landed.

Despite the pleasant warmth, Seth begin to shiver. Inside the enemy's ship.

—We need to get out!

—Seth, it's all right. They saved your life.

—Who, exactly?

—One of the flyers. I think she's the commander. She brought you back here herself.

His thoughts were speeding in too many directions.

—Why didn't we die when that big wave of light came over us?

He thought of how Ritter had dropped, lifeless, as he was overtaken by it.

—I don't know. Maybe it doesn't hurt us because we're hybrids.

I think it's some kind of shield. It goes all the way around the ship. Way up into the sky, too.

—*I want to get out of this thing. I want to see.*

He started pushing against the clingy fabric. He realized his wounded leg didn't hurt at all.

—*I will let you out.*

This wasn't Esta's voice. It had a pinkish light and smelled like geraniums right after they'd been watered.

He felt his body being moved gracefully into a sitting position. A seam of light opened before him. He squinted. The face that greeted him was not Esta's. Dark brown eyes beneath heavy eyelashes. A long sloped face with fine dark hair, and tall oval ears at the top of his head. He was a runner.

—*You are healed*, he told Seth matter-of-factly.

He'd expected to be greeted by a flyer. Was this runner a doctor? Somehow he thought all the runners and swimmers would be caged up somewhere, awaiting orders from their leaders. Weren't they all supposed to be enslaved soldiers?

He swung out his legs and was a bit embarrassed to learn he was wearing only his boxer shorts. He looked down at his bare thighs, touched the place where he'd been shot. All he could make out was a small pink circle of scar tissue. He flexed his leg muscles. A faint twinge of pain was all he felt. Incredible.

The runner stepped back and Seth saw Esta behind him. She smiled tentatively.

All he wanted was to go to her. He hopped down. There was something strange about the way his feet touched the scratchy floor. He felt lighter. Then he understood: their gravity was a bit weaker than Earth's. They must be maintaining it inside the ship. He moved quickly toward Esta, then stopped short. Was it weird to hug her in his underwear? She closed the gap between them and hugged him tight.

"I thought I was going to die," he murmured.

"Me too."

He saw the runner's ears lift curiously at the sound of their voices. The cryptogen couldn't understand what they were saying, and Seth wanted to keep it that way. Nonetheless, he couldn't help whispering.

"Are we prisoners?"

"I don't think so," Esta replied. "The commander picked you up herself and put you on a floating transport. I mean, she could've just killed us if she wanted. They wanted to fix up Siena's collarbone, too, but she was too scared."

"Siena? Where?"

He turned to see her sitting on the floor with Charles. Beside them, Darren stood, trying to make his arms and chest look big, but in the vast chamber, he only looked small—and terrified. All three of them did. They were inside an alien ship, seeing real cryptogens for the first time. No wonder they were shell-shocked.

"Why didn't you guys run?" he asked them.

They'd been ahead of him. Even if they'd been overtaken by the sound shield, they could've just run out.

"There were soldiers everywhere," Darren said, "waiting on the other side, blocking us. They saw my tail."

"And my claws," Charles added.

"They probably thought we were cryptogens," said Siena, "because they started firing at us."

"But the bullets weren't getting through that sound thing," Darren said. "We were safe—as long as we stayed *inside* the shield."

"Yeah, safe," said Siena with a sarcastic echo, looking around fearfully.

Seth followed her gaze. For the first time he took in his surroundings properly. They were on a large platform, high in an enormous space that stretched in all directions. It took him another moment to realize that their platform was actually floating, like similar ones all around him, hovering, or gliding past, carrying runner and swimmer cryptogens. Flyers crisscrossed the air at all altitudes.

Dangling from the high ceiling were countless rows of black sacs like the one he'd been in. Some still seemed occupied, others hung limp, and some of the empty ones were being retracted inside the ceiling.

The full strangeness of being inside a cryptogen ship finally crashed over him. The light didn't seem to come from any one source. The air itself carried an unfamiliar scent. It wasn't unpleasant, but it was so strange it made him anxious. He wished he could push his face into Esta's hair so he didn't have to breathe it.

A floating platform piloted by a swimmer pulled neatly alongside theirs, and the runner who'd released Seth from his sac stepped aboard without a word and was taken away.

Seth watched as the runner was ferried to a nearby row of black sacs. The platform hovered alongside as the runner opened a sac. A flyer emerged, standing tall on the platform and rustling his crimson-and-gold feathers. Looking at him, Seth felt a tremor of fear and awe. The creature emanated such power. The runner appeared to be giving him a checkup. Maybe the flyer had just woken up from his long sleep, years drifting in a synthetic womb.

The flyer seemed impatient and brushed the runner away. Then he turned his head and looked across at Seth, impaling him with a predator's gaze. Inside his head, Seth tasted a whiff of diesel and was terrified the flyer was about to speak to him. To his relief, no words took shape in his head.

It reminded Seth of the way those policemen, and even some of Pearson's soldiers back on Deadman's Island, had looked at him. He was a misfit everywhere, hated by humans and cryptogens alike.

The flyer leapt to the platform's railing and took flight. With envy, Seth watched his powerful wing strokes.

"So what're we going to do?" Charles said quietly.

It was just the five of them on their platform now.

"What *can* we do?" asked Darren. "They've parked us way up here, and it's one heck of a drop."

Seth peered down. Far below, small figures moved around machinery. *Machines of war,* he thought.

"What have you guys told them?" he asked the others.

"Not much," said Esta. "They wanted to know why the soldiers were firing at us, so I told them how we were locked up in a bunker and escaped."

"And then got caught again," said Darren, looking at Esta and Seth balefully.

"Whatever you're feeling," Seth told him, "let's just button it up for now. We've got bigger problems to deal with."

He heard Charles's story, and Siena's, about how they got captured and taken to the sheriff's office in Point Roberts. Darren had been picked up when he made it ashore.

Then it was Seth's turn to tell his story. When he told them that he'd gone back to Deadman's Island, he knew Esta was mulling this information over. He wondered if it made him weak in her eyes. She had refused to go there.

"Listen," he said, lowering his voice further. "Three cryptogens landed at the army base."

"What?" Siena said in astonishment.

"They're rebels. One of them's the one that contacted Anaya back at the bunker. The rebels want to make a weapon that'll take away the flyers' sonic weapon."

"How? Some kind of chemical?" Charles asked.

"Yeah, a virus, I think. Wrecks the transmitters in their brains."

"Our brains, too, right?" Esta said, her face hard.

"Yeah, but so what?" said Seth.

"That'll change everything," Darren said.

"Everything," Seth agreed. "The flyers have these helmets that amplify their sound—that's how they trash cities. But they won't be able to use the helmets if the virus works."

"If," said Esta. "And we're still assuming the flyers are the bad guys. Kind of looks like everyone's getting along in here."

"We can't tell anyone else about this," Seth said, already worried he'd said too much. Hot pinpricks of sweat flared across his back. "Okay?"

Everyone said yes, even Esta.

Seth saw Siena look past him fearfully. He turned to see the flyer who had rescued him. The commander. She flew toward their platform, bright and glorious with her feathers of white and gold and blue. They all moved back so she could land. Her crest bristled like a barbed crown. Seth's legs felt watery with apprehension. He knew what she could do to him, to all of them, without even creasing her forehead.

A platform nudged alongside theirs, like a boat, and a runner and a swimmer now stepped aboard. They stood slightly behind the commander, who gazed at Seth and the others in turn.

—*You are splendid,* she said to all of them.

Her voice made his teeth ache, as though he'd inhaled icy air.

Seth didn't know what to say. Thank you? Why did you save me? What are you going to do with us?

—*Show me your wings,* she requested.

Obediently, he stretched out his arms and flared his feathers, as did Esta. Siena flared her good arm.

—*How fine you all are.*

Her words didn't make his teeth hurt this time—as though they'd adjusted to this new temperature.

There was genuine pride on the commander's beaked face, like she herself had sculpted them out of mud and breathed life into them. Her demeanor was not nearly as stern as the general's. It might have been kind, even. Still, Seth was too overwhelmed to speak.

—*You are afraid,* she said gently to the five of them.

—*Yes.*

—*You are afraid that I will kill you.*

—*Yes.*

—*I will not kill you.*

—*Your plants and animals have already tried,* Seth said.

—*We sent our plants,* the commander said, *and our creatures. We need our own food and atmosphere.*

It was said so matter-of-factly, so unapologetically, that for a moment Seth was confused. A pioneer mission. Wasn't that what Terra had called it? As if it were so wholesome, so righteous.

He said nothing. He didn't want to anger her.

—Our mission has caused a great deal of death, yes?

Her voice was deep inside his head. It smelled like melting ice.

—Yes, he answered.

—Life changes on every planet in the universe. It is inevitable. You are doing it to yourselves. Changing your atmosphere. Heating your planet. Driving your creatures to extinction.

It was the news he'd grown up with: climate change. Arctic ice melting. The oceans rising and turning acidic. Marine life dying. Temperatures rising. Droughts and floods and fires and famine.

—Your world will end, the commander said simply. *We are creating a better one.*

She made it sound like the cryptogens were doing a valiant and selfless thing. They were changing the world, yes, and faster and more efficiently than humans ever could. But it was not a world meant for humans.

—Your world won't include humans, Seth said. *We'll all be dead.*

—Not so, she said, looking at them. *You were made perfect for this new world. You were meant to inherit it. And with us, you will thrive.*

The last word rang in his head. This was so different from everything he'd been told—by Anaya and Terra and the other rebels back in the biodome. They'd made it sound like the hybrids were created as lab rats to test the ecosystem for the cryptogens. But nothing had been said about the hybrids having a place in this new world.

He felt a pulse of that old dream feeling: flying someplace

where he would be safe, where he'd belong, where he'd be loved. He looked at Esta and saw the same longing in her face. Like they'd just shared the thought.

He heard himself ask:

—*Will I fly?*

The commander looked at him, and her beaked mouth opened in a smile.

—*Oh, how you will fly!*

Seth swallowed as a hot, guilty pleasure filled him. Despite what the general had told him, he wanted to believe the commander.

Someone who flew could be free.

Someone who flew could escape any danger and never be hurt anymore.

—*Stay with us.*

The commander was speaking to all of them, he knew, but he had the strangest feeling that she'd just called him by his name. A name that was somehow truer than the word *Seth*.

—*So we're not prisoners?* he asked.

—*You are free to go if you wish.*

Seth saw Siena's face lift hopefully.

"We go outside the shield," Darren said aloud, "and we're dead. The soldiers will shoot us."

"That's why we're not going anywhere," Esta said. "We're staying right here."

CHAPTER FOURTEEN

ANAYA LOOKED AT PETRA in admiration. "That's a brilliant idea! Use the rain! It makes so much sense!"

Before she could share the idea with Terra and the other cryptogens inside the biodome, she and Petra were bombarded with questions from Colonel Pearson's staff in the observation room.

"But how long before their ship can fly?"

"Even if they got there, aren't all the cryptogens already awake on the main ship—"

"Maybe they're all down here now—"

"In which case the main ship might be totally empty—"

"Must be a command crew still aboard—"

"So they'd just blow the rebels' ship apart before it docked—"

"Say they got aboard, how long would it take to culture the virus—"

"Enough!" shouted Pearson, silencing the room. "Anaya, Petra, can you please relay all this to the cryptogens, and find out if it's possible to deliver a weaponized rain from their main vessel."

Anaya needed a moment to rein in her own excitement before she could focus on silent talking.

—*Possible, yes,* Terra replied. *But there will be many hurdles.*

—*The ship needs at least another day to heal itself,* the swimmer said.

Anaya glanced through the window at the ship. The charred crack looked a little smaller, but the shiny scar tissue had not completely covered it.

—*Can you speed it up?* Petra asked.

—*No.*

—*Okay,* Anaya said. *But after that you can fly back to the primary vessel. Will all of you go?*

The thought of all of them suddenly leaving made her feel fearful—and abandoned. She definitely felt safer with them here, especially now that the invasion had begun.

—*No,* Terra said firmly. *Only I will go.*

Anaya swallowed and met the runner's amber eyes. Did it have to be her?

—*I know the machinery best,* Terra elaborated.

—*Will the ship be empty?* Petra asked.

The general's gasoline-tinged words filled her head now.

—*No. There will be a small command crew left aboard. And a landing ship held back in reserve.*

Anaya's spirits plunged as she pictured one of those huge petal-shaped ships filled with soldiers.

—*Awake?* she asked.

—*No. They'll be kept in their wombs until needed.*

—*Will you be able to dock safely?* Anaya asked now. To her, this seemed like one of the most vital questions.

—*We have rebel friends among the command crew,* Terra said.

—*Unless they have been caught,* said the general. *Or betrayed us.*

—*Not betrayed,* Terra said heatedly. *If our friends gave away our plans, it was because they were tortured.*

—*Nevertheless,* the general said, *the commander must know our plans now.*

—*Even without friends aboard,* Terra said, *I might still be able to dock.*

To Anaya, this didn't sound very hopeful. *Might?*

—*Our scout ships are well cloaked, even to our own technology. It might be possible to approach unseen. Once I dock, the ship will know.*

She made it sound like the ship was a conscious being.

—*What then?* Anaya asked. She needed to know every step. Not just so she could relate it all to the impatient grown-ups around her, but so she herself would know what Terra would have to do to survive.

—*I will need to instruct our machinery to culture the virus.*

—*How long will that take?*

—*A day to produce enough virus for a rain. And then a few hours to deploy the seeding pods and create a global weather event.*

—The viruses would be inside the pods? How many of them?

—Tens of thousands.

Anaya imagined the rain pouring down, just as it had on Salt Spring Island, carrying seeds; just as it had when it deluged the army base, carrying eggs. This time—if they were successful—the rain would carry a virus that would rob the flyers of their power. It would fall all over the planet, unavoidable.

—Wait, she said, a worrying thought sliding in, *can the rain pass through the shields of the landing ships?*

—Yes. The shields allow rainwater to pass through.

—But what if the cryptogens just wait it out inside the ships?

She waited tensely as Terra conferred privately with the swimmer and the general.

—The virus will live on in the ecosystem for some time, but you're right—for the fastest and strongest effect, we need them outside the ships.

—How?

—If we destroy the shields, we can lure them out into the rain.

TO PETRA, EVERYTHING SOUNDED impossibly complicated. And risky. After she and Anaya passed it on to everyone in the observation room, Pearson asked:

"All right, so how do we knock out the shield?"

—*The machinery is inside the ship's core,* the general explained. *Difficult to reach, and only accessible to my species. But the shield's transmission tower at the top of the ship can be destroyed.*

—*How?* Petra asked. All her time with the swimmer on the salvage mission had improved her silent talking and made her feel more confident telepathically. But the general's voice in her head still left her a bit shaken.

—*A sonic blast, but I have lost my power. In place of a sonic blast, it would need to be a powerful explosive device, properly placed.*

In Petra's head appeared an image of the landing ship. She zoomed in on a tower jutting from its center. She grabbed a tablet and started drawing it as accurately as she could, including the location where the general said the explosive blast would need to be focused. She passed it to Colonel Pearson.

—*The ship is heavily armored,* the general told her silently, *but without its shield your weapons can damage it. And then the soldiers will come out to defend it.*

"They'll come pouring out like a swarm of wasps," Petra told the room, terrified. "Is that really the best idea? They'll wipe us out!"

"They won't be at their strongest," Anaya reminded her. "Our atmosphere's not ready for them yet, right? They'll still be allergic, and short of breath. They'll be cold, too. It's not a lot, maybe, but it's still an advantage."

Dr. Weber nodded. "The longer we wait, the stronger they'll get. And the weaker we'll get."

Pearson nodded. "Every day we lose more infrastructure to those worms. We lost the Site C hydroelectric dam a few days ago. Without power, without fuel, our ability to wage war plunges."

"Colonel!" one of the staff officers called out. "We've got intel that the Americans are planning a significant strike on the ship over Point Roberts. They're already starting to evacuate the area."

"Does that mean they're gonna nuke it?" Petra asked in horror.

"It didn't work on the big ship in space," Anaya said.

—*What will happen?* Petra asked the swimmer. *If the humans attack the landing ship with the same kind of weapon they fired at your primary vessel?*

—*The ship will strike the missile from the sky.*

"The swimmer says it won't work!" Petra told everyone. "It won't get close enough to wreck the shield or hurt the ship."

She felt a strange wave of relief. At least Seth wouldn't be hurt. If he was alive.

"If the bomb detonates anywhere nearby, there's a lot of people on our side of the border in that blast area," Dr. Weber said. "Can you get the Americans to call it off?"

"Unlikely," said Pearson, "but I'll try."

"Tell them a cryptogen scientist said it won't do anything," said Petra. "That'll get their attention."

"Too much attention," Pearson said.

"We agreed it's time to stop keeping secrets," Dr. Weber reminded Pearson.

The colonel grunted in assent. "Start talking to your CSIS contacts, and I'll start making calls."

"What about Seth?" Petra said.

There was a split second of confused silence. She saw Dr. Weber flinch.

"No one's said anything about the kids trapped inside!" Petra persisted. "We're not even going to *try* to rescue them?"

"Petra—" began the colonel impatiently, but she headed him off.

"I know, I know, not a *top priority* when the world's being invaded, but still, you're going to just give up on them?"

"She's right," said Dr. Weber.

"She's not," said the colonel. "Seth made his choice by leaving this base. We have no idea what's happened to him or any of the others. Likely they're already dead."

Petra felt as if all the air had been punched from her lungs. "No," she wheezed.

Even the colonel seemed to regret his harsh words.

"If we're lucky enough to coordinate the kind of attack we've been talking about—that's the best chance we'll have to rescue Seth and the others. That's the best we can do."

NOT EXACTLY PRISONERS. NOT exactly free.

From their floating platform, Seth watched the ceaseless activity in the vast chamber. It made him think of a wasps' nest, all these hovering spaces and compartments housing a small nation. He saw cryptogen runners and flyers and swimmers being woken from their sacs and ferried away on platforms down to the ship's lower level, where all sorts of war machines were being prepped.

Down there, he picked out vehicles that looked similar to the floating transport platforms, only heavily armored and bristling with weapons. Other, more streamlined vehicles looked a bit like Jet Skis, and must have been for the swimmers. Off in the distance he saw and heard the flash of weapons being tested.

Preparing for battle.

"I thought all the runners and swimmers were supposed to be enslaved or something," said Charles, watching beside Seth. His unshaven face was completely covered by fine hair. "But they all seem to be working together."

Pointedly, Esta said, "Like equals."

"How would we know?" Seth asked, but he'd noticed the same thing.

He'd seen runners give medical checks to newly woken flyers. He'd seen flyers operating floating platforms, and swimmers handling weapons. The only indication that the flyers were in charge was the commander, but even her first lieutenants were a runner and a swimmer, so they obviously had important positions, too. It wasn't at all what he'd expected.

And if he and Esta and the others truly were prisoners, they weren't being mistreated. They'd been brought fresh clothes, made of the same white synthetic fabric Terra and the other rebels had worn when they first arrived. The clothes had seemed shapeless at first, but when he pulled them on, they molded intelligently to his limbs and body, leaving the feathers on his arms and the lower half of his legs free.

He looked at his friends. With their feathers and fur and tattooed skin and tails on full display, they all looked a little more like cryptogens now—and a lot less human.

They were brought food regularly, but also given the choice of being fed inside the sacs, percutaneously. Seth wasn't alone in wanting to eat the old-fashioned way and, like Esta and Darren, had eagerly fed on meat from the cryptogen animals brought to them. Charles ate black grass and berries and vines. Siena held out until her hunger got the better of her, and then she, too, ate meat.

Her collarbone had been repaired. After she'd seen Seth come safely out of the medical sac, she'd finally agreed to go inside herself. She'd been in a lot of pain, for a long time, and Seth was glad she had both her arms back. He still felt guilty, having left her behind on that bridge—flying away without her. Now she had her wings back.

"I think I liked being in a human prison better," Darren said.

"We're not prisoners, Darren," Esta said irritably.

"Well, there were board games, at least," Charles said, trying to lighten the mood.

"I don't have wings like you," Darren said to Esta, "and in case you haven't noticed, they've parked us in midair."

Darren was right. Despite the commander's talk about their being free to leave, no one had offered them the run of the ship. Or explained how to use the platforms that flitted about.

Seth had been watching how the cryptogens operated them. It seemed all they had to do was grip a certain section of the guardrail. So he'd tried doing the same, moving his hands bit by bit along the surface.

And after a while, he'd found the right spot. A musical vibration filled his head. It was asking something of him, but he didn't know what, and wasn't sure how to reply. Anaya had told him about a similar feeling, when she'd touched the walls of the rebel ship. It was similar to the silent talking, but more complicated.

So, yes, they were stranded up here—although there was nothing stopping him and Siena and Esta from gliding down to the ship's lower level. Could they simply find a door and walk right out?

But that would mean abandoning Charles and Darren. And he wasn't going to do that again.

And more vital: he wasn't sure he could convince Esta to leave.

Especially not with humans waiting just beyond the shield, eager to kill them.

Seth turned to see a runner gliding toward them on a platform. He recognized him as the one who'd accompanied the commander, except now he wore white synthetic clothing and a mask fitted over his nostrils.

—*Would you like to go outside?* the runner asked them.

Seth looked at the others, and they nodded as eagerly as he did. There were no windows in the ship, and he was anxious to see what was going on beyond the shield. They all stepped aboard the platform.

Carefully, Seth watched how the runner's hands gripped the rail, but it didn't reveal anything new about how to pilot the platform. It moved gracefully, rising toward the summit of the chamber. Above them, a hatchway spiraled open—and there was the sun.

After the soft, even light of the ship, the natural daylight made him squint. It was cooler outside, and Seth realized the ship generated the same warmer atmosphere as the biodome.

On all sides, the vast ship spread out as a flat gray expanse, except for a small antenna in the very center. A powerful vibration emanated from it and triggered a purple flicker in his mind. When he looked up, he saw the spreading dome of the shield, curving high overhead.

The platform skimmed low over the ship to its very edge, where it set down. Seth had a panoramic view of the entire peninsula and the surrounding sea. The ship itself hovered, one half over parkland, the other half over water.

He'd expected to see tanks and soldiers ranged outside the shield, or battleships offshore, but there was nothing. In fact, the streets of Point Roberts were eerily deserted. He supposed they'd evacuated. Except for the bodies. They were still scattered in the streets, all the humans who'd been crushed by the spreading shield. The guards who'd imprisoned him. Ritter, too.

He thought he picked out the flash of a few military drones, flitting beyond the shield. Could they see him right now? A bunch of hybrid kids, hanging out with a cryptogen aboard an invading spaceship. Once a picture like that got out, there was no chance people would ever trust hybrids. Was that one of the reasons they'd been brought out here? he wondered darkly.

"Check this out!" said Darren, pointing.

Seth turned to look out over the water. Beneath the surface flashed hundreds of swimmers, like a massive pod of dolphins, cutting the water into white furrows. He couldn't help laughing, it was such a joyous sight.

Then he realized they were hunting. In groups of three and four they brought down water striders hiding among the water lilies. The swimmers made it look like a ballet, outflanking the giant insects, spiraling in to chew off their legs, then devouring their helpless bodies.

"And over there," said Charles. "In the big park."

Some runners were cutting down black grass, while others seemed to be seeding new fields. A different group harvested the snaking vines and berries; another stood inside gaping pit plants, propping the mouths open with stalks of black grass while they cut thick fleshy strips from the purply insides.

"In the sky," Esta said.

Seth lifted his gaze and caught flyers circling, then hurtling down on one of those crater-faced rhino things he'd fought in Stanley Park. It was hard to know what actually killed the creature—the flyers' slashing wings, or the sonic blows. They ripped into it with claws and talons, feeding hungrily.

"Yum," said Siena, looking queasy.

—*The food aboard our ship is nourishing,* their runner escort explained, *but it's been a long time since we have hunted and harvested the natural food from our own world.*

"I don't see any of the runners or swimmers making a break for it," Esta remarked. "Wouldn't they try to escape if they were so badly treated?"

Seth had to admit, the cryptogens did look harmonious. The scene looked more like an extraterrestrial Garden of Eden than a military camp.

"They don't look like prisoners," Siena admitted.

"What would prisoners look like?" Charles asked.

"Maybe they're too afraid to disobey," said Seth. "All the flyers have to do is threaten them with sound. They don't need guns or handcuffs. They've got a way better invisible weapon."

But he couldn't quite convince himself. He thought of Terra and the swimmer back in the biodome—they had important jobs. Pilots, scientists. Why would the flyers let the runners and swimmers have jobs like that if they were prisoners or slaves?

And this runner with them right now was obviously a trusted and high-ranking lieutenant of the commander.

"We could ask him," Darren said, nodding at the runner.

"Don't," said Seth. He didn't want to let anything slip about Terra and the other rebels. He didn't want to lead the commander to Deadman's Island.

The runner had been watching them curiously as they spoke aloud, and also with a hint of irritation at hearing them use their own language. But Seth was glad they had a private way to communicate with each other, even in the presence of the cryptogens.

—*We runners and swimmers did not always work together so harmoniously with the winged ones,* the runner told them silently, as though he'd detected their confusion and surprise.

Seth realized the cryptogen wasn't really using the words *runners* and *swimmers* and *winged ones*—the names came instead as a mixture of scent and light and image. It was only his own brain that needed to put human words to these cryptogen names.

—*Long ago there was a war. My kind and the swimmers formed an alliance and waged war on the winged ones.*

Seth stared at his feet, afraid to look at Esta or the others, in case his surprise blazed from his eyes. This was *not* the story they'd been told by Terra or the general. Seth could still see and smell the images the general had seared inside his head. The pounding sonic blasts from the helmeted flyers that collapsed structures and flattened runners and swimmers like wet leaves on a sidewalk. The terror and destruction. The sensations were so real they were like his own memories.

Was it possible they were fakes? A high-budget special-effects extravaganza?

—*The winged ones were more advanced and powerful,* the runner continued, *and we were defeated. But the winged ones were merciful. Even though we started the war, they shared their knowledge with us. The winged ones made our lives richer than they had been before. And now we thrive together.*

—*So you aren't enslaved?* Darren asked.

Seth cut a warning glance at Darren. A sound growled up from the runner's throat. With relief, Seth realized it was laughter.

—*Do I look like a slave?* the runner asked them. He moved his hand to indicate all the cryptogens working together outside the dome. *Do* they?

—*No,* Esta replied, and then aloud said:

"Maybe these rebels have been lying the whole time."

Seth looked nervously at the runner, hoping he understood none of this.

"Why would they do that?" he said, struggling with the uncomfortable idea that he'd gotten everything backward.

Esta said, "Maybe your guys aren't proper rebels. Maybe they're just terrorists who want to overthrow the government!"

"Even if we don't know whose story is true," Charles began, "we know one thing for sure. These guys are here to take over our planet. That does *not* make them the good guys. Are you okay with everyone dying but us?"

Seth looked at Esta and knew her answer. Aside from him, who did she care about? For that matter, who did *he* have? Petra. Anaya. Dr. Weber?

"It's not like human beings haven't overthrown and wiped each other out for a zillion years," said Esta. "What's the difference? At least the cryptogens will leave us alone. They won't dump us in bunkers and mess with our brains."

"How can you be so sure?" Siena asked.

Seth's head flooded with confusion. From the corner of his eye he spotted a second platform skimming toward them. It was guided by the commander herself. She wore a mask over her nostrils and the same aerodynamic armor that Seth had first seen on the general during the landing in Stanley Park. He marveled at how thin her legs were. Her body was light, to let her fly, and her power was all in her mind, behind those penetrating black pupils.

—*There is a weapon,* she told them, coming to a halt alongside.

Seth said nothing, fearing that the commander had found out about the rebel plan to make a viral weapon from Anaya's blood.

—*What kind of weapon?* Esta asked.

—*One that will have no effect on us. Watch.*

She lifted a clawed finger to point at the sky. Seth shielded his eyes and saw a small spark against blue.

"Is that a missile?" Siena exclaimed.

Suddenly Seth understood why the city was deserted.

"It's got to be a nuke!" he said.

—*Should we go inside?* he asked the commander.

—*No.*

The spark didn't seem to move, only grow brighter. For a split second Seth saw its actual shape, a narrow tube aimed right at the shield's midpoint. But suddenly the missile veered and streaked out over the strait. Seth waited for a mushroom cloud to bloom over the Pacific, but nothing disturbed the horizon.

—*It didn't explode,* he said.

—*We disarmed it,* the commander said. *It is now at the bottom of the ocean.*

Seth's heartbeat stumbled, then raced, like he'd been sprinting. He forced a few big breaths into his lungs.

"They were going to nuke us?" said Siena, looking around, stunned.

"They might not even know we're here," Charles said, but he sounded doubtful.

"Bet they do," said Esta. "See those drones everywhere? They can zoom in. They see us. Like I said, the humans don't care about us! This is the only place we're safe!"

Seth wondered who'd ordered the attack. Was it Pearson? And Dr. Weber—would she have tried to stop it? He felt heartsick.

"The cryptogens could've aimed that missile at Vancouver or

Seattle and let it explode," Esta said. "They didn't. Maybe they're more merciful than you guys think."

—*Will you fly with me?*

The invitation came from the commander herself. Seth looked at her in astonishment.

—*I can only glide right now,* he told her ruefully.

From the platform, the commander picked up a slim vest and held it out.

Bewildered, Seth took it in his hands. It was amazingly light.

—*This will let me fly?* he asked.

—*Yes. It gives us extra thrust. Even though you cannot yet flap, the flight vest will give you more than enough thrust. Your wings will do the rest.*

She held out identical vests to Esta and Siena. Esta took hers; Siena shook her head.

Seth slipped it on, shivering with excitement as the armor adjusted itself around his torso, keeping his arms free. He felt a powerful vibration pass through his body.

—*How does it work?* he heard Esta ask eagerly.

—*Talk to it, in the same way you talk to me.*

A light flickered expectantly in Seth's head, as though the vest was waiting for him to give a command.

He spread his arms and ran. *Speed.* He felt the push from the flight pack and lifted his legs. He skimmed low over the ship. *More.* He angled his arms, felt his feathers parting the air, giving him lift. He soared up, leaving the ship below. He felt the steep climb in the pit of his stomach. He leveled out, squinting against the strong headwind, blinking joyful tears from his eyes.

When he tried to turn, a gust broadsided him, and he slewed, then stalled. Plummeting, he flapped in vain.

—*Accept the fall,* the commander told him.

It took all Seth's resolve to pull in his arms and let himself plunge headfirst.

—*Seth!* Esta cried out.

In those few seconds he saw her flying toward him, he saw the stippled blue-and-white water of the strait, the roads and houses and parks of Point Roberts, the vast cryptogen ship, and his friends Charles, Siena, and Darren gazing up at him. Could he even see the expressions on their faces? Was he that close?

—*Now,* the commander told him.

Seth spread his arms, angling his feathers ever so slightly. They caught the wind and he felt himself start to pull out of his dive. Still, the ship's deck was coming up awfully quickly. He rotated his arms more, grunting with the strain, and leveled out. He streaked over his friends' heads and angled his feathers for the climb.

Thrust, he told his flight vest, and with a shout of jubilation, he went soaring back up into the sky.

Nothing dragging him down. Nothing holding him back.

The sheer joy of it!

—*What happened? You okay?* Esta said, cruising alongside him.

—Just a little tumble, he said.

Up ahead he saw and *heard* the purple flicker of the approaching shield, and banked. This time it was a good turn, and he circled, only losing a little height. With his mind he nudged the flight pack for more power and went higher.

Overhead was the shield's dome. With a start he reminded himself he could fly right through it, unharmed.

—Don't, Esta said, soaring close. *The humans will kill you. They'll shoot you down the second you leave.*

There were no military jets that he could see right now. And he felt sure he could outfly them with this flight vest. Burst through the shield and keep going . . . but where? Back to Deadman's Island? But if he went, it would be alone. Even without asking her, he knew Esta would not come. And she was all he had.

She crossed paths in front of him, laughing with delight, and he followed her. Both of them, dipping and soaring and learning how to fly. To be with Esta, wing tip to wing tip, doubled his joy.

Hadn't he been having this dream his whole life? Flying, with others like him, belonging.

This time, it wasn't a dream.

CHAPTER FIFTEEN

WHEN PETRA WAS FINALLY summoned inside the biodome's conference room with Anaya, the large table was encircled by men and women she'd never seen before. Their uniforms were plastered with so many colorful insignia and badges and medals that, despite her nerves, she almost started giggling.

All morning, from their apartment window, she'd watched as more and more helicopters landed at the base, until the field looked like an airport. She knew that the men and women getting off these helicopters came from governments all over the world. They were met by the colonel and his officers and ushered inside the main building, where she figured Pearson would tell them everything he knew.

And only after that would he introduce them to her and Anaya—and afterward, the three cryptogens in the biodome.

"Ladies and gentlemen," said the colonel now, "this is Petra Sumner and Anaya Riggs, both hybrids, both escapees from the bunker facility run by Dr. Ritter."

She felt the hard landing of dozens of eyes and knew she was being examined. Every inch of her scrutinized. Her tattooed skin, her tail. She looked at Anaya for support, and the two held each other's gaze for strength, and also so they didn't have to look at the faces around them. Anaya had shaved her face, but her arms had a thick covering now. Her claws were uncut. And Petra's own face had its full patterning: an intricate black swirl around her eyes and nose and mouth.

There was no hiding anymore, and part of her was relieved, even as she dreaded what all these new people would think of her.

She avoided their eyes and looked instead at their uniforms, trying to find out where they were from. She picked out a lot of American flags, a couple she recognized as Japanese. There was one she thought might be Mexico, and one with the flag of the European Union.

With a start, she recognized the action-figure proportions of Paul Samson, the military intelligence officer who was Dr. Ritter's right-hand man at the bunker. Even though he'd turned out to be a good guy and helped all the hybrids escape, seeing him brought a queasy tide of memories. She gave him a tight smile, which he returned with a nod.

"It's thanks to these children," Dr. Weber said, "that we've developed pesticides, herbicides, a cure for the mosquito bird plague. They are exceptionally brave, and we have a great deal to thank them for."

Petra's shoulders actually jerked in alarm when she heard the first clap. Quickly, the applause spread through the room. Her cheeks flushed with surprise. This she hadn't expected. Her eyes moved across the crowd, and she noticed that not everyone was clapping. Some of the faces remained hard, even hostile.

"It's also through them," said Colonel Pearson, "that we've been able to communicate with the cryptogen rebels you will be meeting shortly."

"And Seth Robertson?" asked one of the visiting officers, a man whose American uniform bore the name tag DONALD. "Has there been any communication from him?"

"No," said Dr. Weber, "not since he left our base."

Donald's eyes turned to Petra and Anaya suspiciously. "You haven't had any telepathic contact with your friend?"

Petra shook her head.

"You can understand," said Donald, "what a grave security risk it poses, having hybrids captured by the cryptogens. Information can be extracted. Loyalties can be turned."

Petra knew what he was getting at: that Seth would betray the humans; even that he might start spying on them.

She was about to object when Dr. Weber said, "I know Seth Robertson very well, and I can assure you that I've never met anyone with more decency and resilience."

"No one is decent and resilient when tortured," said Donald.

Petra hated him.

"And it seems," the officer went on, "there were four other hybrids who were captured with Seth Robertson."

"Esta!" Petra exclaimed. "I knew it!"

"One of our drones captured these images shortly after the landing. Can you identify these other hybrids?" Donald slid a photograph across the table to her and Anaya. She picked it up and glanced at Colonel Pearson for the okay. He nodded.

As she examined the picture, she felt her eyes prick with tears. The resolution was poor, but she had no trouble recognizing the people. On a large floating platform were Charles, Siena, Darren, Esta, and Seth. Seth was lying flat. They were accompanied by a tall runner cryptogen with gray-streaked brown fur.

"They were all at the bunker with us," Petra said, and gave their names.

"The purpose of your visit here," Colonel Pearson told the room, "is to see if we can act together, and decisively, to defeat the cryptogen invasion. Some of you have indicated to me that you've made contact with other rebel landing parties. And you're here because you are at least open to the idea that these rebels may be sincere, and offer us a chance at victory."

Petra figured that most of the countries Pearson had contacted had not sent delegates. The Chinese were not present, having shot down the rebels' ship as it landed and declared it some kind of victory. Petra wondered how they were feeling now that there was a landing ship parked over Shanghai. And what about India and Egypt and Singapore? The Russians were here.

"Surely, Colonel Pearson," said one of their officers now, "you have entertained the notion that you are being fed misinformation and lies by these so-called cryptogen rebels. There is no way of knowing what they are truly saying—your only source is the hybrids, who may themselves have no loyalty to the human cause."

Without meaning to, Petra let out a deep sigh. When it turned heads, she said, "Oh, come on. You really think we're enemies?"

"I think, after what these kids have endured," said Paul Samson, "and the service they've done our planet, they shouldn't have to defend themselves. I think I can speak for the United States"— and here he shot a smackdown look at Officer Donald—"and say that our government has recently changed its position on the hybrids. The cryptogens who landed on our soil, however, have been detained, and haven't been allowed translators yet."

"This will change," said another American officer. "We're shutting down all our detention centers and releasing hybrid children."

Too bad it wasn't sooner, Petra thought bitterly. If Esta hadn't been locked up in Point Roberts, Seth wouldn't have needed to go rescue her.

"We urge all of you," said Colonel Pearson, "if you haven't already, to assemble teams of hybrid translators so we can all have more vigorous discussions with the cryptogen rebels."

"You are more trusting than us," said the Russian. "Our cryptogens are still detained. And we have quarantine the ship that landed, inside an airplane hangar on one of our bases."

"We are very grateful you took this move to contact us," said a woman from the Japanese delegation. "Otherwise all our countries might have proceeded, each of us, alone and fearful. We have been speaking with the three cryptogens who landed outside Kyoto, using hybrid children."

It was strange for Petra to think that, across the world, there were teenagers like her and Anaya and Seth also talking to rebel cryptogens, maybe in a place not very different from this biodome.

"Did they tell you about the viral weapon they wanted to make?" Anaya asked.

"Yes," said the Japanese officer, "though unfortunately, they were not able to create one successfully. Which is why Colonel Pearson's news is so welcome."

"I would suggest that our discussions not include Ms. Sumner and Ms. Riggs," said an officer from the European Union. "For matters of security."

Despite his politeness, Petra could tell that the officer clearly held her and Anaya in suspicion.

"No," said Colonel Pearson. "These two are critical to our plans. And we need them to translate when we move upstairs to the observation dome to include the cryptogens in our conversation. Let's do that now."

Pearson and his officers led everyone out of the conference room and up a flight of stairs to the door of the observation room.

"My hope," said Pearson before opening the door, "is that

after listening to what the cryptogens have to say, we can all agree on a joint course of action."

When Petra entered, the first thing she saw through the window was the general perched atop a dead water strider, tearing savagely into it with his talons and feeding the meat into his gnashing beak.

—*General, you have visitors,* Petra told him, as politely as possible.

The winged cryptogen looked up and, seeing the visitors crowding the observation room, hopped off his prey. There was still a bit of meat caught on the tip of his beak. Petra took in the faces of all the military personnel, hoping they had missed the flyer's table manners. Judging by some of their horrified expressions, they had not.

She realized that for many of these people, this was the first time they'd seen real cryptogens in the flesh. Which was shocking enough without seeing them rip a dead animal apart.

—*Maybe this was a bad idea,* Anaya said to her silently, *bringing them in here so soon.*

—*What can we do?* she replied. *Dress them up in cardigans and slippers?*

Inside the biodome, Terra, the swimmer, and the general drew closer to the observation window. It was impossible not to admire their power and dignity. The three cryptogens faced the dozens of humans in silence.

—We are on display, the swimmer said inside her head.

—Yes, she replied. *Try not to eat anything for a while.*

"A pressing question that has not been addressed," said the Russian, "is why the cryptogen runners and swimmers on the landing ships haven't tried to free themselves. They greatly outnumber the flyers, yes? What is holding them back?"

Pearson nodded at Petra, and she passed the question along to the cryptogens.

—Fear, the general replied. *The runners and swimmers know that any mistake, any disobedience, will result in immediate death.*

—Most of my kind, said Terra, *would rather serve the flyers and survive. Some of us have risen to positions of authority because we won their trust. I was permitted to become a pilot and a scientist.*

—As was I, said the swimmer. *But until now, we've never been in a position where success against the winged ones was possible.*

—If we can destroy the shields of the landing ships, the general said, *and send down a rain immediately after, you must strike the undefended ships with full force.*

After Petra relayed all this to the room, a pensive silence hung over it for a few moments.

"The rebels are asking a great deal of us," said the Mexican emissary, "but what about the runners and swimmers themselves? Once we break down the shields and are, ourselves, under full attack, what help can we expect from the rebels? I can't believe for a moment we have the force or firepower to defeat the flyers."

—*The rebels are waiting for us to raise the lantern,* the general said.

"Raise the lantern, what does this mean?" asked the Russian dubiously.

Anaya had been the one to experience it, so Petra let her friend do the talking.

"It's a telepathic sign," Anaya explained. "It's like a beacon of light and hope. The rebels pass it among themselves. It's a sign to revolt."

"But there's only a few hundred rebels," Officer Donald said. "That's not much of a fighting force."

—*It will soon become an army,* said the general. *Once I pass through the shield and destroy the transmission tower, the swimmer and I will raise the lantern ourselves. When the other runners and swimmers see us together, fighting as one, they will have the strength to rise up, too.*

"And once the rain comes," Anaya added, "the flyers will lose their power."

"This is a very optimistic scenario," said the European emissary. "I won't insult you all by pointing out the possible flaws. Except one. How are the human forces supposed to know which of the runners and swimmers are on our side?"

"A good point," said the Russian. "The possibility of confusion and friendly fire is very great. After all, we cannot see this lantern."

Petra asked the general the question and passed on his reply.

"The general says we should only attack if fired upon first, and concentrate our firepower on the ship itself, and the flyers."

"How long before the weaponized rain?" Paul Samson asked. "I don't know how long our forces could hold out against the flyers at their full strength."

—*I will communicate from the primary vessel,* said Terra now. *And let you know when to strike. I will try to send the rain the moment the shields come down.*

"Colonel Pearson," said the Japanese officer, "my country feels this is the best path forward."

"I am not authorized to agree to plans of any kind," said the Russian. "But I will report back to my superiors immediately and let you know their response."

"As will I," said the European emissary.

"We'll work with you to coordinate attacks against the ships at Point Roberts and Baltimore," said Paul Samson.

"And Dr. Weber and I will continue to work with our counterparts in the countries that aren't here today," said Colonel Pearson.

"With luck," said Dr. Weber, "they might be having their own conversations like this one."

Petra looked around the room. The plan wasn't unanimous

yet, and maybe it never would be. But it was better than nothing, and she felt a flicker of hope. If every step of this rickety plan went okay, they might have a chance.

IN HER SLEEP, ANAYA was aware of someone calling her. It was like a voice whispering outside her door, and it smelled of gasoline and smoke. She woke with a start and sat up, heart hammering, neck damp with sweat. She looked at the bedroom door, saw the comforting line of light underneath. No smell of smoke. Just a bad dream, then.

But there was still an uneasy vibration in her head, and a bullying flicker of light in the corner of her vision.

"You okay?" Petra asked sleepily from her bed.

"Don't turn on the light," Anaya said when she saw her friend reach for the bedside lamp. "You feel something? In your head?"

Even in the dark, Anaya sensed her friend stiffen.

"Yeah. Like something wants to get inside."

"Don't let it."

"Who is it?" Petra whispered, sitting up.

It didn't feel like someone was trying to talk to them—more like *looking* for something.

Anaya was afraid to go to the window, but she couldn't stop herself from parting the curtain just a bit. She looked out across the base. Everything seemed calm.

"See anything?" Petra hissed.

"No."

She checked the two guard towers—and didn't see the usual shadows of guards inside.

"That's not right," she said, then stifled a scream as three slim, winged shapes darted across the sky.

"Flyers!" she whispered, stumbling away from the window.

Petra leapt out of bed and started dragging on clothes. With trembling fingers, Anaya did the same. Was this it—was it happening? Was the whole world being attacked? Or just Deadman's Island?

She rushed across the living room, glad to see that the blinds were lowered, and went to wake up her parents. For a split second she beheld their peaceful, sleeping forms—this would be the last moment they didn't know they were under attack—and then she put her hand on Dad's shoulder.

"I saw flyers outside," she whispered as he and Mom stirred and sat up in confusion. "I don't think anyone knows yet!"

She went back to the living room as her parents hurriedly dressed. Petra was holding the phone limply in her hand.

"No dial tone."

"Where's your dad?" Anaya asked, looking toward Mr. Sumner's open bedroom door.

"Night shift at the hospital."

Dad came in, buttoning his shirt. "Why haven't the guards sounded the alarm?"

"I think the flyers killed them." Anaya gulped.

"Radar, then," Dad said.

"If they flew in low," said Mom, "radar wouldn't pick them up."

All was quiet outside. No alarm sounded.

"Why aren't they attacking?" Petra asked.

"Maybe they're looking for something," Anaya said. Suddenly it became clear to her. "They're looking for Terra and the others!"

Petra shook her head in confusion. "How'd they know to look *here*?" she asked, then trailed off. The sick look on her face told Anaya that they'd both just had the same terrible thought.

Seth. Had he told the cryptogens about the base?

"I've got to warn Terra," Anaya said.

She hoped the runner already knew. Maybe the rebels had been woken by the flyers' probing minds. But what if they hadn't?

"Can you just send Terra a message telepathically?" Mom asked.

Anaya shook her head. "The flyers might hear it; they're listening! I've got to get to the biodome myself!"

"No way," said Dad.

"If the flyers find them, they'll destroy the ship! The virus. They'll *kill* them!"

"I'll go with you," Dad said.

"I'm faster alone."

All her fear disappeared and left no hesitation in her mind.

"Anaya!" Dad made a grab for her arm.

But she bounded to the door and out into the corridor. No

one was faster than her. And one person alone was less likely to be seen than a noisy jeep filled with soldiers. She reached the exit and slipped outside.

The night was still quiet, the air cool against her hot face. She checked the sky, then ran, plotting a course through the shadows.

On the narrow causeway that connected the base to Stanley Park, she opened up, her strides huge. The end of the causeway was gated with a guard post, and she saw the sentry come out, squinting in confusion. She didn't bother to slow down; she jumped, sailing over the guard and the razor wire atop the fence. She hit the ground running.

Glancing back, she caught a silvery flash of three flyers circling Deadman's Island. No thunderclaps crushing concrete or rending metal. Not yet. She cut off the road and went into the trees, vectoring straight for the biodome.

Her feet barely touched the dewed grass. If there were cryptogenic creatures lurking in the trees, she would outrun them. If she plunged into a pit plant, she would jump clear in a flash. She was swift and unbeatable.

Beyond the aquarium parking lot, the curve of the biodome glowed bone white. She reached it in twenty strides. The main door was locked, and she pressed the buzzer until an officer appeared and opened the door.

"What's going on?" he asked.

"I need to get inside," Anaya told him. "There's three cryptogen flyers—they're looking for the rebels!"

"I haven't heard anything about—"

The officer reached for the walkie-talkie at his hip, and Anaya smacked it out of his hand.

"No! They'll pick up your signal!"

The urgency in her voice must've convinced him, because he stood aside. Anaya bolted inside and up the stairs. Over her shoulder she called back, "Open up the loading bay doors. We need to get them and their ship out of there!"

Anaya entered the observation room and hurried past the surprised on-duty officer to the pressurized doors. She buzzed herself through and walked into the moist heat of the biodome. She kicked a questing vine out of the way. There was no sign of Terra or the others. They must be sleeping inside the ship. The hatch, she noticed, was closed. She was afraid to call out silently. Would the flyers hear her?

Breathlessly, she went to the ship's hull, prepared to knock, but when she touched the place where the hatch was, it opened like it knew her. She stepped inside. Three sacs hung from the ceiling, each molded to the very different shapes of the three cryptogens.

She didn't know how best to wake them. Luckily she didn't need to. Her entrance must have triggered some kind of signal, because all the sacs were shifting and opening. Terra emerged first, her curious eyes locking onto Anaya's.

—*Flyers,* Anaya said.

Terra lifted her hand in a sign for silence and touched the wall. The hatch to the ship closed.

—It's safe to talk now, she said to Anaya. *The hull will block our signals.*

—There's three or more, circling the base.

—Someone has betrayed us, said the general with an angry whiff of diesel fumes.

—I don't think they know where you are yet, said Anaya.

—We must move the ship, Terra said.

—Will it fly? Anaya asked.

—It will fly, even if it is not ready to leave the atmosphere.

—Where is Petra? the swimmer asked, zir voice salty in Anaya's head.

—Back at the base.

—If she or any of the other hybrids signal to each other, the winged ones will find them. They will question them. And kill them.

Anaya felt sick. She hadn't thought of that. She needed to get back to the base. To warn Petra, to warn all of them.

—I will go, said the swimmer. Ze hurried to the wall and opened a locker to retrieve a weapon that looked like a harpoon gun mounted on a complicated pivot. Deftly ze belted the harness around zir chest and shoulders so ze could still run on all fours.

—Go, the general told Terra. *Take the ship. I will go meet them.*

The words were loaded with smoke and threat. Anaya knew he meant to fight the other flyers. How, she couldn't imagine, now that he'd lost his sound weapon.

Nonetheless, he took his helmet from a locker and put it on.

It was useless to him now—and possibly deadly, if he tried to attack with sound. All his sonic energy would split his own skull. But his enemies didn't know that. Not yet. When his full battle armor was on, he said:

—*Once the hatch is open, we must be silent.*

He touched the wall, and cool air rushed inside the ship. Through the hatchway, Anaya saw that the loading bay was already wide open, as she'd asked. An army helicopter hovered above the trees, releasing orange streaks of gunfire in the direction of Deadman's Island.

With a screech, the helicopter's rotors folded up like a dead spider's legs, and the machine dropped aslant, crackling through trees. Anaya felt welded to the floor with terror.

The swimmer left the ship and moved with a speed Anaya had never seen before. Darting out the loading bay, ze disappeared into the darkness. The general spread his magnificent wings and hurled himself into the night sky.

Anaya understood he was trying to buy Terra time to take off, to save the ship, the virus, their chances at winning this war. And now Anaya herself needed to go back to the base, to warn Petra, to help Mom and Dad, to do anything she could.

She made to leave the ship when, with a thunderous boom, an entire wing of the aquarium was punched flat into the ground. How long would it be before a blast was directed at the biodome?

Terra pulled Anaya away from the hatch and closed it.

—You're safer here.

The runner was already climbing back inside one of the hanging sacs.

—We're going now, Terra said, seeing Anaya's confusion. She motioned to the sac next to hers. *Get inside. We pilot the ship from here.*

—We?

Anaya climbed in. Instantly the sac molded around her, arranging her body into a crouching position, as if she were about to lunge. She felt a strange expectant pulse against her skin.

—I don't know what to do— she began.

—Listen to it, Terra instructed her.

—I can't see anyth—

And then immediately she could, as if the fabric against her eyes had suddenly become transparent. Except that the view it offered was *outside* the ship. Turning her head, Anaya realized she had a complete wraparound view, above and below, too. And they were already moving, through the loading bay doors and into the sky.

CROUCHED LOW, PETRA RAN through the shadows across the base, toward the barracks where the hybrid kids slept. She figured the flyers would be prodding at their sleeping minds, too, trying to get them to talk, asking them where the rebels were. She'd warn them, then head straight to the hospital.

How would they protect all the patients? Could they move them to the basement or something? Her dad. So much thinner now, and grimmer, too. When he smiled, only his lips moved, and it made his eyes look so sad. She wanted to run to him right now, but she had to warn the other kids first.

From one of the guard towers came a shout, and she looked up to see a spotlight aimed into the sky. Three flyers flashed through the beam, their terrifying helmets gleaming. She caught wings of the iciest blue.

With a horrifying crack, the guard tower and the light and the guard operating it were gone. It took Petra a second to find the dark wreckage on the ground, like shreds of cardboard.

Now, finally, an alarm began to sound, a swelling and subsiding wail.

From the barracks, doors started opening. Soldiers poured out, still shrugging on flak jackets.

"Get inside!" one of them shouted at her.

The hallway was dark except for the emergency exit lights and the clashing flashlight beams of soldiers in combat gear, checking weapons, tightening helmets. Some glanced at her with a frown; most ignored her altogether. She took the stairs. She knew the kids were on the third floor. She started knocking on doors.

"This is Petra!" she shouted. "Wake up! Wake up! Don't use

telepathy! No silent talking! The flyers are looking for you! They'll hear you if you use telepathy!"

Doors began to open and kids peeped out. Some were already dressed, and others were still in boxers and T-shirts, scrubbing their eyes.

One girl stood, looking stricken.

"What is it?" Petra asked her.

"I was talking to Val across the hall."

"For a long time?"

She shook her head like a terrified toddler. "Half a minute?"

"Okay," said Petra, feeling dread. "It's probably okay."

A soldier appeared at the end of the hall and shouted at them to get to the basement right away.

Everyone in the hallway went sideways as if they'd been struck. Petra hit the floor. Drywall and rubble rained down on her as the entire roof peeled off. She saw a flyer, battle armor blazing, circling over them. It plunged down, then flared its wings to make a landing on the debris-strewn floor.

Petra cowered with all the other kids in the roofless hallway. None of the others had actually seen Terra or the general or the swimmer, and before them was this towering cryptogen flyer. A fierce heat came off it, and the stink of rancid meat. Its feathers flattened against its skeletal arms. In its battle armor, it seemed like a monstrous mechanical hawk. The helmet hid the eyes, the beak, the nose, and made the head look huge and misshapen. Its talons gouged the cheap carpeting.

The flyer turned its head slowly to see all the hybrids.

—*How strange you are,* it said to all of them. The words were toxic with contempt. *So malformed. Where are the rebels?*

Petra was the only one, officially, who knew, but there were bound to be rumors.

She winced, and all around her, kids cried out and clutched their heads as the flyer hurt them with sound. She heard their silent garbled pleading.

—*I don't know . . .*

—*Stop, please . . .*

—*They don't know!* Petra shouted over the others.

The flyer rounded on her.

—*You do.*

Agony, like a spiny sea urchin in her brain, throbbing and searing. She dropped to her knees. It was impossible not to plead and beg; they were the only words she could form. The pain ceased.

—*Tell me.*

She wouldn't tell. She could be strong. She wouldn't give away the rebels. And Anaya was there, too! But when the pain came back, harder, she felt herself collapsing. She'd do anything to stop the pain. Then, faintly, she heard another silent voice in her head, one of the runners:

—*The aquarium! I heard they're in the aquarium!*

Petra's pain stopped and she burst into tears of relief, and despair.

—*No,* she said weakly.

—*The aquarium?* the flyer demanded of the boy.

He pointed. *Big building! In the park!*

It was done. Petra knew that the flyer had already transmitted the news instantly to the other flyers. She couldn't stop crying. She tried to find Anaya in her head, searched in vain for her light, then caught a faint whiff of grass.

—*Anaya!* she called with all her strength. *They're coming!*

The flyer must have heard her, because its helmeted head veered toward her in fury. Petra clenched her eyes shut, every tendon and muscle tensed for the final tidal wave of pain.

"Get down! Down!" someone was shouting from the end of the hallway.

Petra turned to see two soldiers with their rifles aimed at the flyer.

Not a shot rang out before the air was sucked away from her nostrils by the flyer's searing torrent of sound. The soldiers flew backward like marionettes; the stairwell exploded outward in a cascade of brick and twisted steel.

Petra lay frozen. None of the kids stood. What good would running do? Her tail gave an impatient twitch. Desperately she looked for places to strike the flyer. Its torso was covered in armor. That left the bony legs, which were mostly protected by metallic feathers. Miss and she'd be dead. Even if she hit, she might be dead if her venom didn't work fast enough.

Petra heard a serrated zinging sound, and suddenly there was a harpoon sticking through the flyer's armored chest. The cryptogen staggered and turned to face its attacker.

Petra turned, too, and her heart surged. It was the swimmer, at the opposite end of the hallway. Ze lay flat against the floor, taking aim once more. She couldn't even see the next harpoon fly, only heard the sound of it unzipping the air before it plunged through the flyer's chest.

—*Sting it!* she shouted to the other hybrid swimmers.

She threw herself at the flyer and struck with her tail. She felt the needle bite into the back of its bony thigh. A runner hybrid launched himself at the flyer and knocked it over. Another runner jumped on the flyer and kicked at its helmet. With a snap it came off, revealing an enraged beaked face. After more tails struck, the face froze in a paralyzed grimace.

The swimmer raced down the hallway toward them.

"It's okay!" Petra yelled as the other hybrids hollered in terror. "Ze's with us. Ze's a rebel! A good guy!"

The swimmer wrenched out zir two harpoons, slick with gore.

—*Is it dead?* Petra asked.

—*Yes. You need to hide now. They will kill you. No more talking. Tell them.*

"No telepathy, guys," she said aloud. "Out loud only! We're *going!*"

Petra heard the swimmer wheezing and worried ze might be injured, and then realized it was because ze didn't have zir mask on. Petra touched the warm smooth skin of zir back.

She heard someone scream. Hot, reeking air crashed over Petra. A pair of taloned feet sank into the swimmer's back and yanked zir into the air. Petra looked up to see an armored flyer soaring away with the swimmer, as though ze weighed nothing at all. The flyer must've stunned the swimmer, because ze went limp and the harpoon gun fell from zir grasp.

"No!" Petra screamed.

—*Go!* the swimmer cried weakly.

The other kids were already surging toward the last remaining stairwell, and Petra was swept along with them. When they reached the main floor, a girl shouted:

"The soldiers told us to go down to the basement!"

"Screw that!" said one of the runners. "I'm not waiting around!"

"They crush buildings!" Petra said. "We'd be buried alive."

"I say we run for it!"

Petra felt the same primal urge. "The park," she said. "We can hide in the trees. Or in the water, for the swimmers. Wait it out."

Petra opened the door and cast a fearful glance into the night sky. No sign of the flyer who took the swimmer. What would they do to zir? Why hadn't they just killed zir—killed all of them—with a sonic blast?

The sky over the base looked clear. Maybe the other flyers were already at the aquarium—she only hoped they hadn't gone straight to the biodome.

Now was a good time to make a break for it. She stepped

outside. The runners bolted into the lead, their powerful legs carrying them weightlessly over the asphalt to the causeway. The swimmers followed.

Overhead came the sound of metal on metal, and when she looked up, she saw two flyers engaged in an aerial dogfight, swerving, diving. One of them was the general. Orange lines of gunfire streaked up into the sky toward them, and Petra traced it back to a gun mounted on an armored vehicle filled with soldiers.

"Don't shoot!" she screamed, running closer. "One of them's ours!"

Maybe they didn't hear her. Maybe they didn't care if they killed one of the rebels. But seconds later, the entire jeep was flattened like a can, and the soldiers with it.

Gasping, Petra looked back into the sky and saw the enemy flyer—but where was the general? Had he been killed? Then he came plunging down from the darkness of the sky, latching onto the other flyer's back. With one powerful stroke of his wing, the general cut off the flyer's helmeted head. Like a giant hailstone, it plummeted earthward. The decapitated body folded up and spiraled lifelessly down.

That, actually, was pretty incredible, Petra couldn't help thinking. She wanted to shout out to the general or wave but didn't, in case she drew attention to him, or herself.

Two flyers down. How many were left? Anaya had seen three. So maybe just the one who took the swimmer? And where was it now?

Above the base, something large streaked silently past in a blur, but Petra made out its unique seashell shape. The rebels' ship! It was okay! It was airborne!

Go, go, go! Petra cheered silently.

And inside her head flared Terra's urgent voice:

—*Aboard with Anaya. We have the weapon.*

Petra's jubilation quickly died. Speeding behind the ship was a flyer with huge wings of white and gold and blue, whose spiked helmet looked like it was made of ice—and was now pulsing an ominous purple.

AS THEY STREAKED OVER Deadman's Island, Anaya anxiously watched the flyer pursuing them.

—*It's going to blast us!* she cried out.

She felt her body become heavy as the ship angled up and accelerated. The sac's fabric expanded to cushion her. Behind their ship, she saw a bright purple flash, and her whole body tensed. But nothing happened.

—*It didn't get us!* she cried. *Why not?*

—*It is sound, and we are now going much faster than the speed of sound.*

—*Oh, right! Yay, speed of sound!*

She couldn't see the flyer anymore, couldn't see much of anything at all, now that they were so high.

—*Are we going back to help the others?* she asked.

As they'd streaked over the base, she'd seen demolished buildings, wrecked jeeps, bodies on the ground.

—*No. This ship has no weapons,* Terra replied. *If we go back, they'll destroy us.*

Mom and Dad. Petra. Everyone.

—*Will they be okay?* Anaya asked, wanting reassurance.

—*I do not know. The general and the swimmer will try to protect them.*

—*There's just the two of them, though!*

—*We're traveling to the primary vessel.*

—*Right now?*

She'd thought they just needed to save the ship, move it somewhere.

—*The commander may put the primary vessel on high alert,* Terra explained. *We need to dock as quickly as possible and start our work. To make the rain.*

Anaya thought of the tender scar tissue forming over the ship's damaged hull.

—*But the ship, is it ready? Healed?*

—*We will find out when we leave the atmosphere.*

She'd had glimmers, over the weeks, of Terra's ruthlessness. Moments when Anaya had felt like a lab rat or a cog in a big machine. The runner, it turned out, was sometimes more like Colonel Pearson than she cared to think. Terra had her mission, and she wouldn't fall out of step with it. Even if it meant leaving her friends to die. Even if it meant leaving Anaya's own parents to die.

They were going beyond the sky. The thought of her parents, in danger, and now so far away, made her eyes sting. It wasn't right. She should be helping them. But that wasn't going to happen. She was in outer space, her body suddenly weightless, the planet a lonely blue curve below her.

PETRA WATCHED THE FLEEING rebel ship and the pursuing flyer until they disappeared from sight. But a moment later came a distant flash of purple, and a rending clap of thunder. Her knees went weak. Had the ship been destroyed?

Nothing she could do. She saw Colonel Pearson and Dr. Weber and a cluster of soldiers moving across the base toward her—and her father! She shouted out and ran. After three strides she was knocked off her feet, and a stabbing pain pierced her hand.

Twisted on the ground, she stared up at the flyer with white and gold and blue wings and the terrifying helmet. One of the cryptogen's talons had impaled her left hand, pinning her to the ground. She felt a spiky mass gathering heat in her head, and prepared herself for the worst.

"Petra!" she heard her father cry out.

Bullets deflected off the flyer's helmet and body armor. The flyer turned its head toward the soldiers, and with a purple spark of its helmet, they flew backward, their weapons mangled together with their bodies. Nearby stood Pearson, who let his pistol fall to the ground and stepped forward.

The flyer regarded him carefully and then, to Petra, said:

—*That one has the look of a commander. Translate for me.*

Petra sensed instinctively that this flyer was absolutely a she, and the power of her silent words was almost painful inside Petra's head.

"She wants to ask you questions," Petra grunted from the ground.

—*What plans were made with the others?*

"The plans we made with the rebels! She wants you to tell them."

"Tell them nothing," Pearson said.

"No!" her father cried. "It'll kill her! Petra, tell it what it wants!"

The flyer's helmeted head followed the speakers, then turned expectantly back to Petra.

—*You have information,* she said. *Tell me.*

Pain spiked through Petra's brain. She flexed her tail.

—*Try to strike me and I will end you,* the flyer warned. *Tell me everything you know.*

A hopeful thought glowed in Petra's mind, despite the pain. If this flyer was interrogating her, it meant she didn't know about the rebels' plans yet. It meant the swimmer hadn't given anything away. It might even mean the rebel ship with Terra and Anaya had escaped unharmed!

But she knew, she knew, she couldn't hold out against the pain that was coming.

Behind the flyer, Petra glimpsed something small in the night sky. Quickly it grew into the blazing white shape of the general, plunging downward. Maybe she made a hopeful sound, maybe she looked too long—but the enemy flyer must have noticed, and whirled, whipping up her wings in defense.

The timing was perfect, and the blow sliced off the general's left wing. He tumbled from the air and skidded across the ground.

The pain in Petra's head abruptly disappeared as the flyer turned her sonic weapon on the general instead. Trying to stand, the general crumpled under the assault.

—*What is wrong with you?* the enemy flyer asked him. *Why don't you fight back with sound?*

The general made no reply, except the terrible choking sounds from his throat.

—*Where is your strength?* the enemy flyer demanded, and pulled her talon free of Petra's hand so she could stride closer to the general.

Petra struck with her tail, but the stinger deflected off the flyer's armor. With a careless backward smack of her wing, the flyer knocked Petra back several meters. She hit the ground hard, winded, but could still hear the flyer silently interrogating the general.

—*If this is a rebellion, who are your other rebels?*

The general made another terrible cry of pain, half moan, half screech.

—*What are your plans?*

Petra glimpsed Colonel Pearson slowly stepping away into the shadows with Dr. Weber and her father. Dad caught her eye and with a flick of his chin made it clear he wanted her to get away, to run. She started to silently scramble backward. She should run, but she couldn't, not with the general so helpless.

—*Why don't you strike back?* she heard the flyer demand of the general again.

Out of the night sky appeared a long floating platform, piloted by the flyer who'd snatched up the swimmer. Petra caught a glimpse of zir, motionless on the deck. Alive, or dead?

The platform landed beside the general, who gave a final cry and was still. With her talons, the white-and-blue-winged flyer contemptuously heaved him onto the platform beside the swimmer.

They're leaving, Petra thought as the platform rose, but the white-and-blue-winged flyer flew off the platform and circled the base.

254

She sent out one sonic shock wave after another. The buildings of the base crumpled under the barrage. Petra bolted, even though she felt like she had no air in her lungs. She saw her father and the others running toward her, joining her. She ran down the causeway toward the park as Deadman's Island was crushed behind her.

CHAPTER SIXTEEN

WITHOUT WINDOWS, IT WAS impossible for Seth to know exactly what time it was. The only hint was the ship's light, which paled at nighttime—or what his body *told* him was nighttime—and grew brighter in the morning. Which was happening right now. In the strengthening glow, there was a lot more activity in the chamber than usual, flyers and floating platforms zipping in all directions.

"Feels like something's going on," said Charles.

"They getting ready to invade?" Darren said.

"God, I hope not," murmured Siena.

Before long, a runner they'd never seen before pulled her platform alongside theirs and told them to board. No explanation was given. Seth met the nervous glances of his friends.

—*Where are we going?* Esta asked the runner.

—*There is something you must see.*

The *must* made it sound serious. Not something they might *enjoy* seeing, but something they were being *forced* to see. Seth's empty stomach gave a squeeze. They hadn't been offered breakfast yet.

With countless other platforms they drifted toward the center of the vast chamber. There, standing on a stationary platform, stood the commander. Beside her—Seth stared in shock—were the general and the swimmer.

The last time Seth had seen them was inside the biodome. Now they were terribly transformed. Both looked physically smaller, and broken. With a surge of horror, he realized that the general was missing his left wing, leaving only a bloodied stump. His remaining feathers were greasy and limp. The swimmer's skin had an unhealthy grayish tinge and was covered in raw wounds that might have been gouge marks. Both of the rebels looked like they'd fought and lost a great battle. Or been tortured.

—Who are they? he heard Esta ask their runner escort.

—Rebels.

Seth felt the other kids staring at him wonderingly, maybe wanting to ask him questions but too afraid even to speak aloud right now. None of them had met the general or the swimmer. They hadn't stood near them, talked to them, and had their voices in their heads.

The commander leapt from the platform and flew tight circles over her prisoners.

—These two traitors were found with the humans! Once my closest friends and advisers, they have betrayed me—and all of you!

Seth wasn't sure how the commander was doing it, but her voice seemed to reach everyone inside the ship at once, more blaring and intense than any stadium loudspeaker.

—They were colluding with the humans, planning to attack us. They were going to wage war on their own kind!

How had the rebels been discovered? Seth wondered. What had happened since he'd left Deadman's Island? And where was Terra? Was she safe, at least? Anxious heat prickled across his back and under his arms. He felt dizzy with nerves.

—They say they are part of a rebellion. I say: What do they have to rebel against? We have all toiled and fought together on many worlds as we've increased our homeland and resources across the galaxies! We have riches! We are stronger together than ever before.

Though he was far away, Seth had the uneasy sense that the general's eyes were on him. He forced his gaze away, terrified that he'd attract attention to himself with his stricken expression—or that the general would speak to him. In his mind, a light flickered weakly, and he caught the faintest whiff of gasoline. That was all: no words, just a scent . . . and a lingering glow at the back of his head. Like he'd just been given something.

—And now we have a new world on which to thrive, the commander continued. *But these traitors would deny that victory to each and every one of you! What do you think of such treachery?*

A terrible chorus swelled within the chamber: growls and gasping snorts from the runners; shrieks from the flyers; rasping, rumbling growls from the swimmers. From these creatures who were normally so silent, it was a terrifying alien symphony. He could only imagine it expressed their outrage toward the prisoners.

—And here are the leaders, the commander said. *We have caught them all.*

Then where's Terra? thought Seth.

—We have destroyed their machines of war, the commander continued. *Their soldiers. All their human allies.*

He almost choked. Petra, Anaya, Dr. Weber.

—They are not so mighty to behold, crowed the commander. *Who would choose to be led by these two pathetic creatures?*

The commander landed on the rail of their platform. Tauntingly, she said to the general:

—Here I am, strike me down!

The general made no reply.

—He cannot strike me. He has no strength! No power!

Why doesn't he fight? Seth wondered. How could he not at least *try* to blast the commander?

Unless he couldn't. Seth's heart tripped over itself. Had Dr. Weber and Colonel Pearson tested their virus weapon on the general? And had it worked? That would explain his powerlessness. The virus had *worked*—and that meant that the rebels and Pearson and all the humans now had a weapon to use against the flyers!

Unless it had been destroyed on Deadman's Island.

Along with everyone stationed there.

With a sweep of her wings, the commander addressed the entire chamber:

—*Maybe, among you, there are some who call themselves rebels. But your leaders would take away all you have worked for. They would plunge you back into fear and uncertainty. They would risk your lives. If we stay united, you are all safe, you are all valued, and here is your home. I know there are rebels among you. I will not punish you. All I ask is that you abandon this futile and destructive cause and become loyal to our one shared purpose!*

Seth swept the chamber with his eyes, wishing he could read the thoughts of all the assembled runners and swimmers. Did they believe the commander? Were they loyal, like their cries and roars suggested? Or were they just playing along, fearful for their lives?

Seth jolted as the general's silent voice suddenly burst into his head.

—*There are many of us! More than you think!*

The general wasn't addressing just Seth, but everyone in the chamber. And his silent voice was just as loud as the commander's.

—*Do not give up hope!* he cried. *Rise up when the time is right! Rise up! Rise up!*

With barely a turn of her head, the commander struck the general and the swimmer with a sonic blow. Seth couldn't suppress a gasp as the two rebels collapsed lifelessly.

—*So it ends,* said the commander, landing atop the corpses, digging into them with her talons, defiling their bodies. *Let us return to our preparations.*

Without a word, their runner escort took Seth and his friends back to their own platform, and left them alone.

"Were those the rebels on Deadman's Island?" Charles whispered nervously.

Seth nodded. "The general. And the swimmer."

He was about to tell them how the general had almost talked to him, and had left him something in his head. But he held back. Why, he wasn't exactly sure. More than anything, he wanted to look and listen to it, right now. But he wanted to do it alone.

"How did the commander even find them?" Darren asked.

"You think the other hybrids are okay?" Siena said.

Seth felt sick. They were asking him, as if he would know. How was he supposed to know?

"I hope so" was all he could say.

"What about the weapon they were trying to make?" Charles whispered. "The virus thing you told us about?"

"The commander said they'd destroyed it," said Esta.

"She didn't say that," said Seth. "She only said she'd destroyed all the rebels' war machines. And the rebels. She might not even know about the virus weapon. And where was Terra? She might've gotten away."

"The runner, right?" said Charles.

"Maybe she has the weapon," Siena said hopefully.

Esta sighed impatiently. "Guys, you can't keep doing this."

"Doing what?" Siena demanded irritably.

"Sitting on the fence. You've got to make a choice. A pretty obvious one. Humans or cryptogens. You're on the fence, but there's not going to be a fence much longer. It's going to be smashed by the cryptogens when they overthrow the planet. So pick a side. Yeah, go ahead and look horrified, but it's the truth."

"Some of us have people to lose, Esta," Siena retorted. "Like families, and friends."

"I'm just thinking of *us*, right here," Esta insisted. "All of us. The commander's offering us a home."

"Oh my God," whispered Siena. "You really do want to join them. You're a monster."

Esta's face hardened. "I'm a *survivor*. Come on, do you guys really care about those cryptogen rebels? They were never going to win—especially not now. These guys here, they're the winning team. And I want to be safe."

She looked right into Seth's eyes, as if to add: "I want to be safe *with you*."

"You really think they'll keep us safe?" He wanted to believe her. How nice it would be to stop worrying and just . . . let it happen. Wasn't this what he'd dreamed about, even as a little kid? A place where he'd be welcomed. Maybe this was it, right here. He had Esta. He had flight.

But he felt something holding him back—like a finger looped

through a belt loop, stopping him from rushing forward into this new future.

"Humans don't care about us," Esta said.

"Not true," said Seth. "Dr. Weber—"

"How many times have they tried to kill us?" she demanded. "They just fired a nuclear warhead at us! What's the matter with you guys? *We are not humans anymore!*"

A deep loneliness expanded through him. In the darkness of his thoughts, only four lonely planets orbited: Esta, Petra, Anaya, Dr. Weber. The only things that kept him from flying off into the cold universe.

He remembered Petra's face the night he left, the pained furrows in her forehead, the pressure of her encircling arms against his shoulder blades.

He remembered how Anaya had come to take his yearbook picture when he sat alone on the grimy school stairs. She'd liked his drawings. If she'd noticed the scars on his arms, she hadn't let on. She'd been his first proper friend on Salt Spring Island.

He thought of Dr. Weber promising to take care of him—more than she could give. But the moment he would never forget was when she'd asked if she could be his foster mother. Even now the memory caught a bit of sunlight in his mind.

But Dr. Weber had left him at the bunker—sure, she said she couldn't help it, but would she have done the same to Anaya or Petra? And *none* of them had come back to look for him when there were bugs and plants and humans hunting him. Even when he did get back on his own, it wasn't long before they'd figured out some new way to use him—test the rebels' virus on him, see if it took away his sonic power.

And then there was Esta. Whose childhood bones had broken easily, just like his. Esta, who'd been dumped at the hospital when her feathers came in, and abandoned. Esta, who'd drawn flying things like him, and whom he'd now, finally, flown beside. He wanted to be airborne again with her, away from everything.

He was tired of weighing his thoughts. Tired of feeling so heavy.

In his chest his heart felt hard, like a fist that wouldn't unclench.

And yet, in the back of his head, the general's sonic message vibrated like a bright box, wanting to be opened.

AGAINST THE DARKNESS ANAYA saw a gray flower with a single petal.

It looked so different from the ship she'd first seen on a monitor, back in Ritter's bunker. Then, it had been in full, terrible bloom. Now, all its petals had fallen earthward, landing in locations across the planet.

—*Why hasn't that one ship left?*

—*A reserve,* Terra explained.

Anaya thought of the rows upon rows of womblike sacs containing cryptogen soldiers, tubes nourishing their sleeping bodies, other tubes siphoning away their waste. The sacs' fabric massaging and exercising the muscles, keeping them strong for battle.

—*Are the soldiers awake now?* she asked Terra.

—*I don't know.*

—*Will they know we're coming?*

—*The commander will almost certainly have messaged the crew.*

Warily Anaya studied the long stem of the ship. It must have weapons.

—*Will they shoot at us?*

—*This scouting ship was designed to be invisible, even to our own technology.*

Terra rotated the ship, and Anaya caught a quick glimpse of Earth. She picked out the west coast of Canada and the skinny point of Vancouver Island. Hidden behind cloud was Salt Spring Island. Homesickness and panic formed a storm front in her brain. Before she could stop herself, she blurted out:

—*Can't you take me back first?*

She knew how scared she must sound, how cowardly. But she found the sight of the cryptogens' main vessel terrifying. She didn't want to go inside.

—*We don't have time,* Terra said. *I am sorry.*

And she did sound truly sorry. Which somehow made Anaya feel a little better. As their ship drew closer, her stomach churned like a washing machine. From inside her sac, she saw how immense the vessel was. The long stem of it was like some impossibly tall skyscraper. They skimmed along the hull.

—*Where do we dock?* Anaya asked.

—*Not in the landing bay. The moment we land, the ship will be alerted to an unauthorized entry. We cannot touch the hull.*

—*So how do we get inside?* Anaya asked in confusion.

—*A maintenance air lock that is not monitored.*

—*You mean, we'll just—*

—*I can bring us very close to the air lock; we will cross the distance ourselves.*

Anaya was aware she was breathing too quickly.

—*I'm not sure I can do that.*

—*I will help you.*

—*Wait, wait, don't we need suits and stuff?*

—*The sac will be your suit. It will give you the atmosphere you need.*

She saw that they had come to a stop, or were at least moving in tandem with the huge vessel. Maybe a hundred meters away was what must be the air lock, a circular blister on the ship's hull.

—*Tell the sac you want to see directly around you now.*

—*Can I do that?*

—*Yes.*

She blinked as she was suddenly back inside the ship, like being returned to her body. She was looking around with her own eyes—except they were covered by fabric—and there were her arms and legs and hands, similarly covered. Her personal space suit. Beside her was Terra, hanging in her own formfitting sac.

—*Stand, and detach yourself. Like this,* Terra instructed her, reaching up and taking hold of the umbilical cord above her head. She clenched it tight and severed it, so she was no longer connected to the hull. Anaya did the same. It reminded her of pinching off the stem of a plant. It was easily done, and the severed ends sealed themselves immediately. *Crazy-smart fabric,* she thought.

It was a bit unnerving looking at Terra, because her face was entirely concealed beneath fabric. Anaya watched her go to the wall and pluck out the translucent disk that contained the sample of the virus weapon. With this, they could change everything.

If they succeeded.

Terra slid the disk into a slim backpack and cinched it tight around her shoulders and chest.

—*We will need to depressurize our ship now,* Terra told her.

—*Okay.*

—*Breathe normally. I am turning off the gravity.*

—*Great.*

She waited to lift off the ground, but that didn't happen, not until she tried to take a step and slowly cartwheeled and hung upside down. She clung to a nearby cable, suddenly dizzy. With a great hissing noise, their atmosphere was vented into space. The air being fed to her inside her synthetic skin was as fresh and abundant as ever. She didn't notice any change in temperature either.

—We'll go out now.

The hatch to outer space opened as easily as a screen door in summer. Anaya stared at the gray surface of the enormous cryptogen vessel.

—Take my hand, Terra said.

Anaya had seen footage of spacewalks, and she knew there was supposed to be a lot more gear than this. Jet packs. Safety lines. Obviously, Terra hadn't seen any of these videos.

Anaya held tight as Terra carefully maneuvered both of them into the hatchway.

—When we reach the ship, you will see a number of rungs, Terra told her. *Grab hold of one. Or you will bounce off.*

—Okay. Have you ever done this before?

—No. Are you ready?

—No, but let's go.

Gently Terra pushed off with her feet. Anaya drifted out beside the runner, trying to look straight ahead. She didn't want to see the vast nothingness around her. The air lock swelled before her eyes.

—Grab hold, Terra told her.

She struck the air lock with surprising force, felt her suit cushioning her, and seized one of the metal rungs. Terra clung to another and was already pressing a hand into some kind of control portal. A hatch silently swirled open in the hull, and Terra tugged her inside.

With a backward glance, Anaya saw their spaceship, looking so small somehow—and then she realized it was actually drifting away.

—*Hey, our ship!*

Terra didn't even look back.

—*I did that on purpose,* the cryptogen told her.

—*What? But we're going to need it!*

Terra had already sealed the air lock behind them. Anaya heard a rush of air as the chamber pressurized, and her body quickly grew heavier as gravity returned. Clumsily she settled on the floor, feeling like she'd run a hundred laps. Terra was hurriedly unzipping herself from her suit, stepping out, and leaving it on the floor like a sloughed snakeskin.

—*I had to jettison our ship,* she explained. *If it were sighted, the crew might realize someone has come aboard. If we can go unnoticed inside, we will have a better chance.*

—*But how're we going to get back?* Anaya asked, bewildered. *How am I going to get home now?*

—*We will make a plan,* Terra said.

—*You mean there* isn't *one? You have no plan?*

—*I do not.*

Anaya's heart gave a panicked flutter.

—*So can we get another ship?*

—*Possibly.*

—*Possibly?* She felt a dual spasm of anger and panic in her chest. *What about my family? What about me? I'm not even sup-posed to be up here! I don't want to die up here!*

—*We need to move, and keep moving. Remove your suit and bring it with you.*

—*I can breathe in here, right?*

—*As well as I.*

Anaya unzipped and crumpled up the suit in her hands. It reduced to the size of a tissue. She put it in her pocket and looked around the small chamber. Apart from the hatch they'd entered, there was only one other place that looked like it might be a door into the larger ship. But Terra went to a different section of the wall.

With her claw, she cut a long vertical incision. She plunged both hands deep inside and pushed outward with a wet oozing sound, creating an opening.

—*This way,* Terra said.

"Not what I expected," Anaya murmured, but did as she was told. She pushed through into a very narrow corridor. Really, it was more like a tunnel. The amber light came from long fila-ments that looked like veins running through the fleshy walls and floors and ceiling. She turned to see Terra sealing the wound behind them. She couldn't even see a scar.

—*What is this place?* she asked.

—*The ship's tissue. We're less likely to be found in here.*

Wires like black vines shifted along the walls.

—*Plant vines?* she asked Terra nervously.

—Similar, but no. Much of the ship is biological.

It was like being inside the digestive tract of a huge animal. Pinocchio in the whale's belly. Coiled tubes made quiet glugging sounds. Others hissed secretively.

Terra led the way. There wasn't space to walk side by side. The walls weren't still. They trembled and puckered sometimes, and made wet swallowing noises. Anaya felt shaky, like her feet weren't touching the ground properly.

—Our gravity is weaker, Terra explained. *You might feel disoriented.*

Disoriented. Anaya couldn't help chuckling. Disoriented was the least of what she was feeling right now. But what Terra had said gave her a pleasing thought.

—Lower gravity means I'll be stronger and faster, right? she said hopefully.

—This is true.

Inside Anaya's head, Terra drew a blueprint of the ship. It was a long cylinder, with a central shaft as a thoroughfare and chambers surrounding it on all sides.

—We are here, Terra told her, making one end of the cylinder pulse. *And the incubators are here.* The opposite end of the map flared.

—Wow. That's a big walk, said Anaya.

—Once we arrive, we will produce a large culture of the virus and deliver it in a global rain.

It sounded so straightforward: Let's just take a nice little amble through the guts of this weird alien spaceship, shall we? Cook up some virus in the kitchen, send a gift basket down to Earth.

The guts of the ship were a maze, passages spidering out in all directions. Sometimes Terra touched a wall, like she was asking it something, but generally she seemed to know exactly where they were going. Anaya tried not to look too closely at the things that resembled lungs, stomachs, brains inside the walls. Fluids and energy flowing through the body of the ship.

—*Can you at least get a message to Petra?* she asked Terra. *Find out if everyone's okay down there? Let them know where I am?*

—*Not yet,* Terra replied. *We can't risk my signal being intercepted.*

Maybe it was panic, or the busy map still swirling in her head, or the low gravity, but every one of her senses was raw, and she suddenly felt nauseous. Her vision began to spin and accelerate like she was on some terrible carnival ride.

She stumbled against the wall and gripped the spongy surface with both hands for support. Immediately she felt a cool sonic shimmer in her mind. It reminded her of touching the hull of the small rebel ship, or being inside one of the sacs—like connecting to something big and vast and mysterious. Like someone asking you a question and waiting for you to respond.

The curious vibration in her head became more urgent, even hostile. And she realized her hands were stuck. When she tried to pull free, she saw that the fleshy tissue of the wall had actually grown *over* her hands.

"Hey!"

She jammed her knee against the wall so she had some leverage, then pulled back with her full weight. Nothing. With a jolt, the wall tugged her knee in and dragged her hands deeper, up to the wrists, then the elbows. It all happened so quickly. Off-balance, she staggered face-first against the wall. The spongy surface began to swallow her.

"I'M SURE ANAYA'S OKAY," Petra said. "I saw Terra's ship fly over the base, and she talked to me and said Anaya was with her and they had the weapon."

"I saw it, too," said Pearson. "And I also heard a sonic blast afterward."

Petra looked at the stricken faces of Mr. and Mrs. Riggs. Why did the colonel have to go and say that? She was trying to be positive for Anaya's parents. She'd heard the terrible thunderclap noise, too, and it had made her feel sick.

"Have you had any reports of a crash in the area?" Dr. Weber asked the colonel.

"No."

"Well, that's good news!" said Petra. "It means the ship didn't get blown up!"

"We have virtually no communications right now. We're not getting reports on much of anything."

They were assembled in one of the many large tents hastily set up among the ruins of Deadman's Island. All night and well into morning, they'd searched the rubble for more survivors. Luckily, all the hospital patients had been evacuated before the cryptogens annihilated the buildings. Her dad was with them now, helping set up the field hospital inside Stanley Park. Lots of soldiers had been injured and killed. All the base's vehicles and weapons had been destroyed.

"You didn't hear anything else from Terra?" Mrs. Riggs asked her.

Anaya's parents were leaning against each other, like it was all they could do to stay upright and keep breathing. Petra wanted to lie and tell them yes, Terra had told her they were fine and somewhere safe. Instead she said:

"No, but they were out of my range by then."

"Or keeping radio silence," added Dr. Weber hopefully.

"So why haven't they come back yet?" Anaya's father asked.

"I wouldn't, if I were them," said Pearson. "I would've gone straight to the main vessel."

"Really?" Petra said. Was their ship even properly fixed? She didn't voice this aloud.

"Terra has the weapon," said Pearson, "and the time to use it is running out, especially if the cryptogen leaders know about their plans. The general and the swimmer were still alive when they took them away—they'll be interrogated." His lined face was grim. "Likely they will reveal things."

Petra winced when she remembered the swimmer being hoisted brutally into the air by the flyer's talons. The general crumpled and moaning on the ground. They'd both been trying to protect all of them, the humans.

"So Anaya and Terra are probably on the big ship right now," Petra said, wanting desperately to believe her own story. She looked at the Riggses. "Anaya is super strong. Honestly, the bravest of all of us. She'll be fine."

Anaya's mom smiled tenderly and stroked her cheek. Petra had almost never let her own mother touch her like that, and regretted it now.

There was a patter against the tenting, and Petra made out the telltale shadows of the mosquito birds.

Pearson stood. "We need to get that protective netting back up. Stay inside." He looked at the Riggses and Petra with what was almost tenderness. "We are going to assume Anaya and Terra have reached the ship and are going ahead with our plan. We need to do the same on our end. Try to get some sleep till then."

Petra doubted she could sleep—did people sleep after something like this?—but she did, zipped into a sleeping bag for two oblivious hours. Afterward, she visited her father at the field hospital in Stanley Park and helped out there. They were taking a break together when Colonel Pearson found them and said, "Let's talk."

There was a jeep waiting for them outside, and they were driven back to Deadman's Island. Inside the command tent, a small group was waiting for them: a grave Dr. Weber, and a couple of solemn officers Petra recognized, and some soldiers she didn't. She glanced nervously at her dad; this all looked pretty serious, but what wasn't these days?

"I've spoken to the US military command to coordinate our next steps. We agree that we need to act quickly. Our resources, fuel, and manpower are only going to weaken. We're losing the fight against the cryptogenic plants and bugs. The worms are taking out more of our power stations, our factories. The more factories go down, the less pesticide and herbicide we manufacture. And there's a new factor: the air is getting more toxic for us. Which means our troops aren't fighting at full strength unless they have oxygen. So. You see my point. We need to strike now. We're proceeding with our plan to bring down the shield of the landing ship."

Petra seemed to be the only person confused by this.

"But how?" she said. "The general and the swimmer were supposed to plant the explosive."

"Very true," acknowledged Pearson. "We need to deliver the explosive another way."

Petra drew in a breath as she realized what was coming next.

"Hybrids can pass through the shield, too," she said. "Like me."

CHAPTER SEVENTEEN

—HELP! **ANAYA CRIED OUT** as the wall swallowed her.

She could scarcely shift her legs and arms. Where was Terra? Why wasn't she dragging her out? Moist things slithered and burped against her face. Her eyes clenched shut. It was like being engulfed in quicksand. What if all this pulpy stuff started going up her nose? Right now, she could still breathe, but how long would that last?

—You're too deep for me to reach, she heard Terra call out.

Too deep? How thick was this wall? She wasn't sure she was moving anymore, but the wall was definitely tightening around her.

—It's squeezing! she shouted silently. *Where are you?*

No answer. And all the while, there was a shrill wail in her head, like the wall was angrily interrogating her.

She heard a terrible wet rasping sound, like raw meat being cut with a serrated knife. Suddenly, something clamped around her left hand, and she gave a strangled scream as she was dragged face-first through the living wall and—

Out into a different corridor, where she collided with a swimmer cryptogen who still gripped her wrist. The swimmer stood tall on two legs, his jaws wide, his chest blazing red. Anaya pulled free and lost her balance. She hit the floor and scrambled back, trying to get out of range of the swimmer's venomous tail.

Crouched, she was about to leap and aim a clawed kick at the swimmer's chest. But in her head bloomed a light that went from pale yellow to a blazing orange in a split second. The lantern! The sign of the rebels! She faltered.

Behind the swimmer Terra burst into view, leaping down the corridor toward them. The swimmer turned and the two cryptogens actually embraced. Friends. With relief, Anaya sank back on the floor.

Brushing away the yolklike goo that streaked her body and clothes, she glanced at the wall and saw it already resentfully sealing itself up, making disapproving smacking and swallowing noises.

—*What just happened?* she asked Terra, getting shakily to her feet.

—*I am sorry,* Terra said. *This was my mistake. I should have warned you about touching the walls.*

—*The ship did not recognize you.*

These words came from the swimmer and were accompanied by a flicker of cloudy aquamarine light and a swampy odor. His chest no longer blazed red, and Anaya now noticed the intricate silver pattern that covered his smooth body.

—*It saw you as an infection,* the silver swimmer explained.

Infection! Maybe it was just a bad translation, but Anaya supposed it was accurate enough. She was an alien life-form here.

—*Why did you bring one of them aboard?* she heard the silver swimmer ask Terra disapprovingly.

—*It was unforeseen,* Terra replied. *Have any of our other teams returned?*

—*No.*

—*None of them?*

The disappointment and anguish in her words were heart-wrenching.

—*And how many of us are left up here?* Terra asked a moment later.

—*I am the last,* the silver swimmer replied, and Anaya felt the grief emanating from his silent words. *After all of you left for the planet, there was an investigation, and many were tortured and killed. Were you successful, at least? Do you have the weapon?*

—*We have the weapon,* Terra said.

—*Then we have a chance!* the swimmer exclaimed, standing tall, his chest swelling with a deep growl that Anaya assumed was jubilation.

—*Can you shut off the alarm?* Terra asked.

In Anaya's head, the wall's aggressive vibration had stopped, but for the first time she was also aware of a persistent wail sounding through the ship.

The swimmer put his hand to the wall, and a few seconds later the alarm stopped.

—*Soldiers are on their way,* the swimmer reported.

—*Can you convince them the alarm was an error?* Terra asked.

—*I will try. But we need to hide you first.*

—*Has the reserve ship been awakened?* Terra asked.

—*Not yet. It's still just a command crew. Small, but vigilant. We need to move now.*

The silver swimmer led the way, and Anaya fell into step behind him, keeping her hands close to her body so they wouldn't graze the walls. She listened as Terra quickly told the silver swimmer what had happened on Earth, and how they had left the general and the swimmer during the attack on Deadman's Island.

—*I fear for their lives,* Terra said.

Anaya felt a sick clenching in her stomach. She forced herself to pay attention to the here and now.

—*Are we going to the lab?* she asked.

—*No,* said the swimmer. *The soldiers will be coming from that direction. You two need to hide while I talk to them.*

He touched a wall, listened, and with a knife cut a long incision and parted it wide. Terra went through first and reached back for her.

—*Come through. You may find this startling.*

Anaya took Terra's hand and let her guide her through the opening—

And stifled a scream because she felt like she'd just been tugged out of the window of a skyscraper. Below her was a vast drop and she was staring right down into it, about to plunge. And yet she didn't. Her feet were planted firmly on the skyscraper's side, and so were Terra's, and both their bodies jutted horizontally out over empty air.

But in a radical shift of gravity and perspective, the side of the skyscraper was suddenly the floor, and she was simply standing upright. Terra steadied her as she swayed dizzily. In confusion, she looked back at the opening she'd just emerged from, and now *it* was in the floor, and the silver swimmer came through and seemed to effortlessly flip ninety degrees so he was standing upright beside them.

—*I don't understand this,* Anaya said, *and please don't explain it to me.*

Before her, a long circular corridor stretched away endlessly in both directions. Anaya wasn't great at guessing distances, but she figured the corridor's diameter was about the length of a city block. From the map Terra had drawn earlier, she guessed this must be the ship's central transit route. Right now it was deserted.

The silver swimmer knelt and healed the incision he'd cut in the floor, then stood and walked toward a metal platform that reminded Anaya of one of those window-washer rigs for skyscrapers, only bigger. She realized it was hovering a couple of inches in the air and didn't even shift when the swimmer stepped aboard.

—*Hurry. The soldiers will be here soon.*

The moment Anaya hopped on with Terra, the platform silently shot straight up. She fought the urge to close her eyes. Belting along the corridor, they crossed paths with a few other flying platforms that Terra told her were automated transports, carrying cargo to various regions of the vast ship.

The silver swimmer suddenly steered them higher toward the ceiling—but of course, *ceiling* wasn't the right word because there was no proper up or down. Still, when the platform tilted over on its side, Anaya couldn't help gripping the guardrail tightly, even though she wasn't at any risk of falling. Her feet stayed firmly planted on the platform, which was now hovering beside a huge doorway.

—*Go inside and wait till I come back for you,* said the swimmer.

As she followed Terra through the portal, she prepared herself for another mind-blowing sensory readjustment, but none came. She was simply walking down a wide entranceway that quickly brought her out onto a catwalk overlooking an enormous chamber. Immediately she recognized it from the images Terra had shown her.

Suspended from the ceiling were thousands upon thousands of sacs, hanging at different levels, containing cryptogen soldiers.

—This is the reserve ship! she said in astonishment. *Why'd he leave us here?*

—They are still asleep.

Still, Anaya thought, there must've been *somewhere* better to hide.

Crisscrossing the chamber at different altitudes were skinny catwalks. As she watched, one retracted, accordion-like, into the wall, and another extended, spanning the chamber.

—This is not typical, Terra told her. *Those catwalks usually come out only when they are waking the soldiers.*

—But the swimmer said—

From the bottom of the chamber, a flyer with green-and-gold wings swooped up and landed on a stretch of catwalk not far away.

Terra tugged Anaya behind the cover of some cables, and they both peeped out as the flyer proceeded to check one of the sacs with an instrument.

—We need to get out of here, Anaya said.

When she turned back the way they'd entered, she glimpsed a runner with yellow-white fur walking through the entranceway, gripping a rifle. Anaya shrank back against Terra.

—Is it a rebel? she asked hopefully.

—No, Terra replied, leading her silently down a set of steps to a lower level of catwalks. *They must be doing a search.*

Anaya saw several new catwalks stretch themselves across the chamber. But the one directly above them began to fold itself, taking the stairs with it.

—*Where now?* she asked Terra.

Terra was moving from one sac to the next, touching each briefly.

—*What're you doing?* Anaya asked.

—*We need to hide you.*

—*In one of those? There's already* people *inside!*

—*That's what will keep you safe.*

She felt a vibration beneath her feet, and her eyes flew along the catwalk. A few hundred meters away, it was folding itself up with alarming speed. In seconds, they'd have nothing to stand on.

—*Follow me!* Terra said.

Anaya pelted after her. She made the mistake of glancing back—and saw that the catwalk was gaining on them. When she faced forward again, Terra wasn't there. Too late, she realized that her rebel friend had leapt across to another catwalk.

—*Jump!* Terra called to her.

But she'd lost her chance. The way was now blocked by dangling sacs and cables. All she could do was keep running. Up ahead she saw a dead end where the catwalk slotted back inside the wall. She didn't have long.

Desperately she unzipped the nearest sac and saw a flash of feathers. She choked back a whimper. A flyer. No time to be choosy now. She squeezed herself inside just as the catwalk disappeared beneath her feet. Fighting back revulsion, she pushed herself deeper, the sac expanding to accommodate her. She zipped herself inside.

Total darkness now. She felt short of breath, but fresh air fizzed into her nose from the miraculous fabric. She made herself small, folding herself away from the sleeping cryptogen, trying not to cut herself on the edges of its wings. She was glad she couldn't see its face. This felt like the weirdest, wrongest thing in the world.

She pictured herself from the outside, dangling inside a sac like some monstrous fruit or cocoon. If someone was looking, would they see her stuttering heart against the fabric?

Was someone looking?

The idea was so paralyzing she stopped breathing for almost half a minute.

If those two cryptogens had heard her and Terra bolting along the catwalk, they'd be searching right now. And what if this sac thought she was a big infection, like the walls of the ship had? What if it started singing like some annoying fairy-tale object, and gave her away:

She's in here. Tra-la-la! Over here! Tra-la-la-laaaaa!

The flyer's body was cold against her, stealing her own warmth. Unexpectedly and urgently, she had to pee. She knew the sac was supposed to take care of stuff like that, just slurp it away, but she was in clothes. She'd wet herself and it would smell, and that might wake up the flyer.

A bony knee kicked her back.

That was normal, wasn't it? People shifted in their sleep all the time. Terra had promised it wouldn't wake up. Anaya stayed very still. Tried to take tiny sips of air, panic stomping around her head. Nowhere to go, except a drop of hundreds of feet. Where was Terra?

The flyer twitched an arm, and Anaya squeaked as a feather sliced her shirt and nicked her shoulder blade. It wasn't deep, but she could feel the stinging, wet line of it. She heard a sniff from the cryptogen. Then, from deep in its throat, came a low unearthly drumroll sound.

This thing was waking up. A single thought rampaged through her head:

Out, out, out.

Where was the zipper pull? Her fingers found it and pulled wildly.

She spilled out. It all happened in a split second. With a shriek she grabbed hold of the closest thing—which was the flyer's ankle—with both hands. Her lower half dangled outside the sac, kicking uselessly, and the flyer was getting dragged out with her. She caught a glimpse of the dizzying plunge awaiting her and closed her eyes. But she didn't fall. When she looked up, she saw the flyer holding tight, its head and shoulders still inside the sac, desperately trying to scrabble back into it.

—Let go!

The flyer's words were like a stunning blow inside her head. The cryptogen kicked, trying to throw her off, but she held on for dear life.

Anaya looked all around for a safe landing place. No catwalks in sight. Could she grab hold of some cables?

She could sense the flyer weakening, then slipping.

With a shriek they fell together. There was a clapping sound, and she saw the flyer's wings extend and start to flap desperately. But with her added weight, they were still falling, though more slowly.

—*Let go!*

These words weren't from the flyer. She looked around and saw, below her, a floating platform with Terra and the silver swimmer rising toward her.

She let go of the flyer's ankle, and fell—

And landed on the platform in a crouch, Terra grabbing hold of her to keep her from flying off as they accelerated, weaving through the dangling wombs and cables and catwalks. When she looked back, she saw the green-and-gold-winged flyer in pursuit.

—*We're being followed!* she shouted silently.

They burst out into the ship's main corridor, narrowly avoiding an automated transport, and the flyer veered after them but couldn't keep up with their hurtling speed. Anaya was relieved they were out of range of its sonic blast—though if it had been wearing its helmet, it could've crushed them by now. Maybe helmets were too powerful to use inside the ship without fatally damaging it.

—*Where are we going?* Anaya asked.

—*To the generators,* the silver swimmer answered. *The command crew knows there are rebels aboard.*

—*Won't they try to stop us?* Anaya asked.

—*We have something to discourage them,* Terra said, and pulled back a sheet of fabric. Lying on the floor were three pods that must have been severed from their cables.

—*Who's inside?* Anaya asked, worried they'd start moving.

—*Three high-ranking flyer warriors,* Terra told her. *We will keep them as hostages.*

—*Are they going to wake up? Because that other one woke up, and you told me it would absolutely* not *wake up.*

They were still barreling down the corridor, and suddenly two flyers were coming toward them. These ones wore armor and helmets. Their silent voices blared in Anaya's head like a loud-speaker.

—*Stop or we will attack!*

Anaya held tight as the platform accelerated. The walls of the corridor were a blur. In her head she heard Terra telling the fly-ers to move aside and hold their fire, unless they wanted three of their slumbering leaders killed.

For a breathless second Anaya couldn't tell if the flyers were moving out of the way, but at the last moment they must have, because the platform blasted past, unimpeded.

Anaya thought she could see an end to the corridor, though it didn't seem to be getting any closer. Suddenly the platform tilted and turned upside down and Anaya gave a squawk. It took her a few moments to reorient herself, and by then the platform had slowed and was skimming through a hatchway into a large chamber. The moment they stopped, the silver swimmer jumped off, ran back to the entrance, and did something at the wall that made multiple doors clench shut.

Stunned, Anaya looked around. It was like a laboratory and a multilevel biodome combined. There were hovering terraces of black grass, terrariums filled with pit plants, suspended spherical pods that contained more cryptogenic creatures than she could ever imagine: bugs, fish, birds, mammals. She wasn't clear whether they were dead or in some kind of torpor. Containers glittered from the walls, filled with liquids and squirming things.

Between all these different areas and levels ran tubes and cables, so the chamber looked like one of those optical illusions of impossible stairways going up and down but never meeting. In one section of the room were stacked rows of huge vats. It was like everything she'd ever imagined a mad scientist's lair should be. After all, this was where all the mad science had happened: all the seeds and eggs that had rained down on her planet. They had come from this place.

—*Are we safe here?* Anaya asked tentatively.

—*We will likely die here.*

—*What you just said, that is* not *good for morale! Maybe a little optimism?*

—*Optimism is a delusion,* Terra replied, *but I will never give up, and that is all we can do. Now we need to get to work.*

SETH WAITED UNTIL EVERYONE else was asleep.

Esta liked sleeping inside one of the sacs, but the others preferred the floor of the platform, like him.

He inhaled and opened the general's box in his mind.

The contents told him the story of what had happened on Deadman's Island when the flyers attacked. Seth saw it all, as though he were witnessing it himself. Enemy flyers searching for the rebels, destroying the aquarium. Anaya boarding the ship with Terra and escaping from the biodome. So she was safe! And Terra, too, and did that mean the weapon went with them?

He watched as the general fought the other flyers in the air above the army base, cutting off one cryptogen's head, giving chase to the commander herself as she pursued Terra's ship and tried to bring it down.

Heart hammering, he saw how the swimmer had saved Petra's life—and the lives of all the other hybrids—harpooning one flyer before getting snatched up by another and chained on a flying platform.

And then Seth watched as the general dived down to attack the commander, who was about to kill Petra. Seth saw the commander sever his wing and beat him with sound before heaving him aboard the platform and returning here.

There was more. Seth wished he could close his eyes during

the next bit, when the general was interrogated and beaten, but the best Seth could do was open his eyes briefly, to dull the intensity of the images, and try to breathe deeply and not cry out of sympathy.

Next came the general's words in his head:

—*There is one you can trust.*

Seth knew that the cryptogens didn't have names like humans did. They had sensory signatures: a unique smell and quality of light. What he received now was a whiff of ginger and a wavy reflection like sunlight off a pond.

—*He is a rebel,* came the eerie voice of the dead general. *He will contact you. Trust him.*

Seth felt like he was being given a responsibility. An order to fight.

—*And do not trust her,* came the general's voice once more.

In Seth's head flickered an image of Esta.

—*She was the one who betrayed us,* came the general's final words. *She told the commander where to find us.*

"YOU'RE NOT A SOLDIER," Colonel Pearson told Petra, "and there's no time to train you, so the plan we've come up with is very simple."

"Okay, good," Petra said.

Yesterday, against her father's objections, against her own gut instincts, she'd said yes, and volunteered to pass through the cryptogen shield and plant an explosive charge on the landing ship.

The moment she'd agreed, she felt like she'd split from her own body and was watching herself from afar. This morning she still felt slightly unreal, awaiting her orders in the command tent with Pearson and the other officers involved in the mission. She was glad her father wasn't here to argue with them about child soldiers and tell them they should find someone else to do it. She *was* glad, though, that Dr. Weber was sitting in. Her kind face made Petra feel a little better.

"What we're thinking," said a female officer whose name tag said CAPT. FOWLES, "is to lower you on a line from a helicopter."

A helicopter. Every time she'd been on a helicopter, she had not had a good time.

"Have you ever done any rappelling or mountain climbing?" Fowles asked her.

"An indoor rock-climbing wall, a couple of times," she replied.

"Great," said the captain, picking up a harness from the floor. "So you'll wear one of these, and we'll lower you. It'll be a passive drop: we'll control your speed, you really won't need to do anything. We'll lower you right through the shield, and when you touch down on top of the ship, all you'll need to do is unhook

yourself from the line—we'll show you how to do that in a bit—
and deliver the charge to the site."

"Sure," said Petra.

"So here's the device," said another soldier, whose name tag
said LT. JAMES. He passed her an object about the size of a brick.
"It's okay, you can hold it. It doesn't go boom until we tell it to.
Not too heavy, right? You put it at the base of the transmission
mast and flick this switch here." He actually flicked it and Petra
leaned back. "Don't worry, it's not armed yet. And that's it. You're
done."

"You hook yourself back onto the line," Captain Fowles said,
"and press this little button on the harness, here, and that tells us
you're hooked on and ready to come up. Simple."

"No problem," Petra said. "I must've done this, like, ten times
at least."

She had to make a joke of it; it was the only way she was going
to get through this. Nonetheless, a troubling thought occurred
to her.

"But won't they hear the helicopter up there?" she asked.

"The Americans are supplying one of their new stealth helicopters," Pearson said. "It's incredibly quiet and has almost no
radar profile."

"Thing's virtually invisible," said Fowles.

"You're also going in at night," Pearson added. "The cryptogens are only active outside during the day. Farming, hunting.

Outside, they still need to wear masks, and it's cold for them, especially without sunlight. Our drones haven't noticed any sentries posted outside the ship. They know they're impregnable behind that shield. I don't think they're too worried about anyone or anything getting past it."

"There's one thing I want, though," Petra said. She'd been thinking about it since the moment she woke up. And, if she was honest, it was probably a big reason *why* she'd agreed to do this crazy thing at all.

"I want to rescue Seth and the others."

She looked around at all the serious grown-up faces.

Pearson compressed his lips and stared her down. He had a good stare. "No chance, Petra."

"Just listen first. I can send him a message. Or get one to Charles. I can tell them we're coming, and maybe they can get out. And we can lift them off with me!"

For the first time, Dr. Weber spoke. "There are five hybrid kids there, Colonel. It's reasonable to want to save them."

"It's completely unreasonable," he replied coldly. "Because Seth is a traitor."

"What?" Petra cried.

"How do you think the flyers found us?" Pearson said. "They knew *exactly* where we were and what they were looking for. Someone told them, and the only person who knew was Seth."

Petra was shaking her head. "No . . . he wouldn't do that."

"We have surveillance video of him flying above the ship, Petra. Wearing a cryptogen flight pack. Flying with Esta."

The image caused her an almost physical pain. The two of them in the air. Like something from one of Seth's dreams.

"So what?" she said, blinking to keep from crying. "Doesn't prove anything."

"Petra, it looks like he's cooperating with them. They're teaching him how to fly. I can't see why they'd do that unless he agreed to help them. Seth must've traded them information—the information that led them here. He could've escaped, but he chose to stay."

No. Seth might've had his heart scrambled by Esta, but not his brain. He wouldn't have signed on with them. When he'd left—and she'd *let* him leave—he said he only wanted to rescue Esta. That was it.

"You drove him away!" she said viciously. "You were going to test the virus on him. If you'd just rescued Esta yourself, he'd be here right now, fighting with us!"

A charged silence hung over the group. Petra counted it with her racing pulse.

"At least let me send him a message," she said.

"Even if you're right," said Pearson, "even if Seth is loyal, that message might be intercepted. It's too risky. It endangers your life, and our entire mission. No messages, agreed?"

"I can't believe you're just going to let them all die in there."

"This is war, Petra."

"What about all that stuff about never leaving your guys behind? All that stuff?"

"You need to agree, Petra, or we're not letting you do this. We'll find someone else."

She looked at his unflinching expression and knew he meant it. She swiped away the tears blurring her eyes.

"Agreed," she said.

CHAPTER EIGHTEEN

—*DOES THE COMMAND CREW know what we're trying to do in here?* Anaya asked Terra.

—*If they don't already, they will soon suspect,* the runner replied as she and the silver swimmer unceremoniously dragged the three bagged flyers across the chamber and plugged their sacs into a bundle of cables.

Anaya eyed the sealed hatch nervously, imagining the soldiers who must be massing on the other side.

—*Won't they just blast the doors open?* she asked.

—*They'll be worried about killing the flyers.*

Anaya wondered if these three hostages would be enough to deter the cryptogens from attacking. She hoped these slumbering flyers were really, really important.

—*What are you doing in here?*

The unfamiliar voice in her head smelled like pipe smoke and glimmered like embers, and Anaya spun around to see a stooped runner with grizzled fur emerging from a tangle of machinery.

—Are you the engineer on duty? Terra asked him.

—Yes, and who are you?

The grizzled runner's eyes took in Terra and the silver swimmer, then rested on her, Anaya, almost fearfully. She had to remind herself that this runner had probably never seen a creature like her before.

—We need to make a new rain, Terra told the grizzled runner.

—Under whose orders?

In answer, Terra created a flare of light that appeared in Anaya's head, too. It was the rebel lantern, and even though she'd seen it twice now, it still made her breath snag and filled her with hope.

—No, snapped the grizzled runner. *I'll have no part in your rebellion. No, no.*

—You have no choice, the silver swimmer said brusquely.

—I am content, said the runner. *I have my life, and I want to keep it.*

Anaya watched Terra and the other rebel, wondering how they were going to deal with this.

—We are giving you a chance to fight for true freedom, said the silver swimmer.

—I am too old to fight, said the grizzled runner fretfully. *Open the hatch and let me leave.*

Anaya felt a pang of pity for the stooped runner.

—No. That is not possible, Terra said. *Leave and they will kill you. Like it or not, you are involved.*

The old runner's eyes turned longingly to the hatch, and then he gave a heavy sigh.

—*Tell me about this rain you want.*

—*It will rob the flyers of their power.*

—*Truly?*

—*Yes, if we can make it fast enough.*

From her backpack, Terra produced the translucent disk filled with the virus weapon, and Anaya watched as she talked privately with the grizzled engineer. They inserted the disk into a section of the wall and, placing their hands on various consoles, began their work. She heard machinery start to whisper and gurgle. After a while, the older runner stalked off to another tangle of machinery, making discontented grunts.

—*What's happening now?* Anaya asked Terra.

—*The virus is being sent to the vats to be cultured. When we have a critical mass, we will load it into the seeding pods and launch them.*

—*What about the weather event to make the rain?* Anaya asked.

—*The pods themselves have the machinery to create ideal weather conditions. Only then will they release the virus into the rain.*

—*So how long will all this take?*

Time was still tricky to convey between them, but Anaya got a sense of less than a day. Again her eyes flicked nervously to the hatch.

—*Will we last that long?*

—I don't know. But I will tell our friends on the planet to prepare.

Anaya's heart leapt.

—Can you find out about my parents, and Petra?

—No. My message must be swift, to try to avoid detection.

Anaya waited and watched Terra's face. Her tall ears gave a twitch and her forehead creased in alarm.

—What's wrong? Anaya asked.

—I cannot reach the general or the swimmer.

—Maybe they're out of range?

—Or dead.

Anaya swallowed. She and Terra had flown away from Deadman's Island while it was under attack. Her last glimpse of the swimmer was of zir darting into the night with zir harpoon gun. The general had soared into the night sky with his armor and helmet, knowing he could no longer strike with sound. Did they even have a chance? Did any of the *humans* have a chance?

—Try Petra, Anaya said anxiously.

Terra's eyes lost their focus for a moment, and then she said to Anaya:

—She is alive. I told her to prepare for the rain.

Anaya let her shoulders relax and almost started to cry. Petra. She regretted every mean thing she'd ever done and said to her friend. If they survived this, she would be the perfect friend forever. And if Petra was alive, there was a decent chance her parents and the others were, too.

All Terra and her team had to do was hold tight, keep the cryptogens on the other side of that hatch, and let loose with a global rainstorm.

The light in the room flickered out, and the burbling machinery suddenly went silent.

"THEY'RE OKAY!" PETRA CRIED out. "They got aboard the big ship! And they're going to send rain!"

Terra's grass-scented voice had taken her completely by surprise, blooming in her head loud and clear and just as quickly disappearing before she could ask a single question.

"Who just talked to you?" Dr. Weber asked.

The two of them had been busy stowing their few belongings beneath the bunks in the crew quarters of the HMS *Carr*. Off the coast of Vancouver Island, the frigate had become their new base of operations.

"Terra, it was definitely Terra!" Petra said, unable to stop smiling.

"You're sure?"

"And Anaya's up there, too!"

"We need to tell this to the colonel," Dr. Weber said, and together they made their way through the cramped companionways of the ship. Eventually they found Pearson on deck, talking with Captain Fowles and some other officers.

"There's the USS *Sanders*," an officer said, with a pair of binoculars to his eyes.

On the horizon, Petra caught sight of the outline of a massive aircraft carrier. It was very impressive, but she didn't care about that right now. She blurted out everything Terra had just told her.

"And you're sure about the timing?" Pearson asked. "Twelve hours?"

"Time's always a bit wonky," she admitted. "But yeah, I'm pretty sure."

"Doesn't leave us much time to prep," said the colonel, "but this is good news, very good news." He turned to the other officers. "Let's set a meeting with the joint military command."

They left her with Dr. Weber. The bracing, salty breeze made Petra suddenly homesick for Salt Spring Island but also amplified her happiness and hopefulness. They could win. She looked out at the aircraft carrier. She'd overheard soldiers talking about all the fighter planes and helicopters it carried. And she knew there were still more battleships coming, to form an armada. All waiting to unleash their weaponry on the cryptogens' landing ship.

Once the shield came down.

And that was up to her. She'd been trying not to think about it. Every time her mind wandered too close to it, she started to short-circuit.

"I don't think Seth betrayed us," she said to Dr. Weber.

"I don't either, Petra."

"When the attack starts on the ship, do you think they'll leave any time for Seth and the others to escape?"

"I don't know. They may—" Her voice faltered. "They may already be dead. I think we have to be ready for that possibility."

Petra knew it was war, and that one kid or five didn't matter much when the survival of the human race hung in the balance. It would be incredible luck if Seth and the others got out of there alive. The best chance would be if the rain came fast, and the flyers lost all their power, and the runners and the swimmers turned against them right away. Or . . .

She could break her promise to Pearson.

Dr. Weber didn't want to lose Seth. And neither did she. She returned to her bunk and pulled the privacy curtain. She turned herself in the direction of Point Roberts—or what she thought was the right direction. She quieted her mind.

And couldn't do it. She couldn't send Seth a message.

She clenched her fists in her blanket and growled into the pillow until her eyes burned. She'd made terrible decisions before, like trusting Dr. Ritter in the bunker, and feeding him information that he'd ended up using against the hybrid kids, especially Seth. Like diving into the water and eating water strider eggs, so Anaya's mother ended up getting bitten by a mosquito bird, and almost dying. And her latest disastrous decision: letting Seth run away from the base to rescue Esta. She could've stopped him. She *should've* stopped him.

Making another bad decision wasn't going to change things.

Pearson was right. Sending Seth a message could ruin every-thing.

—*THEY'VE SHUT DOWN OUR* power, Terra said.

—*I'm surprised it took them so long,* the silver swimmer remarked. *The chamber's ventilation fans have shut down, too.*

The grizzled runner came back looking grumpier than ever.

—*The cultures will die if we can't power the vats.*

—*Is there a backup generator or something?* Anaya asked.

The old runner gave a visible sigh, plucked a knife from his tool belt, and muttered silently, as much to himself as anyone else:

—*The flyers never did bother themselves much with the ship's guts. That was work for runners and swimmers. But it means we know the guts better than anyone. And no one knows the guts better than me. . . .*

He made a sound that might have been laughter and headed for the wall. He cut an incision, jumped into the pulpy mess, and disappeared from sight.

—*He's sane, right?* asked Anaya.

—*I'm more worried he might be trying to escape,* the swimmer said, hurrying over and poking his head into the opening. *I cannot see him.*

Anaya's heart sank. In her head came the scorching voice of a flyer from beyond the chamber's sealed hatch.

—*You are powerless. And your atmosphere will expire soon. Open the hatch or you will suffocate.*

—*No,* replied Terra.

—*We will blast the door open, then.*

Anxiously, Anaya turned to Terra, wondering how she'd respond.

—*Against the hatch,* Terra said, *is the sleeping body of the commander's second-in-command. If it were known that he was killed by your blast, while lying defenseless, the commander would be most displeased. As you know, she is not merciful with those who displease her.*

It was a convincing speech, and was met with a sullen silence.

—*Good work,* Anaya said to her. *Do we really have the second-in-command?*

—*I have no idea. We took three random flyers. We did not have time to discover who they were.*

The lights came back on, and with them, the encouraging hum and glug of machinery and hiss of air from unseen vents. Shortly after, the grizzled runner pushed himself out of the wall, coated in goo the color and consistency of rice pudding. How could he navigate his way through all that stuff? But he had, and had gotten power and air back for them.

—*Helps when you know your way around the guts, yes?* he said triumphantly.

—*If he can come through the walls,* Anaya said to Terra, *can the flyers?*

—Yes, and that may be their next plan of attack.

Terra's furred face creased with sudden worry. She leapt to the wall and put her hand against it.

—They're coming now.

SETH WALKED PAST THE field of black grass with Esta and Charles, Darren and Siena. The cryptogen shield fell over a large part of Point Roberts and the surrounding coastline, including a big park where masked runners were cultivating and harvesting black grass.

Seth supposed this was his yard time, to get some fresh air, maybe to try to trick him and his friends into thinking they weren't really prisoners.

Esta smiled at him, like they were enjoying a pleasant stroll in the park. He smiled back and hoped she couldn't tell he was faking it. It was hard for him to meet her eye now.

Knowing what she'd done.

Maybe it wasn't true. Maybe it was a lie, but how could he find out without revealing he'd been contacted by a rebel? He hadn't even told the others what he'd learned from the general's message. He was too worried they'd let something slip—and he didn't even know what he was supposed to do with this terrible news yet. Esta, a traitor.

"Why don't we just run for it?" Darren said impatiently.

"Don't think we'd make it very far," Charles commented.

Seth agreed. All around them were runners and flyers, and they were definitely being watched by the two cryptogens who had escorted them outside on a floating platform.

Still, the urge was strong. Make a break for it. Would there ever be a better time?

"Go ahead," said Esta, "but I don't think you'll get a happy welcome on the other side of that shield."

—*Do not run.*

This voice had never bloomed in his head before, but he recognized it instantly from the general's message. A gingery scent, a lacy white light.

—*Who are you?* Seth asked, looking around.

—*You don't need to know yet.*

—*We want to escape.*

—*If you try, you will be caught and punished. And you will not get a second chance at freedom.*

—*What do you want?* Seth asked.

—*Your help. Before he died, the general said we could trust you.*

Seth wasn't sure he wanted to trust anyone ever again. So he asked:

—*The commander said we'd be safe in the new world, after the invasion. Is that true?*

—*No. She fears you all.*

This surprised him. *Why?*

—*You are stronger in some ways. Your bodies. Perhaps even your sonic weapons.*

This was truly startling news. *Really?*

His face must've given him away, because he heard Darren ask, "You all right?"

"Fine," he said.

"You're not talking much," Esta said.

"Yeah, sorry, I'm just stuck in my own head," he said, and realized he had no idea what anyone had been talking about for the past minute or so. He didn't want to lose his connection with the rebel, though.

—*Is the commander going to kill us?* Seth asked.

—*She will breed your hybrid kind as forced labor. You will join the runners and swimmers as her eternal laborers.*

Seth stared out at sea, trying to keep his face calm. So much for the commander's promise of a new world in which they could all thrive together as equals.

—*Why aren't you all rebelling?* he asked.

—*We will. But we need to destroy the shield first. There is a plan to send a rain from our primary vessel.*

—*A rain?*

—*You are aware of the weapon the rebels were trying to create?*

—*The one that steals the flyers' sonic power.*

—*Yes. A rebel team is aboard the vessel, creating it now. We need* to destroy the landing ship's shield so the humans can attack and drive the flyers out into the open.

—*This is incredible! So why don't you guys just wreck the shield?*

—*Only a flyer can do it. With a sonic blast. Without the general, we have no flyer rebels aboard this ship.*

Seth grimaced. Ah. So he was needed again. He was useful.

"You talking to someone?" Esta asked, jostling his arm.

"What? No."

"Because I know your face pretty well, and that's the look you get when you're silent talking."

"I'm just fried, all right?" he said testily. "I feel like my head's going to explode. I don't know what we should be doing anymore."

"Then let me decide," Esta said, and kissed him on the cheek.

—*I will show you the way to the shield,* the rebel was saying.

—*I can't go anywhere. They left us stranded on our platform.*

—*I will teach you how to fly it yourself.*

Very quickly, the rebel taught him a sonic password, like a little song. Seth repeated it to him until he had it memorized.

—*Yes. After that, the platform will be in your command. Now here is the map.*

In his head, another small glowing box appeared.

—*After you destroy the shield, you can escape with your friends on the platform. But not the one who betrayed us.*

Esta.

—Are you sure she told the commander where to find the general?

He still cradled a wilting hope that Esta was innocent.

—The commander herself told me it was your friend, the rebel said.

Seth glanced at Esta, who was watching him curiously. He dropped his gaze.

—I can't leave her behind, he said.

—You must, said the rebel. *She's a threat that must be eliminated, or she'll betray us again.*

CHAPTER NINETEEN

THE HELICOPTER WHISPERED THROUGH the night sky. It was certainly the smoothest, quietest helicopter Petra had ever been inside. The cabin was lit by a pale blue glow; even the extensive cockpit controls emitted only a spectral glimmer. She took a peep through the small tinted window and saw only darkness as they crossed the strait toward Point Roberts—and the cryptogen landing ship. It was time.

She'd made her good-byes to Dad on the frigate's helipad; he'd wanted to come along, but she'd begged him not to. Having him here would make her feel too much like a little kid, and she needed to feel invincible right now.

All day, ships had been gathering in the Strait of Georgia, waiting to launch their attack the moment the shield came down. And she knew that around the world—Japan, Mexico, France— other armies were quietly launching similar missions, using hybrid kids to bring down the shields of the landing ships—and hoping for rain.

Her thoughts flew up to Anaya and Terra, beyond the sky. She wished they'd send her just one more message, telling her they were still safe, that the rain would come, right on time.

Her eyes skittered nervously across the people sharing the cabin with her. Captain Fowles and Lieutenant James, and Colonel Pearson himself. Weirdly, she felt comforted that he was here. Pearson was pretty badass when it came down to it, and even aliens might think twice about tangling with him. But it also made her think the mission couldn't be so dangerous, since surely the army wouldn't want to risk losing a colonel.

In her headphones, the amazingly calm voice of the pilot said: "Five minutes."

It was a good thing she hadn't eaten any dinner; she would've thrown it up by now. She licked her dry lips, stared at the floor, breathed.

"Let's get you rigged up," said Captain Fowles.

As Petra stepped into the harness and started fastening clasps, she was glad her hands and mind had something to focus on. Mounted in the cabin ceiling were the winch and spool of cable that would lower her. She'd already practiced how to clip the cable onto the harness, but she did it some more now, on and off, on and off, until she could do it in a matter of seconds, without even looking.

"One minute," the pilot warned them serenely.

She was dressed head to toe in black. They'd even made a kind of black sleeve for her tail. Fowles handed her the gloves.

"It'll be cold up high," she said.

Petra slipped them on. Her hands were trembling. The lieutenant helped her on with the backpack that contained the explosive device.

"When it's in place, just flick the switch," he reminded her. "Simplest thing in the world."

"Yep."

"You're going to have one heck of a story to tell," Pearson said, giving her a rare smile.

"I'd rather have no story and survive," she said.

More intensely than ever before, she missed Anaya and Seth. Over the past months they'd been through so much together, and they were strongest that way. She didn't want to be doing this alone.

"I think you're one of the bravest people I've ever met," Pearson told her.

Petra swallowed, afraid she might start crying.

"I liked the old Pearson better," she said. She didn't want anyone being kind to her right now. She wanted orders, terse, barked. Pearson was happy to oblige.

"You have one objective," Pearson said, looking at her sternly. "And only one."

"One objective, got it," she said, feeling a deep stab of guilt.

Late yesterday, she'd broken the promise she made to Pearson and herself. She'd sent a message to Seth. She wanted to help win this war, yes, and save the human race, but she could *not* go to the landing ship—the place where Seth was being held prisoner—and just *leave* him there. Especially since it was her fault he was there in the first place.

So, last night in her bunk, sleepless, she'd searched for Seth's telepathic light.

Was it another terrible decision? Maybe. Probably.

It had been incredibly difficult to find him. Her head had filled with static, and she'd realized she was seeing the flicker of thousands of cryptogens communicating telepathically. But she forced herself to focus only on Seth's silent voice, the scent of it, the light: the things that were as unique as the whorls of his fingerprint.

Only one of him in the world.

Where was he? She'd felt exhausted, and hopeless—maybe Dr. Weber was right: he was already dead.

But then she'd found it. His light. It was so frail, like a wisp of smoke from an extinguished candle.

—*Seth? Seth!*

She listened fiercely. No reply. And tried once more before all trace of him evaporated.

—*Seth! Come on!*

—*Petra?*

In her joy she'd sat bolt upright and banged her head on the underside of the upper bunk.

—*Yes, it's me, Petra! Can you get outside, on top of the ship, in four hours?*

She felt like the connection between them was weak, the

worst phone connection in the world. She hoped he could hear all her words.

—*Four hours?* he said back to her.

—*Yes. I am coming to rescue you. Just be on top of the ship!*

And she'd let their brief wispy connection dissolve.

"Approaching target," said the pilot now.

She removed her headphones. She tested her straps and harness line. Darren would've loved to do this. This was the stuff he'd been dreaming about. Special Ops. She couldn't help smiling. He'd be so pissed when he found out. If he ever found out.

"Good to go?" Pearson asked her.

"Good to go."

The lieutenant slid the door open and cold night air punched its way into the cabin. Captain Fowles nodded at her and helped her step backward outside, onto the landing strut. Shivering, she did not look down, not yet. She doubted there'd be anything to see, they were so high.

She got the thumbs-up and stepped off.

They'd warned her it would be fast, but that hardly prepared her for the insane plunge as the line unspooled. She would've screamed if she hadn't been paralyzed with terror.

In her head was a deep, building thrum, and she realized she must be approaching the shield. She pried her eyes open. Below her was a faint purplish film suspended in the air. The noise inside her head became more intense and terrifying as she hurtled toward the shield. She tensed as she struck it. The noise inhabited every bone and tendon and tooth in her body—it could break her, destroy her—and then she was through it, and it was fading.

She stared down, still not able to see anything. She suddenly felt very exposed—all that air around her, and what if a flyer was nearby and plunged toward her? With one sonic blow she'd be pounded into a pancake.

Finally she made out the ship, which was coming at her with worrying speed. She hoped they knew what they were doing up top—and that the sensor on her harness was working. Immediately she decelerated and a second later made a smooth landing on the ship's surface.

She unclipped herself from the line, which hung there, swaying slightly in the breeze, like a strange playground swing.

Slowly she turned in a circle. A few hundred meters away was the shield antenna. It created a dangerous purple vibration in her head.

One objective, Pearson had told her.

Not true.

She looked all around for Seth and the others. There wasn't anywhere to hide. No walls or slopes, except for the throbbing shield antenna. She felt like she was standing in a huge field, waiting for a lightning strike. As for doors, there was no sign of them, not that she could see. How did people even get out here?

She crouched and headed toward the antenna. Halfway there she heard a spectral hiss and pivoted. Light shone up from an opening in the ship's hull.

Silhouetted against the light was a head.

"Seth?" she whispered.

Anxiously she made her way back to the winch line. What if it wasn't Seth? Her gaze was welded to that silhouetted head. Her shaking fingers fumbled with the hook, ready to clasp it back to her harness and push the button if something terrible came out of that hatch.

"Seth," she hissed. "Say something. Please."

A lone figure climbed out and stood, still shadowed by the light from the hatch. She saw the jagged edges of feathers. Was Seth so tall? Were his legs quite that thin?

"Petra?" It was Seth, absolutely Seth, hurrying toward her. "I half thought your message was a trick!"

He grabbed her by the shoulders and she threw her arms around him, hugging him tight. Behind him, more figures emerged from the hatch. In the wash of light, she saw Charles, Darren, and Siena. No Esta.

"Awesome," said Darren, looking at the harness. "We getting airlifted out?"

She knew Pearson was watching everything from the helicopter. She could imagine his fury right now. There would be a lot of swearing.

Back at Ritter's horrific bunker, she'd watched, helpless, as Pearson ordered the helicopters up before all the hybrid kids were aboard. She wouldn't let him do it again. She'd send them all up and go last.

"C'mon," she told Seth, shrugging off her harness and holding it out to him. "Put this on, and I'll hook you in."

She wanted him in that helicopter before anything went wrong. She wanted him safe.

"Siena first," Seth said.

"I'm a feminist," said Siena, "but yeah, hook me into that thing."

Hurriedly Petra clipped her into the harness, hooked it onto the line, and pressed the button. Siena was reeled up into the air, fast.

"Where's Esta?" Petra asked Seth.

"Asleep. I hope."

Something must have happened to her, or between them. Petra didn't care what the reason was.

Charles was watching the hatch anxiously, like he was afraid something was going to come through any second. Darren's eyes were fixed on the sky, waiting for the empty harness to come back down.

"I've got a bomb," Petra said, nodding at the transmission antenna. "We need to blow that up, and when the shield comes down, the army hits the ship with everything they've got."

"And then the rain comes," Seth said.

"How'd you know that?" Petra asked him in surprise.

"What rain?" Charles asked.

"I'll tell you later," Seth said. "Here comes the harness."

"Looks like you get to be Special Ops after all," she told Darren as she helped strap him in.

"Thanks, Petra," he said, and then his eyes looked past her shoulder.

She turned to see Esta walking toward them in the cold predawn light.

"What's going on?" she asked.

Petra pushed the signal button, and Darren was hoisted high.

"Who's up there?" Esta asked, squinting into the sky. "Is it Pearson?" She looked at Petra, then Seth. "You weren't even going to tell me you were leaving?"

"Why would I have told you?" Seth asked her. "You want to stay here!"

Petra noticed something new between them: fear. Seth was scared of her now.

"You want to stay here, too," Esta said to him. "You're making a big mistake if you leave."

"Listen," Petra said, trying to make things better. "You can trust Pearson now. Things have changed. Everyone's working together. Humans and hybrids and the rebel cryptogens. No more tests on hybrids. You guys'll be safe!"

Esta scoffed. "Yeah, right! And did Pearson actually *tell* you to rescue us?"

"Yes!" Petra lied. "That's why I'm here."

"But it was okay to leave *me* behind—just like last time?"

"Come with us," Petra said, feeling like she was dealing with a dangerous and unpredictable animal. She hated the idea of Esta in the helicopter with them. What if she blasted everyone with sound?

The empty harness dropped back down, and Petra went to steady it, but Esta got there first. She held the line in her clenched fist, like she just wanted to be helpful.

"We don't have much time," Petra said, fighting the tremor in her voice. "Seth, you want to go next?"

She wanted him in that helicopter, away from Esta.

"Charles first," he said.

Why was Seth so reluctant to go? A terrible thought crept into Petra's head. Did he really not *want* to? Was he plotting something with Esta?

Petra started helping Charles into the harness, aware that Esta was watching her every move.

"Up you go," said Esta as Charles was lifted into the sky.

It was just the three of them now.

"What's in the pack?" Esta asked her.

Petra said nothing. Maybe she could get Esta to go up next.

"Tell me."

"Nothing," Petra said, and a grenade exploded inside her head and she crumpled at the knees. She heard Seth telling Esta to stop. Her vision twisted into a pretzel, went black for a second. When she could see straight again, Esta had wrenched off her backpack and was holding the explosive device.

"See this?" Esta said to Seth. "She was going to blow us up!"

"It's for the shield," Petra grunted, getting to her feet. "And it doesn't go off until we're all out of here." She looked up and saw the harness returning. "You go next."

Esta's wing flashed out and slashed through the cable. The harness clattered to the deck along with the clasp. The severed end of the cable swayed uselessly.

"You're crazy!" Petra raged. "That was our way off!"

"We don't need a way off," Esta said. "Seth and I can leave anytime we want."

Petra looked at the two of them, not knowing what to think. The sudden pain in her head made her choke. She couldn't even scream, couldn't beg for the pain to stop.

It stopped. She saw Esta stagger back, one hand clamped to her head, looking at Seth in astonishment.

"You hurt me!"

"Leave her alone, Esta," Seth told her, and then he stumbled back, wincing as she struck him with sound.

"Why can't you make the right choice?" Esta said, and Petra saw that the other girl was crying. "It's so simple, and you keep picking the wrong people."

Petra watched as the two of them faced off, and realized neither truly wanted to hurt the other. She grabbed the severed line and tried to fasten it somehow to the harness.

—*Petra,* came Darren's panicked voice in her head. *Pearson says you need to place the explosive—*

—I need to fix the harness first! Can someone tell me how—

—Petra!

—Just tell me how to make a freaking knot!

—Petra! Darren shouted again. *There's cryptogens—*

She was suddenly, terrifyingly aware of a tall flyer with white and blue and gold wings standing a few feet away. She knew this flyer; she was the one who'd cut off the general's wing. Beside her were a runner with a rifle, and a swimmer with a harpoon gun.

—Commander, Petra heard Esta say. *This swimmer hybrid helped the others escape, and she was trying to destroy the shield's transmission tower.* She held up the explosive device for the commander to see. *Seth and I stopped her.*

In dismay Petra looked at Seth, whose eyes flicked to Esta. What would he say? He said nothing, and Petra's heart crumpled.

—Go! she yelled to Darren up in the helicopter. *Now!*

She saw the line disappear as the helicopter reeled it in, and hoped it was already very far away.

—Take her inside, the commander said.

The cryptogen's silent words were like cigar smoke inhaled directly into her lungs. She coughed, her eyes watering. Never had she felt so desperate. She hadn't delivered the explosive to the transmission mast.

She hadn't rescued Seth.

She had failed Pearson and the entire planet.

CHAPTER TWENTY

HIGH IN THE SHIP'S vast central chamber, Seth stood uneasily on a platform with Esta. Beside them were the commander and her two armed lieutenants, the runner and the swimmer. The commander held no weapon—she didn't need to, because she had the most powerful one of all inside her head.

Slightly below them, all alone on a second platform, was Petra, looking utterly desolate. Though he couldn't hear her sobs, he saw her shoulders shaking. He wanted to speak to her but didn't dare.

Around the chamber circled more flyers. Platforms crowded with other cryptogens jostled for position. Seth felt sick. It was just like the execution of the general and the swimmer.

The commander leapt from the platform to address the chamber. Her voice blazed in Seth's head, filled with power and fury.

—Look! The enemy sent her to destroy our shield. She is one of those that we created, to share our future! She is ungrateful, like the other three who escaped. We sheltered them, protected them from the humans who would have tortured and killed them. We healed them.

And they betrayed us, and conspired to destroy us. But their plan was stopped by this brave pair.

Seth watched the commander circle over him and Esta.

—These two are truly grateful for the new world we are making for them. They are loyal allies.

Seth's unease intensified. Outside on the ship's deck, Esta had lied for him, but he wasn't convinced the commander believed her. The story seemed flimsy. Hadn't the commander seen him and Esta battering each other with sound?

—Therefore, the commander continued, and this time Seth knew he was being addressed directly, *the execution is yours to carry out.*

He understood now. His eyes met Petra's. How could he ever live with himself?

—Do it, Esta told him. *If you don't, the commander will know you're disloyal.*

Into his head burst another voice, the ginger-scented words of the secret rebel.

—Strike her, the rebel said. *You need to live. You need to destroy the shield.*

He was twisted with misery. In his head were two voices from different sides, both asking him to do exactly the same, terrible thing.

—Strike!

This was the commander's voice now, blaring inside him.

"Yes!" Seth agreed.

A life's worth of fear and grief and betrayal and rage was all right there, vibrating furiously in his mind. He stoked it until his head felt like it might split open. He looked away from Petra and welded his gaze to the commander's sleek feathered head, and only then did he release the sound.

He had no idea how powerful he was compared to a true cryptogen. He was only a half thing, and probably weaker.

But the commander reeled back in the air as if blasted by a cyclone. Her wings buckled and she spiraled limply down through the vast chamber. Had he killed her? Seth gulped air, his heart pounding in his ears. It was like all the oxygen in the chamber had evaporated as everyone watched, stunned. Then a dozen or more flyers plunged after their commander, trying to catch her before she hit the ground.

—*You fool!* the rebel's voice said in his head.

On the platform, the commander's two lieutenants were staring at him in shock.

—*What have you done?* the swimmer cried, leveling the harpoon gun at him.

Instantly the runner lifted his rifle and shot the swimmer in the back. Seth barely had time to feel confused before the runner grabbed Esta and hurled her, shrieking, over the side of the platform.

"Hey!" Seth cried, reaching out too late to catch her.

He peered down to see Esta, arms spread, half tumbling, half gliding down through the tumult of the chamber. He looked back at the runner, bewildered.

—*She is not our friend,* the runner said, and right away Seth recognized the gingery voice and aquatic light of the rebel who'd been talking to him secretly.

—*You?* he said in astonishment. The commander's lieutenant was a rebel?

A cracking pain blinded Seth as the runner struck him hard across the head with his rifle. Seth's knees buckled.

—*Stay down!* the runner barked at him. *Pretend you're unconscious.*

Gasping in genuine pain, Seth barely needed to pretend. He didn't try to wipe away the blood streaming from the wound in his forehead, just lay sprawled on the platform.

—*What's the plan?* he asked.

—*I'm taking you to the shield core, to destroy it.*

He opened his eyes to slits. Through the guardrails he could see Petra, all alone on her platform, forgotten for the moment in all the mayhem—but she wouldn't be forgotten for long.

—*We need to rescue my friend!* he told the rebel runner.

—*No.*

—*Then I won't destroy the shield!*

He was trembling and meant every word of it, and the runner must have realized it, because he put the platform into a steep tilt and rounded back, smacking against Petra's platform so hard she nearly went flying off. She looked at the runner in terror, then down at him.

—*It's okay!* Seth said to her as the runner grabbed her roughly.

She was dragged aboard the platform and hurled to the floor beside him. He slid his hand into her cold fingers and squeezed.

They were hurtling through the chamber now, and he heard the runner blaring to everyone that he had caught and killed the rebel murderers.

—*I did not think your sound would be so strong,* the rebel said privately to the two of them. *You are as powerful as us, maybe more so.*

—*Did I kill her?* Seth asked, hardly daring to hope. *The commander?*

As if in reply came a great rising roar from the chamber, and when he cracked open an eye, he saw the commander rising on powerful wingbeats. Even from this great distance, she seemed to radiate heat, like something white-hot removed from a forge.

—*Where is he?* the commander cried out to the entire ship. *Bring him to me!*

The commander's words made Seth wince in terror, and his hands went icy.

The platform sped on, into some quieter portion of the ship, and skidded to a stop against a wall.

—*Stay down,* the runner told them.

Seth watched as the rebel used a claw to make a deep cut in the wall. Pushing both hands inside, he widened the incision.

—*Go through,* he told them. *To the shield generator.*

A map quickly drew itself in Seth's head.

—*The transmission tower outside is too heavily guarded now,* the rebel said. *But the generator is still vulnerable to a sonic blast. You'll need this to destroy it.*

From a locker he passed Seth a helmet, and an armored flight vest.

—*What will* you *do?* Seth asked him.

—*Once you destroy the shield, I will raise the lantern and start this fight. And hope that you humans honor your pact and fight with us.*

—*We will,* Petra told him. *Once the shield's down, they'll hit the ship with all they've got. You need to get everyone out, right away.*

—*Yes,* said the rebel. *And hope for rain.*

—*And hope for rain,* Seth repeated, thinking of Anaya.

—*Quickly, go now,* the rebel said. *Don't touch the walls.*

Seth pushed through the strange, woundlike opening, followed by Petra, and then it was sealed up from the other side.

"Don't touch the *walls?*" Petra whispered, looking around the fleshy corridor in horror. "I don't want to touch *anything.* I feel like I'm inside someone's body. If this is what the future looks like, it sucks."

Seth quickly pulled on the flight vest and excitement vibrated through his body. He held the helmet in trembling hands. He was almost frightened to put it on.

"Just do it!" Petra hissed. "We need all the firepower we can get."

He was suddenly, overwhelmingly, glad she was with him. The helmet was snug, encasing his entire head. There was a moment of darkness until his eyes lined up with the holes—or sensors, he wasn't sure. But now he could see.

"Okay, that's pretty freaking scary," Petra said. Her voice sounded muffled.

A hot tremor sang through his whole body. He felt suddenly like he had eyes in the back of his head, because he was seeing in all directions—which was impossible, until he realized it must have something to do with the helmet. His sight and hearing seemed to fuse: objects glowed and hummed. He saw and heard everything, knew the exact distances between them and himself.

"Whoa," he breathed.

He felt strong and protected. Untouchable. He wanted to shout. He wanted to smash things up. He could do amazing, terrible things in this helmet. He feared it. He liked it.

"You look exactly like one of them," Petra said, a little uncertainly.

"I'm not," he said, needing to reassure himself.

He followed the map the rebel runner had given him. The place was like a hedge maze made of living, pulsing tissue, but luckily he didn't need to make many turnings.

"This is the spot," he said, stopping where the corridor took a sharp jag.

With his wing he cut a deep gash in the wall and plunged in. Even before he came out the other side, he felt the tectonic rumble. He stumbled out onto a broad catwalk encircling an enormous shaft that could only be the ship's core. And suspended in it was the source of the rumbling sound.

The shield generator was the size of a blue whale stood on its tail, a vast stretch of muscle and fat and veins and tendons and organs, all of them humming and vibrating. The sound was now painful, like the terrible pressure in his head as the shield had waterfalled over him after the ship landed.

It was like a living thing, great currents of purple energy crackling over its surface and traveling up the shaft to the transmission mast.

His gaze focused on the generator's center. Anger was never hard to find in his head. This time his anger was about Esta. He thought about how she'd changed and how he couldn't change with her. She'd become something ugly, but he couldn't stop loving her. Not just like that, not so fast. His anger trembled brightly in his head, and he felt the helmet encouraging it, amplifying it until he feared his head might explode.

"Do it!" he heard Petra shouting at him.

And maybe he was shouting, too, as he unleashed himself at the generator's mighty muscle. The noise deafened him: a cannon's echo in a tin can. A gaping hole opened in the generator, wet machinery exploding everywhere. He aimed higher and blasted open the top of the shaft so he could see the night sky. The transmission mast crumpled and the last of its purple light flickered out.

"Holy. Crap," breathed Petra beside him, grabbing his hand. "You did it!"

A shrieking alarm sounded through the ship. He stood, gasping and spent, beholding the wreckage he'd created.

"We need to get out of here," Petra was telling him. "The army's going to hit the ship hard. As soon as the shield's down. That was the plan."

Seth shivered and looked around the shaft. A transport platform hovered farther along the catwalk, and he grabbed Petra's hand and ran for it. He moved his hands along the railing until he felt it sing to him, and gave the command the rebel had taught him. They lifted.

As he guided the platform up through the shaft, he heard a flicker of light in his head.

"Hear that?" he said to Petra.

"The lantern!" she replied.

It was a jubilant blooming of beautiful light, like a sunrise, now blazing in his head, and with it, the message to rise, to fight for freedom. Seth had no idea how many runners and swimmers would answer the call, and how many would remain loyal to the commander.

He flew the platform through the hole he'd blasted in the top of the ship, past the debris of the transmission mast, and into the coming dawn. He climbed high. Below, a few flyers were already circling, overseeing armored platforms of runners leaving the ship. In the water, he glimpsed the quick shadows of underwater vehicles.

"Take over," he said to Petra.

"What?"

Quickly he showed her where to grip the platform, told her the silent command to communicate with it.

"Fly back to the base," he told her.

Her look was one of total astonishment. "Where are you going?"

"To fight with the rebels."

"No, no, no, that's not the plan! The humans will shoot you! You look exactly like the flyers!"

"I know. So the winged cryptogens will never see me coming!"

His flight armor, his helmet: it was a perfect disguise. He would pick off one flyer after another before they knew what he was.

"You don't need to do this!" she said angrily. "The rain's going to come!"

"What if it doesn't?" he said. "This might be our only chance."

"I don't get it!" she raged. "First you turn away from all of us, and now you're fighting for us?"

"Lesser of two evils," he said.

He jumped off the platform and silently asked his flight suit for power as he spread his wings.

—*Seth!* she yelled up at him. *Remind me never to rescue you again!*

—*This planet's the only home I'm going to get,* he told her silently as he sped away. *I figure it's worth fighting for. And a few of the people on it.*

CHAPTER TWENTY-ONE

IT WAS JUST THE four of them.

Anaya, Terra, the silver swimmer, and the grizzled runner engineer, who had trouble even moving himself around. They weren't much of a fighting force. Especially against the flyers. Just one of those guys would be enough to kill them all.

—*We have some time, but not much,* said the silver swimmer.

—*They don't know their way around the guts like we do,* the engineer pointed out.

—*There must be weapons somewhere?* Anaya asked.

—*On the landing ship,* said the silver swimmer. *Even if we could get there, they are locked up. Only flyer officers can access them.*

Anaya looked around the cluttered room. There would be plenty of places to hide, at least. But how long could they stay hidden?

—*Can you wake those things up?* Anaya asked the engineer, pointing to the pods and vats of slumbering cryptogenic animals.

—*Those are invaluable specimens,* he said, shocked at the idea. *We harvest important cells from them.*

—How about we let them do some fighting for us? Anaya said. *Just this once.*

—The flyers will simply kill them all, the engineer said.

Anaya remembered how Seth had finished off the giant rhino thing in Stanley Park, blasting it with sound.

—Are there any they can't *kill with sound?* she asked.

—Yes, that one, Terra said, and pointed at a specimen so terrifying that Anaya almost couldn't look at it. She didn't know if it was mammalian, a giant bug, or an incomprehensible blend of both.

Worriedly, she asked, *You didn't put any of those on Earth, did you?*

—No.

—We were saving it for the next rain, the silver swimmer added.

Anaya looked back at Terra in shock. *The* next *rain! You never told us about that!*

—I did not want to worry you. I was also hoping we would defeat the flyers before that stage.

—Okay. Well, can we wake it up and let it loose?

—You want to rouse this creature? the grizzled engineer asked. *Insane! Do you have any idea how she eats her prey? She—*

—Wake her, the silver swimmer said. *We can take our platform high and hide.*

He nodded to a shadowed area of the chamber, cluttered with hanging sacs of specimens.

—Very well, said the engineer glumly.

—Anything else we should let loose? Anaya asked.

The engineer glanced back at her askance. *This will be enough.* He put his hands to a control surface and Anaya heard a wet rattling sound. When she looked over, she saw the cryptogenic beast trembling in its sac.

—Get on, said the silver swimmer from the platform.

Anaya and Terra helped the stooped engineer aboard, and they lifted high into the chamber, nudging into the cover of dangling tubes and sacs. Anaya could no longer see the sac holding the animal, but she heard an unnerving clicking, like many pointy limbs tapping against a hard surface. With a burst, liquid splashed against the floor.

—This was a poor idea, grumbled the engineer.

Anaya craned her neck but still didn't see the creature anywhere. She wasn't sure she wanted to. She'd forgotten to ask if it could climb.

From different locations around the room came a sound like serrated blades cutting through watermelon. Anaya saw a wing slash its way through the wall. Moments later, a flyer pushed through the gash, followed by a runner with a rifle. Elsewhere, more flyers cut their way into the room. In all, Anaya counted eight flyers, two armed runners, and three swimmers. They stood quietly, taking in the chamber, looking and listening.

All that greeted them was the hum of machinery and the *drip-drip* from the sac the cryptogen had just burst from.

Where was it?

Anaya heard a shriek, and when her eyes found the source, all she saw was a flyer's legs being dragged into a tangle of cables. From out of sight came the sickening sound of metal and meat and bones being mangled.

The flyers must have given silent orders to the two runners, because they reluctantly advanced toward the eating sounds, rifles at the ready.

The creature moved so quickly it was impossible to get a proper sense of it. One of the runners got a shot off before it was overwhelmed. The second fell back in terror but was snagged by a long limb and dragged toward the creature. It seemed to have more than one mouth.

After that, the beast pounced from one cryptogen to the next, ripping and killing. Gunshots and harpoons hardly made it blink—and by this time, Anaya had found things on its body that were definitely eyes. Only the flyers remained now, and they must have realized that their sound weapons were useless, because two took to the air and the others rushed for the walls. The ones that remained on the ground were caught and torn apart before they could escape into the ship's guts.

Then, as Anaya watched in horror, a hidden pair of wings unfolded from the creature's body. No one had said anything about this thing flying! Airborne, it was ungainly and didn't seem to have much power or speed.

The two surviving flyers circled above it. One of them passed close to Anaya's hiding place, and she tensed, waiting for it to pass. It didn't. It swerved back. Anaya could tell by its expression that it had found them.

—*Up here!* the flyer blared to its companion, and then was coated by some kind of paste the color of guacamole.

In confusion, Anaya looked down and saw the cryptogenic beast directly below. From some organ in its body, it unleashed another jet of green spray. A terrible shrieking welled from the flyer's beak. Anaya could see fumes rising from its feathers and realized its wings were melting. The flyer plunged into the eager limbs and mouths of the creature.

The other flyer landed near the main hatch and made a valiant effort to unlock the doors. It didn't even have time to place its hands against the wall before it was inhaled and eaten.

—*And what happens now?* said the engineer with a kind of grim satisfaction. *Now that we've all had our fun. What do you propose now, hmm?*

Anaya watched the beast by the hatch as it choked down the remains of the flyer, then regurgitated the feathers. The thing was a killing machine, but now that they'd turned it on, how did they turn it off? She looked around the chamber at all the other creatures, all the other plants.

—*There must be some way of killing it,* she said.

—*This,* said the engineer simply, pulling a small dart from his tool belt.

—*What's that?* Terra asked.

—*Poison. Take me closer, please.*

—*No,* said the silver swimmer.

From his tool belt, the engineer drew out a metal straw and slipped the dart into one end.

—*My aim is good, but not that good. Closer. This is as good a moment as any. She'll only get more aggressive as she wakes up fully.*

—*She seems pretty awake to me!* Anaya said.

—*Just a little closer,* the silver swimmer said, and moved the platform out from their hiding place, and a bit lower. The creature didn't seem to notice.

—*Closer,* said the engineer, raising the straw to his mouth.

The platform slid through the air. The creature whirled in a crouch.

—*Not that close!* wailed the engineer.

The creature leapt, and even though the platform was reversing madly, Anaya realized with dead certainty that the beast was about to land on top of them. The engineer staggered off-balance against the railing.

—*Shoot it!* Anaya yelled at him, then realized he already had.

When she looked back at the beast, it had gone limp in the air. It bounced off the platform's hull, then dropped to the floor, lifeless.

Anaya felt like hugging the engineer.

—*You're a surprising fellow,* she told him.

—*Nothing compared to her,* the engineer said, looking at

the dead animal with genuine regret. *A shame to kill such a rare specimen.*

The silver swimmer set down the platform, and they all hurried toward the tight cluster of incubator vats.

—*How close are we?* Anaya asked.

—*The culture's nearly ready,* the engineer said, listening to his sonic instruments.

—*What happens next?* Anaya said hopefully. *Explain it to me.*

—*Once we have enough culture,* Terra said, *we fill the seeding pods.*

Terra pointed to row after row of transparent pipes. Each pipe was filled with what looked like giant transparent beach balls.

—*They are designed to enter the atmosphere.*

They didn't look very strong—she couldn't imagine them withstanding the scorching heat of reentry.

—*We program their trajectory,* said Terra, *and in the high stratosphere, they create the conditions for rain.*

—*They make clouds,* said Anaya.

—*Yes. And then they release their cargo.*

Eagerly she pictured it. The virus released into the clouds, mingling with the rain, pelting down over the planet. Every raindrop that hit the flyers would infect them, robbing them of their sonic weaponry.

She only wished she would be back on Earth to feel that rain on her face.

The silver swimmer made a low liquid rumble in his throat.

—*What's wrong?* Anaya asked him.

—*The command crew has just given orders to wake the reserve ship. They'll be back for us, with thousands of soldiers this time.*

HUNCHED AGAINST THE WIND, Petra sped out over the water on the cryptogen platform, heading back toward the armada of ships.

She couldn't believe she'd gone to all the trouble to rescue Seth, and he'd just flown off into danger again! How was that for gratitude? Or even good sense?

She was reassured by the solid bulk of the human ships, the aircraft carrier's huge cliff of metal rising from the sea. All those jets, ready to slingshot off the deck, the attack helicopters lifting. The battleships bristled with gun turrets. And there was her own frigate, the *Carr,* where her father, and the Riggses, and Dr. Weber were waiting. But she knew all that metal wouldn't stop the sonic carnage from the flyers' helmets.

Her head was filled with a chaotic crackle of telepathy coming from the cryptogen ship. She caught the occasional flash of the lantern, that amazing beacon that was supposed to summon the runners and swimmers to the rebel cause. But she also caught the shouted orders from the flyers, who smelled like smoke and scorched rubber and devastation:

—Battle formations!

—All units, seek out the source of attack.

—Annihilate weaponry.

—Kill everything.

Glancing back, she saw platforms like the one she was piloting, except outfitted with armor, pouring from the landing ship. Masses of flyers circled overhead. Beneath the ship, the water churned as swimmers and aquatic vehicles plunged into the sea. She felt terribly confused. It looked like everyone was still following the flyers' orders.

She turned back to the human armada. Was she running away from the fight? But what else could she do? She had no weapons. Her platform wasn't even armored. She was basically driving a flying shopping cart. For the first time she wondered if the humans would open fire on her.

—Petra! Petra!

The voice belonged to Charles, and she glanced over to see the stealth helicopter flying alongside her. Was that someone waving at her through the window?

—Hey! she called back.

—We're headed back to the ship, Charles told her. *Stick with us so you don't get attacked. We've told them not to fire on you.*

—Thanks!

—The shield's down! Did you guys blow it up?

—It was Seth. He did it!

There was a slight hesitation before Charles asked:

—*Where is he?*

—*Fighting for the rebels,* she answered with a sick heart. When she looked behind her, she felt even sicker. The air above the cryptogen ship was absolutely blackened with flyers now. It was like a giant wasps' nest had been kicked open and released millions. Somewhere in that turmoil was Seth.

As she neared the HMS *Carr*, a shrill alarm reached her over the water.

—*What's happening?* Petra asked Charles.

—*Tomahawk cruise missile launch.*

White smoke boiled from the decks of the battleships, and missiles leapt from their launch tubes. Orange blazes in the pale blue sky, they arced and started to fall toward Point Roberts like shooting stars.

None of them reached their target.

They exploded in the air, nowhere near the cryptogen ship. The flyers must have intercepted them. Despair swirled through her. Maybe they wouldn't be able to strike the ship, even without its shield.

Fighters and helicopters tore past overhead, on their way to Point Roberts.

—*Come on, Petra,* Charles told her. *We've got clearance to land on the frigate.*

A flash in the sky drew her gaze. It looked like a flock of

migrating geese, except they were fully armored flyers, in an arrowhead formation. On the battleships, gun turrets angled high and began thumping fire into the sky. A few flyers spun, smoking, down through the air.

Not invincible, she thought with grim satisfaction.

With a terrible scrapyard crunching sound, the command tower of the nearest destroyer crumpled, as if an invisible fist had squeezed it. Huge dents were pounded into the ship's midsection. Smoke curled from inside, pale, then black.

"Oh my God," Petra breathed.

She hadn't thought it would happen so quickly. The total destruction.

She looked back toward Point Roberts, at the churning mass of flyers protecting the cryptogen ship.

When would the rain come?

What if it didn't?

Not far behind her she saw the water swell weirdly and caught the flash of swimmers beneath the surface like a pod of dolphins. Each of them was riding a vehicle that looked like an underwater Jet Ski.

They were headed toward her—but she knew their target could only be the HMS *Carr.*

—*Petra, hurry up!* shouted Charles.

She had to do something, even if it came to nothing. She skimmed the platform to a stop above the cold water of the strait, then dived in to intercept the swimmers.

WHEN SETH SAW THE missiles fired from the battleships, he was filled with hope. But as their bright flare came closer, armored flyers shot straight toward them. One after another the missiles exploded high above the ship, creating tarantulas of smoke and debris dripping through the sky.

There were so many flyers, circling protectively at different altitudes. Even though he was armored and helmeted, he was afraid to go too close, in case they noticed he was different. He worried his heavier legs and talon-less feet might give him away—or maybe they'd have some other way of knowing he was only a hybrid.

Suddenly, from below came dashes of blue fire, and he looked down to see two armored platforms of runners firing up at the flyers.

Rebels! It was beginning!

The runners wore breathing masks over their noses; they were still weak in Earth's atmosphere, but they fought on, blasting skyward. Their barrage took the flyers by surprise, and many were struck and fell, smoking. The air smelled like a slaughterhouse. Retaliation came almost at once. Seth gasped as a huge thunderclap pulverized the rebel platforms, punching craters in the earth below.

Seth felt faint with terror and guilt. Had he just helped set a massacre in motion? He saw another group of flyers streak out over the water, in the direction of the human fleet.

He angled his wings and sped after them. The air was cool against his feathers, but his head and torso were warm inside his helmet and armor. His chest swelled as his breathing quickened. In his head was the bright vibration of the flight pack and the helmet, awaiting his commands. Such speed he had! Such a view before him!

Over the strait, he gained on the flyers. Artillery fire from the ships below blossomed all around him. Ahead of him a couple of flyers were hit. He swerved wildly, losing control. Recovering, he caught back up to the formation—in time to see the battleship's command tower crumple and the hull breached.

His fear and anger boiled in his head. In front of him were all the flyers. His helmet told him their distance. He had one chance before they turned on him. Could he destroy them all in one blow? He remembered what the commander's rebel lieutenant had told him: his sound weapon was powerful, maybe even more powerful than theirs.

He felt the murderous vibration in his head swell into a torrent. He heard his own thunderclap. The flyers before him crumpled like origami birds, except for one that was tumbled through the air by the blast's concussion. Seth sucked in air and angled himself down at the surviving cryptogen flyer. It righted itself and swerved to come at him head-on.

—*What happened?* the flyer shouted. *Did you see what—*

Seth unleashed another burst of sound that drove the flyer's crushed body down into the water.

He was panting. He'd killed them all. The helmet made it so easy.

You had to do it, he told himself, and he looked down at the human fleet. The battleship was sinking, but he'd saved the other ships. For now. And he had his strategy. Surprise and destroy.

—*Seth!*

He swerved, ready to unleash sound, before he recognized Esta's voice. Her voice had once filled him with such joy. She circled around him, armored, helmeted.

—*It's not too late,* she cried out. *Fight with us!*

—*They're just going to use us as slaves! They're going to kill everything and everyone we know!*

—*I don't care. I care about you, that's all. Stay with me.*

—*Stay with* me! he countered.

Swirling around each other in the air like some aerial ballet, tighter and tighter.

Let's leave, she said. *Right now. Fly away. We both have packs and helmets. No one will bother us. Just you and me.*

Seth felt the temptation. How he felt the tug of it!

He wanted to feel like he had in the boat, drifting in fog when they'd kissed. The two of them against the world. But he didn't feel that way anymore. He couldn't, not after what she'd done.

—*No,* he said.

—*No?*

He heard the despair in her silent voice, and the kindling anger, too.

—I'm not going to strike you, he said.

—I won't strike you ei—

A bruising flash of light sent him tumbling backward through the air. Gasping, he righted himself and looked around wildly.

—Esta! Esta?

All he saw was a small swirl of debris. A bit of a helmet. Esta's red-and-blue feathers, fluttering down.

CHAPTER TWENTY-TWO

HEART POUNDING WITH HOPE and anxiety, Anaya watched as the incubator vats released jets of the virus into the seeding pods, filling one after another.

Faster, faster, she thought.

Once loaded, the pods were shuffled along their pipelines to the outer wall of the chamber, where they were torpedoed into space. There was no window, but Anaya imagined them speeding toward the bright ball of her planet, blazing through the atmosphere, and starting a rain that would save them all. If they weren't already too late.

—*Thank you,* she said to Terra. She turned to the engineer and the silver swimmer, who'd been working together on some other bit of machinery. *All of you, thank you so much!*

The alarm that had been sounding through the ship stopped suddenly, and Anaya looked worriedly at the hatch and the walls. Very soon, something terrible was going to happen.

She knew better than to ask Terra if there was a way out of here.

A ship to take her home.

There was no escape route, no waiting ship, nothing that would save them from the coming attack. The idea of dying was so vast, she couldn't really believe it, not yet anyway. Maybe that would come later. Right now, all she cared about was seeing every last seeding pod blasted into space.

—*Put your skin back on,* Terra told her abruptly.

—*My skin?* she asked in confusion, then remembered the sac she'd traveled inside aboard the small spaceship, the same sac she'd spacewalked in. She yanked it now from her pocket and flapped it out.

—*We're going outside again?* she asked nervously, pulling the fabric up over her legs.

—*No. It will protect you.*

—*How come you guys aren't putting them on?* She shrugged the sac over both shoulders.

Like a mother zipping a child into a snowsuit, Terra zipped Anaya's sac up all the way. She was blind for a moment before the miraculous fabric snugged against her body and face and started seeing for her.

—*I still don't understand wh—*

One of the pipelines stopped moving along its seeding pods.

—*Is it broken?* Anaya asked worriedly.

—*I stopped it,* Terra said, and knelt down to pull up a hatch in the pipe. She put her hand on the top of an empty seeding pod, and it opened. She took a belt of tools and leaned inside.

—*What're you doing?* the silver swimmer asked the runner. *You're slowing us down!*

—*It's done.* Terra turned to Anaya. *Get inside.*

Anaya stared, uncomprehending. A small flare of light appeared in her head. It was like the strange glowing box of information Terra had sent her, like a gift, when they'd first started communicating.

—*What did you just give me?* she asked.

—*Instructions. If you want to go home, go now.*

—*In* this?

—*Trust me.*

—*But what about you?*

—*The pod barely fits one.*

—*Get in another one, there's lots!*

Terra shook her head. *We need to stay here to make sure the work is finished.*

Anaya felt a huge squeeze of sadness at her throat.

—*No, it's not fair—*

—*You were never supposed to be up here. It was a mistake. Get inside.*

She threw herself against Terra and hugged her, and felt herself being hugged back. She wanted to go home, but it felt so wrong to leave like this.

Firmly Terra guided her down inside the pod. It was a tight fit, knees up to her chin, shoulders folded in, arms wrapped around her legs. She felt a breathless squeeze of panic and started shivering, but the fabric warmed her, and fresh air filled her nostrils. In anguish she watched as Terra sealed the pod's hatch.

—*What will happen to you?* she asked Terra.

—*I have a plan.*

—*Will I see you again?*

—*Maybe.*

The pipeline started to move again, shuffling her toward the launch tube. Through the transparent pipe she saw the door to the chamber blast apart, and flyers soar into the room. And then she was plunged into the darkness of space.

PETRA HIT THE WATER, the cold like a vise clamping around her heart and lungs. She swam furiously, afraid of freezing solid. Within seconds, she felt warmer, and calmer.

Her eyes adjusted, her pupils widened. Rising around her were high groves of seagrass, some clustered with water strider eggs. She kept her eyes open for wolverine-squid things, but even they weren't her main worry right now.

Taking shape in the murky distance was the approaching platoon of swimmers.

She swam to meet them head-on, singing the lantern to them.

—*Stop, stop, stop!* she cried.

They did not stop.

—*We're friends!* she cried, flashing the lantern like crazy. *We want to help you fight the flyers!*

They kept coming on their jet speeders, which she could now see were mounted with guns.

A harpoon sliced past, narrowly missing her shoulder.

—*Hey, I'm flashing your stupid lantern!* she bellowed. *You're supposed to be starting a rebellion! Not sinking our ships!*

Nowhere in her head did she see a return lantern, not even a feeble flicker. They couldn't all be loyal to the commander, could they?

She dived deep into the shadowy seagrass before they could take aim again.

—*She's the traitor!* came a voice that smelled like an open sewer. *The one who tried to destroy our ship!*

—*Just the shield!* Petra cried back from her hiding place. *The rebel leaders are sending a rain that will take away the flyers' power.*

—*Lies!* came the bilge-water voice again.

He must be their captain, Petra thought.

—*We're fighting the flyers, just like you!* she said.

Slithering through the grass, trying to stay hidden, she couldn't see anything. Were they even looking for her?

—*Ignore her!* ordered the captain. *Proceed to the target and destroy it!*

Peeping up from the grass, she saw the platoon about to pass straight over her. She pushed off and grabbed the underside of a jet speeder, catching a ride unseen.

—*Don't do it!* she cried out. *If you destroy that ship, you'll be killing hundreds of your allies.*

—*And if we disobey orders,* came another voice, *the commander will execute us.*

—*She's soon going to be powerless!* Petra said.

—*Find this traitor!* demanded the captain. *She must be underneath one of our vessels!*

Petra knew that if she had any hope of stopping them, she had to make an Oscar-winning intergalactic speech right now. In a language that wasn't her own, and with which she'd always struggled.

—*The rain's coming,* she said, *and it has a virus in it. It will take away the winged ones' sonic weapon. They won't be able to use their helmets, or hurt you anymore. Very, very soon!*

She was promising things that might not come true. It didn't matter. What mattered was preventing them from blasting the ship apart.

—*I heard about this plan,* came a different voice in her head.

—*When will it rain?* asked another voice.

—*Find this traitor!* the captain roared again.

The underwater flotilla of speeders slowed down, and Petra saw several swimmers coming toward her, armed with harpoon guns.

—If you kill me, she cried, *if you sink our ships, you're only help-ing the commander win. You're weakening yourselves. If you want your freedom, let us help you! Fight with us and we can defeat the flyers together! If we can't fight together, we will all fail! Please!*

Hands grabbed her and dragged her, kicking, off the under-side of the speeder. Before her appeared a large swimmer with marbled skin patterning. It had to be the captain. He aimed his weapon at her.

—Please! Petra said again, the only word she could utter.

She almost gulped water as a harpoon went through the cap-tain's heart. Blood unspooled like a red ribbon in the water. The captain floated lifeless.

—We need to listen to her, said the swimmer who'd fired the harpoon. *Haven't we dreamed of a chance like this? We left our planet as slaves, but we don't have to return as slaves.*

One by one Petra's mind filled with small pulses of light, pale at first, like someone breathing on the embers of a fire, like a kid learning a new song, soft at first and then faster and louder as they gained confidence. It was the light of a dozen swimmers, ready to fight, raising their lanterns.

FURIOUS, SETH WHEELED IN the sky, glaring down at the human battleship and the gun turret that had just killed Esta.

It would be so easy to crush it, to punch a hole right through the ship's hull.

They didn't even know who they'd killed. They'd thought she was just another enemy. Through his deadly helmet, he saw the turret swiveling to take aim at him. He could make it easy for them, stay nice and still.

His heart ached. That big, stupid muscle in his chest didn't have the good sense to give up and just stop beating.

But with every thump his rage grew. Banking, he soared back toward Point Roberts. He knew what to do with his rage.

He urged his flight pack to give him all its speed and aimed himself into the center of the flyers churning above the landing ship. Inside his head was a pressure so intense he thought his head would explode. He released it and it felt like world-cracking sound blasted out from his eyes, his mouth, his fingertips. Before him, flyers dropped like swatted flies. He was shouting, terrible words spewing from his mouth.

He pulled up and away, gasping at all his destruction but wanting to mete out more.

Because what he was doing was not enough.

All around him, humans and rebels were being annihilated. Jets crumpled like paper airplanes before they could even release their missiles. Helicopters spun flaming to the sea. On the ground, the runners' armored platforms burned—whether destroyed by the flyers or humans, he would never know.

Scattered across land and sea were bodies so mangled they were hard to recognize. Over the water, formations of flyers flew low, to finish off the human fleet.

He would be recognized soon. He would lose the advantage of surprise.

From the thickening cloud overhead, two fighter jets broke through, their wings heavy with missiles. Seth—or was it his helmet?—could anticipate what would happen. It was like seeing five seconds into the future. He could tell the fighters were headed for Point Roberts, to strike the unshielded ship.

From all directions, flyers closed in on the two fighters. A single thunderclap tore a wing off the first jet, sending it spinning earthward. The remaining jet veered, but the flyers were locked on it. Seth swooped down behind them and began to crush them with sound. Not fast enough. But seconds before the jet was annihilated, it released its four missiles.

Clear their way, Seth thought.

With a burst of speed he pulled alongside the missiles, sending devastating thunderclaps at every flyer he saw. Two of the missiles were destroyed, but two survived. They exploded against the hull of the landing ship in flaming blisters.

He veered away, hoping to hide himself in the aerial mayhem, but a terrifying chorus filled his head.

—*A traitor!*

—*He's wearing our armor!*

—Kill him!

—I will kill him.

This voice Seth recognized.

He looked to his left and saw the commander, her icy wings of blue, gold, and white cutting the air toward him.

CHAPTER TWENTY-THREE

CRAMMED INSIDE THE SEEDING pod, Anaya saw the cryptogen vessel shrinking into the darkness. It was the only way she knew she was moving at all. She felt no sense of speed yet. Floating all around her were thousands of seeding pods, like bubbles in oil, glinting in the sunlight.

But she knew they were all moving, hurtling toward Earth.

She was *hurtling* through space inside a giant beach ball! What did she think she was doing? Suddenly she was gulping in panic. Her sac hissed out more air for her.

Hurriedly she opened the glowing box Terra had left in her head. The first thing to emerge was Terra's familiar voice:

—*Your oxygen supply is very limited. You have only what is left in your sac. Try to breathe calmly.*

Breathe *calmly*?

The idea of running out of air was terrifying; nonetheless, she forced herself to slow her breathing, taking one deep breath, and then another, until the erratic thumping of her heart eased and steadied.

Better.

Warily, she returned her attention to Terra's glowing box, hoping that whatever popped out next would be a little more encouraging. Diagrams unfolded themselves in her mind like a set of alien Ikea instructions, only more complicated. Luckily, they came with customer support.

—*I have programmed the pod,* Terra's voice said, *to splash down in the harbor.*

Anaya saw an aerial map of the Deadman's Island army base. That was good.

—*These pods were never designed to land.*

That was *not* so good. She checked her breathing.

—*But it should retain its integrity with a water landing,* Terra's voice said. *As you enter the atmosphere, the heat will be intense.*

"How hot can it get?" she wondered aloud. These pods had to be shielded, or they'd burn up during entry. And they must be insulated, too, or their cargo would die: the seeds, the eggs. The virus that was supposed to save them all.

But me? she wondered.

—*To protect its cargo, the pod is programmed to automatically cool its interior with nitrogen gas during entry. Such a thing would kill you. You must override the controls.*

"How?" Anaya shouted, and had to force herself to drag her attention back to the images and voice in her head. These instructions might be the most important ones she'd ever have to follow.

—*Your sac will protect you. But it has its limits.*

So it was up to her, somehow, to keep herself at the right temperature.

Too hot and she'd fry. Too cold and she'd become a corpsicle.

To calm herself, she gazed at the beautiful blue ball of Earth. Home. She was going home. But the planet was rapidly growing, and she knew that before long she'd be smashing into the bright shell of Earth's atmosphere.

She placed her hand against the wall, following Terra's instructions. It took her a few tries to find the right spot—the place where she felt a sonic connection with the pod's machinery. She followed its almost musical circuitry in her mind until she found the controls for the automatic nitrogen spray. She turned it off and figured out how she could command the gas coolant herself. She made it give a tiny hiss, just to be sure, then turned it off.

"I am in command of a beach ball," she murmured to herself.

Around her, the other pods began to glow like amber beads. Hers was starting to shudder like a truck over a gravel road, then boulders. As the pod shook violently, gravity returned with a vengeance. Her suit hissed and inflated to cushion her as the ride became rougher still.

And with the angry orange glow that erupted around the pod came the heat. She hadn't expected it so fast and furious, like a blast from an opened oven. Hand against the wall's control surface, she sent out a sonic command, and a blast of nitrogen gas filled the pod. She felt her body cool, and suddenly she was frigid, teeth chattering. She pulled her hand away to break her connection with the ship. The gas stopped and dissipated, leaving ice crystals glittering on her synthetic skin.

She wasn't cold for long. The pod was now ablaze with fiery light as it bulldozed its way through the atmosphere. So hot again. The pod trembled violently; her hand lost its place on the wall and she struggled to find it again. There.

Another blast of nitrogen, longer this time, because she still felt hot, like her insides were baking. It got cooler, then viciously cold with very little warning. When she tried to pull her hand away from the controls, it wouldn't move. In horror, she realized it was frozen to the wall. She was too cold to tremble this time. She couldn't feel her fingers. Or her entire body, heavy and numb—and still the cooling gas was blasting into the pod.

—*Stop! Stop!* she cried out to the machinery, but maybe something was broken, or it didn't understand her half-frozen brain, because the gas kept pouring in.

She felt like her very lungs must be freezing. It was so hard to take a breath. Even her heartbeat was now a slow, congealed thump. The amazing cryptogenic fabric could not save her from this icy death. Her vision started to wither.

Something struck her pod, hard, and with her dimming eyes, she saw another pod go ricocheting off hers like a billiard ball in space. But the blow had been enough to knock her frozen hand away from the wall. The hiss of gas stopped. Her skin was rigid with ice, and she couldn't move a muscle.

Thaw, she pleaded with herself.

The fiery aura around her pod was fading, yet there was still enough heat to melt the ice on her suit. Tiny droplets danced off her and she could soon move her fingers, then toes, arms, and legs.

At the same moment, the terrible rumbling stopped, and she was through! Light poured past her and she heard and felt the wind buffeting the pod. Oh, how good it was to be back in the sky!

She was still so high. The stratosphere, she remembered from physics class. Alongside her fell hundreds of other seeding pods, speeding toward the cloud covering below to do their work.

With difficulty she lifted her heavy hand to the wall to check her location. It took her a moment to understand the map that appeared in her head. She made out the shape of British Columbia, but the pulsing blue line of her trajectory did not lead anywhere near Vancouver, but far to the north. This wasn't right. . . .

With a sick lurch of her stomach, she realized that the other seeding pod must have knocked her off course. She was going to land hundreds of kilometers away from Deadman's Island—and not on water but land! Could the pod even withstand the impact?

She was breathing too fast again, and told herself to slow down.

Your oxygen supply is very limited.

Anaya turned her attention back to the instructions Terra had left for her.

—If your trajectory is altered, came Terra's voice, *there is little you can do to correct it. One procedure might work.*

Anaya listened and thought it must be a joke, it seemed so ludicrous. But Terra had never told a joke. If this was her only chance, so be it.

She rearranged herself in the pod and, on all fours, started running like a hamster on a wheel. Despite her fatigue, her powerful legs still had strength in them, and the pod began to rotate. And as it rotated, it drifted in the direction she needed to go.

She gave a huff of laughter, because she'd once joked to her father—so, so long ago—that she should just live in a bubble because of her allergies. Just roll herself around everywhere.

She could only manage thirty seconds before having to rest, heaving for air. With her hand she checked her position and saw that the trajectory now took her closer to Vancouver. But she wasn't there yet.

She did another crazy hamster run. Around her, the other seeding pods were trailing streams of vapor. As she watched, these wispy streams thickened and gathered into bright fluffy clouds, and then darker ones.

She was flashing in and out of cloud now, but caught sight of a seeding pod disintegrating in a glittering flash. Off to her left another pod evaporated, then a third, leaving its payload of viruses churning in the air.

Water droplets spattered against her pod and streamed off in rivulets.

It was happening. The rain was beginning!

She checked her position again—closer, but still not quite there.

She felt hot and breathless and realized it wasn't just from the running. The steady hiss of fresh air around her nostrils was now a stutter. Her oxygen supply was running out.

The clouds darkened further. A flash of lightning jaggedly divided the sky.

She must be close now. She checked again. In her mind, the glowing blue line on the map took her right over Vancouver's harbor. She was on course.

The cryptogen fabric clung against her sweaty skin, against her face, against her nostrils. And she realized there was no more air at all now. She was going to suffocate inside this thing!

Her pod punched through the dark-bellied clouds. Things flashed past. Was that a jet, a helicopter? And flyers! Flyers flashing through the sky like a plague of malevolent angels.

She hit something in the air, and her pod went spinning, then ricocheted off yet something else, like a pinball in some infernal game.

—*Petra!* she cried out. *Seth! Can you guys hear me? It's going to rain! I'm coming back, but I don't know if—*

And then she couldn't talk anymore. All she could do was close her eyes tight because she was in a machine never meant to land, and she only hoped that Terra was right and she'd survive the landing.

WAITING BENEATH THE WATER'S surface, Petra gazed up at the warped shadows of approaching flyers, skimming low in formation toward the fleet.

—*They're coming!* Petra cried to the rebel swimmers.

—*We need to take them all,* said the swimmer lieutenant. *Or they will send for reinforcements.*

From their jet speeders the cryptogens took aim with their harpoon cannons. In a burst of bubbles, a spray of narrow missiles zipped through the water, broke the surface, and exploded in the midst of the flyers' formation. Broken bodies spiraled to the sea. But Petra saw two survivors, circling.

To her left, a sonic blast cratered the water and Petra felt like she'd been hurled against pavement. A rebel swimmer floated nearby, crushed and lifeless.

—*Deeper!* someone shouted. *Go deeper!*

Petra grabbed hold of the nearest jet speeder as it dived toward the ocean floor. Around them, sonic bursts pounded the water like depth charges.

The water darkened, and she realized that she needed to breathe.

—*I've got to go up!* she cried.

—*They will see you!*

She couldn't help it. She'd stayed down longer than ever, and she'd reached her limit. She was only half swimmer, and her human half needed air.

—*Take this,* said the swimmer who'd saved her life. He offered her the dead captain's speeder. *But don't surface here.*

—*Thank you,* she said, gripping the controls. They were similar to the floating platforms', and she felt the machine awaiting her sonic orders.

She sped closer to shore, angling gradually toward the surface, until she couldn't wait any longer and veered straight up. She stopped just below the waterline and tilted only her head above the waves, gasping air into her withered lungs.

Her eyes darted everywhere. Another formation of flyers shot toward the fleet, skimming low to avoid the ships' guns. Ahead of them they sent blasts of sound rolling over the water like giant bowling balls that smashed against the sides of the ship. The aircraft carrier sat crookedly in the water.

Above her in the sky: fire and thunder and spinning, smoking wreckage. Flyers skirmishing with helicopters and fighter jets.

And somewhere among it all was Seth.

She knew in that moment she had to stop him before he got killed.

Silently, she called out his name, again and again, but couldn't hear or smell his telepathic light and scent.

She needed to get up there somehow, and it wasn't going to happen with a jet speeder. She looked around the wreckage-strewn sea and spotted an armored platform, hovering adrift about six feet above the surface. Its runner crew was dead.

She jetted over, and when she was below it, she jumped for the platform—and missed by a few feet. She splashed down in defeat. It was out of reach, but she wanted it. She dived deep, to the bottom of the strait, crouched low, and pushed off. She kicked with all her might, rocketing straight up, her body undulating like a true cryptogen, and when she broke the surface, she sailed so high, she nearly brained herself on the underside of the platform. She caught hold of the grilled floor and swung herself over the side, and aboard.

"Sorry," she whispered as she shoved off the dead runners. She gripped the controls, felt the expectant hum in her head, and angled the platform to the sky.

Just then, in her head, a familiar light glimmered. Not Seth's, but—

Anaya's?

. . . coming back . . .

—*Anaya?* she cried out.

But the voice disappeared so quickly she couldn't be sure.

Bursting out of the clouds came something pale and round like an icy meteor. It plowed a deep furrow in the water and finally came to rest, bobbing on the surface.

Petra thought: *A new egg?*

Because there was definitely something moving inside, something purplish gray and wrinkled and bloated.

THE IMPACT WAS SO intense Anaya must've passed out, and when she came to, her cryptogen suit was protectively inflated around her like an enormous airbag. She unzipped her head and inhaled hungrily.

She'd made it! She was alive!

Water slapped against the transparent pod.

And overhead a battle raged. It was like a volcanic eruption, the sky churning with smoke and flame and charred debris. She caught a glimpse of fighter jets and helicopters and flyers—so many of them!—flashing and clashing thunderously. Armored platforms with runners streaked through the sky, shooting lightning. Some seemed to be attacking the flyers—rebels!—and some seemed to be firing on each other.

She looked wildly all around. She was low in the choppy water and couldn't see land, but far in the distance she made out the deck of a huge ship, maybe an aircraft carrier. Where on earth was she?

And was it raining? She looked at the top of her pod and couldn't tell if that was rain, or just spray.

Shouldn't it be raining by now?

She had to get out. But go where? And how? Where was the shore? And that aircraft carrier looked a long way away. But she couldn't stay here, bobbing in the water like a sitting duck.

The decision was made for her. The pod seemed to be melting.

This thing that had plunged through Earth's atmosphere in a billion degrees was now leaking. Before Anaya could open the hatch, a geyser of cold water from below filled the pod and rolled it over as it sank below the surface.

Trapped, Anaya flailed to find a way out. The salt stung her eyes, and she could barely see in the dark water. Where was the hatch?

She felt something grab her arm and pull. She gasped in surprise and was about to inhale water when she was dragged with tremendous speed toward the surface. The moment her head was clear, she gasped air.

"Got you!" Petra cried, grinning beside her.

Anaya flung her arms around her friend, and they treaded water together. She was laughing and crying all at once.

"Thank you!" Anaya said into Petra's damp neck. "I would've drowned!"

"I thought I heard you in my head, and then that thing landed, and I didn't recognize you!" Petra said. "You were all wrapped up in one of those sac things!"

Despite the thick hair on Anaya's body, the water felt frigid, and her teeth were chattering.

"Come on, out you get," said Petra.

Anaya saw the platform hovering at water level a few feet away. With her friend's help, she bellied up onto it, shivering herself warm.

"Did you do it?" Petra asked, climbing up beside her. "The rain?"

"Yes!"

"Then why isn't it raining?"

"It will. I saw it happening way up in the sky!"

"Better be soon," Petra said. "We're not winning!"

Anaya looked all around. Behind them was Point Roberts and, hovering above it, the massive cryptogen landing ship, smoking but still intact.

"Is Seth still inside?" she asked Petra worriedly.

"No," her friend said miserably. "He's up there."

"What?" In confusion, Anaya angled her gaze to the churning aerial battle. "How?"

"He has a flight pack and a helmet. He wanted to fight!"

"No! He doesn't need to do anything! The rain's going to finish this! We need to stop him before he gets killed!"

"I know!" Petra wailed. "I was on my way to find him. Maybe he'll listen to you! Try!"

—*Seth!* Anaya called. *Seth, the rain is coming! If you can hear me, get away from the fighting! Find somewhere safe! Seth?*

"Anything?" Petra asked.

"Nothing."

"Pearson wanted me back aboard the frigate," Petra said. "But I'm not leaving Seth behind all over again."

Anaya felt the weight of her friend's gaze and knew she was

waiting for her to agree. Did the two of them really stand a chance up there? They'd probably get killed within seconds.

She looked out at the fleet. An aircraft carrier was crooked in the water, an oily slick spreading from its hull. One battleship was a smoking wreck, and the other one spat fire up into the sky, trying to keep the flyers at bay. Her eyes settled on the smallest ship in the fleet, bearing the Canadian flag, and she felt like her heart would burst.

"Are my mom and dad on that one?" she asked Petra.

Her friend nodded. "My dad, too."

It wouldn't be long before the flyers descended on it.

"Seth's all alone," Petra said. "And he's been alone so much. I can't let him be alone again. You don't have to come. But I'm going."

Anaya gave a quick nod. "I'm going with you."

In desperation she turned her face to the swollen clouds.

"Come on!" she shouted hoarsely. "Rain!"

—*LET ME FINISH HIM,* the commander shouted at the other flyers as she circled Seth. *This is the one who struck me. Look at him, hiding in our armor like a coward.*

Seth struggled to get the commander in his sights as she banked and dipped, but she was a faster and a better flyer. And even with the flight pack, he was starting to feel the hard burn of fatigue in his shoulders and the center of his chest. He realized just how much work his flight pack had been doing for him. It had tricked him into thinking he was really flying himself.

He saw a chance and unleashed sound at the commander. His thunderclap was met by hers and their sonic blows collided in a great crack. The concussion bowled Seth backward. It took several seconds to right himself in the air.

—*You were never meant to fly,* the commander told him.

So the general had been telling him the truth all along. He was too heavy. Built wrong. He would never thrive in the air. He felt suddenly so tired that he was tempted to fold up his arms and let them rest. There was simply too much weight to carry.

—*Seth!*

In his head fluttered a voice like something from a dream. It was Anaya.

—*Seth, there's a rain coming. . . . Get away. . . . Find somewhere safe—*

The commander's blaring voice obliterated Anaya's—but not the strength and hope Seth now felt surging up through him.

—*You were only intended to be a slave,* the winged cryptogen said. *And now you will not become even that.*

He sensed the violent vibration growing in the commander's helmet and launched a counterblast. The deafening sonic collision was more powerful this time, and he saw several other flyers caught in its radius spiraling earthward, crushed.

—You think your power is equal to mine? the commander said, and he smelled the scorched fury in her silent voice. *You have pretended at being one of us, but you aren't.*

—I'm more, he said savagely, and struck again.

His blast met hers in a deafening thunderclap that came perilously close to him this time. His ears rang. The vision in his helmet dimmed. He would not win this battle. He was so exhausted. She would annihilate him, or get bored and let the other flyers finish him off.

A sudden gust buffeted him and he heard a rumble of actual thunder from the dark-bellied clouds. Water spattered his armor. Then came the deluge, rain clattering against his feathers, streaming off his wing tips.

Even as he struggled under its weight, he was overjoyed.

This was the rain.

He felt it drench every inch of exposed skin, his arms and hands and legs. And with the wetness came a raging itchiness. It was so crazy-making that he couldn't stop himself from trying to scratch at it, his wings collapsing as he clawed his skin. Tumbling through the sky, he saw the commander and the other flyers doing exactly the same thing.

He wanted to peel off his own skin, now erupting in welts. His breath rasped in his narrowing windpipe. He couldn't fill his lungs. In the air, but suffocating. He didn't understand. This was not what the rain was supposed to do.

He was aware of a helicopter blasting away at the flyers in their helplessness.

And suddenly the rain stopped, and with it, the itchiness. He could breathe properly again.

The commander dived down at him.

—*Was that the weapon meant to destroy us?* she asked mockingly.

Was it? Seth's head swarmed with confusion. Had the weapon failed? Had it done nothing except trigger a violent but short-lived allergy?

Before him the commander beat her wings so powerfully she was practically standing in the air. He saw her helmet glimmer violet and knew she was about to strike, and it would be devastating. With his last remaining strength he kindled a vibration in his head—and was overwhelmed by such stunning pain that he blacked out for a second.

When he came back to himself, he was tumbling, and so was the commander, trembling like she'd just experienced the same agony he had.

—*Kill him!* the commander shouted to the nearby flyers.

Seth didn't try to fight back. Not because he'd given up. But because he suddenly understood that the pain in his head had been self-inflicted.

It was working.

The rain was working.

It had turned his own sonic weapon against him.

All around him, flyers reeled in pain as they tried to blast him with sound, slewing through the air, terrible shrieks issuing from their beaks.

—*Kill him!* the commander cried again.

—*We cannot!* one of them wailed.

—*The pain is overwhelming!*

—*Do it!* the commander said.

Above him, Seth heard a muffled thunderclap as a flyer's helmet exploded. Off to his left, another bloody explosion, and a second flyer fell, headless, to the earth.

—*What have you done to us!* the commander shrieked, flying down at him and slashing at his armor with her sharp wings.

Seth rolled, fending off her blows as best he could. He felt his flight pack loosen and saw that it was trailing fluid that spun away through the air.

He was losing speed.

And he was beginning to fall.

"THE RAIN!" ANAYA CRIED as it struck her face.

She'd never been so happy to get soaked, even as the terrible itching crawled over her body.

"What's happening?" Petra cried, scratching furiously.

"It's okay!" Anaya told her. "We added an allergen to the virus. It won't last."

"This is worse than what water used to do to me!" Petra cried, bending to scoop up some seawater to splash all over herself.

The deluge ceased, and with it, the welts and itching.

"Look!" Anaya said, pointing up at the sky. "It's working."

Flyers were tumbling down like limp puppets.

"Their own weapons are killing them!"

"Shine the lantern!" Petra said. "You're better at it! Tell everyone!"

In her head Anaya summoned the blazing light of the lantern, beaming it out to anyone who was listening.

—*The flyers can't use their helmets anymore!* she cried silently. *They've lost their power to strike with sound! Tell everyone!*

She heard the lantern echoed back to her, over and over, like a song she couldn't get out of her head. She sang it till it must have echoed in every head for kilometers. The lantern, the sign to fight for freedom.

In the air, the flyers were in disarray, fleeing from the remaining helicopters and jets that streaked through their ranks. Out at sea, the battleship released a new barrage of missiles, and this time they reached the cryptogen ship unhindered. Rebel runners on armored platforms flew high to join the fray, unleashing lightning. From the water, rebel swimmers shot a surge of harpoons up at the flyers.

Anaya looked at her friend, barely daring to say it.

Petra did it for her: "Are we winning?"

"I think we're winning!"

"But Seth!" Petra said urgently.

Anaya called out silently, again and again, without a reply. She scanned the sky—which was foolish, because how would she ever be able to pick him out in all that chaos?

—*Anaya! Petra!*

The voice was Seth's, and it took her a moment to track him in the sky.

"There!" she said, pointing.

Far from land was a tight knot of flyers, pressing in, flying apart, knotting up again, like a vicious flock of birds. And she realized they were all attacking Seth. And now he was plummeting.

"We're going!" Petra shouted. And with a burst of speed, the platform soared up toward him.

CHAPTER TWENTY-FOUR

STRUGGLING TO STAY ALOFT, Seth saw islands below and realized how far he'd strayed from Point Roberts and the mainland.

The commander came slashing down on him again. The blow caught him across the backs of his calves and sheared off feathers. A trail of blood spiraled behind him.

He was flightless now. It was all he could do to glide.

When the commander came at him the next time, Seth was ready and struck a blow to her head, powerful enough to knock off her helmet. Her exposed beak snapped, her predator's eyes blazing in fury. He rolled out of her way.

Not much time left now.

An island was coming up fast. Below was an open field, and Seth aimed himself at it.

He hit the ground and skidded across grass, feeling like he'd been broadsided by a truck. Gasping, he couldn't move for a few moments. His eyes darted wildly. Where was the commander? Groaning, he slowly got to his feet, amazed none of his bones were broken. His first thought was to reach the cover of the nearby trees, and then he realized he was standing on a school field.

The school itself was so overgrown with black vines it took him a moment to recognize it.

He was back on Salt Spring Island, on the same field where pit plants had once swallowed him and Anaya and Petra.

He started to limp toward the trees. He'd forgotten to take off his helmet and he was glad, because it told him where the pit plants waited below the earth.

The commander crashed down on him, knocking him to the ground, her wickedly sharp talons planted on his chest.

Her face was sharpened with anger—and fear, too. He could see that now. Her weapon, her devastating sound weapon, was useless. In quick bursts her breath whistled through her swollen nostrils, and Seth realized she was having trouble breathing without her helmet.

This was not her atmosphere. Not her world.

—*What have you done to us?*

Her words boiled in his head like oily smoke.

With one taloned foot she clutched his helmet and ripped it off his head, and transferred it to her own. In that moment, when she was slightly off-balance, Seth grabbed the foot planted on his chest and pulled hard.

The commander was light—those wonderful hollow bones that allowed her to fly—and she staggered off him. Seth scrambled up, feathered arms flared.

They circled each other and came clashing together, using their wings like swords. Sparks flew from their metallic tips. The smell of fireworks filled Seth's nostrils.

One slip and he'd be sliced in two. But he remembered all those hours training in the bunker, striking at punching bags. He leaned in harder. He drove the commander back, one step, two, then cut a huge gash in her armor.

She flapped her wings and lifted out of range. Seth flapped, too, but could not rise. Without a flight pack, he was earthbound. He felt the shame of it—the foolishness of thinking, all this time, that he might fly. A mocking shriek came from the commander.

She flew down at him, striking his arm so hard he felt it break.

Broken arm, broken wing, broken boy.

He staggered for the trees, his arm searing with pain, but she knocked him down again. Flat on his back, he watched her come again, lifted his good arm to fend her off. He would not look away.

Something blurred through the air and struck the commander with such force she was plowed twenty feet across the field. Anaya landed near her in a crouch and kicked her again. Seth heard the sound of cracking bone.

A platform set down, and Petra jumped off, raced toward the commander, and struck her with her barbed tail before she could rise.

But rise she did, slashing out with her unbroken wing, driving the girls back.

Petra lunged in and stung her once more, but the commander's good wing lashed out and Seth heard Petra's cry of anguish.

"Petra!" He scrambled up and raced toward her. He saw blood drizzling down her legs but didn't know where it was coming from—and didn't have time to check because the commander was still standing and cutting at the air with her metallic feathers.

Seth saw her helmet flicker violet as she prepared to strike them with sound—had she forgotten she'd lost her sound weapon? Or was she simply desperate? She staggered backward, shrieking, clutching her head in the self-inflicted agony.

Terrible words torrented from the commander's head into Seth's, scorching images so foul he wished he could blot them out. She vented all her fury on him until her motions became sluggish. She stopped slashing out with her wing. She swayed.

—*You vile, vile creatures,* she raged at them.

A huge yellow tongue hit her from behind, and Seth looked up to see a crater-faced rhino creature at the edge of the field. It began to drag the commander toward it. Shrieking and clawing, the commander fought the whole way.

Seth saw her helmet flicker violet once more, and this time he knew it was no mistake. The commander was snapped inside the rhino creature's mouth and then both creatures exploded from the force of the commander's suicidal sonic blast.

ANAYA FELT COMPLETELY UNREAL as she sat in her school cafeteria, sipping a can of ginger ale from a smashed vending machine. She was hairy from head to toe and had clawed hands and feet. Normally this would have been her worst high school nightmare imaginable, but right now it didn't matter one bit. She and her friends were alive.

After taking shelter in the school, Anaya had sent a message to Charles, who was aboard the Canadian frigate, and it hadn't been long before a helicopter touched down on the roof, carrying Mom and Dad, Petra's father, Dr. Weber, and a few soldiers.

"Is there going to be a scar?" Petra asked, lying facedown on a nearby table while Dr. Weber took care of her wound. The flyer had cut off her tail, leaving only a stump. Outside on the field, Anaya had tried to bandage it as best she could, but it was bleeding a lot.

"Let's not worry about that just now," said Dr. Weber, finishing her sutures.

"Best day of my freakin' life," said Petra cheerfully.

Anaya wondered if they'd given her some pills, because her friend looked really relaxed—and delighted, actually. After all, Petra had wanted that tail off since day one.

At another table, Petra's father was stitching up the gash in Seth's leg. His broken arm already rested in a makeshift sling.

Anaya smiled across at him, feeling almost guilty that she had no major injuries of her own.

"What's going on out there?" she asked Mom and Dad again.

They were sitting on either side of her, smushed very close, like they were going to stay like that their entire lives. There had already been tears and a hundred kisses on the cheek and forehead, and they'd called her all her old baby names (plus a new one: Little Astronaut), and she'd told them, hurriedly, about what had happened aboard the main cryptogen ship, and her insane reentry. But she was impatient to know what was happening over Point Roberts, right now.

"Honestly," said Dad, "we don't know much more than you. Our only news came through Colonel Pearson. And there wasn't a lot of it."

"Everything was happening so fast," Mom said, "and we were mostly belowdecks." She shuddered. "The sounds were terrible."

"Are we still winning?" Petra piped up. "That's what we want to know!"

"We're still fighting," Dr. Weber said, bandaging Petra's wound. "The colonel told me that most of the runners and swimmers have turned on the flyers, but not all. And they still have some very powerful weapons. There've also been reports of flyers leaving the battlefield."

"You mean deserting?" Seth asked.

"We hope so," said Dr. Weber.

Anaya didn't like to think of flyers finding places to hide, planning some terrible counterattack.

"We've also got reinforcements coming in now, from other bases," Dr. Weber added.

"So the Battle of Point Roberts is our victory," said Petra. "Can we just say it, please?"

"We don't know that yet, Petra."

"Look, we killed their commander!" Petra said boastfully. She had definitely been given some pills. "Seth dueled with her, and then Anaya kickboxed her and broke her arm, and I paralyzed her, and then she got eaten by a rhino thing and blew herself up! I'm calling that a victory, okay?"

"Even if we won here," Seth said quietly, "there's nine other ships on the planet."

"But it rained all over the world, right?" Petra said, unwisely trying to sit up, then wincing and lying back down. "That means all the flyers are knocked out."

"How about the rest of the world?" Anaya asked Dr. Weber.

Dr. Weber looked over as she put her instruments away. "It's chaos. We only know little bits so far. But we were hoping you might be able to help us with that. Have you heard anything from her?"

Anaya shook her head. In all the tumult, she'd barely thought of Terra. Now she felt almost overwhelmed with sadness. Terra had saved her life, sent her home, and she'd just abandoned her and the other rebels aboard the ship. Her last view of the runner's face had been as the hatch exploded and flyers swarmed into the laboratory.

"If you could—" Dr. Weber began.

"I doubt I even have the range! I mean, it's all the way out in space. I probably couldn't do it."

"Could you at least try?" Dr. Weber persisted gently. "After all, you two had a very strong connection."

It was those words that undid her. "I'm just afraid," Anaya choked out through her tears. "I'm afraid she's dead!"

She felt her parents' arms around her, Mom murmuring comforting things, and Dad telling Dr. Weber, "You've got to give her a bit of time, she's been through so much."

But when Anaya had cried herself out, she wiped the damp fur of her face and said, "No, you're right, I need to try."

She closed her eyes and waited for it to darken behind her eyelids before opening up her mind. Immediately she was barraged with cryptogen chatter—so many silent voices, some joyful, some agonized, some vengeful. She tried to be especially attentive as she sought out the sensory fingerprint that belonged only to Terra. Right now, it was like searching for a pebble on a rocky beach. She sensed many other runners, but none were Terra.

She sat a moment, feeling like a tiny candle in a window that opened onto the vast universe.

Fighting back her worst fears, she said, "I can't find her."

But Terra found *her.*

Anaya's head was suddenly filled with amber light and the smell of fresh-cut grass.

"It's her!" she shouted aloud to the others, and then blocked out their voices so she could concentrate.

—*Are you all right?* Terra asked her.

—*Yes! Are you? What's happening up there?*

When Anaya had escaped in the seeding pod, she'd felt like she was abandoning Terra to certain death. But it turned out the silver swimmer and the grizzled engineer had already improvised a weapon. From one of the huge incubating vats, they'd rigged a powerful hose that sprayed the virus directly onto every flyer that had burst into the laboratory.

The effect had been instant: the flyers who tried to use their sound weapons, despite the terrible warning pains, died as their heads exploded. Terra had raised the lantern and had been joined by most of the runners and swimmers. The grizzled old engineer, meanwhile, was already busy releasing more of the virus into the ship's central ventilation system. It wasn't long before every single flyer in the vessel was powerless.

—*We are in command of the ship now,* Terra said.

Anaya felt awash with relief. *Oh, that is such good news! And down here? Do you know what's going on down here?*

All over the planet, Terra told her, other battles were raging. Maps and images flared in Anaya's mind. Quite a few countries had managed to destroy the shields of their landing ships and force the flyers out into the weaponized rain. Outside Tokyo a damaged landing ship had tried to take off but had been grounded by what was left of the Japanese and Chinese air forces, working in cooperation. Elsewhere, flyers had abandoned their ships outright and fled to mountains or rain forests, sometimes taking human hostages. In other places, humans and rebel cryptogens, with the help of hybrids, fought together as allies. But there were still battles where rebels and humans fought each other, despite attempts to make peace and forge an alliance. Everywhere, there were terrible losses on all sides. Anaya tried to block some of the images in her head.

—*But the flyers are losing,* Terra said. *Any that have fled, we will find.*

—*What will you do with them?* Anaya asked nervously.

—*Aboard the ship we've arrested and imprisoned them. They're unconscious in their sacs, awaiting the journey home.*

—*Home?* Anaya asked in surprise.

—*Yes. This was always our hope. Not to conquer another world. But to return home.*

—*What about all the flyers there?*

—*We will try to negotiate with them. And if that fails, we have the virus, and the ability to send another rain.*

—*So you're going?* Anaya asked, feeling foolish the moment she asked.

—*Yes,* Terra said, *but not quite yet.*

ONE MONTH LATER

CHAPTER TWENTY-FIVE

"CAREFUL UP THERE," MOM called across to her.

"I'm fine," Anaya said, with an amused shake of her head. After all that had happened, it was funny that Mom worried about her standing on a ladder.

The two of them were clearing the black vines off the walls of their house. The vines were dead now, yellow and brittle, their berries withered. She felt a twinge of sadness about the berries—they'd tasted so good!—but definitely *not* about the wrinkly acid-filled sacs that trapped and devoured small animals.

Three weeks ago, it had rained again, across the entire planet.

This rain had contained not seeds or eggs or viruses, but an herbicide and pesticide that Terra had engineered—improvements on the ones that Anaya's dad and Dr. Weber had developed first.

As quickly as the cryptogenic plants had grown, they'd withered and died. No more black grass taking over farmers' fields, no more seed-spitting water lilies changing the atmosphere. No more vines strangling forests and snaring food for the voracious pit plants that waited under the soil for their animal and human prey. The worldwide deluge was so effective that not even the plants' pollens were left to reseed the planet.

And within days, the cryptogenic insects were decimated, too. Gone were the mosquito birds with their terrible plague. Gone were the giant water striders and all the horrifying bugs. The titanic borer worms were taking longer to get rid of, because they were so deep beneath the soil. But Terra had said it was only a matter of time before the pesticides worked their way down to them.

The mammals were a different question. Any cryptogenic creature that was born, not *hatched*, on the planet was immune to the last rain. There was no chemical spray for them—not one that wouldn't harm humans, anyway. So everyone was still on high alert for things like the crater-faced rhino creatures, or the wolverine-squids Petra had described. Anaya still shuddered whenever she imagined them.

And a few other species had been sighted, too—but nothing compared to the number Anaya had glimpsed inside the crypto-gens' laboratory, waiting to rain down on Earth.

"They said they spotted one of those rhino things at the north end of the island," Mom said from her ladder.

"They're supposed to die out pretty fast, without the crypto-genic plants and bugs to eat."

"Yeah, well, from what I hear, they're happy to eat humans, too. So for the time being, we've still got some invasive species on our island."

"Like me," Anaya said.

"You are a *pleasant* invasive species. And you are staying inside until they kill that thing. Unless you have an armed escort."

"Do Seth and Petra count?"

"No."

"Even though we're like galactic warriors now?"

"Nope."

Anaya ripped some vines off her bedroom window and peered inside.

It was a bit like looking into a stranger's room. There was her unmade bed, just as she'd left it the day she'd been evacuated from Salt Spring. Her clothes scattered on the floor. Her shelves of books. An unfinished homework assignment on her desk. When she thought of going back to all that, she caught herself sighing.

She knew things were going to change.

Some changes would be her choice. Like maybe getting laser hair removal. Or her claws filed down regularly.

Other changes would be forced on her.

Earth plants were coming back. And that meant flowers and pollens and spores. That meant allergies.

"Lunch is ready!" Dad called from the front door.

It was their first proper day back inside their own house. Salt Spring Island had never been a Spray Zone, so things had gotten pretty bad over the past months. Some of the islanders had tried to tough it out barricaded inside their own homes, but most of them had banded together in the town's few office buildings, the hospital, the community center—the places with the thickest walls, which were easier to defend.

After they'd returned to the island, Anaya and her family were put up in the middle school, along with Seth, and Petra and her father. There was so much work to do. It drove home to Anaya how very, very lucky she'd been, living on an army base where there were always meals, electricity, and running water. And safety—or as much safety as it was possible to have in their overthrown world.

On the island, so much of every day was making sure there was enough clean water, enough food. Was there enough ammunition, enough gasoline for the generators? Was there internet? No? How about shortwave radio? Was there enough medicine for the sick and wounded? There were turns keeping watch from windows and rooftops, day and night. And when they were sure the cryptogenic plants and bugs were gone and it was safer to venture outside, there was no end of work.

There were roads to be rebuilt, pit plant craters to be filled, power lines and water lines to be restored, fields to be cleared of dead black grass. And there were fewer people than usual to do the work.

Anaya had been shocked at how many islanders had died, people she'd known all her life, kids she'd shared classrooms with. What they'd suffered on Salt Spring was echoed and amplified all around the world. They'd probably never have an accurate global death toll, but the estimates mounted day by day and were almost too harrowing to comprehend.

In the kitchen, Dad had found some canned soup and warmed it on the barbecue, which, amazingly, still had some propane left.

"Most places in the Northern Hemisphere, it's too late to get a new crop in for this year," Dad said over their simple meal, "so it's going to be a very tough winter. But"—and he looked at Anaya with a grin—"that's incredible, what Terra told you about the dead black grass. Turns out our little invasive dude's even more amazing than we thought!"

"I know!" Anaya said, smiling at Dad's boundless enthusiasm for plants, even alien ones. "Talk about a silver lining."

Yesterday, Terra had told her how the black grass could be used as a fertilizer. The process had been complicated, and Anaya had transcribed it as best she could and forwarded it to Dr. Weber.

"I'm also pretty excited about its potential as a green fuel," Mom said.

"Let's hope humans do some of the heavy lifting, too," Dad said. "Rebuilding with clean energy—so we don't face another extinction event with climate change."

Anaya took another spoonful of lentil soup. Rebuilding. There was so much of it to do. Power plants, highways, hospitals, factories. They said it would take decades to rebuild. But next year there would be a new crop: grains and cereals and fruits and vegetables to feed the hungering countries of the world.

After lunch she went to the bathroom and looked at herself in the mirror.

She'd let her fur get quite thick again and knew she should haul out the hair-removal cream and the razors. She'd need lots of razors, which were in very short supply right now.

She sneezed, and then again. Her old allergies. She closed her eyes.

Yes, she would change.

But not everything.

Not the new strength in her legs and body.

Not the ability to talk silently with other hybrids.

Not the different person she'd become in the past months.

"OF COURSE IT *WOULD* grow back," said Petra, slouched dejectedly on her bed.

She finally got the thing hacked off, and, *hello,* back it came. It hadn't taken long either. After a few days she'd noticed a pressure against her bandage and felt around with her fingers. It was just like that terrible first time when she'd noticed a knobbly bit sticking out from her tailbone. A few weeks later, it was already several inches long.

"Well, at least there won't be a scar," Anaya said, obviously hoping for a laugh.

Why was this so hard for her friend to understand? Didn't she know how much agony this had caused her?

"I do not want a tail!" she said. "I think I've been quite clear about this."

"You have," Anaya said. "And don't take this the wrong way, but right now, I don't think it ranks as one of the world's biggest problems."

"I can't sit down in most chairs! Not to mention the fashion nightmare of having to alter every piece of my clothing. We're talking about a long, venomous *reptile* tail, okay? It's a big deal! It's not a little bit of plush kangaroo fur—"

"Hey," Anaya objected, "I am *totally* covered with fur unless I sh—"

"Or some big ugly toenails," Petra continued.

"Claws!" Anaya corrected her. "And they're not so ugly, are they? Really?"

"I guess I could get it cut off again," Petra said, "but—"

"—it'd just grow right back."

"Yep." Petra sighed. Could she live with it? She had for a few months. "It has been useful in some tough situations."

"Could come in very handy," her friend agreed. "Date not going well? Just sting the dude and walk away."

That made Petra laugh. "Okay, that would be pretty good."

"I'm sure one day you'll meet some charming person with a tail of their own."

"Ha ha. Yeah, I know, I'm just supposed to accept who I am and all that. But I can't help noticing *you've* shaved."

Her friend touched her smooth face with a self-conscious laugh.

"See?" said Petra. "Fitting in is important to you, too. You want to make a good impression the first day back at school and all that."

"Oh my God, school."

"Yeah," said Petra. "And imagine me walking down the hallways with my tail. 'Oh, sorry, Jessica, did I get you? Just stay there, it'll wear off. Total accident, sorry.'"

She figured she was different enough without the tail. The impossibly smooth skin was not so bad at all. Most people would kill for skin as smooth as hers. The patterning was another thing, and she was still trying to decide whether to have it lasered off. Or maybe it was cool?

"You won't miss anything?" Anaya asked her. "You know, when the world goes back to normal?"

She felt a quick squeeze of the familiar sadness. One thing would never go back to normal. Having Mom in her life. It had been wonderful to finally get back into their own house and start putting it to rights, but every room had memories of her mother; she could tell her dad felt them just as strongly as she did.

"Oh, sorry," Anaya said, wincing. She must've realized what was going through her head. "Stupid question. Sorry, Petra."

"It's okay, I know what you meant. And yeah, of course there's other stuff I'll miss. Swimming. But Dad said we might be able to put in a pool—and fill it with special water. You know, the burning acid water I like."

"Pool party for one," said Anaya.

"But the best thing," Petra said, "is that Dr. Weber said she could set me up with a lifetime supply of my own water. Baths, showers, the works."

"I'm glad she's moving here," Anaya said.

Petra had already heard. Apparently, Dr. Weber had found a place on the island to rent. And Seth would be living with her; she was going to be his foster mother after all.

Which meant Seth would be going back to school with them in September.

"Yeah," Petra said, smiling at Anaya, "I'm pretty happy about that."

IT WASN'T HARD TO climb the fence around the Mount Maxwell lookout.

Seth walked closer to the drop-off. At six hundred meters, it gave a sweeping view over Salt Spring Island. The drop was not quite sheer, but rocky all the way down.

He shifted closer to the edge. He couldn't stop thinking about Esta. The way he'd felt when they met, the first person exactly like him in the whole world. He remembered their first silent conversation across the cafeteria. He was haunted by the promises they'd made each other in the boat in the fog. He felt a deep, wordless emptiness.

He wished he'd forget.

He didn't want to forget.

He thought about things she'd said all the time. How there'd never be a place for them here. The humans would never trust them, never love them.

Seth jumped.

It was a warm day and he felt the thermals rising up from the hills and fields, and they lifted him as he spread his feathered arms. It was five weeks since his arm had been broken, but it had already mended, amazingly fast, not like the old days. Down he glided, banking to the east, the wind pushing him. He reveled in every sensation.

Even if he couldn't fly, not properly, he had this at least. It was not so bad a consolation.

He set down neatly on the street in front of his new house, where Stephanie Weber was waiting. She lowered the binoculars she'd been using to track him.

"I don't know how many of these jumps I want to agree to," she said. "It's pretty nerve-racking."

"I could take up hang gliding or BASE jumping, maybe," Seth said. "Would that be better?"

"Let me think about this. Come on, everyone's here."

He followed her through the cozy little house to the backyard.

He'd been expecting Anaya and Petra—but *not* Colonel Pearson, who looked as stern and stiff as ever in his uniform. Surprisingly, Seth felt glad to see him.

"Stephanie was kind enough to invite me to your . . ." He gestured at the patio table set with refreshments while he searched for the right word. "Send-off, I guess."

It was a send-off, but they weren't saying good-bye to each other, but to the cryptogens. Over the past weeks, while the runners and swimmers had been making repairs to their landing ships and waiting for their hulls to heal, they'd also been tracking down the last of the flyers, and even helping get rid of the borer worms and other cryptogen animals.

Some groups of humans had been happy enough to work alongside the rebels, but overall, the cryptogens were treated with extreme suspicion. Most people would be very happy to see them go. And for the cryptogens' safety, Seth was happy, too. He knew they'd never be welcome on Earth. Frankly, he wasn't convinced he and the other hybrids would ever be truly welcome.

But this afternoon, so Terra had told Anaya, the last landing ship, the one over Point Roberts, was ready to return to the main vessel. It was Anaya's idea for the three of them to be together to watch it depart.

"I actually have something for you three," Pearson said, "and Stephanie suggested I give them to you in person."

He handed a small box to each of them. Seth opened his. It was a very shiny medal.

"I know you kids might not care about medals, especially military ones, but you've earned them. I hope at the very least they'll remind you of your exceptional bravery and courage. I was wrong about all of you, from the very first. Especially you, Seth. And I'm sorry."

Seth didn't know what to say, and he noticed that Anaya and Petra were similarly speechless.

"Thank you," he finally said.

"They're leaving," Anaya said abruptly. "I just heard from Terra."

With the others, he turned his attention to the southeast. Dr. Weber raised a pair of binoculars to her face and pointed.

"There."

It was just a small line on the horizon, but it quickly thickened and spread. Seth still marveled at the sheer size and unusual shape of it. Its ascent took it right over the island. It was high enough so that they didn't go weightless, but it still made him feel light-headed as it passed directly overhead and blotted out the sun.

Then the sun came back, and the ship had disappeared into the high cloud, and Anaya was crying, and Petra already had her arm around her. Petra waved him over, so he went and joined their hug. He liked having their arms around him.

"It's silly, I know," Anaya said, half laughing through her tears, "but I won't have her voice in my head again."

"It's not silly," Seth told her.

It was an incredible thing, to have someone share space in your head. He thought of all his dreams and couldn't imagine being without them.

"You'll have me," Petra told Anaya, then added mischievously, "But you used to say you hated it when I got inside your head."

—*And I hope there's some space for me in your head,* Petra said silently to him.

—*Yes,* he replied. *Always.*

—*Excellent.*

They all had some drinks and brownies and talked about all the things that had happened, and the even more things that still needed to happen to return to normal.

"I should be getting back to Deadman's Island," said the colonel after a while. "But, Seth, I wanted you to have this."

From the table he picked up a package sealed with the insignia of the Royal Canadian Air Force and handed it to Seth.

"What is it?" Seth asked. It was large but not especially heavy.

"Thought you might like it," Pearson said. "It's classified, but I know you can keep a secret."

He gave Seth's shoulder a squeeze as he said good-bye to them all and departed through the back gate.

"Well? Open it!" Petra said.

Seth unsealed the package and pulled out an armored vest.

"Is that—" Anaya began.

Whispering in disbelief, Seth said, "A cryptogen flight pack!"

"So you can fly!" Petra said.

"Oh, that's great," groaned Dr. Weber.

"It is," said Seth, grinning. He could almost feel the rush of wind in his ears as he soared higher.

He was half human, half cryptogen, but for the first time in his life, he was starting to feel whole.

ACKNOWLEDGMENTS

With thanks to my wonderful editors, Nancy Siscoe and Suzanne Sutherland, and their respective teams at Alfred A. Knopf Books for Young Readers and HarperCollins Canada, who helped these books to thrive.